THE WOLF AND THE LAMB

The Wolf and the Lamb

Lukas Allen

Lukas Allen

The Lamb

A young member of the Organization begins her journey the next day. She had drifted from her noble roots, and instead is a gunman for hire, fighting back the damned and unholy that have arisen again strongly in the world. She sleeps soundly now, having a dream of flying as an angel, as someone whispers to her in the night...

Ol*iv*ia, Ol*iv*ia, Ol*iv*ia...

1

Just call me angel… your morning angel…

I yawn, get off the bed, and listen to the music in my head for a little longer.

Gawd, I loved Juice Newton!

I looked into the mirror, brushed back my hair, checked the scars on the side of my face to make sure it wasn't moving anymore, and went to wash up. I passed the boarded up windows, and made sure they were still boarded up.

I looked down at my body in the shower. Gawd I was skinny, but I suppose some men find that attractive. Any man would love to get a peek of *this*… I was sure of myself. I was a woman, now, and not some idiot kid hiding in her dad's closet from the murderers… No, the murderers should be hiding from me.

I sang in the shower. Really believed I could've been a singer, as I was younger. Something down the lines of a female Johnny Cash. I suppose I could still pursue those dreams… I had a lot of content to sing about… but it's been ages since I played guitar.

I decided I'd give her a little go, after I got all nice and dressed in my combat suit.

I sang as I twanged the guitar, stopped, said, "Oh, that's not the right key…" and then continued playing in the right key.

I smiled. I could definitely be a young female Cash, no doubt about it!

I went off to work, with my shotgun on my shoulder. Had to upgrade from my dad's old shotgun to this sweet baby… A real, working, combat shotgun, completely matte black, just like my combat suit.

I stood guard as they ushered in *more* refugees… I'm sure the economics people in charge will get all huffy again over this, but it was worth it for that *one* smiling girl who gave me a flower. If anything, I made sure to keep track of where she stayed. Always helps to win over a peace officer, sure does.

America wasn't the place it once was… If we didn't have the higher ups, I suppose, the whole thing would be a tribal fuck all with no respect or care for anyone, afraid of the monsters in the night and even worshipping them.

Hehe. I killed plenty of those monsters, one even with my bare hands. Well, I suppose the knife *really* did him in, but I had to put the fucker in submission hold first. Vampires are like that, y'know?

I got a call on my walkie that someone called "Shine or something" wanted to meet me.

Ohmygawd! Shien! I still owed her for helping my mother escape that cult! Not sure what she exactly did, but I *knew* by the look in her eyes that night that she sure as fuck didn't do nothing.

On that night, she was dripping in sweat. Her pupils were dilated far past anything I've ever seen, even past the druggie boys when we had those trip fests on the farm, and she kept saying these weird words, that I think weren't even Japanese.

I went to intake, and saw them questioning my Japanese American friend.

I instantly broke out into a smile, and went to hug her, shotgun bouncing around on my back.

She smiled that familiar sinister smile, and returned the hug.

She said, "Can we do this somewhere private? Your friends are very… forthcoming, but I really need to speak to you alone."

"Of course, my good bud. Guys? Quit pestering my friends and go check if we got enough drinks for Her Majesty."

The guys looked abashed, but smiled and nodded to me. They knew Her Majesty loved her cold water…

They were good guys. Almost too good. I was sad that a lot of them would be shipped off with the rest of the refugees, away from this outpost, and away from me.

Stupid Her Majesty and her dictational rules…

I was just getting close to one of them, too! A good guy called Jasper. He needed help with his shooting, and I sure was happy to oblige! I frankly just told him to get a haircut. You know, to get the hair out of his eyes. But we still kept seeing each other after!! He looked mighty fine in a buzz cut, yessiree.

But now, even after I waved to him in passing with Shien to a more secluded park bench, I know I'll miss the dude. He had such an innocent smile…

I sat down with Shien, and she got straight to the punch, like she usually did.

She said, "There's a certain prophecy about…"

"Oh, am I the 'chosen one' or some shit? Wouldn't be a bad change of pace."

"Not particularly… Actually, I think if the whole thing was gone and forgotten about it'd make it a hell of a lot easier for everyone. The spirits are writhing, and I've been away speaking to the last of some monks, and taking their guidance…"

Shien was an occult specialist, just like myself. Although, while she did the more finesse parts like calming a spirit and letting them pass on, I did the muscle work and kept any "forceful interaction" back. It's part of the reason I'm still at this outpost, because just out of reach of civilization… were the specters and the damned.

Shien continued, "You're not really the chosen one. I'm not sure anyone is, because I found a play on words in the old texts that state, 'The one around is the chose one.' So I'm really just sure that if someone wants to fulfill their prophecy, they can be damned if they care and go about doing it."

"Um. I'm not really sure about the whole religious aspects you talk about a lot."

"I know, I know… But you are very wonderful at keeping me- people from getting killed. It's part of the reason I needed to see you. Because if all else withstanding, even the damned old dweller in my dreams keeps asking about Olivia Lamb, and always seems depressed when I tell him I don't know…"

"Well golly! An old dweller asked about me?? What's he look like? I want to know the new face I'm going to be working with!!"

"You… You won't be working with an old dweller. He's just a dream figment, anyway." Shien said.

"Oh… So why is it you want to see me, then?"

Shien smiled wickedly, and said, "We're going to stop this prophecy before some damned evildoers *do* intend to start it. I know this, an eruption of the Earth, with the spiritual crossing into reality, won't be good for anyone."

I smiled cheerfully, and said, "Yay! Let's get all packed, and we can go into No Man's Land like all stars!"

We smiled together, and went about to do what we said we'd do.

2

The only reason I could afford to live in the crappy, boarded up house I did live in is because I had the paperwork, passed down to me by my father, of genuine property in the U.S., and they paid me accordingly. Shien wiped off the dust on the railing, and asked me if all places in the U.S. were so homey still.

"Nah, but I gotta take what I can get, y'know? I sometimes rent the place out for company parties and the like. Good ol' capitalism. Been living here for years now anyway, and it's nice to have a mantle to hang my shawl up on and the like."

"I see... I don't have many belongings, trust the spirits to guide my way, but I noticed that that's quite a heavy bag over your shoulder."

"Well, yeah! Gotta have a lot of stuff. There's polluted water every which way, and game isn't as easy to come about as it was. After that brief exponential growth of animals, which was really just them running away, we've had hard pickings in the wild."

"To get here, I lived off acorns and water from this beautiful stream seeming to erupt from the rocks." Shien said.

"That? That's the ol' Good Water Stream. We're thinking about exploiting it and redirecting it, but you didn't hear that from *me*..."

"A shame. A shame filthy corporations still feel like they need to put their hooks into everything."

"I know… I mean, I think I know. I don't agree with every decision Her Majesty pulls, but it keeps people guided. Without her and her megalomart super corporation, we'd just be a bunch of schmucks in the wilderness, and she's got a lot of pull with people in the Capitol, too…"

"Oh yes. Americans are stuck living in a pseudo utopia as every resource is being drained for the few ones who can afford upper class relationships…"

"Yeah, kinda. My mother is drifting along in that society, making ends meet by the sound of it. She's secretly been trying to land another husband, some douche who has a few more cans of beans than her… I keep telling her to come out to the outpost with me, but no, she says she wouldn't *dare* live in the wilds like me. I half the time agree with her, and wish I was behind those big walls, too."

"I trust that you are the only protection we need?"

"Nonono. We're going out with a *convoy*. Scouting people, who are looking for more people or resources. It's by where you said the shit was going to go down, so we'll just follow along until you do whatever you need to do."

"*We.* Whatever *we* need to do. I need complete assistance in *all* manners that come up, if we don't work together, then we may as well call it quits right here and now."

"Alright, alright, I understand. As long as you don't throw me in a volcano, or sacrifice me in whatever else methods to appease those old dwellers of yours."

She smiled wickedly, and said, "If that happens, I'll be sure to let you know. Perhaps I should tell you there's a carrot on a stick down in the volcano?"

"Haha, no thank you, missie. I don't do this for the carrots. This is to get us straight on Gawd's good book, since without you I'd be another orphan lady in crumbling America."

"Very well. I shall note the favor noted."

"No problem, Shien. Still wish I could take orders from the Organization… but they got no pull anymore, no power. If I can *actually* help a few of those orphan kids, make sure they're set up for life, I can do that here, instead of anywhere else."

"Suit yourself. Although, like a roaming paladin, or estranged good witch, we are everywhere you *truly* need us. I think you should reconsider your Organization connections, perhaps at the end of this long, grueling journey."

"Hm. Well, I promise I'll think about it, if anything." I said.

3

I had to ask, *had* to ask, Shien about the old guy.

"Hunter Wolf? I hear he's living in Australia right now, besides taking strange trips to Gods know where in between. Here, look, he sent the Organization a picture of himself and his ostrich." Shien said, and showed me a picture on her phone of Hunter lounging on a plastic lawn chair on the beach, wearing some shorts and ridiculous Hawaiian t-shirt in shades with an ostrich beside him.

"Ha. Old weird dude." I said.

"Politics say that he's one of the next up for leadership in the Organization. He keeps declining the offer, which happens to only gain him more support." Shien said, turning off her phone immediately to save batteries.

"That's good of him… I'm glad I crossed paths with him, well, you know, not *really*… but I'm glad he finished what he started. Without him I'd still be raging and raging, trying to kill anyone who even *looked* like the bastard that killed my father… I've got more of a sense of peace now, yeah."

"To me you still seem like a very wild and upstart woman, wondering which way to go every time the convoy leader loses his footing…" Shien said.

The convoy leader was looking around himself, looked at a map, and then continued down the route he was going down. We followed him, marching behind the truck that carried much needed supplies and space for supplies.

I continued the conversation, and said, "That's *Wallace*. Don't say something like that, in case you *actually* want to get lost..."

"Oh, I just thought the people of America still listened to their primal calling, to roam the highways and such without a care in the world. I did not know we were going specifically to the ruins of an old town to hack up any farmland we can get, and take the proceeds to a corporate midway that sells its citizens to the highest bidder..."

I slowed my pace, and she stopped behind me. I soon stopped too, and just looked at her.

I had a desperate look on my face, and said, "Please, Shien, you're not supposed to talk about that. It's no good for morale."

"Oh? You all wish to be homeless bikers instead still? Believe me, that would be a wonderful change to this sort of conventional ruggedry that doesn't even allow one to look at the natural landscape rolling by..."

"No... That thing you said about selling the refugees. That's not what we really do!" I said.

"Isn't it? Hardly a shame, hardly at all. We all need good working hands and joyful fresh faces in the workplace..."

"It's- It's just that we get the people to where they need to go, and that's that. Some need workers, some need craftsmen, and we make sure they get there!!" I said.

"Ah... I see. Her Majesty's rule is complete and nonnegotiable, even to hearty and good souls who once forsook all evil and corruption." Shien said.

"That's- I'm- I'm still like that!! I just do it for the right cause now, you'll see!! Just... *March, soldier!*"

Shien sneered at me with a wicked look on her mien, and marched in a ridiculous fashion past me. I sighed and rubbed my face... The guys were looking, and I didn't need to be drummed out because of my *ridiculous* traveling associate...

4

I was still grumbling to myself at the stuff Shien said, on the ground in my sleeping bag as she was a bit aways from me in her own.

But... she was so... *right.* I had been losing my way, just for the extra snacks I could trade for little mementos, little things that proved my time meant something to me...

I had started up a photo collage, of faces I would never see again. Pictures of me and the guys, pictures of my old family from when I was a child, pictures of the landscape and wildlife I happened to cross paths with. I'd never see any of them again, and I was whiling away my time working for *Her Majesty...*

She always said, through her little workers, that I was essential in keeping this area secure. Said that Base 64 could keep going with people like me. I thought she meant my skills hunting the evil around the area, and didn't expect it to be routine congratulations given to *anyone* working for her, despite the wording being different for each one here.

The guys talked and joked about seeing their families in the Capitol. Said they just had to go through one more tour, before they could get them whatever they wanted. I just did it because... kind of because I thought people needed me. For that little girl who gave me the flower, and people like her. The ones who *couldn't* stand alone in the darkness, the ones who *needed* a helping hand in these hard times.

I don't know… I just grumbled to myself until I fell asleep.

I shouted my frustrations at an old dweller, saying that this was all a waste of time, and that no one needed me, that I may as well walk off into the distance and *die...*

Cthaklc just said, "**W**here *would you* go?"

"Um… Did you not hear me? I said I would die."

Cthaklc just shrugged, and read the almanac, as he was doing. He pointed to a clipping here, right here, that said in the 1940s turnip growth would be surprisingly bountiful.

I nodded, and said that was neat.

He continued to read, absorbed in that small little book.

I turned away, to look at the farm of my dad's that I grew up on.

I walked around the sunflowers, and said hi to the cows.

"Hello, Olivia." a cow said.

I waved to her, and continued to walk through the sunflowers.

So bright… the sun looked through the fields… so bright…

I woke up in the morning suddenly to one of the guys shaking my shoulder.

He said, "C'mon, Olivia. Sun's shining."

"Oh… Ok. Thanks, Tom."

I looked at the sun barely peeking over the horizon, and got ready for today's march.

5

This wasn't good.

Wallace called me up to the front, and asked me about the scratch marks on a nearby tree.

I didn't want to tell him, but it was my duty to.

"They're werewolf markings, sir."

A quiet descended on the convoy, and Wallace looked to them, then back at me and cleared his throat, "Er, about how many of them, soldier?"

"This looks like an alpha wolf's mark, so at least a pack of three or more. You can see it by the length of the claw marks. Now, the next full moon should be a week away, but we still don't want to run into any of them in human form. Werewolves... ain't particularly friendly folk." I said.

Someone in the convoy said, "Werewolves? Chupacabras and fairies, too?"

A few of them laughed, but Wallace stared daggers at the man, and they shut up. Wallace gave a little speech to the men, as Shien watched, him stating that things had changed in the good ol' U.S.A., and that myths were in fact real, at least these days. "Chupacabras are a little further south, right, Lamb?"

I nodded my head, and Wallace continued.

"And if there are any *damned* fairies, you either beg they offer you peace, or tell the man to quit being such a nut and get dressed proper, you hear?"

The men muttered yes sirs, and I went back to Shien.

She told me that was a very well done speech, hard to find in such a rural part of America.

"Oh, well he was just kidding about the fairy thing." I said.

"Was he? I've known to never cross one of the fae. They are very capricious, if they do not get what they want." Shien said, and walked forward with the others.

"Ha! Ha…" I laughed, realizing there really was so much of the world I didn't know about…

Us two trailed in the back, as I begged the specifics about "fairies," and Shien was strangely happy to oblige. She seemed like she was in a bad mood this whole trip, but seemed happy to dump her knowledge of the subject on me.

"When I traveled Europe there in fact were many secret portals to the Fae." Shien said, "Not even a thimble's length in actuality, so any human would have a far more difficult time to get through them. The kingdoms of the Fae are closely guarded secret, usually reserved for moon struck lunatics or little children. A fae could ask you something big or small, from eternal love to a short smile, sometimes even where your treasure is hoarded so that they can either steal it, or burn it down.

"The nature of Fae is rather reclusive, and I believe, if they ever went to America, that they were hunted down and devoured by our more primal spirits and ancestors, often seen depicting Native American tribal poles. The spirits are ever at war with the fae, who play tricks on them and get them lost in the afterlife.

"If a fae asks you for *anything,* understand that that could not be what they truly desire. They could actually be asking for the opposite thing, in a sing song riddle, or may just want to see you give up or die trying. Know that true bargains with the fae are everlasting and unbreakable, and if you *do* gain something you desire from a fairy, pixie, or other fae creature, then you should be very sure to hold onto it close, unless the object or feeling gets tired of you and desires to pass back into the realms of Fae."

"…How do you know so much about this?" I asked.

"Books, Olivia. As well as my own exploring here and there. The lunatics really aren't that bad to talk to, much more preferable than idiot children, and sometimes divulge a secret or two if you are willing to listen to their heartbreak and trauma."

"Oh. Kids aren't that bad!"

She looked disapprovingly at me, and we continued to walk forward. I had a great bounce in my step, after listening to this hidden lore, and had daydreams all throughout my head about what I'd ask for from a fairy or Fae creature.

6

"Hey look! Mushrooms! Gosh, it's been so long since I had some good shitake..." a soldier said, reaching down to a speckled reddish brown mushroom in the grass.

"Don't!" I yelled out, "Those are amanita mushrooms! They're really poisonous!"

He looked back at me, and wiped his hand on his shirt, even though not touching the mushroom. "Just doing my job, Lamb. Don't need to shout so hard."

I knelt before the amanitas, and plucked one of them, shoving it in my pocket.

"Whatch you do that for...? Didn't you just say-"

I poured a bit of my drinking water on my hand, and said, "I did. But it's never too bad to have a little poison, eh? Could come in handy if those werewolves try to eat us, or if someone gets on my case, and I slip this into their rations..."

The man gulped, nodded, and said, "You sure are a scary scout, Lamb. Say, how'd you get those scars on your face...?"

I walked forward as the man followed, and I said, "You wouldn't know, even if I told you. Do you know what ghasts are?"

"No, do you?"

"Yes, I do. They're ghosts who still have a very corporeal form in our plane of existence. They're more commonly called 'ghasts' when they are out of the form they are possessing, and often have long nails or a weapon they can use to harm someone who spooks them."

"So a poltergeist. Got it."

"No, no, no. A poltergeist is generally a mischievous spirit, who either haunts a place because of someone who wronged them or is genuinely just bored in the afterlife."

"But in the movie, everything was trying to kill them because of that poltergeist. So they're Native American?"

"I didn't say that. They could be, but you probably will never know, and usually the person blames whatever the poltergeist did on themselves, thinking they just forgot about it, except in cases like that movie. But then the person usually just blames someone else, instead."

"So a Native American slashed your face? Why'd he do that?"

I sighed, and said, "No, a *ghast* slashed my face. It was this whole mass resurrection/possession thing, in an old, defiled church, and after we caught all the possessed bodies, and were cutting them down with silver bullets, the ghast got out of a body, and cut me, riiiight here, and it left the scars you see."

"Oh. So that's why it's so white. Cuz ghosts are white...?"

"I guess. Believe me, it stung for days, and I couldn't wash it or bandage it hard enough, no matter what I did. I suppose it's a nice battle trophy, eh?"

"Sure comes with a story. I only wanted some mushrooms, not to know every little detail about you. Although..." he snorted and grinned, trying to talk suave and sexy, "Maybe you can tell me more about poltergeists sometime? I really loved that movie as a kid."

He continued that idiotic smile, and I patted my pocket with the mushroom, saying, "No thanks. But I could slip this into your morning coffee if you don't back off. Let me know if you see any more of them, ok? They're a great find."

He gulped, got a little pale, and said, "S-Sure thing, Lamb. S-Sure thing."

I smiled, and went back to walk beside Shien.

7

I saw a rabbit walking on two legs. I did a double take at it, and it was hopping on all fours when I looked again.

I told Shien I'd be right back, and she waited on the trail for me.

I followed that rabbit. Thing looked pretty tasty, no doubt about it.

It looked back at me, and somehow looked... annoyed?

It ate some grass, and I was pulling out my shotgun...

It looked annoyed still, and ran away before I could take aim.

I sighed. Guess we'll be eating dried packet rations tonight again...

I walked with Shien, and as we were talking, I fell into a hole.

I just fell, and fell, and fell.

I thought, as I was falling, shit. This was probably going to hurt a lot.

I closed my eyes, waiting for impact...

And landed on some pretty four leaf clovers all around me, *huge* ones, that were so very comfortable to land on.

The rabbit, who was huge, was pointing at me to a leprechaun, and the leprechaun smacked a bludgeon in his hand, and went up to me. He began reading my rights.

I guess he was sort of a cop...?

I said, "Look, I'm sorry for chasing your rabbit, but I was just very hungry! You gotta understand!"

The cop leprechaun shook his head, and slammed handcuffs on my wrists, dragging me with him.

They slammed the jail cell door behind me, as I looked out on a world of Fae through the cell bars.

Wow. A huge, brilliant, mushroom castle... that I was in the dungeon of.

I was later, after being fed only a piece of candy corn, dragged before the Fae King and Queen.

I was thrown in front of them, handcuffs still around my wrists, and slowly got up, looking at the most beautiful people I've ever seen. They even seemed to sparkle, somehow, and somehow even their emotions were beautiful to me.

It was extreme rage.

They claimed that I was an invader, a no good doer, an evil hunter, and a malicious human.

"Hey!" I said, "I'm only one of those things! Well. Maybe two, but I'm not evil! It's very difficult to live up above, in the land of... humans! We're all very hungry, sometimes, and gotta hunt to survive!"

They fluttered their wings in anger, and the Queen said, "Whatst thou give for your freedom? Whatst thou give, for justice?"

I looked at her. Was it some sort of riddle?

I just said, "I don't really have anything to give. All I can say is I sure won't be hunting no more bunnies that hop around on two feet."

The King and Queen deliberated my argument, and the King nodded. He said, "It ist hard to tell the difference between what ist yours, what ist ours, and what ist theirs. But what will you give?"

I felt the mushroom in my pocket, and offered it to the King and Queen.

They gasped.

I looked worried at that gasp which seemed to last forever, and the Queen said, "You knowst of our kind? We are the Third Generation of Amanita Fae, Brother and Sister of the Final Realm, and All Realms Beyond."

"Um. I know not to take your words in vain, or your kindness." I said, and knelt before them.

They applauded me, as did their Fae court, a fairy undid the shackles on my wrist, throwing them to the ground, and the King said, "Please, rise, rise. If you would wear our banner, in the world of the humans, we would be forever grateful. Please, what ist it that one as you could desire?"

Was this some sort of Fae wish?

Even though I had been thinking about it all day, I still had to take a moment to decide...

I wanted to see my father again... but no, I don't think I'd truthfully ever do so, and I've made my peace with that.

I wanted to eliminate evil... but if I asked that, where would it end? Evil is always blurred and shrouded, what could seem good, could really be not, and what could seem evil, could really be your best friend. I knew better than to muck about with the realms of morality.

I only humbly asked for my freedom, the freedom to wear their banner in peace, and if I ever desired aid again, that I would be able to humbly ask for it once more.

"Granted." they both said, but the Queen also said, "Oh. Take some money or something, too, and just please give the rabbit what it deserves next time."

I slowly nodded, kind of confused, and a hole opened up under me, as they tossed in mushroom bits after me.

I thought.

This was going to really hurt, this time...

But I was just fwooshed forward, like being pushed, out of the hole and into the light of day again.

I was right behind Shien, as she was continuing our conversation, and she said, "You seem kind of quiet, Olivia, are you ok?" and looked back at me.

I stared incredulous at her, and picked up the mushroom bits scattered around me.

I saw that damned bunny in the distance seem to smirk at me, and I left it some of the mushrooms, which it hopped up carefully to, and ate from.

I looked at that damned little guy. Looked cute, but I wasn't feeling so hungry as I had been. That candy corn really filled me up actually.

I asked Shien to give me a tattoo at camp that night, had all the equipment myself, of an amanita mushroom on my bicep. She did the artwork wonderfully, and I flexed looking at my shroom tat.

8

We got to a town, and found *beautiful* fields of pumpkins and grain, with a kindly old lady sitting on a porch and offering us alcoholic pumpkin juice.

Wallace and I took a sip from the offered cups, and while he looked like he was going to spit it out, I sighed in comfort as the chill of good homebrew caressed my psyche.

Wallace asked her more specifics, and she said her boys were all working the fields still, in this abandoned, desolate town, which seemed to be completely taken over by this family in favor of making the grandest farm I'd ever seen. Empty lots were now booming farmland, the parks rolled by with produce, and it was all thanks to this lady and her family.

Wallace nodded to some of his men, and said, "Looks good enough. We'll be sending more people soon to appropriate what we can. You should come with us, Miss, it's not safe outside of the outposts."

She looked flabbergasted at him, a look of complete, utter shock and awe, as he tried to grab her by the hand and drag her to the truck. She hit at him, and while I tried to calm her down, she spit in my face.

I stopped, wiping off the spit, as she screamed for help from her sons.

Some men came up to the truck, wielding pitchforks and scythes, and our men settled into formation, aiming all of their guns at the young men. They dropped their tools and surrendered, and a few of our guys snapped handcuffs on a few of the unruly ones, and shoved them behind the van to be marched back to Base 64.

Shien was looking at the whole scene, arms crossed, with complete, everlasting disdain.

I felt the red go to my face looking at her looking at me like that, and simply told Wallace I would be checking around the town for any hint of the supernatural...

They... rounded up all of these poor villagers, and grabbed whatever produce they could to be piled up in the van. Shien followed me as I walked off briskly.

She said, "We can go to the sacrificial zone now. Much better than being here."

I rubbed my eyes, and said, "I know what you're thinking, but those people will be thanking us, when they're in the Capitol..." hardly able to believe my own words.

"It doesn't matter in the grand scheme right now. We need to go, and while it would be almost pleasant to be left alone from your militarized friends, I think we shouldn't linger in this place for very long without due purpose. The spirits... I can already feel the spirits of old America whisper in discontent at what is happening."

"Ok... As long as they don't be whispering my name in the night, or some shit..." I mumbled, walking behind a briskly walking Shien.

9

We looked around the "sacrificial site." It was a large, seemingly volcanic, hole in the ground.

I looked down, as it blasted steam upwards, and asked Shien what we were supposed to do now.

She looked at some old, old parchment, mumbling to herself. She said, "By the timeframe given from this manuscript, people should already be traveling to the area in droves and jumping off into the pit..."

"Maybe its all a bunch of hogwash? Something that was supposed to happen, but never would?" I said. I continued, "Like the whole Revelations bit in the Bible? I sure ain't seeing no Horsemen in the skies, but if it feels like it's the end of the world, then it sure is today."

"No... No. I don't think so... I'm pretty sure... Yes. It can't be something so stupid like the last bit of the Bible, planning doom for all..." she said, searching the manuscript hard, but sighed, and sat down by the volcanic pit. She said, "I suppose it could be... I guess this was all a waste of time, Olivia."

"Good. I'm glad the worst isn't really the worst, when it comes down to it. Now, I know you've got a lot of problems with my work... but I'm gonna work *really* hard on getting those people some good farmland, somewhere they can call home, farthest away from petty corporate greed that I can."

"That's good of you, Olivia. I admit the whole thing rubs me the wrong way. Even in the Land of Freedom, freedom doesn't seem to come free."

"I know, I know… I'm sorry you had to go through all this with no big shebang at the end. I'm sure you must have been really worried, if those spirits crossed into the mundane and caused all sorts of ruckus. Might leave you out of a job, eh? If things are so bad they're not worth fixing?"

She smiled slightly sinisterly at me, and said, "I think I could manage, even if worse comes to worst. You know, I have not a bad hand at divination, and may start the trade up just to be able to purchase fare away from this continent."

"Ooh. Care to read my future? I'm a Pisces." I said, sitting down before her by the volcanic pit.

She gestured to my palm, and I offered it to her.

She felt the lines on my palm, very delicately, but thorough, finding the exact meaning she needed to from the scars on my skin.

She shut her eyes, feeling only the skin on my palm, and said, "I sense a very difficult birth, a rupture in time that will never be still…"

"Oh yeah! My mom did have a bad birthing of me. I came too soon. Was close to being a stillborn, actually."

She continued, "The stars will never favor one such as you, born in the month of darkness and despair… destined for it, throughout all the time you walk under the sun…"

"Um. Ok."

"I cannot speak for your future, but it seems you will have a great part to play in all manners coming forth…" Shien opened her eyes, and said, "That's a usual gimmick, to say that a person has a great part to play still. But where was I…"

She shut her eyes again, as I giggled.

"Hmm… I see a redheaded boy… No, bald? Is he an old man?"

"That's *Jasper!* He used to have long, rolling red locks... What's it say about him, hm?"

She felt my palm, felt it again, and opened her eyes. She looked into mine, and said, "He's dead, Olivia."

"Wh-What??"

"I'm sorry, Olivia..."

She just hugged me immediately. I didn't believe her words. I couldn't. Everything would be fine, for everyone, especially at Base 64.

Then someone approached from behind us, and I immediately had my shotgun pointed into the wilderness, asking who's there, and that they better show themselves.

A young woman with dazed eyes, flowers in her hair, looking like she just came from the farm we were just at, walked towards us.

"HALT! Don't move, Miss." I stated.

She continued to walk up to me, in that strange daze.

And jumped into the volcanic pit, before I could stop her.

10

I heard a roaring and rumbling coming from that pit, and the wind started to scream in my ears, almost pushing us down as we were by the pit.

Shien shouted, *"This is what was prophesied!! We need to leave, before something catches us here!!"*

I looked down at the pit, back at Shien, as the night was coming down. I heard long howls in the wind, and followed her as we ran from the sacrificial site.

We got back to the convoy, and the old woman was struggling under the grasp of some of the guys, and she said, "Where's Olive?! She's not here, we can't leave without her!!" The men tried to ask her what she looked like, where she was last seen, and the old woman just continued to panic, saying, "She never was a right one!! She never was very happy!! We can't leave her, we *can't!!*"

I said, "I'm... sorry, Miss. She jumped into that hole in the ground, down east a bit aways."

The old lady looked into my eyes. She had complete despair enveloping them.

She collapsed to kneeling, mumbling, "Not Olive... Why Olive? Not Olive..."

There were more howls in the wind, and I had my hand on my shotgun, *ordering* the men to march *right now.* We needed to leave this place, as fast as we could.

The farmers behind us marched solemnly in the convoy, as the old woman cried in the truck. I had all my instincts opened wide, for whatever would be in the night. The full moon looked down on us, and seemed to mock me as it did.

Damnit. This was never supposed to happen. Shien kept reading the prophetic text by the light of her phone, growling in anger and wrath. I asked her if she could help, or needed help, or something.

She just said, "I *wanted* to *stop* this!! The 'chose one' shouldn't be some random suicidal girl that this fucking convoy pissed off!! IT should've been me!! And I was supposed to deny it, and allow a new age of freedom for all!!"

She mumbled and growled, and I took my eyes away from her to see a large, dark, howling form on the hill.

I looked into its hungry, lupine eyes. Werewolves.

They raced down the hill to us, all four of them, and I ordered all as a unit to shoot at the heads!! Into the eyes, anywhere you see a weakness!!

The men followed my command, and shot at the werewolves. A werewolf got too close, the alpha by his size, and lunged at a man, dragging him into the forest by his neck as he tried to scream.

The farmers started to panic, and the old lady cried out, *"RUN! RUN FOR YOUR LIVES, MY CHILDREN, RUN!!"*

This broke the spell of obedience on the farmers, and they rushed off into the wilderness, to be devoured by the werewolves, by the sound of it.

But there was a horrible snarling, coming from the other side.

I looked into the wilderness and nearly dropped my shotgun by the unholy thing I saw in the darkness, revealed only briefly by my shotgun flashlight.

That.

That was…

It couldn't be.

Shien shouted out, "Chupacabras!! Everyone, keep moving forward!!"

The chupacabras and werewolves were fighting each other over the remains of those farmers, slicing at each other with those long talons and roaring something fierce.

11

We ran.

We kept running.

Until, finally, the morning sun shone down on us.

I breathed a sigh of relief. That was Base 64, far into the distance... Could only really tell by the smoke coming from the buildings, and the lights, which kept shining even in the brilliant light of dawn.

We kept walking. Wallace looked a little worse for wear, taking a nasty bite from a werewolf that if I wasn't standing over him just then, shooting my shotgun at its eyes, the thing would've mauled him to pieces right then and there. Shien was frowning, instead of smiling wickedly, and seemed to walk with a dazed expression to the outpost with us. A lot of the men were praying, strangely. I thought that religious ideology that came into the base would do everyone some good, but they still seemed so scared.

The old lady just sat in the back of the truck, with a listless expression on her face, being bumped slightly this way and that as the truck turns.

When we got close to the outpost, I noticed a few sad mourners, a family dressed in black, as a body was paraded out of the base.

The hand fell off the cart, and the father, by the looks of him, nudged it back on.

My face went white. They were taking Jasper... away...

I asked the father what happened, and he looked at me sadly and said, "Suicide. Are you… Lamb? Olivia Lamb?"

"I-I-I am."

"Thank you for being with my son when you could've been. I… don't think he could take it, after his mother died, and he got the news that your scouting party had perished…"

"W-We didn't perish, though! See, we're all fine, every one of us!! Mostly. Some got killed off by the beasts, and some… just ran. I'm so sorry, Mister Laserfiche."

He just looked at me with an expression of heartbreak, and continued to follow the cart, which Jasper was picked up and placed in the back of a van. The father told me they would be taking him back to the Capitol, and wished me luck.

The van drove off, and I couldn't help but burst out crying.

I just got to my boarded up house, slammed the door, and moaned as loud as I could.

Shien followed me, opening and closing the door behind her, and simply sat on a chair, looking off into nothingness.

I ran to my collage by my bed, and pasted the picture of Jasper right in the center, where he should be, smiling to me after he got his buzz cut.

I simply looked on at all those smiling faces. Jasper. My dad. The rest.

Why would he kill himself?? There must be some sort of foul play, just had to be. Someone must've been picking on him, or, no, coerced him into suicide.

I ran around the base, trying to find any bit of info I could about Jasper. I found out that we were claimed a failed mission as soon as we crossed a certain border when the werewolves struck, where Base 64 could not contact us. For all they knew, we were dead. I continued to look, and I met friends of Jasper's who this event took completely off guard. They knew he had a mother that was very sick, but did not know Jasper was as well. In the end, I was before Her Majesty herself, and she slammed the suicide note before me. She was scowling, and I peeked at the note, trying to glimpse any bit of truth.

The... The man said he was just depressed, couldn't go on living in today's time. No matter how hard he tried, he just said he wanted to blow himself up. Told me... *me...* Olivia Lamb... that he was very sad to know I lost my life on a scouting expedition.

"We... We didn't die, though." I told Her Majesty.

"You are formally relieved of duty, Miss Olivia Jetson Lamb. There will be no more need of your talents. Whatever you say will have no more bearing on your position here."

"But- If I wasn't there, telling the men what to do, we'd all have been eaten!!"

"Again, whatever you state now will have no bearing on your position. Unless you'd like me to press charges, I can make a formal inquiry into how you got the position you *had,* and how you were so grossly incompetent during so."

I was white in fury as Her Majesty stared daggers into me, and turned my back on her, leaving the suicide note of Jasper's, and going to pack whatever I needed from my house, to never come back ever again.

12

I flipped off one of those religious sect people who pitied me, who stated I was a degenerate and a whore.

I just rested my bag on my back in a more comfortable position, and left with Shien out of Base 64, where I had spent so much time at, foolishly believing I was doing some sort of good.

They confiscated my combat suit, my shotgun, anything I used in a professional capacity, and I sold, gave away, or traded the rest. I suppose things were tough to come by, but they could've treated Black Betty a little nicer. She was a good shotgun, a pretty shotgun, and didn't need to be handled so roughly.

I had sold the house back to the corporation that gave me it, getting a little bit of notes that they promised would hold their value. I would've preferred just some extra food, and traded some of the notes for just that from the quartermaster. He and I had a pretty good standing, as I was an avid trader and barterer, always giving whatever I could spare to the refugees, so he gave me a little more than what the notes were worth.

Shien said, as the gates of Base 64 shut behind us, "That was a good trip, all and all. I learned that if something is prophesied to happen, you'd be a fool to go about stopping it. That *is* why they're called prophesies, and not wishy washy wishes."

"I think if you weren't there, warning us about the chupacabras, things would've been much worse off."

"Oh, that was just something I picked up from my past. From meeting Hunter Wolf, believe it or not. I learned to recognize the beasts, and always do a little research about local fauna and wildlife wherever I go before heading out."

"But they were so quiet. Not like the werewolves. If they, I suppose, didn't have a run in with the werebeasts, we probably would've all been murdered in our sleep by them anyway."

"I suppose. Anyway, what is it you wish to do now, Olivia? The world is opened to you, and you no longer need to take the yoke of your elders who happen to hold only financial power over you."

"I don't know. I suppose I could rent my services out."

"As a whore? Like that priest person suggested?"

"No… If I don't need to. When things get rough I don't mind having to look the other way and let the man finish, but I was talking about renting out my *skills.* You know, stuff I learned in the Organization."

"You wouldn't mind working for them on the side? They're reopening a lot of positions that they held, with members falling off left and right. Need anyone they can get, just like Hunter Wolf says."

"Hmm… As long as they don't fuck up my life with those orders. I'm getting kind of excited for this life of freedom bit, so nobody better come along and take it."

"Ha! I think a life in the Organization would do you well. They're a lot more relaxed than what they had been, especially with Hunter Wolf's guidance."

"So he's really the big boss now, huh?"

"No, but a lot of people come forth to him to ask for aid or advice. He never intervenes directly, but always seems to know just who to talk to.

If anything, he's a perfect company directory, since we all go and talk to him about things anyway."

"Hmm… You think you could set me up with an interview with him?"

"Sure! I'll give him a call right now, see if he's busy."

"Just like that, huh?"

She motioned me to be quiet, as she got on the phone and called Hunter Wolf.

I heard a cheery voice on the other end as Shien smiled wickedly at the person on the other side.

She made a formal application for me to Wolf-

Wolf pshawwed her down, and asked if he could speak to me himself.

Shien offered me the phone, which I took.

I heard some strange bird sounds on the other end, and Hunter Wolf said, "Lamb! It's been too long."

"Hi, old dude. What's new?"

He laughed uproariously, and said, "I'm trying a hand at ostrich farming. It's hard to do… because besides their temperaments, they just get this look in their eyes when the blade is about to come down… Smart birds. It's why I keep my best gal, Chickie, by my side most of the time. Couldn't kill her, no matter how helpless she looked. Isn't that right, Chickie? Aren't you a good little birdie? Yes you are!"

Wolf seemed to be talking off the phone to his ostrich.

He continued, clearing his throat, "But how are you, Lamb? Still alive, by the sounds of it. I'm so, so sorry that our paths crossed when you were younger, and that werewolf- Christian, the werewolf, slew your father like that… If there was anything I wish I could do over again, it would be that moment."

"Oh, it's ok… I was really just calling about a job."

"For me?"

"No, me, dummy! I hear you've got a lot of pull in the Organization. I'm not about to give up my free will, but having someone tell me where to go and what to do slightly wouldn't be a bad thing. Just give me a little advice, old man. I just got drummed out of my unit for Gawd knows what, and I've got all of cursed, good ol' U.S.A. at my feet."

"Hmm… How's your mother, by the way?"

"She's fine, I think. Living in the Capitol."

"You don't want to see her?"

"I… I kind of do. Is that a bad thing? Just tell me who to kill and how to kill them, and I'll be right on it, Mister Wolf!!"

"'Mister' Wolf? I've never heard anyone ever call me that, I think. Unless I was in trouble."

"Er… Old man! Please give me something to do, and then pay me to do it!"

"Go see your mother, Lamb. I think family is very important, and if you still need some spending money, I'll let…" he went on to talk about who and whom would pay me, give me orders, and the like, "…and if you really feel like it, maybe I can teach you how to be an ostrich farmer. It's not as easy as it looks!!"

"Thankyousomuch, Wolf! I'll talk to you later, if that's ok?"

"Of course! Stay safe, Lamb."

I smiled and hung up, giddy with glee, as Shien smiled wickedly.

13

I hooked up with Wolf on social media, in the sparse internet connectivity that I could, and he posted allll sorts of pics of his girlfriend, who looked almost younger than me!! Still the same age, that Charlotte looked, as I had seen her before... She certainly had a good bod, and beautiful blonde hair, that's for sure, posing and dancing around in that bikini in the night's light...

I laughed at a gif of her dancing eternally, back and forth, in a looped video. What a gal.

Oops. That's where coverage ended, as we passed another made up border.

The toll man looked pretty seedy, and wouldn't take the notes I got from Base 64.

He said, "What's good that gonna do me? I's need some good bread, dude."

"...Who do you work for, again?" I asked.

"...I'm the toll man!! I'm the specific and only toll man on the road, and if you wanna cross this 'ere highway, you answer to *me!*"

"...Can we go around it? I don't think we have enough rations to feed you, if we're gonna get to the Capitol."

"...You could, ya, but you might as well go back the way you came, if you can't cross this 'ere booth. This highway is a sacred an' important piece of American history, safest in the country, so if you wanna get past me, I'ma need something that can feed my belly."

"I don't think it'd be that hard to cross it. Just go around it, over there, by the looks of that crushed in fence."

"...That there's where gremlins go, yeah, who don't pay no tolls. I'd make 'em, but you ever seen a gremlin? Sharp little teeth, ugly fuckers. Look just like the kids down the road, 'f you don't mind me sayin'."

"...I can spare a packet of bread that'll last you a week, if you got anything more to give."

"'Ey now, who's the toll man and who isn't? Whaddaya mean, if I got anything to give?"

"Whatcha got? This is good bread, fresh baked and very hearty."

"...Can I see it?"

I pulled out a package of the bread, fresh baked around a week ago, but still pretty good if dipped in some water.

He drooled at the bread, but said, "That ain't no good 'nuff. I need, at least two of those if you wanna cross this 'ere toll."

"Oh, I'll give the man some bread if he really needs it..." Shien said, reaching into her bag.

I motioned her to be quiet, and continued to haggle.

"Why! Do you know what flour this is? This is Sir Louriflower flour, special from the best bakery... around here."

"Don't look like a flower." he said.

"Nonono, you know, the grain and wheat that's used to cook the bread? *That's* the flour that went into this here loaf."

"Sir... Sir Louriflower? 'E some sort of knight?"

"Oh yes, used to fight windmills and the like, but started hunting dragons. All the best flour is named after Sir Louriflower!"

"...Don't like those windmills. Kill all the birds, and are jus' so ugly."

"I know!! That's why Sir Louriflower specifically hunted them down. Was one of the most renowned windmill hunters in all the world, just like in the storybooks until society collapsed. Then, he *had* to go hunting dragons, unable to commit to his true calling, you know, maidens to feed and the like."

"...Used to be a librarian, I did. Never read a single book, and I'm proud of that to this day."

"Quite a good calling. I used to love going to the library and just getting a fresh drink of water, and looking at the comic books of the talking cat..."

He perked his head up, and said, "I got some o' those books! The little weirdo cat ones, too! Been no good to sit on, sleep on, nor even eat, but I can trade them for a bit o' that good Sir Louriflower bread you got."

"Ooh. Then I'll give you a tip with the bread... dip it in your coffee."

"Coffee?"

"Yeah! It's some old knowledge passed onto me by my grandma."

"Got a pot brewin', if you'd care to join me."

"You have *real* coffee??" I asked, as he got out of the toll booth with a steaming pot of coffee.

He poured the coffee into three cups for us three, and said, "Yeah. Some rich bitch came down this road, and just dumped all the stuff at me feet. Glad for the coffee, but it sure don't feed me."

We sat and drank coffee with the toll man, dipping our bread in the coffee and making jokes all day. I learned from him that apparently that evil woman, Her Majesty, was traveling down this road, and she's the one who gave him the coffee...

We waved the toll man goodbye, with his pot of coffee and big bag of bread, with some books in our bags and some good stories he told us in our heads.

Later in the night, Shien and I sat by the fire off the highway road. It was a grand fire, a roaring one, but Shien just seemed to shut her eyes and meditate as I roared by the roaring fire.

"Wooowee! What a great night. That toll man sure was right, this road is *safe!* No people as far as the eyes can see, yet not a single disturbing sound in the night… Bless that illiterate fucker, bless him."

Shien shifted, as she meditated.

I waved a hand at her, and sat by the fire with my books. We used some of the more boring, philosophical ones for tinder, but I just loved this gawddarned talking cat. It felt like I was opening up a piece of my childhood, smelling that old book smell and seeing that cat make jokes.

I was getting sleepy by the fire, as Shien just seemed to meditate…

I looked at that blaze which was slowly turning gentler, kinder, smaller, with a smile on my face…

I saw, before I drifted off to sleep, Cthaklc sit beside us by the fire.

He looked at me, with his tentacled face, and said, "Is *this* a good time?"

I nodded, falling asleep, and Cthaklc shrugged. We watched the Native Americans ride by on their motorcycles, popping wheelies and whooping down the road…

14

Shien asked me, after I accidentally brought up the subject, "Did you once have to work as a whore?"

"Er... Not particularly... Just after things got real chaotic, remember? There was this fire, this beautiful fire, and food, meat, good stuff, with everyone happy and drinking booze... I wandered over to that fire, and quickly saw that the only way to get what *I* wanted, was to give the dude who was holding me what *he* wanted. It was a wild night, and I'm thankful I don't really remember it, but I suppose that's the closest I've ever had to sell myself."

"I once did so for a kabuki theater performance. Pure curiosity, I assure you. I wanted to get into the entire role of the geisha, and he paid me, I performed, and I continued to perform throughout the night. It was an enlightening experience, and I was even offered a permanent stay by the... headmistress, I suppose you'd call her. But like I said, it was pure curiosity."

"...It's not a good feeling, is it?"

"I thought it was rather... interesting. I happily doled out my services to the man, and he happily responded. I see it more as a work experience, rather than anything I could call recreational."

"...I hated it. I hated being before this douchebag, that I could've snapped in half if I really wanted to, but he was part of... their society. All those people, all dancing and drinking together… They were together. I was completely alone."

Shien sighed and rested a hand on my shoulder, as I was consumed by memory, sucking dick, bending low, all that, just for a piece of meat and somewhere warm to sleep.

"It was so good when people were a little more respectful, y'know?" I said, and we kept walking.

"I don't think it ever really changed. People are still rude, distasteful, expecting more than their fair share… At least the wildlife seems to have taken a firm hold on the world, nature has bit back, with fangs, and we no longer may hear her cries unanswered."

"Haha! I guess that's one way to put it. I believe that there's a distinct 'essence' in nature that shouldn't be there now… All the vampires, were-wolves, chupacabras… They don't belong in our world."

"Perhaps we do not belong in theirs."

"Hmm… I don't know, but if one tries to steal my life, I'm gonna be fighting back with all I got."

"Quite primal of you. Do understand that we don't need to be calling out for this fight, however. If it needs to happen, it will."

"Yeah, yeah, I understand. Prudence. I don't like to hide from things, though, just know. I don't like to be hidden in the bushes, or a closet, and wait until the monster has enough time to really do something bad."

"That's understandable. Anyway, were there any men in your life besides that poor young man who happened to die back at the outpost?"

"Hmm… There were high school dudes, but y'know, they were just high school dudes. When I graduated high school I dated a cutie, a real pussy actually, who thought I was a barista, instead of already working for the Organization. This was around the time you met me."

"Ah yes. The cute, wide eyed Lamb in her pubescence."

"Hey! I wasn't *that* young! Anyway, the guy ditched me when everything started collapsing. Spouted all this BS about being together forever… but just packed his bags with his mommy, and left. My mom was already swept up in everything, and I couldn't latch onto my mother like *him*…"

"Sometimes… and I don't say this as a pickup line or anything, I've found women to be much stronger, and more pleasurable, than men."

"Woah now, missie, that sounded like quite a pickup line, if you don't mind me saying so, especially with that long look of desire you just gave me."

Shien smiled wickedly, and said, "What look?"

I just laughed, and said, "Whatever. Do whatever you have to do to give you that good feeling down below. I've never been that desperate, but you do you."

"Desperation? Really? So, you're saying you would rather spend another night with that man you sold yourself to, than me?"

I looked into her eyes for a long second.

She smirked.

I said, "Cut it out. We only have a few more nights of this, and you better keep your hands to yourself."

She raised her hands in the air, and paraded before me. I laughed.

15

I quickly averted my gaze as Shien took off her shirt to be more comfortable. She wasn't even wearing a bra!!

"Are you ok, Olivia? I don't have some strange marking on me, do I?"

"Er... No!! It's just... ever since you said that weird little lesbo thing, it's been making me..."

"Uncomfortable?"

"Uncomfortable. That's the right word." I said, with my back to her.

"I'm sorry. Thank you for letting me know. I don't plan to be restricted to clothing forever, but I'll make sure to keep it a private moment to oneself."

She put back on her shirt, and I turned back to her and sighed.

She said, "I told you it wasn't a pickup line."

I rolled my eyes, and said, "You make me wonder, ok? Is that ok to say? I usually don't *ever* think about that shit, but just know, you kinda make me do so."

"Am I forcing you to do so? Tying you down, and having my way with you?"

"No..." I said, trying to avoid her gaze.

"Then know I never will tie you down to have lustful relations, without your permission. Is that good enough?"

"See!! See, just there, you did it again!! It sounds like you're *offering* to do that, and not setting boundaries like a proper person!"

She looked at me quizzically, and said, "I thought that's what I was doing."

"You're too wordy! You get tied up in your words, and swirl around in them, and don't know where the truth really is!! I don't want to have sex with you, by the sounds of it you don't want to have sex with me, but I can't tell by all your swirly words!"

"Hmm... Are you sure this isn't something personal to you, and not me?"

"No!! There you go again, shifting all the blame and pressure on me! Ever since we met again, you've been like a very wordy moral compass, and even though I admit it's not so bad all the time, I don't need a moral compass for sex! Just... Keep me out of your fantasies!"

She huffed, crossed her arms, and said, "I never had any fantasy in mind. In fact, I find the truth of what you and I do to be far better over some silly daydream."

"We don't do anything, though!!"

"We've been making a beautiful journey through beautiful America. I'd say, based on my previous romances, that if you *weren't* feeling a tad romantic towards me, then I should take it as an insult. Although I tell this as your friend, Olivia. Nothing. Changed. I'm still your grouchy mentor and you're a nice student, ok?"

I felt the red go to my face, and said, "I ain't no plush butt student, eager to sit on your lap."

"Why, with that boney butt, you'd probably prefer it if I sat on your lap."

I growled at her, and she growled back.

I went off... to get more firewood.

<h1 style="text-align:center">16</h1>

We walked the day in silence. I looked back at Shien once, and she made an obscene gesture of flicking her tongue out between two fingers.

I grumbled at that.

We just ate food, kept walking, ate food, slept.

Ate food, kept walking, ate food, slept.

I kinda wished I never talked to her about sex. We could've just been bullshitting like we used to, but instead she's gotta get weird with her lesbomancy.

She stared into the fire, and said, "If you had to choose between an incubus or a succubus, which would you choose?"

"Neither, cuz they're both foul abominations that don't belong in the world of the living." I said, staring into the flames.

She sighed at the fire.

She said, "I fell to one who could be one, and then the other, then more, and other. It was a shameful moment for me, that I will never forgive myself for."

I looked at her, staring into the fire sadly.

She continued, "It's one thing to have sex with a living person, or even another thing to have sex with a ghost, it's a whole 'nother thing to have sex with a demon."

"Why? Aren't demons just dead bad people?"

"I suppose some could be. Some are truly awful creatures, that only tempt you with that dark feeling you desperately crave, but can never have. Even if you are fulfilled, and satisfied, from having sex with a demon, it is only a brief rest before the craving returns, and with it all the suffering that one could ever desire."

"…Sounds pretty messed up."

"It is. I thought I could command the demon to do whatever I wished. Was getting into darker magics and occult spirits, you see. It offered me very slight power, invisibility, magic I never thought possible. This being, it turns out, despite being given different names in different cultures, was Duke Sallos, a largely beneficent creature for many humans. But altogether unwholesome for me."

"…What did the bastard do?"

"He not only tempted me, but allowed me to have fulfilled urges, most especially if I would come down to his domain. I would be giving up on life, as a human, like *that.*" she said, and snapped her fingers. She continued, "I later only saw this for what it was. A suicide of very grand measures. But… the dreams… the meetings… they were like something out of a story book, a grand, lustful, erotic story book, tailored for only me. Even now, I am filled with an overwhelming feeling of nostalgia as I talk about those days, sometimes even think about them."

"…Continue."

"I had finally, after summoning this demon to Earth, with very well done bindings and precautionary measures taken, had what I wanted for so long. I had sex with this creature, and then the pits of Hell reached out for me. I had never been a Christian. I had never given demons of Satan their true respect. But then, as he smiled, so handsomely, after being oh so fulfilled, I had a shuddering feeling of the world without me.

"As if I was never here, had never been here, and would continue to never be here.

"I had to turn the demon, whom I called my love, down, and he only smiled, and respected the decision.

"Do you know how horrible that feels??"

"To be gone. That does sound scary... That sounds terrifying. Like life never even mattered."

"Invisible to even the Gods. But worse... was just that smug, understanding look he had given me. The 'oh, ok, that's fine, miss out on grand, beautiful, dirty sex and just go on being a human, ladida.' I wanted this!! I *needed* this. And *I* was the one to cut my dreams short."

She looked sadly into the fire, and I felt stupid for my little feelings of sexual insecurity.

I sat beside her, and just hugged her. She felt warm, and smelled pleasant, as she turned her face into my shoulder.

I only hugged her, and I thought I saw a smile in the flames.

I just stared at it until it went away.

"No one's gonna do that again. Just... to fuck with you that way... I mean in your head. Dude sounded like a righteous prick, and if I can help it, none of my friends are gonna get fucked in the head by a demon." I said.

She laughed, and returned the hug, saying, "Thank you, Olivia. I think you've given me a bit of relief over that whole incident. It was something I've regretted for years."

I smiled at her, and she kissed me on the cheek, and I allowed her, then allowed her to get up, and go to bed in her sleeping bag, as I watched the night and the fire.

17

I saw something left by the fireside.

"Um, Shien, you left your medication." I said, picking up the bottle of pills.

"Oh, I won't need them anymore." she said, already making a start down the road.

"I really think you should take your medication, Shien, trust me, I hear that does a load of good. And seriously, I don't need you doing something crazy if I need your help down the road. Seeing hallucinations, throwing shit, whatever, you don't need that crap."

"They didn't stop hallucinations for me. They started them. Those are pills that increased spiritual coalescence in my body, allowing me to see and interact with ghosts, spirits, and oni."

I looked back at the pills. Big yellow and black ones. I saw Shien continue down the road, and I hurried after her with my bag bouncing on my back, "But why leave them? Isn't that your job, and favorite thing to do, anyway?"

She looked at the pills, looked forward again, and said, "The time has come that those pills are now worthless. They won't do anything, anymore. The veil has been lifted, permanently, forever."

"…Because of that suicidal chick?"

"Yes, and also because I failed. I did not stop the prophecy, nor deny it, or absolutely do anything."

"It's not your fault." I said, walking beside her, still holding the bottle of pills.

"It pretty much was. I believed that the prophecy could be accepted, fulfilled, and also denied, by anyone who dared try. Turns out it was fated for that girl to kill herself, and things would turn up for the worst anyway."

"Nothing's written in the stars, and fate is just a toy used by fat chicks who can't get dates. I don't care if I'm a Pisces, and I'm pretty sure no one cares. Fate is what you make of it, I always knew. If you want to bow your head down and listen to 'fate,' then really that's an excuse to not give a shit or take part in the world around you, and blatantly accept that you really, by fate's purpose, have no purpose."

"Very aptly said. I believe there is some truth in your words. Still, perhaps if it was not a prophecy, it was at least a warning that if one more soul, a 'pure soul arisen from the flowers themselves,' killed herself in that spot, going back to the ashes from whence she came, that the boundaries of living and the dead would break, tearing all asunder. I already know that I can see ghosts without the pills. I saw them last night, wailing, howling, and laughing in the wind."

"Sure that wasn't just the wind?"

"The wind, no matter how talkative it may be, never used to call me a 'cunt' before."

"…Sure it wasn't someone pulling a prank?"

She sighed, and continued walking, and said, "No… The bastard ghost kept doing it all night, I looked for him while you were sleeping, and he popped out of the ground and said, 'Boo, cunt!' scaring me onto my butt on the grass, and laughed away in the breeze. That's how bad things are now."

"Really? That doesn't sound that bad. Kind of mean, but probably just a silly poltergeist... that somehow you could see... and also talk to... a lot..."

"You've never seen a ghost besides the ghast that slashed your face, correct?"

"No... but I did a bit of research on them with the Organization when I could. If it helps, the ghast was also under the light of the moon, and I still could barely see him, but when he cut me with those nails, it sure as hell hurt."

"That's going to be happening a lot more now, and I'm sure they're all writhing in the moonlight still, endlessly following the Ghostly Parade, or anyone they care to, to find their way back to the afterlife. The smart ones won't try to get back to Earth, but the temptation is quite palpable."

"What's the Ghostly Parade?"

"Used to be a grand gathering of ghosts and spirits, all on their way to the afterlife, or from the afterlife to briefly visit humans for a spell in times of offering and when the veil is thin. They march in the Parade, specters, demons, spirits, ghosts, and oni, and none remember what they saw if they did see the Parade, the ones who weren't swept along with them to continue on to the afterlife."

I felt a shiver cross my spine, from the wind I think, and we continued to walk down the road.

I pocketed the bottle of pills anyway, thinking maybe I could sell them to some druggie or something, but still hoping those ghosts stayed far away from *me...*

18

"Wow! Lookit those walls!" I said.

"What are they hiding, you think?" Shien said.

"Lots and *lots* of people. C'mon! Let's get in line!"

We got in the long line to the Capitol front gates. The walls were *enormous,* 'bout skyscrapers high, and only a small entry was there for us to get in. It took all day, waiting in line, but we eventually got to the front.

"Identification?" the cop said at the front.

I pulled out my papers and old driver's license, and Shien pulled out her passports stating she was a Japanese citizen as well as American.

The man looked at the passports funny, and took a long time reading my papers.

"Sorry, but these don't state you can enter the Capitol." he said, handing back our ids, and then waving for the next people to come forth.

"But wait!! I'm Olivia Jetson Lamb, did a lot of work on Base 64! Everything I need to get inside should be there!" I said, shoving the papers back into the man's hands.

He raised his eyebrow at me, and looked at the papers again. The people behind us looked peeved.

54

He still gave me back the papers, and said, "Even so, I can't allow entry to every corporation scumbarrel that shoves identification in my face that, for all I know, could be fake."

"I ain't no corporation scum! At least not anymore!" I argued.

"All the scumbarrels get free entry, the bosses anyway, but if you ask me we don't need their kind to do our jobs in America." he said, waving for the next people to come forth.

I stepped in front of them again, and their donkey heehawed at me.

"What's a scumbarrel? And please… mister… My mother's in there, all alone… She's sick, needs some medicine." I said, with a teary look in my eye. I was even able to squeeze one out, that ran down my cheek. Nailed it!

He looked kind of grossed out, and said, "If I had a dollar for every woman that's- A scumbarrel is a gunman of the corporations, just like you claimed to be. Now take those pitiful crocodile tears away from me, and go back to your scumbarrel friends."

Shien said, "I can't come in, either?"

The cop shook his head, said, "The Japs are all well and fine to have around, but not their spies and secret agents, which from these fake passports it looks like you are."

"They aren't fake." she said.

He glared at her, and said, "If you don't want me to read your rights, and you can see how we do things in *America…* Then you'll get out of my face."

"¿Por qué tardan tanto, mama?" a child sitting on the donkey asked his mother.

He waved for them to come forth, and we stepped out of line. The people with the donkey just sauntered happily into the Capitol, after briefly showing some papers.

"What do some backwater farmers have that we don't? It looked like they were from Mexico." I said.

The cop glared at me, and said, "Class, if anything. Now get out of my sight, before I have to write you up."

I said, as he was helping the next people, "Listen, I got some notes from Base 64, I could give them to you if you let us in."

"Trying to bribe an officer..." the man said, as he wrote something down on a pad of paper.

I frantically tried to think of something, before I had to run, instead of negotiate.

I tried to pose sexily, and said, "Aww... man... I hate getting written up... Want to meet my friends, instead?"

He raised an eyebrow, stopping writing.

"I like to call them Tit and Tat..." I said, rubbing Tit.

He continued to write, saying, "Soliciting an officer..."

I took out the pills, and said, "Please, at least give these to my mother. She's very sick, and I spent a long time trying to find medicine that would help her. She lives on Nixon Street, and her name is Martha Lamb. My friend here is a doctor, but I'll have to send her back home to Japan without her help, I guess..."

I gently pressed the pills into his hand, and sighed, walking away with Shien.

The man shook the bottle of pills, and said, "Wait! I don't want to have to go to some sick woman's house. I'll write up a temporary pass for you, and you can get in."

I smiled wickedly with Shien as my back was turned, and turned back, saying, "Thank you so much!! You don't know how much this means to me. I'll tell my mother about you, say you saved her life. You are Mister...?"

"Officer Canoli. Just please, get in, get out. Ok?"

We smiled and nodded, and he handed the pills back and wrote a pass for us to come in.

19

Before going to my mom's house, I got the notes exchanged for old American bills, only really used in the Capitol these days, but woah did I get a lot of them! I ran a hand through the money, stating to Shien that I was rich.

"I'd say the American dollar is worth only about half of what it was before, so I suppose you're only half rich." Shien said.

"I don't care!! I'm gonna buy all sorts of stuff for Mom, get her a big chicken dinner, and some nice souvenirs for us!! Gonna be swell! She'd probably love to meet you again, mhm, after you helped save her from that cult!"

Shien slowly smiled gently, and she followed me as I sauntered down the road in a rich lady's step. The houses were so beautiful, old ramshackle things put together with whatever people could spare, but they had a colorful look to them, the old bits of sheet metal and scrap metal, and I passed the old memorials in glee. Never been to the Capitol before, but it sure had changed!

I bought a whole chicken dinner, just fried up that day, and even bought a chicken dinner for that bum!

Soon, more bums were around me, asking to be fed, as I paraded the chicken dinner through the street, and I gave them little pieces of the chicken here and there. Soon, the whole thing was just bones. Oh well! I went to get another!

I knocked on my mother's door, and she opened up with a bedraggled look in her eyes, in a maid's outfit, but smiled genially at me and offered her arms opened immediately for a hug. I hugged my mom close, chicken under my arm, and introduced her to Shien, asking if she remembered her.

My mom looked at Shien inquisitively, and said, "Um… You went to high school with Olivia! Or… college?"

"I didn't go to college, Mom. Couldn't after the world turned over." I reminded her.

Shien shook my mother's hand and introduced herself. She said her and I never really had the chance to take up academic studies together, but would be glad to educate me more where she could.

"A tutor! I'm so glad you're continuing your education, Olivia! Hard to tell what it's good for nowadays, but I'm so proud of you!" my mom said, and hugged me again. I shrugged to Shien, and my mom took the chicken dinner from my hands and into her house, where we followed her.

She was soon carefully devouring the chicken, as we made all sorts of conversation!

She offered us her bed and a guest one, but Shien shook her head and said she could sleep on the couch. My mom smiled gently to her, and thanked her very much since she always tended to sleep crooked on that thing.

I went to sleep in the tiny room beside my mother's, up a ladder and on the next "floor." I looked out at the smoke and lights in the night through metal frame open window, and sighed out.

Cthaklc appeared at the foot of my bed, and asked me, "**Who are they?**"

I looked at the big mansion, the White House as it was once called, and realized I didn't really know.

Then I passed out immediately, falling asleep.

20

Shien was looking kind of crooked as us three sat for breakfast with my mother, which turned out to be beans.

"These are the tasty cola flavored cans. Don't waste a drop, now!" my mother said.

I snarfed down the beans, as Shien carefully drove a spoon through her bowl, she looked at me as I nodded to her devouring the beans, and slowly raised the spoon to her mouth and took a bite. She made a really weird face, as she chewed on the beans, but then ran her spoon through the bowl again and again, shoveling the beans into her mouth, and I nodded to her.

My mom gave us some soda to drink, caffeine free, and left off for work. She worked as a maid in anywhere they needed her. Apparently had a job up in the White House soon, later in the night. I gave her some cash, about half of what I had, and she squirreled it away somewhere, but said she still needed to work for a living. It's all reputation, she said.

As she opened the door to leave the house, our beans all eaten, a cop was staring through the opening looking at us.

"I told you two to leave, Olivia Lamb." Officer Canoli said.

My mother said, "Why, whatever do you mean?"

"I'm glad to see you're looking so fit and fine, Miss Martha Lamb, but I only gave your daughter and her doctor friend a temporary pass."

"What! She's my daughter, and she can stay with me, so there."

"I'm sorry, but you know things are tight right now. Can't let people in without special work permits, and-" the cop said.

"Shame on you! By the Housing Act from when the Capitol was first being built, it *clearly* states that anyone of origin here can allow blood related family to stay with them, at least one, but up to five. This happened when the Capitol was first being *built*, mind you, and I have all the documentation of legally *buying* this house, *living* in it, and *working* from it. And to drive off a doctor!! You *know* we need as many of those we can get! The Ol' Hack, Brother Bob's, doesn't do it for everyone with their hatchets and saws!! Do you want *another* epidemic to happen, while there are free, good doctors around to prevent it?!"

"Er... No... Not at all!! I'll... I'll take your word on the Housing Act..." Officer Canoli said, looking abashed.

"I would, if I was you!! And look it up later too, when you can!! Now, if you'll *excuse me,* I need to head to the Queen Lizard herself, to have her only *temporary* quarters swept out!"

"Oh... That one scumbarrel woman? Do you need an escort?"

My mother smiled nicely, and took the officer's arm, saying, "It *does so* help to have a friend in the occupation of peace, *it does so.* Please, let me tell you all about my daughter, who got top grades in her class, who is just now even *learning* from that doctor, to better herself and the world around her..."

She closed the door, and they walked off down the street.

I drank down the soda after the beans, and Shien said, "Is everything 'cola' flavored, here?"

"Just about! Love it or leave it!"

She frowned, and sadly drank her coke with me.

21

Shien went to the library to look up any subject she could get about spirits coming forth, breaking the veil as she says, but I was whiling away time in a gift shop.

"Forty bucks!! This hat has even got a stitching problem on it!" I exclaimed.

The blonde haired cashier shifted in her seat, but frowned and said to me, "If you don't like it there are plenty 'I heart D.C.' shirts."

"Those are fifty bucks!! And they're all too short, too! I'm a medium, and the things only come up to my breasts!!"

The cashier shifted again, and remained silent, as I looked around some more.

There was... a gnome, in a snow globe. It held the American flag sternly up to the sky, as little flecks of snow fell around him.

Hmm... Only twenty five bucks. I guess I'll take him.

I paid for the gnome, and walked out with him, but as soon as I crossed the threshold, I dropped him as I was shaking him for the snow.

He shattered on the cobblestones, and I looked for help back at the cashier.

She was counting her cash, and simply shrugged at me.

I grumbled, and tried to salvage the gnome if I could-

Where'd he go?

I looked around. Maybe he rolled away.

I saw a hole in a bakery wall, of way overpriced bread that didn't even feel that good (you know it's good bread by how it feels) that some gnomes were making their way into. A big one was helping the little ones up into the hole, and then shoved his big ass through the hole as well.

I carefully walked into the bakery, looking for my gnome.

I peeked under loaves of bread and other pastries, looking in the corners and under baskets for a hole.

The cashier kept trying to make small talk with me, trying to get me to buy some bread.

I ignored him, and continued to look for any secret gnome hole.

"Look, if you won't buy anything, can you please just leave?" the cashier said.

"No... I'm looking for my gnome..." I mumbled, picking up a loaf of bread that had a little hat next to it, sure he'd be there, but nope.

"Gnome?! Gnome? Gnome." the cashier said.

"Yeah... Was about yay high, had a cute hat on and a long beard..." I said, talking to the cashier and showing him the size of the gnome with my hands.

"...Gnome... Damned gnomes..." he muttered.

"What did you say?" I asked.

He looked frightened for a second, and bid me to come with him into the back.

He said, as we were in a backroom, tons of failed baking experiments done all around us, "Look, I don't need another inspection, can't afford it. The gnomes keep telling me my bread is bad, and I don't know whether to believe them. I just really need a doctor, and I'll give you a few loaves if you just leave."

"...What if I got rid of your gnome problem?" I asked.

He gasped, and said, "You can do that?! I'd pay you all the bread you can take with you."

I smiled and shook his hand, asking him more about the gnomes.

"Well, they say my bread is bad. Can hardly get any sleep, no mam, because they keep telling me to wake up at the crack of dawn and get to work..."

"Um... I think you should listen to the gnomes. If you don't get up early to raise the dough, you're never gonna make any good bread."

"But I just do that the day before. Prep work." he said.

"Well... I mean, you can *do* that... but the baker at Base 64, that's where I used to work, always said that if it's really not properly refrigerated and totally secluded the dough will overrise. Best bread is made all in due process. Gotta make it fresh."

"But all my other experiments!! I want to make the finest pastry I can, the most marvelous specimens of delicious, exquisite baking, the perfect doughnut, the finest cannoli, croissants, even a churro here and there for our Mexican friends... If I can't do that, what's the point of making bread?"

"Even if you make good, normal, plain buns, people will flock to you for them. Good bread is its own good reward."

"...Anyway, I'll be sure to take your words under advisement, but please, please, please get rid of the gnomes. If you don't, I swear I'm *this close* to going and locking myself up somewhere, or even going to Brother Bob's so they can hack off my head."

"I'll look around." I said, and he sighed and went back up front.

22

I heard quiet mumbling in the store room.

"Look at this… Not even good flour. Piece of shit flour, piece of shit bread."

"He doesn't even let the ingredients bind together! Just takes it wet or dry, lumps it around, *barely* molding it, and then sticks it in a pan and calls it quits!"

"He even gets the ingredients all wrong, too! Just guesstimates, for every batch!"

"Bastard fucker doesn't even use oil. Just *scraaaaapes* the bread out of the pan."

"And if they're not undercooked, they're burnt! I don't know how this guy can waste his time on all that other crap. Can't even make a pound of bread for us."

"It's all the stupid Blonde Witch's fault. If she never set us loose on this place, saying we'd get our weight in bread and then some, we wouldn't *still* have to be here in this *stupid* hovel of a bakery."

I had peeked around the corner, watching the gnomes speak.

A small one, my little guy, pointed up at me frightened.

They all looked at me, and one said, "Crap. We gotta blind *another* lady who saw us? We can't keep doing this."

"I hate hearing their eyes pop."

"And the crying."

"And wiping off the jelly on my pants..."

They were slowly walking up to me, hands raised before them, and I jumped out of hiding and said, "Heyyy guys, don't mind me. I want to help!"

They slowly lowered their hands.

"Are you an agent of- BEGODS. Look at that tattoo."

They gasped as they saw the tattoo of the Amanita on my bicep.

"You're an agent of the Blonde Witch, and her horrible entourage." my little gnome guy said, "I barely escaped."

They patted my little guy on the back, one saying, "It's not your fault for getting locked up so long. But now you gotta be the one to blind her, you know the rules."

The little gnome was crying, getting ready for a fight with me.

I stared at him, and I went down to pat him on the head, saying, "I won't hurt you- *WOAH!*"

He threw me to the ground with immense strength, and was crawling up my neck.

He looked me in the eyes as he was going to blind me, and cried out, "I *can't* do it!! I *can't...*"

He burst out crying, and I carefully placed him back on the ground beside me.

The gnomes all sighed, and the big one said, "Well now we gotta reason with her... What do you want, Agent of the Amanita Fae? Can't you just leave us alone?"

"What have you got against the Amanita?" I asked, sitting up next to them.

"They give all sorts of powers to people who don't need them, who frankly only make a lot of crap in our lives unbearable." a gnome said, "The Three Sovereigns of Amanita are no good for a lot of Fae, and we are secretly plotting a rebellion with others who want them overthrown."

"Well it's not so secret now! Is it?"

"Oops."

"Three? I only saw two sovereigns." I said, "Brother and Sister, by their titles."

"What you don't know, is," a gnome said, "the eldest brother is a horrible sorcerer and Fae enchanter. He either walks amongst the people disguised, or sits in his sorcery tower trying to gain complete control of the galaxy. We won't bow down to people like them, anymore! We're free gnomes, and we intend to stay free."

"Hmm. Tell me about this Blonde Witch."

"She traps good gnomes and others like us, selling us as mementos to snot nosed kids and ugly tourists." the big gnome said, "We could not stop her, nor free our other kin. Instead, we made a bargain with her, if we could get some *good* bread in our belly, we'd be able to overthrow her and free all the gnomes. But this place only has crappy, bad bread!! If anything by now we've taken it as an insult, and BYGODS we are going to have our good bread, one way or another."

"Are you sure she wasn't just mocking you, since you all look so scroungy, hungry, and skinny?"

"...I suppose she could've been... We aren't very happy here, nor very healthy amidst all the humans. We need to be in natural wildlife, or on some good lawns at least." the big gnome said.

"Well, I already set the baker on the right track, but stay right here. I'm going to free your friends I saw in the shop."

"You'd *do* that?? We'd be ever grateful for you if you set our kindred free. With our combined power, we should be able to strip the Blonde Witch of her powers, and none need fear her ever again." the big gnome said, and I shook his hand, a deal made.

I smiled, and went back to the gift shop.

I looked at all those poor gnomes trapped in snow globes, and I "accidentally" knocked the shelf loose, spilling all of them onto the floor, shattering their containers.

The blonde haired cashier gasped, and said, "*What* have you *done??* You're going to have to pay for those."

"It was only an accident. I'll be sure to get you a loaf of bread?"

She looked disgusted at the sound of "bread," but soon gnomes charged the shop, liberating their dazed kindred, and all stared at the cashier in fury.

She swooshed her blonde hair around, and said, "Listen, why don't you come back when you're fed in your full power-"

"Never, Blonde Witch. We are going *home!!*" my little gnome said, and all the gnomes waved their hands, and started to hum.

The Blonde Witch screamed, as her hair turned into a natural brunette.

She cried as she saw it falling out of her head.

The gnomes shook my hand, one by one as they passed, and the big gnome said, with the little gnome by his side, "We'll be toasting you forever onwards. If you ever want a drink of our gnome brew with us, stop by, any time. And please, get something else on your bicep than a horrible poisonous mushroom."

"I'll get a little gnome sitting on top of it, then."

The two smiled at me, and poofed invisible, leaving the shop as the cashier screamed at her balding head.

I went back to the baker, and he said, "So they're gone?"

"Yep! But instead of the current bread you have, I want you to keep working on it, and when you have some fresh baked buns for me, just send them to my mother Martha Lamb on Nixon Street."

He smiled, tears in his eyes, and just shook my hand over and over. He said he'd be sending me good bread, and not bad bread, every week to me he could.

When I got back to my mom's house, I got Shien to tattoo a cute little gnome on the amanita mushroom, fishing from a little pond beside him.

23

"Now don't have any parties!" my mom said, and winked before leaving in the night. She always had a real lax hand when it came to my parties...

Didn't matter in the end. None of the party people showed up when I was all alone, when their loyalty was truly tested. The end of the world, was the end of the world, and I could excuse most of them for their choices of abandoning me when I was going to hold the most raginest, the most hardcore, party on Earth. In fact, only some Organization agents came by, but quickly left as they had duties elsewhere, only stopping by briefly.

My mother was going to the White House to be a maid during a huge party there. As soon as there's a mess, it needed to be gone, my mother said. I just hope none of the higher up people of the Capitol made any trouble with her. I honestly just hoped no one gropes my mother and then gets away with it under political disguise...

I thought she still looked very good, even the cultists did from our past, as she was a sex offering that was going to be murdered.

I got a call from "Organization" on my phone as it said from the caller id, and I picked up.

I got in touch with a woman who always seemed to mumble off with her words. "What?" I had to ask her, for the thousandth time.

"Sorry… It's just a new job… I don't think without Wolf I'd (mumble mumble mumble…)"

"Just act like you're shouting at me, then." I said.

She breathed in, and shouted, "THERE'S A VAMPIRE IN THE CAP-ITOL, AND IF YOU DON'T KILL HIM, SOMETHING BAD WILL HAPPEN!!"

"What sort of bad?"

"THE LEADER WILL ANNOUNCE A FULL CHANGE OF GOV-ERNMENT, IN FAVOR OF HIMSELF BEING SUPREME CHANCEL-LOR FOR LIFE!! THE VAMPIRE IS THE ONE WHO IS GOING TO CHANGE HIM, AND GIVE HIM THE POWER OF IMMORTALITY AND THE ALLEGIANCE OF ANY SUPERNATURAL FORCE THAT STALKS THE COUNTRY!! WE'RE GONNA PAY YOU GOOD, FOR THIS ONE, EVEN THOugh we don't have much money left, and (gasp) but THE ORGANIZATION NEEDS YOU!!"

"Ok. So a vampire. Probably at the White House, amiright?"

"Yes. During a party that is going to happen tonight, probably later on in the night sometime."

"Anything else I should know? What's he look like? How will he approach?"

"I'M SORRY, BUT IT'S COMPLETELY UP TO YOU NOW, GOOD LUCK!!"

She hung up, and I rubbed my ear from all the yelling.

I talked it over with Shien, and she slammed a fist in her palm, and nodded her head. "I think some delegates from my country should be at that party, and I think, unless they've forgotten, that they still hold me in high regard for unposessing the Emperor's wife."

"Wow. They probably gave you all sorts of high honors for that." I said, as we left my mom's house, locking it shut with a key she gave me.

"Not… particularly. It was a very hush hush matter, but it was one of the things that got my citizenship in Japan. Even though it's very nice to be able to travel the world with special Organization visas, there's nothing so nice as having another home waiting for you, just across the water."

"Ok. If they can get us in, then maybe *I'll* join you as a citizen there, too."

"You're thinking of leaving the country?"

"Yeah! I grew up here, worked here, seen the Capitol, good enough for me. I wanna explore the world! Just gotta get one of those ostrich omelets from Wolf, too."

Shien smiled wickedly, and said, "That sounds wonderful, Olivia. Let's take a cab there, if we look good enough for the occasion?"

She waved a hand at her leather jacket and skinny jeans, and I looked down at myself at my camo jacket and cargo pants.

"Um. Let's swing by that dress maker's, just down the road from here. Still looks like they're opened." I said.

24

"That's a great design, and I'm afraid it's the only thing we have in a small. Some tourists just ate up my whole inventory today! I'm in such a great mood." the dressmaker lady said.

Shien looked at her white, I <3 D.C. dress in distaste. She asked, "Is it supposed to be a 3, a heart, an ice cream cone, or a penis?"

"It's emoticon!! You know, I, heart, D.C.! It's tradition in America to get these cheesy shirts with stuff like that, and I just made a dress out of that idea!" the dressmaker said.

Shien looked back at her strapless back, but said she'd take it, and try not to burn it after the first night.

I paid the woman for Shien's dress and my turquoise, sparkly dress, getting some cheap costume jewelry for Shien and I, we dropped off our clothes at my mother's, getting hooted at by a few bums, and we took a cab to the White House.

Shien wore high heels, but I kept on my black cowboy boots. If I needed to slay a vampire, I didn't need to be tripping on my heels. I looked around my new, black purse for stuff I thought might be able to help me slay a vampire...

Lockpicks. Always pretty handy when breaking and entering.

Sawed off post stake. Found it under my mother's house.

Knife. Always keep a handy knife on you.

Money. May help, who knows?

Shien looked at the knife, and cleared her throat. She said, "I don't think that would be very wise to bring in such a high security gathering."

"Aww… But I'm a security officer. It's a good habit." I said.

"Still… Just maybe… ditch that."

The cab let us out in front of the White House, and I dropped the knife down a gutter drain. Didn't want this to be traced back to me if somebody uses it for ill purpose. I had another back home in my bag anyway.

There were all *sorts* of people walking into the White House, even pimps, thugs, gamblers, politicians, lawyers, all sorts of scum like that. Guess nothing really changes, eh?

Pimps were offering their ladies to politicians, and I saw a few politicians pay for a few ladies, then continue onward to the White House.

I was set to let them do that dirty business out here away from me, but one pimp grabbed Shien's wrist and started speaking Japanese to her.

Shien spoke in sharp Japanese back, and struggled against the man.

I grabbed him in a headlock as he was taking out his knife, and threw him to the ground.

I stamped a boot on his chest, knocking his wind out, and told him, "Get the fuck out of here before I kill you."

He nodded, and ran away down an alley.

"Thanks, Olivia." Shien said, trying to fix her hair again, "He thought I was someone named Katy. Do I look like a Katy to you?"

"Not at all. Let's just get past those guards before any of his friends show up."

We walked past the guards, quickly, quietly, carefully. All the whores, led by the politicians, seemed free to take anything they wanted with them into the White House, but I was stopped and my purse looked through.

They looked at the stake questioningly, and I said, "Just some trash I found. I keep… a collection."

He shoved it back in the purse, and shoved the purse back in my arms.

Shien immediately spoke in friendly Japanese to a few out of the loop delegates. They were looking on in shock at the "depravity" they were muttering about. They bowed to her, as she bowed back, and she accepted a short Japanese man's arm who led us into the White House.

They talked all through the night, and Shien motioned politely towards me.

"Inspector Kaguwa, at your service, and this is Ambassador Shiori. I am so, so, so, so very pleased to meet someone who helped banish the malevolent oni in the Empress, and her associates." he said with Shien in his arm, and shook my hand.

I kept my lips shut, as they continued to speak in Japanese to each other, and I told Shien I was going… to look around. She nodded to me, and I began searching for entry and exit points a vampire could use.

Hmm. I looked at all the windows. If it was a talented vampire it could probably turn into a bat or a shroud of bats to fly up here to them.

There definitely were all sorts of hidden entries and exits in the White House, so I searched around some bookcases, hoping for a secret book that opened a hidden passage, before giving up on that plot. If one decided to go through one of these entries, then I hoped the security would meet the challenge.

I saw the big, fat, Head Chancellor as he was now called, instead of President, kissing a woman in a back room. She stroked his combover, and I was glad at least she wasn't my mother.

So that was the guy… Would be easiest to kill him now instead, but it's all timing in these Organization tasks. If I did that now, I'd only be thrown in a cell and executed. If I do it when he does become a vampire, I'd be celebrated as a hero. If I wait too long, the whole Capitol could be doomed.

But then... she started sucking at his neck. Gross.

But the man looked hypnotized as she did so, with a super ugly expression of delight on his countenance.

I saw the blood drip down from his neck, and the woman paused, and licked it back up, catching my eye in the doorway as she did that.

I ran as quick as I could, as she called for security.

I was soon dragged before the woman, who was now crying with hidden fangs, at the body of the Head Chancellor, bleeding from the gashes in his neck on the floor.

Their rifles and pistols were all pointed at me, as she said she saw me slash at the Head Chancellor.

Inspector Kaguwa knelt before the body, and said, "These are bite marks."

"Traitors. Traitors, all of them." the woman said, but a doctor knelt before the Head Chancellor, bandaging his wounds as quick as she could. The vampire grabbed a pistol from a guard, and said, "If you will not execute them, allow me..."

She pointed at me as I saw my life flash before my eyes, moving out of the way as quick as I could. Ambassador Shiori was shot instead, the blood splattering all over Shien's white dress.

The woman continued shooting, saying, "TRAITORS, TRAITORS, TRAITORS, ALL OF YOU!! *HAHAHAHAHAHAHAHAHAHA!!!*"

She continued to shoot with lightning speed and immaculate accuracy, taking out the guards and then starting to fire on the guests, grabbing a rifle and mowing them down as they ran, laughing and laughing as Shien, Kaguwa, and I hid behind a desk overturned as everyone ran.

The Head Chancellor moved, and the woman stopped firing to kneel before him, saying, "I will finish you, good, noble, loyal soul. I will finish you now."

She bit at the Head Chancellor, ripping off the bandage and completing the vampiric transformation, by taking all of his life with her bite, ripping down the side and feasting on the blood.

I rushed out of hiding then, and ran straight towards the woman as she looked up at me.

I tackled her off of the Head Chancellor, as the Head Chancellor's bloodless body started to move.

The vampire roared and immediately turned me over, as I went for her heart with the stake, running forward away from me.

But Shien tripped her.

She fell flat on her face, and I jumped on the vampire's back, thrusting the stake, *hard*, into her back, right where the heart was.

She screamed out a death moan, and I got up off her corpse.

Then the Head Chancellor grabbed me with two surprisingly over powered arms, threatening to rip me in half limb from limb, as I grunted and screamed, the sweat rolling down my face.

I felt something pop, and the vampire Chancellor threw me to the side, where I slammed against a wall.

He went to the window, as huge bat like forms flapped before him.

He laughed, a horrible laugh, and they carried his huge, fat form, all three of them, and flew him out of the White House.

I couldn't move my left arm, as it was dislocated from its socket. Shien rushed up to me, and said, "This will hurt, ok?"

I just screamed as I touched my arm with my other hand.

She grabbed my shoulder and in a quick motion shoved my arm back in its socket.

I screamed.

Inspector Kaguwa picked me up, and rushed me out of the building with Shien following.

People were in a panic, but I saw my mother peeking out of a side closet. She gasped and ran up to me immediately, intercepting us.

We stopped for a second as she felt my face, asking me if I was ok, and then Kaguwa kept running with me and Shien, and my mother followed in her maid outfit.

25

I saw that fat bastard Chancellor flying away from us in the night...

And I suppose, the anti air cannons saw him too.

They shot missiles at this unidentified flying object, and two of the vampire bat things dropped the Head Chancellor, as he went tumbling to the earth with the third one beneath him. Smush, the Chancellor went on the vampire bat monster, as the other two fled.

We hurried over to check, and found the Chancellor getting up from the fall, the bat smushed like a fly, twitching here and there. The chancellor was stretching his fat body, jumping around, and throwing punches at us.

I got out of Kaguwa's arms, and asked him for a knife.

I stretched my popped in arm, felt just like a bad bruise actually, as Kaguwa handed me his knife.

I wielded it before me, stepping back and forth to the vampire monster's roars and then his charging.

He was closing the gap fast, and I dodged out of the way of his headbutt, but didn't make it away from that fat arm smack me across the face.

Blood was streaming from my nose, and I saw the instant bloodthirst in the new vampire's eyes.

He started growling, and leering his fangs, looking like he was going to pounce on me.

He pounced, as I dodged out of the way again, nicking him with the blade, lunging in again, cutting at his suit into the flesh, at his neck, at his eye, stabbed him hard in the stomach.

The vampire did not care that I was ripping him apart, and continued to roar and try to catch me. I suppose if he wasn't so fat he'd be far faster, not only with the unholy strength he had.

He grabbed a fat hand on my neck, choking me.

I stabbed the knife into the joint, and quickly broke the arm, escaping the grip.

The arm was dangling from the vampire, as he roared hard at me.

Then the gunshot came from the White House steps.

They were protestors, shooting down the Head Chancellor, as well as security guards taking aim.

He turned back at them, roaring, and someone threw a torch at his face, and it caught fire to his combover, probably because of whatever cheap spray he used to keep it up, and the vampire was soon flaming in the night.

It was running for a monument's pool, trying to douse himself from the blaze, but I ran behind him, fast, and stabbed him in the heart with the blade, jamming it deep into him and leaving it there.

He gurgled, and fell into the water, scorched to a crisp, and he did not get out of that water ever again.

At least until they fished it out, taking his body away to the morgue.

Already, cops were detaining people and questioning them, and I stood beside Kaguwa, Shien, and my mother. I said to Kaguwa, "Very nice blade. Was that silver in the spine?"

He said, "It was. It was a very special gift given to me by a governor… my father."

"Just know, silver works better, at least for vampire hunting, when it's on the *tip* or the *edge*. The tips tend to break off more or dull quicker if they're silver, but it's so hard to slash a vampire to pieces, you know? Just need one good thrust with a silver blade, and then they're usually out for the count. But, the blade worked with silver in the spine, if shoved in deep enough."

"…Thank you, Miss Lamb. I will be telling my government about the loss of the Ambassador. There's a good sushi place down the road, would either of you care to join me?"

Shien said as long as it wasn't soda flavored. Kaguwa assured her it wasn't and we both agreed-

My mother said, "Olivia Jetson Lamb!! No *way* are you going *anywhere* else!! I'm going to take you home, make you some of that ravioli you liked as a kid, and then you can stay right there!"

I protested, but Shien said, "I think you deserve a rest out of sight, Olivia. Please, allow us to continue to work. We'll be speaking directly to authorities from my country, and also try to smooth things over with this whole incident."

"…We will? Oh. We will! Yes, need to talk to a lot of people." Kaguwa said.

"I'll be talking directly to the Organization. Now, what kind of sushi do they have again, Kaguwa? They better not be fish raviolis like I saw once…" Shien said, in her still bloodied white dress, taking Kaguwa on the arm as they made conversation and went to the sushi place.

My mom just took me straight home, sat me on the couch in front of the TV, tucked me in under a blanket, and soon gave me ravioli to eat, just like what I had when I was a kid.

I watched a silly movie, as she soon went to bed, and texted Wolf about what happened.

"If they tell you that you can't have a weapon, just flip a badge in their face really quick. I see that happens in the movies." he said.

"Nah, I don't think that would've worked. But you should've seen me!! I was jumping around, left right left, and took that fucker, both those fuckers, down with barely any help!!"

"I admit I'm a bit jealous, Lamb! Two vampires, one fresh turned and the other a woman from the older Soviet era. Quite a good job! Oh, shit, Charlotte is going to"

I waited for a while, after asking him how he knew the woman was a Soviet? Spoke in perfect English to me, even throughout the mad cackling.

I waited awhile, watching the old movie of Cthaklc trying to save the princess. He kept popping up sometimes, in stranger and stranger places. He asked the princess, "**Will *you* lov*e* me?**"

She said, from her tower, "Yes! Yes! I love you, Cthaklc!"

They kissed as he ascended the tower, and he wrapped his tentacles all over her neck from his face.

Wolf texted back, and not in his usual way. "Say, babe, how long've we known each other again?" he said.

Huh? I told him (who was obviously Charlotte on the phone now) that we met just last week, on that dating site.

I laughed my ass off at the old man who was probably getting chewed out by Charlotte right now.

26

I gulped next morning that I got a friend request from Charlotte on-line. She sent me a smiley face, saying, "That was quite a funny trick you pulled! But don't worry, it only helped Wolf's and my relationship in the long run. Seeeee you!"

I carefully accepted the friend request, and found out that Charlotte actually had tons and tons of friends, a lot of them Organization people, but also a lot... who had very strange looking profiles. I carefully liked her picture, of her staring off the bow of a ship, the wind blowing her hair back in the night.

Huh, the picture smirked at me when I liked it. I liked it again, just to see the effect. Neat. How'd she do that?

I went out for breakfast with Shien and my mother. Shien hadn't come home last night, so I assume she was either working hard, or maybe playing as a geisha again with Kaguwa. She seemed pretty happy, but I honestly didn't know if that was because she got laid, or if she actually *was* just working all night. Either way, it was nice seeing her just watching the people pass by, smiling not wickedly this time, and eating breakfast sandwiches with us.

My mom took the day off just to be with me, and she showed me all sorts of the best places in the Capitol. Where tourists were allowed to one part on top of the wall, the ancient books and the Declaration of

Independence and the Constitution, all the people she knew, which she treated like her best friends, from either coffee shops to hospitals.

I got a text from Charlotte, asking me what's up.

I said, oh you know, just hanging out with my mom.

She said, "I wanted to ask you what you think of this new Organization roster I put together."

I said sure, I'd take a look. She sent me to a link that I wowed at. It looked so professional all gold and black, with absolutely every Organization member's pictures, some smiling joyfully with their kids, others with a grim, bleak look. I saw that Charlotte had proclaimed herself as a "freelance agent" and that all the changes to the website were done by her.

And then there I was, with my years of service, starting from just before I graduated high school to where I was now. It was like I never left.

I had tears in my eyes, and kept scrolling to see the "Head X" to be Hunter Wolf himself.

"We're going to put this out at the next unveiling of the Organization's new leadership. Since we need to pay you, I was wondering if you'd care to take a trip out to meet us in Britain at the birthplace of Orson Lions, the founder of the Organization." she texted, "Of course we got you the gold, but please come see us, ok? This is a formal invitation."

"Gold?"

"What you get paid with. We've basically got a whole new mint of gold pieces, because even if money from everywhere is crumbling to be less than cigarette paper, gold holds its value. It's something Wolf thought of."

"I accept!! I can't wait!"

She sent me a smiley face with fangs, and I told Shien the news!!

27

We got some soft, firm, delicious, awesome rolls sent to us by the baker guy, with a big "Thank you!" letter underneath them. They were so good, we ate all of them that morning!

I hugged my mother goodbye, as we were going to take the train to the port. She had tears in her eyes, and kept on hugging me. "There will always be a home for you with me, Olivia, with lots of hugs." she said.

I said, "Oh, I don't want to be constantly living with my mother, now! I got things to do! People to see! If you ever need *anything,* just give me a call, or call the helpline from the Organization. They'll either let you know I'm dead, or let you know I'm blowing you off."

She laughed under her tears, and hugged me good one more time before we got on the train.

We waved her goodbye, and I saw a familiar face on the train! Granted, he looked pretty sad and lonely, but I cheerfully went up to Wallace and asked him what he was doing here!

"Olivia Lamb! It's so nice to see you! Even though sometimes I wish you'd just have let that werewolf eat me, instead of saving my life... But Olivia Lamb!" he shook my hand, "I'm... going to get treatment, in London. Apparently there's all sorts of people there who can help people... in my condition."

"Oh, because you're a werewolf now? We're going to London too!"

He waved me down, motioning me to be silent, and we sat in a booth as the train started away. He said in a hushed whisper, "Don't speak so loud! No one is supposed to know about that!"

Shien sat beside me, and said, "How will they help you? I've heard that lycanthropy is incurable."

He looked at Shien, and said, "Oh... You're that lady who was with Lamb. Still around, eh? I don't have a clue, but this is one of my last few hopes. If they can't, I'm just hoping they can set me down at a nice private island, *completely* private, where I can't hurt anything anymore..."

Shien said, "I was always curious of werewolves, not directly because they were always stated to be very dangerous, but I was wondering-"

Wallace pulled up his sleeve, and showed off the large bite scar on his arm.

We looked at it, and Shien gently touched his arm, before he rolled back down his sleeve.

"Well, we're in for a trip, ladies! I hear this is the smoothest liner to London, fastest ship still on the market, and we should only be stuck in each other's company for about a week. Say, why are you going to London? Old pals? It would hardly surprise me, since it's you, Lamb."

"Well, I work for a once secret Organization of monster hunters again, and we're traveling to London to see my old friend and new boss take up command! Gonna be swell."

"Ah. Ok... Maybe our reasons to go there are somehow connected." Wallace said, "I honestly thought you must've been one of those weird militant girls growing up, with odd fascinations on occult monsters and horrible fiends. Came in handy on our scouting trips once or twice, as you know well. Say, how are you feeling about Jasper? It was everywhere around the Base, after we found he killed himself because of us, that claimed failed mission on our end."

"Oh… I still get a bit sad when I think about him, but I'm sure he'd want me to continue my life. It makes me sad, that he couldn't do that too." I said.

"Yeah… Still wish my wife was alive, when I think like that. Just let the grief be, and you'll find some method of releasing it, if you keep on living."

"Thanks, Wallace."

He smiled a sad, lonely smile, and we talked about other matters.

28

We boarded the creaky old cargo ship, all three of us, and I saw a familiar face tugging a wheelie bag up the ship plank too.

Her Majesty. *Still* around too, it may seem...

I locked eyes with her once, and she seemed to get a little flustered. I smirked on that, and then planned on ignoring her for the rest of the trip.

She nearly tripped off the plank, which I was really hoping she would, but her little workers who looked like servants grabbed her before she could head into the brink. Darn...

Shien and I settled in our conjoined quarters, looking at the porthole that was just water level. I slammed my bag onto the bottom bunk, and Shien climbed up to the top, to read for a spell.

I sat there bored for a while. Maybe Cthaklc would show up.

I continued to sit there, bored.

Then I remembered something awful that I had completely forgot about. Damnit... my dreams had been getting progressively worse and worse, how could I forget about this... I suppose since I didn't have a werewolf in my company before.

I rushed out of the room, telling Shien I'd only be a minute. She waved a hand at me, ignoring me to look at her book.

I looked all around for Wallace, and asked which room he was in. The sailor didn't seem to know. I described him, "Big guy, not too big, with short brown hair and a sad, lonely look? Has a five o' clock shadow now?"

"Hmm… Oh, are you talking about the Beast?"

"No, I'm not talking about any sort of beast. I'm talking about Wallace."

"…By the sound of it, seems like you're talking about the Beast. Go down to the cargo hold, and for God's sake don't let him bite you."

"He wouldn't bite anyone!! Bye." I said, rushing off to the cargo hold.

I found Wallace there working with a few sailors, setting up some sort of… bindings. Huge chains, attached to the walls of the ship. A radio was playing old music from the side.

"Yes, just like that. A little more taught, I don't need to be able to escape by slamming the chains over and over and breaking them from the friction."

The chains were wound up tighter, and Wallace went down on his knees, and let them shackle them onto his arms and legs.

He spotted me then looking on in horror, and he said, "Lamb! Please, just let me be alone. You don't need to see this."

"…Can't they just lock you up in a nice, private room somewhere?" I said, walking before them.

"No! That only will mark up my trip expenses, anyway, and no one would like to clean up that room after that…" Wallace said, "Please, good sirs, continue."

They continued to wind the chains up, and soon Wallace was slammed against the wall, completely chained up, unable to move his arms or legs an inch.

"…Do you need some water or something? Maybe some food?" I asked him.

"No, I don't need to eat anything. But I actually could use some water, if you wouldn't mind letting me sip from a glass." he said.

I took out a bottle of water from inside my purse, and went slowly up to Wallace and let him sip from the bottle. He was drenched in sweat, and I wiped it off with my sleeve.

"Now, please, just let me be alone, Lamb. Thank you, everyone, for doing this for me."

A sailor said, "Thank you for the tips, Beast."

"My pleasure… My pleasure…" Wallace gasped out.

The sailors all left, and I shut that damned radio off.

I waited in front of him, sitting on the one chair in here, as he struggled and moaned with a horrible fever seeming to break on his brow.

He broke from his feverish sweat for a second, and locked eyes with me with a look of horror in them. "Please, leave, Lamb. Please."

I shook my head, and just continued to sit on the chair, letting the full moon peek in through the porthole window.

He struggled and strained against the bindings, dripping in sweat, and soon I saw the claws extend from his hands, the fur grow from his five o' clock shadow, down the entire length of his body.

His face elongated into that of a long muzzle, and he opened his lupine eyes at me, and growled.

Upon seeing me, he strained even more against the bindings, and let out a long, horrible howl.

Shivers crossed my skin, as he stared at me with such… hunger.

He snapped his teeth at me, as I stayed put on the chair.

I looked at the radio in my hand again, as he howled under the light of the full moon, and I slowly turned it back on.

The song was an old rock song about Little Red Riding Hood and the Big Bad Wolf. The Meteors, I think.

But music soothed the savage beast, and he settled calmly against the bindings, listening to the music.

I had stayed with Wallace all night, and saw the werewolf transformation break under the light of dawn. He gasped and howled once more, and then settled to sleeping in his bindings against the wall.

Aww… I'll get him some breakfast.

I got continental breakfast for the crew and its passengers, steak and some ok looking bread with some veggie mix. I ate mine down quickly with Shien, with Wallace's on the side of the table. She said I looked tired, and I nodded, oh yeah, I was tired.

I still went back down to Wallace with the breakfast, and he sniffed in the air and seemed to wake up at the smell of that. I tried feeding him a piece of steak, but he said, "Please… no meat…"

I then just fed him the bread and veggie mix.

I undid the bindings, and he slammed onto the floor, sleeping. I placed his coat on him, over his strained and sweat stained clothes, and let him sleep as he desired, his music still playing.

"It's a beautiful day in the North Atlantic Ocean, this is NATL Pirate Radio, telling you what you want to hear, and playing the music you want to listen to." the radio said, "Oh, we've got reports that merfolk are taking an interest in travelers through our wet ways to lands unknown, so either keep your ears plugged from their singing, or let the women do all the work on your ship. It is 7:45 AST, keep your ears open on our radio, or keep them shut when you see a beautiful fishy looking woman in the depths. Next song, Keelhauled, by Alestorm."

I let the upbeat sounding pirate rock play, and went to go *finally* sleep…

29

I woke up around noon, found Shien wasn't around, and I went to explore the ship.

I stopped around a corner where a woman was berating and insulting one of the sailors. She said, "I paid top dollar for this cruise, you're telling me there is *no* alcohol on this ship??"

"Sorry, mam, but alcohol isn't good for the crew in times of great difficulty."

"*What* difficulty?! Seems like you're all sleeping at your posts, like there's *nothing* even in the water but sharks!"

"...Um, it's a beautiful day, mam, and maybe you should spend it on the bow, maybe take some pictures? Ladies love to take pictures on the bow."

"Never! I wouldn't *dare* even be seen by the public in this leaky tub you call a cruise liner!"

"Maybe on the keel, then..." he mumbled.

"*What* did you say??" she said.

"Nothing, miss. Just please, let me do my job."

"Hmph!" Her Majesty hmphed, and stormed past the sailor, past me, as he continued to scrub the deck.

I walked up to the sailor, and said, "Hi. Don't mind her, she's just an awful bitch. Where's the Captain, by the way? I'd like to know of all the places he traveled."

He looked at me, smiled, tipped his cap and said, "Well howdy, miss. Do believe he's down with some special company today. Gotta tell you at least, that was some fine looking Japanese lady that walked off with him, knew all about boats, too. Would expect it from one of the Japs, but it's so cool to have someone who knows about that stuff on board."

"Thank you. This way?"

"Right down the aft, miss. Big cabin, but not too big."

"Thanks!" I said, waved him goodbye, and went to the cabin.

I found Shien… drinking, with the captain of the ship, a young man actually, with one eye, who looked like a pirate captain to be. Was in the middle of telling Shien about how he's glad he still had all his limbs, and that the sharks were only hungry for his eye the day he was shipwrecked on a desert isle.

"Oh? Why not your entire head?? How did you manage to escape with only one eye??" she said, sitting before him at his captain's desk.

He slammed his foot on the desk, and said, "Got balls of Stahl, Shien. Balls of Stahl. I went straight for the shark's eyes meself, and I think he took it as an insult and went for mine too."

"And in the isle of cannibals, how did you survive, then? Perhaps eat a few of your crew?"

"Never would I insult my tastebuds with my crew's scurvy meat. I drank, as we're doing right now, and when I took on those cannibals in drunken rage, even if I had some ok meat by their standards, they cowered in fear and ran. Continued to drink, and I'm not sure what really happened afterwards, but none of my crew was carried off ever again! I think the cannibal chief's wife had a might good looking bod on her as well, but I can only remember it in flashes under me one eye."

"Very noble. Maybe you have a few cannibal children somewhere, or maybe-" Shien said.

"Bahhh. If I got cannibal children, I'll shoot meself with my pistol myself. But that's up to the Gods of the Sea now, and not me. Always give Davy Jones his due, and Poseidon, and all them fuckers down below."

"I'm sure Ryujin is happy for any offerings-"

"Don't care if Ryujin can suck me shit. As long as Davy Jones gets his due, and Poseidon, and all the Gods of the Sea, then that's all that matters." he said, and noticed me by the door, "But well, well, well... Look at this! We've got another fine maiden on the voyage."

"Hi, guys! What's that you were saying about an adventure with sharks and cannibals?"

I settled down before the captain with Shien, as he told the entire story again, Shien completely enraptured, as she drank, just as she had been before. I was quickly offered some rum, as well as some more rum.

30

Golly... What an awesssshome little adventure... Not only the Chief's, as we soon called the captain, but my owwwwwnnnn as wellllll...

I stumbled down the aft of the ship, drunk, and looked up at the less full moon in the sky. I smiled at that. Woweeeee... Look at all the stars. No lights around us but that of the ship's, and it was soooo prettttyyyyy...

Shien stayed with the captain, getting nice and comfy with him in his cabin, always listening to his stories even if he repeated some bits, and I got the fine notion of getting some dick of my own.

Ooooops! Should I say that? I don't know, but I was dreaming of... Wallace... as he looked so *ferocious* as a giant wolf...

I found him sitting on the floor by his bindings, with only a sleeping bag for a bed, drinking some tea.

I said, "You gonna do it, or meeeee?"

He looked at me surprised, and said, "Um, what, Lamb? Thank you for staying with me all through the night. That's really something, and you're quite a gal for doing so."

"Gonnnna take off your clothes, or me. Duh." I said, standing before Wallace with a drunk smile on.

He looked at me even more surprised, and said, "As your commanding officer I don't think that would be right! I-I-I don't even sleep without looking at a picture of my wife, before I go to bed!!"

I sat beside him, nudging into him in sweet, sweet drunkenness, and asked if I could see her.

He took out a pocket watch, and showed me his wife inside. She was a pretty woman, eternally accompanied by the click, click, click of the pocket watch beside her.

"Noooo kids?" I said.

"No... She died because of some- Some raiders. Gangbangers, hoodlums, thugs. Killed her because we wouldn't pay them after the world went to shit... I was always at the ready with my gun, but I got a call from a nice lady further down the block who needed help with her heating..."

"She what, yourrrr mistress?"

"She was about 85 when I met her. I found her dead, just her time is all, and went home to find... it was my wife's time, too. They didn't spare her, even if they *took everything we had...*"

He clenched his fist in frustration, and I gently took his fist and laid his palm on the side of my face, right on my scars.

I said, "Let's give you your money's worth. Not even sommmmeeee kids, and she got offed."

He looked into my eyes, with his hand on my scars. He gently stroked it, and said, "You look really, really beautiful, Olivia."

"Thanks. Now getttt them pants offff, I needa get some lovin' into me." I slurred.

We kissed, and soon the night was what it was, a glorious stream of lovemaking, under the light of the stars through the porthole.

I snuggled up with Wallace in the morning, and he gently tucked me back in under the sleeping bag as he went to piss in a bucket.

I watched him for a while, and said, "They don't even give you a bathroom? You're a Beast, I'll give you that, but seems kind of primitive."

He clenched off his stream, and turned to me, and said, "A Beast is all I'll only ever be, now. I... I think, anyway, I killed some people at Base 64..."

"Quit being so mopey, Wallace. I want to see you cajoling with the other passengers when you feel up for it, too. Some fresh air and sunlight ought to do you some good!"

He smiled to me, naked as he was, and I rubbed Tit and Tat, and stretched out of the sleeping bag.

He tried saying, "Know, as your commanding officer, I want to say-"

"You're not my commanding officer anymore, Wallace... Didn't the head bitch Her Majesty tell you? I was formally discharged."

He continued to smile, and continued, "That you are really, really fun."

"Thanks! I try to be. It's the least people need in this world." I said, and got dressed back up.

31

Wallace kept making eyes at me, as I smiled and winked back, and he continued to tell stories to the passengers, a few kids, who thought he was really neat, being a werewolf in the cargo bay. He showed off his bite scar, and continued to tell stories about Base 64, even with me in some of them, and he pointed me to the kids and they wowed at me.

They ran up to me, and I crouched before them, saying they were really cute kids. They said, "We're pirates! Arrrrr."

I said, "And I'm the captured maiden! Oh please, someone save me!" I said, fluttering my eyelashes and putting a hand to my breast.

"Er… No! We don't give our maidens to no landlubbers! Do we?"

The other kid said, "No! Come with us, Miss Maiden, we've got some torture and interrogations to do on you, for your treasure!"

"Yeah! Your treasure!"

I followed them as they took me by the hands, and smiled and winked at Wallace one more time. He sat on the side of the ship, and smiled and winked back.

I ran down the ship from the kids, laughing my ass off with them, and they tackled me down and pointed their imaginary swords at me, and I surrendered.

They continued to ask me for my treasure, and I said, "With the Captain! Go see! And just be sure to call him Chief, and let him drink his hooch in peace!"

They smiled and laughed, and ran off to the captain's cabin.

I got up, still laughing, and the parents came up to me and introduced themselves. They told me they were taking the trip to Britain to bank on long lost relatives of theirs, and hope they can find a better, more peaceful land than the U.S.

I nodded, and said that things sure have changed.

I talked with them for a long time about what I used to do in the U.S., be a peace officer, and they listened to my stories politely. They thanked me for being one of the few good ones, if anything.

"Whaddaya mean?" I asked.

She said that they had to pay exorbitant fees to many "peace officers," and he said as long as his cousins from his great grandpa remember him, then things will be alright. Easier to protect, Britain was, than the whole of the U.S.

I sighed, and thought of the ship we were on. Easy to protect, from anyone prowling on dry land-

I heard the singing come from the side, and the husband was enraptured by the song. He walked off to the side of the ship, as the wife and I did curiously, and I saw some bitches with fish tails on some sharp rocks singing to us.

I saw Wallace dive off the side.

The captain was yelling at his crew to put in their earplugs, and get the damned passengers who weren't ladies below deck. "Ladies! It's up to you to keep your man at bay, so hop to it!" he yelled, with his earplugs in.

A few of the men passengers were wandering to the singing, and the women passengers begged or pleaded with them to come back below deck with them. Her Majesty was trying to command her male attendants to stay back, but they still wandered to the, even to me, beautiful singing.

I just, y'know, wouldn't be swimming as fast as I could to the singing like Wallace was.

A man was shouting at the captain, saying we should go to pick the Beast up, but the captain just said, "WHAT?!" as loud as he could, as the other man tried to tell him under his earplugs. In the end I was pointing off the bow of the ship, pointing at Wallace. The captain followed my finger, and saw Wallace swimming to those bitches on the rocks.

Damned mermaids… not even any decency, big, naked boobs that looked like plump pillows, no little shells on them like in the pictures…

I tried to take command if I could, but I didn't know shit about ships. Shien actually came out, looking still kind of ruffled up from the captain, and took command with visual commands, waving her arms this way and that in sailor code, and the ship turned to Wallace.

We were getting close to the rocks, and I threw a rope out for Wallace. "Wallace!!" I yelled out, over and over, but he didn't seem to hear me, instead focused on the mermaids' singing.

The captain gave me his pistol, and I took aim at the bitch with the hugest tits, and I shot her down.

Then, the mermaids started screaming an angry, screeching sound, and dove off into the water.

Wallace looked confused for a second, as most of the men without earplugs in were besides a gay couple and the kids, and Wallace dove down into the water, after the mermaids.

I shouted, "No!!" and jumped after him into the water.

I dove, and below in the vast, empty expanse of the sea, I saw a mermaid kissing him, him struggling to escape as she took all his breath away.

I swam to that mermaid, and tried to punch her as hard as I could. I just was underwater, and she grinned at me with large, sharp teeth, and took a bite out of my arm instead.

I grunted in angry agony, but swam with Wallace up, as he wasn't breathing or fighting anymore.

I gasped in the air, swallowing in water, and swam for the rope with Wallace over my arm. I held onto him fast, as they dragged us up with the rope.

I sputtered up water on the deck, and checked to see if Wallace was breathing. He wasn't, but Shien came up and quickly did CPR for him.

He sputtered up water, and I kissed him quick, feeling that he was alive.

He broke free of my kiss, and continued to gasp in air.

I stroked his wet hair, as he continued to gasp, and then took him down below decks, to my quarters.

32

He said, "I... thought I heard my wife singing to me..." as I gave him not salt water to drink.

"I guess that's a pretty common attraction." I said, checking his pulse. It was pretty normal, but still beating hard and fast.

"You're... You're not mad at me?" he said.

I said, "Hell no! If I saw some big chested dudes singing out in the water, I'd be wondering what they were doing there too, same as you!"

"...Thank you, Olivia. I'm so, so sorry... I just couldn't help myself! It was like-"

"Like you were following your cock, and not your head?" I said.

"...A little bit, yes. I just didn't know how anything could be so beautiful, and I had to know how."

"...Well, at least we know curiosity is one of your flaws... But remember that curiosity killed the cat."

"...Yes, I'm familiar with that euphemism, even though curiosity is all we ever followed, as scouts."

"True. Just know that not every big breasted naked fish person wants you for your heart. More for the flesh on your bones, actually." I said, rubbing the now bandaged bite on my arm. Hoped I wouldn't turn into a mermaid for this, like a werewolf.

He held my hand, and said, "You're really awesome, you know that? I wanted to tell you… about some of my fantasies as a scout with you in mind-"

I just kissed him quick, and said, "Please don't. Then *I'd* have to tell *you* about more than half my fantasies with men in my time there…"

He smiled, and said, "It's a lonely life, isn't it?"

"Not really, because I thought you were really all such good guys. Best friends, if I could call you all that with the phrase being used mutually."

He smiled sadly, and said, "Ever have a fantasy with me exclusively?"

"Er, it's kind of embarrassing…"

"C'mon, Olivia, we did the deed, mutually, at least you can get whatever harbored feelings you had on the table."

"…Well… It was after you got lost again, and then-"

"*I* got lost?" he said.

I looked at him seriously.

He smiled ridiculously, and said, "Of course I got lost! Of course I got lost. Of course I got *lost*…"

"…Well, that didn't matter much, because I could guide you. We'd be leading the convoys, you and I, and you'd never get lost again. You'd have that pecker of yours pointed in *exactly* the right direction, and I'd always help you follow through…"

He wrapped an arm around me.

I continued, "And we'd find beautiful places, things I always imagined. I've found a few of them, but not every one of them. Specifically I'm looking for that unicorn grove I always imagined in my youth, and we'd be so happy when we found all of them! Just unicorns, frolicking around, and then we could get close and comfy under some unicorn hidden grove… Remember, this is a fantasy, mind you, and you were always the first one to look up at, when we were scouting…"

"I always saw you looking! Because I was always looking back... Sometimes just to see if I went in the right direction, but a lot of time to get a look at you."

I nudged against him, smiling, and said, "That sounds like a corny phrase not created by the man who 'looks at his wife every night before bed...'"

He rolled his eyes, and said, "It's not like I didn't think of things, out alone in the woods."

"Ok. I can get that. Now, let's get something straight, I got *no* fish parts underneath my belt, and I want you to remember that..."

I rolled with him in my bunk, and we made love again.

33

Shien looked tired of being groped by the captain, but said it was worth it just to get *one more* story out of him... She said she's never found anyone so interesting, out alone amongst the sea like that. I asked her if any of his stories were really true, and she said, "I'm not certain, but I'm thinking of being his agent just so he can get some of those stories on print. Would be worth it, to see my name besides such an *enthralling* character..."

"Hey now, you've already got me for that! The journey is almost done, anyway."

"I hope so, because between you and me, the ol' Chief really knows how to take a lot out of a gal..." she said, yawning, "Now I just want to sleep, and not think of *any* man in my bed..."

I looked up at her, with an arm over her eyes in her bunk, and asked, "Did he give you head?"

"Gave me all I ever wanted, and then some, all that... Now let me sleep..." she said.

I giggled, and went off to go meet Wallace. He was enjoying the fresh sea breeze, as he looked out to the land far away on the horizon. I snuggled up next to him, and he squeezed me close. Said, "There, I'll be safe again. There, I won't have to worry anymore."

"We gonna still see each other, after?"

"I don't know, depends on what they need me to do. I'd love to, but I know you've got all the world before you, and don't need to be tied down to me."

"I *like* being tied down... Gives me a sense of security. Still, I'll always write you, whatever you need to do..." I said, and he squeezed me close some more.

We just watched the land get very slowly closer and closer to us, enjoying the sea breeze.

I finally got connection as we were approaching the land again, and got a text from Charlotte asking if the journey was substantial.

I said it definitely was, and got further detail about the grand Organization event happening.

A passing ship wooted at us, as we were getting closer.

Wooted?

Sounded like a bunch of women were screaming at us, cheering in delight.

The captain came out and saluted the seemingly all women crew on the next ship over.

They stopped next to our ship, and we threw the anchors down with the land so close ahead.

I asked the captain what was the hold up?

He said, "Damn, woman, those are the crew of the *Cherry Pop.* Shame to let the maidens go off into the seas, without giving them a fair farewell!"

"...Um, can we just tell them hello and keep going?" I asked.

"No, mam! We *need* to give those maidens what they are duly looking for! They're going off to hunt krakens and sea serpents for some scientific society, that the Sea Gods only know of!"

I looked off at the head of their ship, and saw the Organization's symbol on it, two lions, male and female, back to back.

We met the Captain Sherry of the Cherry Pop, as she *leapt* off her ship and to our own in a boarding kind of manner, and she informed us that she was going to be taking our men and drinking all of the captain's ale. The men cheered, but the captain said, "Not *my* ale. Who do you think you're speaking to?"

"The ol' bastard who calls himself captain of this ship! That's you, isn't it, sweet cheeks? So, tell me... how've you been doing with all the mermaids showing up on our radar?"

"Er... Had barely a problem with them! This lady, this lady here, even shot one of them with me own pistol!" the captain said, pushing me forward.

The tall, burly, blonde woman under a captain's hat said, "This scrawny wench? How come you couldn't shoot her yourself, Captain Cute Cheeks?"

"Er... Would be a shame, to do a lady like that in... with those big peepers and big- But that's why this chick shot her! Was trying to steal her man, she was." the captain said.

"Really. And who might you be, miss? Could use another good shot on the Cherry Pop! Tell 'em, ladies!"

The women on the other ship all cheered, and I said I was Olivia Lamb. Shien appeared beside me, and said, "I didn't expect the Organization to already be scouting the seas."

The Captain Sherry said, "Of course we are! The Organization takes a concern in *all* manners suboccult and spiritual... even monsters of the deep! We're off on an expedition to hunt down the great sea serpents of time, the krakens of the dark abyss, around the world to the end of the world! Tell 'em, ladies!" The ladies from the other ship screamed out louder than before.

"Hm. You're not going to the grand festival?" Shien said.

"No need! We know who our boss is, and it's that crazy sonofabitch vampire hunter called HUNTER WOLF! We do this for the WOLF, gals! Here here!"

And the ladies screamed some more.

"Anyway… We're just looking for some cheap supplies, maybe a good party for the ladies…" Captain Sherry said, "Would be a shame to let this crew of all females out against the depths of the sea without having a bit of fun, first…"

I said, "You're all female to keep the mermaids back, right?"

"Hm? Of course not! We're just *better* at the job than men are! All of these gals, sea wives and sea hookers, and we've had enough! Don't need no man to do our job, and if those mermaids start a' singing, we're gonna thrash them so good they won't know which way is up on the ocean floor! We can do anything that a man can, well, most anything, and that's why we've stopped off with your ship!" she said.

The captain stated that we could unload some of our supplies for such a grand voyage to the Gods of the Deep, and the ladies all cheered, the men cheered back, and we had a night of partying before we got to land, and before they went off to the deep sea.

34

Blip...

Shien asked if I was alright, as she stumbled beside me.

Blip...

I got so drunk, I was sober again. And the fights these gals could pull off... the guys were all taking bets, and after I won again and again, Captain Sherry decided to take me on...

Took me down in the first minute. Just slammed my head down with a takedown, smashing the table beside us...

Blip...

Wallace ran up to me, after disentangling himself from another horny sailor lady, and said, "Shien! Olivia! I really thought you could take her, I really did."

Blip...

He asked me if I needed to lie down, and I said, "Just need some air... blip... Just need a bit of air..."

I wandered down the ship, not certain where I was going. Wallace looked worried, and Shien said just to let us walk for a bit. Wallace said, "Nuh uh. Every lady here wants to stick their hands down my trousers and then some. Good for the crew, but I only got eyes for you, Olivia."

Blip...

I told him to go have some fun, but he just walked slowly behind us as I walked slowly, really feeling my head pounding, but feeling so sober... So sober I was drunk... No wait, wasn't it the other way around?

Blip...

In the end, Captain Sherry herself ran up to me, pounding me on the back and saying that was a good fight. I got into a conversation, stating that was truly rational to take me down at the start, that's what you should do...

"I knew you were going to try that. Took all my gals down with barely a fight, because you got to their head first. Literally. Smacked Betty Sue unconscious, and went for Mary Anne like she was a featherweight..."

Blip...

"But you can't bet on the first thing being so easy like that. That's why I hardened myself for your wailing uppercut, and went down after you after that. It was the second hit, and not the first."

"But you're such a boss woman, I bet those sea krakens and wailing mermaids won't know what hit them, when coming after you..."

"Haha! I do hope so. Just remember, when you gotta grit your teeth and take the punch, it doesn't have to be the final swing. You're a good gal for taking up the Organization's mantle like that, but still need, besides your weapons, a lot of good experiences. Be open for the experiences to come."

I slammed her on the back, which she took unwaveringly, and I said I'd keep that in mind.

Blip...

35

I woke up in my bunk, scarcely remembering how I got there, then hurried out of bed to see Britain approaching, getting dressed quickly.

I saw the port of London approach, and I looked around for Shien, around the cheering passengers who were cheering at the people on the port, some family, lovers, best friends, or new bosses.

I found her waiting on the captain, as he had spent a long night with Captain Sherry the night before. He just grumbled and turned over in his bed, as I told him the port was closing in. Shien shrugged at me, and took some of his booze before we left the ship.

We waved at all the people of London, and were ignored after that. Nobody was looking for us, but we were looking for the Organization transport that Charlotte promised.

We found them, after ditching looking for them by the port, by a tea and biscuits place down the street. The guys were sipping from their tea by the black limo, and we waved at them. They straightened up immediately, and called out our names before opening the door of the limo.

We got in, and they took us around London, which I thought was a lot more ragged and dirty than all the postcards I had ever gotten. The Big Ben had already came tumbling down... Its remnants were sacred parts of the old street we passed, never moved. We passed the old churches and new surveillance systems, even more high tech than what they had before. The many cameras and soldiers in the streets didn't really make me feel safer.

I texted Wallace in the car, after leaving him with some tough looking hairy people by the port. He said... things were enlightening, if anything, and texted me no more after that. I promised we would meet after the Organization party.

After the guides, the two guys in front of the limo, quit showing us all the classic, cheesy parts of London, they took us to a hotel so we could wash up.

It was a nice place, probably more than I had ever been in, like a piece of the old world, but I still was nervous all night, thinking what I'd say to the Organization and Wolf when I could. Shien told me to quit being so nervous, that she was going to do the hard part and address the new Spirit Department, if anything.

"Spirit Department?" I asked.

"It's a new thing that Wolf thought of, and I accepted command on the fly. After I told him about the spirits breaking forth out of their boundaries, Wolf immediately offered me the position. I had scarcely notion of what to say, since I usually work alone, anyway, but we'll see how it turns out."

"I think you'd be a good spiritual advocate, Shien. I haven't seen a single one since our failed outing by that pit, though."

"They tend to stay away from you. Say you've been cursed, some say blessed, and some just don't want what you're selling. Which brings up what I wanted to ask you, what *are* you selling to spirits, Olivia?"

Shien looked me seriously in the eyes, and I was a bit shocked at the look.

"N-Nothing at all! I don't have a single idea what you're talking about."

She just looked into my eyes searchingly, and then blinked, and shrugged. She said, "Ok... But be careful in times to come, ok? If any spirit tries to offer you something you shouldn't or can't have, *tell me right away, ok?"*

"O-Ok, Shien." I said, and then we went downstairs to go the Organization party.

I was looking for Wolf, at this gathering of a huge ballroom. Didn't find him, but saw Charlotte handing out masquerade masks to us. I shook her hand, meeting her again finally, and she said, "The masks are symbolic of the time of hiding on our end to be over. When it is midnight, we'll all take off the masks and *really* party! How cool is that? Something I thought of."

"Very neat, Charlotte." I said, putting on my mask with Shien doing the same.

A heavy orchestra of classical instruments played for us with a chorus, the heavy metal guitar and bass playing beside them. They sounded enchanting and masterful, like something old but also new.

I bumped into an old, old man who had a masquerade mask on, as Shien mingled with the rest of the party. He said, "Pardon me, miss! My name's... Fox. Norman Fox, at your service."

He shook my hand, and I noticed the large fangs on the edge of his lips. I asked him... "Are you a vampire?"

He continued to smile, and nodded, saying, "You're not supposed to figure that out so fast, like the rest of the people here, but yes, I am the oldest vampire alive."

"Wow! Really?? Shouldn't I like, kill you, then?"

He laughed uproariously, and we got beers from the side. He said, as he sipped his beer, "I don't think so, but people like Wolf do. If I couldn't keep helping as I'm doing, I'd gladly take the stake through the heart. You're Miss Olivia Lamb, aren't you? A pleasure to meet you, finally, Lamb."

"You too, old, old man! Say… When's Wolf finally gonna come out of hiding?"

"Beats me. He's probably still upstairs." Fox said, sipping his beer, "Should be out among the people, he should, but I'm certain he's got all the world counseling him right now."

"…What do you mean…? Oh, whatever, I'll go see myself."

"Quite good of you, Lamb. We'll all be down here." Fox said.

I got to the stairs, looked back at Fox who raised his beverage to me, and then I continued on upwards.

I looked out through a room, calling out, "Wolf? Are you there?"

I kept looking through the room, and saw Wolf talking to an old man who still looked even as strong as Wolf was, on the balcony.

I heard them say, Wolf first, "So you really think I can do it?"

"No, but do *they* think you can do it?" the older man said.

"I think so. Took forever trying to ignore them, then deny them, and now here I am." Wolf said.

"It's all the *countenance*, man. You have the face for the job, the motives, the means, the necessity. If anyone could do it, it would look like it would be you. And that's really all that matters. Do you think I had anything but a crossbow, like you did, when I first started the job? Because I didn't. I just had the job, and that's all that matters."

"And that's all that keeps us going, too."

"Yes. Very much yes. If you can keep all these souls to keep moving, then you've done your job far better than anyone before you. I was very certain things would fall, as we went on only taking charity donations for our essential job, hell, I was only doing so myself as I was young, alongside the Church with my arms opened for any piece of passing bread, but things somehow got brighter and better for us, and what was only a group of four is now an amassed membership of twelve hundred people. Even more, in the old days, but I'm very glad it has kept going so far past my own life."

"Thank you, very much, for your guidance, Orson Lions." Wolf said.

I had to step out of hiding by then, but when I did, Orson Lions blew away in the wind, and Wolf looked at me contently with his hands in his pockets.

36

Wolf put on his masquerade mask, that of a large wolf's, and we went back down to the festivity. I had so much to ask, but he simply thanked me for being here.

We danced for a bit, Wolf and I, and then he whispered that he had to make a speech. I nudged him forward to the stand, and he smiled back at me.

He started his speech, taking off his mask before midnight.

"I am Hunter Wolf. Many of you know of my exploits, against the forces of the damned and unholy. No, I shouldn't say exploits… I should say necessity. It is a necessity that I did what I did, for everyone, for all of us, and everyone who cowers at their bedside unable to deal with the horrors of the dark.

"I was offered, again and again, to be another economic slob at the head of the Organization, only there as a figurehead, to take a cut, and allow us to continue to fall into disarray.

"But I will not allow us to fall so low.

"We are the last light in the dark for many that we have crossed paths with. The world has changed, more for the worse than the better. Even the damned have none but us, as we seek to rectify corruption and greed, wickedness and decadence, murder and mayhem."

Charlotte was clapping and woo wooing at Wolf at that.

Wolf continued, "And I wish to continually extend the arms of Orson Lions, our founder, who was born in London, in this grand event. We will not only help those who have been cursed by wickedness and evil, we will be a strongarm against hunger, disease, and cruelty. We *will* make things brighter and better in the world, by my father's life, who was cut down by a vampire."

People around started cheering, and urged him to continue.

He continued, "It is no secret to many of you that I lost everything as a young man, that my life's purpose was set and founded in the cruelty I had to endure. It is no secret that I lost everyone who mattered, as an Egyptian monster of old *slaughtered my family in horrible malevolence...*"

He gripped the stand hard at that.

He continued, "But I was given a place in the world by the Organization, and with our previous leader, the female descendent of Orson Lions, Lovely Lions, dead at the old age of 78, I have agreed to take up leadership of my home, to be the heir that Lions didn't have available, and continue to guide the Organization to new heights.

"I accept the call of the Organization.

"We, *we,* will carry out our slaughtering, our desecration of the damned, of all the ungodly that stand in our way. In any person's way, who simply wishes to have a good life, with nice nights and nice days. *We,* like the wolves in the story books, will be the ever gnawing hunger, but for goodness, for purity, for the light of the dawn, that we all need. I urge you, and thank you all, to and for this calling. *We,* will let the houses of unholy crumble under our breath, and sanctify the ground once again for glory under God.

"Thank you, all of you, for dedicating me for this position, in one way or another, I will not allow myself to fail you. Never before, and never again.

"I am Hunter Wolf. And I accept the call of the Organization."

We were silent for a good bit. Then a few people started clapping, then cheering, then all of us were. Wolf nodded to us, and said the time of hiding for the Organization was over, and we all revealed our faces from our masquerade masks. People smiled and laughed at each other, and we continued the party, far into the night. It was 12:01.

37

I told the limo driver, one of the guides, to continue around the block again in drunkenness. There was something I missed.

I saw that there was a werewolf club opening, with furries, freaks, and all manners of degenerates (that's what the sign said) invited to come party.

I told the limo driver to stop in front of the bar, and he didn't judge, said he would be just around the back. The limo driver drove off to the parking lot, and I stumbled inside.

Woah. Was that real?

A werewolf waitress paraded past me, going to give some people in costumes their drinks. They said she had a great costume!

I stopped the waitress, and I said she had a great costume too, in my drunken stupor.

She snarled flirtatiously at me, and I could see the edge of her lupine lips curl into a smile.

I blinked, blinked again, and then stumbled to a lonely seat at a table by myself.

It was quite an event just to look around at all these strange, awesome looking people. There were people who had super realistic costumes, getting drunk as a Wolf (that's what we started saying after Wolf started drinking) and partying all throughout the bar.

"Olivia!" someone growled from behind and above me.

I carefully looked up, and saw a horrible, monstrous face above me, drooling at the sight of my skin.

He kissed me softly on the cheek, though.

He sat before me, and said, *"Like it, hun?"*

I blinked.

I blinked again.

Then I recognized the color of his fur, the color of his eyes, and I gasped.

He grinned and snorted in his lupine form, and I gasped out, *"Wallace??"*

"Yeah, babe. These guys and gals- They're just amazing, aren't they? Gave me an injection, said I could be my wolf form whenever I desired, whenever I wanted..."

"I-I thought you wanted to get rid of it, though."

"Hm? You see these muscles? I'm a goddamned super wolf with these! And listen to this, just listen."

He howled at the ceiling, and everyone howled around him, bringing goosebumps to my skin.

I stuttered out, "Y-You're not even wearing any clothes!!"

"Hm? Can't see anything under all the fur, can you? Well how about we fix that... Howbout it, babe? You can bang a real, happy, lucid werewolf!"

He growled flirtatiously, and while I admit it *was* kind of a turn on...

I had to decline, as he looked at the werewolf waitress pass by.

I held his claws, and said, "You do whatever you need to do, babe."

He looked back at me and snorted, *"What?"*

"I like that you can find peace with yourself. But just call me when you feel like being human again, ok? I don't feel like committing bestiality, at least not currently in my life, and would love to see you smiling again as a human again."

I smiled gently, but he ripped his claws away from me, saying, *"Forget it. There's tons of great girls here anyway. I'll see you around, little Lamb."*

I frowned, but got up, and walked away.

I ran to the limo.

I got in, and started crying.

I told him no, I didn't feel like going around the block again, and he took me back to the Organization ball.

I sniffled, getting out, going to find Shien and go home-

Where was my home? Was there even such a place?

Still, I gasped as I saw Wolf talking delicately with Her Majesty outside of the ball.

I marched up to them, as for so long I had marched for Her Majesty, and told her to leave.

Wolf said, "…This is one of our backers, Olivia. Meet-"

"I know who she is. And I know for sure as Hell I won't be working for you if you take her support."

Wolf looked at me seriously, then back at Her Majesty.

He said to her, "I'm sorry, but we won't be able to continue our dealings. I think we're just about settled up, giving a little more to you on our end, and we can settle things right now."

Wolf took out a many folded piece of paper from his pocket, as Her Majesty stood aghast, and he burned the paper with his lighter before her.

She stuttered out, "By dear God, Mister Wolf! Think about what you're doing!!"

"If a trusted member of my Organization feels so strongly against you, then I am one to take her counsel, and not trust foreign hands in our weapons and security dealings." Wolf said.

He dropped the burning parchment to the street, and Her Majesty just looked at it for a while.

She snarled out, *"Then I would be firm in choosing your enemies as well, dear Wolf.* Unless you'd care to renege on this decision. I assure you, we have copies of the contract-"

"That are only worthless copies, now null and void. I don't think we'll need your services, nor ever really did, Miss-"

I snarled, *"Get. Out.* Go far away from here, *Your Majesty,* and get the hell out of my life."

She looked repulsed at me, but said that we haven't heard the last of her, and shuffled away to her car, where her attendants welcomed and consoled her.

I said to Wolf, "Thanks, Wolf. That bitch deserved far more than a burning of a contract."

He sighed, and shoved his hands in his pockets, saying, "Would've been difficult without her in the last few months, without getting weaponry and the like where we could. But, there are always new arms dealers."

"Again, thanks. She's been lording over my life for too long, and I couldn't bear to think that she'd be lording over here, too, where it really mattered."

Wolf smiled at me, somehow still looking so sober after drinking so much, and he beckoned me back into the ball.

He told me about ostrich farming, saying the good eggs come from the more wild birds, just like his Chickie, and that he can't wait to get back home to Australia again.

"Weren't you an American?" I asked, as I stumbled in his arms.

"Yes, but... I've learned to look at a grander picture. We're all humans, Earthlings, and we deserve to be able to stand hand in hand, one and all."

"That's a good way to look at it- I think I'm gonna throw up... Something about seeing Her Majesty brings that out in you..."

Wolf scrambled away to find me a bucket, grabbing one from behind the bar, and put it before me, as I threw up, and puked, hurling and hurling, and wiped my lips when it was done, and said, "That feels a lot better. Thanks, Wolf."

He smiled at me, and went to dispose of my puke. What a guy, now my boss.

38

I got a letter from Wallace in the morning, that Shien dropped off in our hotel room.

I looked at it, and it looked like someone was trying really hard to write…

Then turned into the immaculate writing of Wallace, and he asked if we could meet, at least one more time.

I asked Shien how she got this letter, if she had seen Wallace, and she said, "No, I didn't see him, but I found that letter on the balcony."

I stroked the letter. Still smelled very musky, like Wallace's musk.

I went to the place he wanted to meet me, that the guide took me to. We passed the farmland of Britain, beautiful, secluded places, hardly taking a beating at all when the world collapsed, and parked in front of "Airy Dairy Farm."

I got out, and walked down the road, as Wallace had promised me he was further in.

I found him, in his human form, drinking tea with a good looking farm couple, just out on the lawn on a patio table and chairs. He still had that five o' clock shadow something fierce.

He looked at me, and shouted out, "Olivia!" and ran up to me, picking me up in a hug and smiling in glee. I laughed in delight, and kissed him on the cheek.

He took me by the hand, and said, "I've got really something for you, something my furry friends told me about. I just can't wait to see the look on your face!"

I asked him, "Was it hard? To be a human again, at least to write that letter?"

"I think so, yes." he said, looking at me, "The words just didn't seem to form right in my head, no matter how hard I tried. They say that should pass and I should be completely functioning if I keep taking the shot. Is a wonderful, beauteous blessing, the medication and treatment they have for people like me."

"I'm really, really happy for you! I didn't even know such a treatment was available. In the old days, if I had to deal with a werewolf, I may as well give it a shot in the head with my shotgun over shots and therapy!" I said, still smiling so happy.

He laughed, and said, "We're the Werewolves of London, babe. Or the Munchmunchers, or the Scratchhausen, or- We've got a lot of names for ourselves… But anyway, can we go see them, good people?" he said, talking to the farm people. They nodded happily, and Wallace laughed in glee, and took me further into the farm.

I saw all the cute chickies and duckies, and the goats baaaing at me, and I said I was glad to see a good farmland again, no matter what he had in store for me.

We kept walking down the farmland, going through some dense foliage, and then I gasped.

There were two unicorns, frolicking in this grove.

Wallace just motioned me forward with a smile, and I stumbled before the beautiful creatures.

I put a hand out to a unicorn, that wasn't a fake unicorn with a stupid plastered horn, I could tell just by looking at it, and it nibbled my hand lightly.

I stroked the beautiful creature slightly, and just sat before it. This was always what I always wanted as a little girl, and to be in their presence just then felt like something holy.

They soon ignored me, going further down this hidden grove, and started having unicorn sex, but I didn't mind... I was happy that soon even more of them would populate the Earth, bringing beauty to all.

Wallace sat with me, as those unicorns neighed and neighed doing the deed, and he said, "So what do you think, Olivia? They're specially bred and raised on this farm, being one of the few ones in the country."

"They're magical..." I said, in a daze.

He just sat beside me, as those horny horned horses humped each other, and I just thought of all the things I believed in as a kid... fairies... gnomes... and now unicorns. They were all real, I just had to look hard enough in the world to find them.

We eventually walked off, I in Wallace's arms, so happy, and he paid the people their fee for showing us this sight. The man said, "You don't want that unicorn meat? It's good meat, very invigorating."

"Er, no, not right now-" Wallace said.

I stared up at Wallace, and gasped.

He shifted his eyes back and forth, and grinned stupidly. He said, "I can get you some, too?"

I yelled at those farmers, saying *how dare they* kill something so beautiful and majestic, and they only looked back at my furious yelling, as Wallace held me back from them.

He struggled to get me to the car, and I had half a mind to punch him in his windpipe, and then slaughter those farmers like they were doing to those poor unicorns...

I simply sat in my seat, and said, "Drive." to the guide, leaving Wallace to spout sorrys and apologies to me as we drove away.

When I got back home, I just went to a mass with Shien...

We sat in the pews of the old church, and I enjoyed the British take on everything. Basically just everything Christian with a British accent, but it was neat to hear.

I went for communion, but Shien stayed back. Said it wasn't good to cross gawds and intertwine religions. I didn't believe so, I thought it was good to have all religions, and let them all give you a helping hand. I took my piece of wafer, said amen, had a sip of wine, and went back to my seat.

I followed Cthaklc to my seat, and he turned back at me, did a double take, and said, "**Where are we going?**"

I just shrugged, and then I sat back with Shien, losing sight of Cthaklc for some reason.

We left the mass, as I thought about the story of Adam and Eve that the priest told. I bet Wolf would know all about this sort of stuff, being so religious. Some people can mock you for your religion, usually claiming they have the same religion themselves, but if they do, scold them, or punch them for trying to take away your belief. Belief is a hard sought thing, that not everyone can achieve.

I just looked at the sky, now so clear, outside of the church. No air travel, nothin', and I thought maybe there was a Gawd up there looking down at me as well.

Shien walked briskly down the side of the church, and I wondered where she was going. I followed, trying to catch up with her, but she kept walking, seeming like she didn't want to be followed.

We got to an old graveyard, and Shien sat before a particular grave. The words were worn off from erosion and time.

She prayed, in her Japanese way, bowing over and over, and I just sat beside her and mumbled some sort of Christian prayer. I continued to mumble little bits of prayer I knew, and then I saw the ghast get into Shien's body.

She breathed it all in, in the light of day, as I sat beside her, and looked down at her own body in shock, mumbling something in a British accent, *"I need the Sword. I must have the Sword!! I need the SWORD."*

I stared at her, thinking how to disentangle this situation peacefully, and Shien stared at me so fervently and seriously.

She said, *"In the ruins of the old faithful, against the workers of wickedness and blight, is the sword for the Light. What did the snake say, that is only true for the Light?"*

She then breathed out, letting the ghast go back into the grave, as she continued to mumble prayers, seemingly unaware of what happened to herself.

"This is the grave of Saint George the Dragonslayer." Shien said slowly, wiping some ectoplasm and spittle from her mouth.

I looked back on the grave. It was just a common headstone, nothing great or marvelous about it.

"Do you know the story?" Shien said.

"Guy killed a dragon to save a princess, right?"

"Er… That's about the gist of it." she said, "There's gonna be a whole mess in Britain, most likely in London." Shien said, looking to me, "I believe it *could* be a dragon, but maybe something more akin to what you are usually assaulting…"

"A *dragon??* No way! Just found out unicorns are real, and now *dragons??*"

"It's not a good thing, Olivia. It's a very, very bad thing." Shien said.

"Er… Ok. I just thought it would be neat to see one, is all."

"And he would probably like to see you, either scorched to a little crisp, or as his offering on a plate. I need to tell Wolf, the Organization, my Spirit Department-"

"Woah now, big girl, take it easy. You're breathing kind of fast. Just take it one step at a time." I said, trying to calm Shien's panicked breathing.

She breathed in and out slowly once, and looked at me for re-assurance.

I said, "Ok now, that's better. Just call Wolf, and I'm sure he'll get everything handled."

She immediately got up, bowed once more to the grave, then took out her cell phone, and called Wolf.

She said a dragon was approaching from the northeast.

39

"Saint George would come out of his grave himself to fight the dragon if I didn't stop him..." Shien said, as we walked back to the church.

"Wouldn't have been a bad thing, but he's probably better sleeping like he is." I said.

"An undead is a tricky thing, as you know well. They scare a lot of people, cause media blackouts, and are really hard to kill."

"Oh yeah, I know that. It'd be cool to meet ol' Georgie himself though, eh? Y'know, get to know another monster hunter like us."

"I admit, it does have a sort of appeal, but I don't think I'd like to care for an undead as my charge for the rest of my short life..." Shien said, "But anyway, he gave me directions for a sword. The Sword."

"'The Sword?'"

"A dragonslayer's fabled weapon, hidden in the remains of Old London, which happen to be... in the sewers. Care to check it out with me? Oh... and do you know how to use a sword?"

"Yeah, kinda..." I said, abashed, "Just like a big knife, right?"

She stared at me for a second, and I sighed.

"Ok, no, but who does, amiright??"

She took out her cell phone, and called Wolf again. Said we'd need a prima quality dragon slayer, who knew how to use a sword, pronto.

We got to the sewer entry, a large pipe, and found Wolf waiting for us himself, with a sword of his own.

"Is this good enough, Shien?" he said, swishing the sword around in an arc, like he always used to know how to use a sword, and always will.

"Fantastic as always, Wolf. Please, follow me as I tell you what I know."

We followed Shien as she stepped through the sewer water, and I looked down at my wet shoes and pants in distaste. Nasty business, being in the sewers... Besides monsters commonly hiding out in the sewers, there was sickness, and filth, and rats.

Saw a few of them scurry along before us, and I felt my hair stand on end. Nothing, *nothing,* I hated more than rats.

Wolf and Shien didn't seem to mind, and Wolf said they were rather good rodents, who if weren't sick, were great at keeping sickness and filth back from the waste, refuse, and disgustingness that piled up from humanity.

Shien just told us, "In the ruins of the old faithful, against the workers of wickedness and blight, is the sword for the Light. I take this to meaning there's an old church up ahead, and something there against wickedness, probably any intruder, with the Sword awaiting."

Wolf said, "Very well. I brought my crossbow, and the sword as you suggested, but can you tell me any more about the dragon?"

"Check your radios, if you need to. It should be all across the country-side by now."

Wolf put in some earphones, and listened to his radio in his pocket.

He looked grim, as I looked at his face, and took out the earphones, and texted... Charlotte.

She immediately texted back.

Wolf said, "We've already got agents all across the country, still hanging around, and are setting up a perimeter against the dragon."

I was sort of awed, wondering how he did that so fast, and I knew it wasn't just words just from the look of him and the feeling I got. We were rising. The Organization was standing tall against adversity, even after the first night of our new leadership.

We kept walking the sewers, and Shien mumbled before a wall, saying, "Some old English riddle, I think. I couldn't really catch the words the priest said…"

"Oh!" I said, "But the serpent said to the woman, 'You will not die.' Is that what you're talking about? The priest sure made a long sermon about those words, stating instead we wouldn't die from God's will, and not the serpent's…"

The wall crumbled before us, probably because of how loud we were being, and we passed further into a hidden part of the sewers.

There was a huge, old Christian church awaiting before us.

Wait, I don't think those were Christian only symbols. Looked very strange, almost Roman.

Shien said, "This is an old church that was converted to Christianity from Roman religion. You can see the large bowl of offering, right over there, and… are those gargoyles? I didn't think they originated in this time."

We looked up at the gargoyles.

They looked back.

Wolf immediately had his sword and crossbow out, as I had a pistol and a knife.

The gargoyles flew down before us, as we shot at them, one of us using silver bolts, the other silver bullets.

The gargoyles just looked more annoyed, and flew down before us, blocking off our escape. The one blocking our exit rasped, *""In the ruins of the old faithful, against the workers of wickedness and blight, is the sword for the Light. Are you the light? Or the wickedness?"*

I thought for a second about their riddle, but Wolf roared, shouting, *"I am the LIGHT! THERE WILL BE NO SWORD FOR FOOLS, NOR ANY THAT CROSS ME! I AM THE WOLF!!"*

The gargoyles simply bowed before him, and a man- No, a skeleton arose from the dank darkness of the church, and raised a sword to fight.

Wolf arose to the challenge with his own sword of silver steel.

They clanged blades together! They fought and swore at the other! The slashed, parried, blocked and evaded!! The skeleton had a deep darkness in his eyes, but Wolf had so much brightness in his own. Eventually, Wolf fought the skeleton to its knees, and held his blade at its neck, head bowed, each of them.

The skeleton dropped its dull, rusty sword to the ground, clanging as it did, and fell over to be with the dust and ashes once more.

The gargoyles shifted, but continued to bow before Wolf.

We continued further on into the church, and found a sword in stone, instead of an altar.

What a beautiful piece of metal, that shined somehow, even just with our phone lights and the opening of light drifting down into the sewer. It had long etches on its blade, beautiful workmanship, that I suppose only George would know the full meaning of.

We pondered at how to remove the sword, but Wolf-

Wolf just grabbed the thing, shimmied it a bit, and pulled it from the huge stone. "It's all in the hilt." he said, "Where you want to direct the blade." He sat down by the stone to inspect the Sword, and said, "There's a sort of… poison, on the blade still. Very old, maybe only get one more use out of it still, but one more use is all we may need."

Wolf sheathed his own sword, and continued off with us through the sewers with the Sword. The gargoyles allowed us to pass, flying back up their belfries and screeching at us, maybe goodbye? Probably just as unholy monsters that will continue to linger on through the eras, never noticed, never seen, but eternally remaining.

40

Wolf struck the dragon with the Sword one more time, and it fell off the rooftops, and to the streets.

Wooh!! What a fight! We had missiles shooting at the dragon left and right, wherever we could catch the thing, as it burned down the town of London to smithereens!! People were scared, hiding in their houses, but the Wolf in the night kept the monster back.

I got off the roof, after using up my entire cartridge of bullets and then the extra, and looked at the huge, black dragon moaning out a death moan. Wolf was beside me, and he shut the dragon's eyes as it died.

He dropped the Sword to the earth, and I picked it up and followed him with it.

"Poison is no good for anyone. Please, take that to a museum or something..." Wolf said, back turned to me.

I stopped. Shouldn't he be congratulated? Rewarded? Loved? No one dared make a peep from the houses, and I recognized a certain theme for us as monster slayers. There was no good reward for us. The only reward came from the Organization, so we could keep living and do what we do.

Wolf walked off with his black suited people, people who were just blasting shotguns and shooting missile launchers, and I stared at the Sword in my arms.

I threw it by my bag in the hotel, seeing Shien cut her hair from when the dragon breathed fire at her. It looked very nice, super short, almost shaved off, and she frowned at herself in the mirror. She asked me, "I don't look like a tomboy, or some butch?"

"Not at all! Just here, you missed a spot on the back." I said, and took the scissors from her hand and snipped off the back pieces she missed. She stroked her hair in the mirror, after I was done, and said thank you.

She flirted with me for a second, holding me in her arms, and said, "I could use a cold drink of something nice. Or a cold drink of you. What do you say? Wanna get drunk?"

I laughed at her smiling so sweetly, not wickedly like normal, and I said sure, we can drink all the rest of the night.

We drank, and drank, and I didn't really mind if she felt me like she did. Felt… sort of comfortable…

Like a big sister, most of the time, until she kissed me.

I kinda wanted to kiss her back, and I kinda did.

I broke free, and looked out the window again. I said, "So all that, for all of us, what would you do?"

She snuggled up to me, and said, "I think I'd decapitate the Queen, and claim myself as her adopted offspring… I really like you, Olivia. I know, that's weird, and gross to you, and unprofessional, but I don't think I'd be who I am today without our travels… Just a great time, all throughout, that I had. Like I was, and am, fully accepted by you, no charge necessary and no prior experience needed."

"Well, we've got a lot of things to do! I think we can still see each other, don't you?" I said with her in my arms.

"I don't think so, Olivia. Gonna have to train all the rookies, and you should look at doing something like that as well… At least take a class or two, something that can benefit everyone, and not take lessons from me in silly spirits…"

"I really like what you've been telling me, though! Great stuff about those gods of sex and love, mhm. I think I'll use those a lot in the future, to get a good guy…"

"Who are you looking for, exactly? If it wasn't Wallace, then who?" she said, looking up at me with her in my arms.

"I don't know, really. I think I'll just keep looking, until I find what I want…"

"Would you like to find me, if you could again?"

"I'd find you all over again, everywhere I could. I mean it, Shien. I sort of thought of you as an old grouch, especially when we first met, but you're so… *cool!* And funny, too. You act like you're not, but then you pull off the serious face and make me laugh like nothing else! I really love it when- I mean, I like it when I can laugh."

She giggled at me in her arms. I kinda wanted to kiss her again.

So I kinda did.

It was soon a very rough night.

I couldn't fight off these nonplatonic urges of mine, and she just turned the music up, and we kept fucking.

"Ooooohhhh… right there, Shien…"

"Right here?"

"Right there- Ohmygawd, please do that again…"

"Mmmm… you taste so good…"

"I can't stand it anymore. Just please use the- Oh yessss…"

"I can keep going for as long as you like, Olivia! Tell me what to do!"

"I like it when you can- Yeah… Be yourself."

And we kept on going, throughout the night, only stopping to drink more and talk sweetly.

41

I kissed her goodbye, as I was still blushing red.

I mean, she wanted to *hold my hand* down from the hotel!! I did, sure, but it was kind of embarrassing.

She waved me goodbye, blowing me one, sweet kiss, that I imagined felt so nice, and drove off with the Organization agent, to do her job, leaving me for good, I thought, but only desperately. I knew I'd see her around, planned on doing so.

I had frantic, unwholesome thoughts that said I was now a lesbian, or a whore, or something along those degenerate lines, but I pushed them back, happy that I could at least spend one more night with my good, good friend.

I got all warm and fuzzy, so good feeling, imagining what we did in our hotel room again...

No, I'm not a lesbian. I'm at least a bisexual, I guess. Wouldn't mind if Shien had a cock, so there.

But then she'd look so... off. I don't think a cock was in Shien's style...

No. I'm not a lesbian, and those feelings didn't matter. It was just fun. Not like I would do that with anyone but Shien, anyway.

But I still wanted to do it...

No.

Grr...

Was this what gay people think?!? Was I now a gay person?!?

Hmm... I shrugged that thought off pretty fast, as I walked through the rain starting up. Gay people usually go through years of trauma, abuse, and struggle, just to find who they are...

Didn't they?

I grumbled in the rain, and ran off to hide under a bus stop.

A big double decker bus stopped before me.

I shrugged, and got on.

I paid the bus driver a gold piece, and he shoved it in his pocket gladly. Great that I got so much cash now from the Organization, no longer worthless paper bills, but pure, soft, gold. I sat in the bus next to Cthaklc, who looked a little concerned where the next exit was, pointing at his ticket. I told him that... Wait... There's no Love Village, at least not around London.

He just stared off into the rain, pressing his face against the glass, and I nervously sat beside him.

What did Cthaklc want? Who was he? Why was he appearing to me? I planned on asking him all of these things and more, but he just turned to me and said, "**The rain is parting fast, isn't it?**"

I told him no, looked like quite a downpour, and he looked out on the rain in content.

We continued to travel, until we got to pure darkness.

Pure. Utter. Darkness.

Cthaklc gleefully rushed to the door. I quickly went up behind him, and said, "Love Village? This place don't look like it got no love."

He looked at me confused, and pointed at his ticket again. I shrugged, as he left off the bus.

Then I blinked, and I was sitting on my seat, looking at the rain, unsure of where Cthaklc went.

"Laaast stop, chaps, take allll your stuff." the bus driver said.

I realized I was the only one on the bus. I thanked the bus driver, and um… asked him when the next bus will come by?

He said, "Not another 'til tomorrow, lady. Thank you for using the Worminall Terminal, best metaphysical transport throughout London. Did you take all your stuff?"

I nodded.

He told me, "Well go on, then!"

I got off the bus.

The bus drove off in the rain, as I stared back at it, trying to shield myself from the rain.

42

I heard a long howl in the rain.

Wallace?

I walked off the street path to that howl, and soon was hiding under a large oak tree, checking my phone gps, wondering where I was.

No reception.

Grr... *Why* can't the world be as easy as it was?! Didn't need this shit, no one did. Just gotta grit my teeth and get through it...

I heard another long howl, and hurried forward.

I saw and heard a werewolf, punching and slashing at a tree, and howling with all his might.

I gently walked up to Wallace, in the rain, and said, "Hard night, bud?"

He turned, growling at me, but immediately stopped as he saw who it was, whining a little bit like a dog.

He just sat under the oak with me, and we just sat together.

He whimpered some more, and soon began crying, then grabbed me and drenched my shirt in tears, along with the rain.

I tried to pat his broad back, but just stroked his fur instead.

He said, *"They're all gonna leave me, Olivia. Every one of them."*

"Hey... Those werewolves seemed kinda seedy if you asked me. At least too hairy for any normal person."

"Not them. THE BASE. All of them in the U.S., said I was worthless... Even my parents don't want to see me anymore..."

I just stroked his soft, wet fur, and told him to shhh, shh, it didn't matter now, he was in a better place, with people who accepted him for who he was.

He sniffled his large nose, and said, *"But not you, though."*

"I'll always love you, Wallace, no joke. You wanna know why? Because of that warm, human side in you, even if you're a monstrous beast now, even if you always will be... I *liked* you, even back at Base 64, because you *cared* about the troops, about... me..."

I smiled sadly, and just let him sniffle, looking into my eyes with those huge ones.

He said, *"You just think I'm a beast. Called me... bestiality."*

"I mean, I'm not against it!! Would sure love to fuck a werewolf, mhm, but I couldn't speak that out in the open like that!!"

"You've seriously gotta know where your priorities are, Olivia. What's it matter if I'm a werewolf? Would it matter if I'm an actual wolf? I'm a person, same as you, and not... a bestiality..."

I looked at that sad argument, but found some truth in his words. I had been demonizing him, just because I had some hangups, that really didn't matter in the grand scheme.

I stroked his muzzle, and tried to kiss him.

He wrestled out of my kiss, and panted, looking at me with a weird sort of accusing face.

"...What?" I said.

"Not the time or place, Olivia. Thank you for the gesture, but... I don't think this is the time nor place."

I frowned sadly, and we just sat in the rain together, sitting alone.

43

We walked back to London as the rain stormed in the night. Weird sort of place, Britain, if it wasn't raining, it was storming.

We ran to the next dry patch, as the light of the lamps shined down on us.

He sniffled, but didn't howl as some cars passed us.

"I can make it my own way, Olivia. You should try to hitchhike."

"Nah, I don't mind. Just want to make sure you're sleeping somewhere safe."

"Suit yourself. Let's try to get somewhere warm, then, and just ignore stupid Britain and its weather..."

He ran down this pure patch of wet grass, as I chased him, and we continued to hike off the side of the road in the rain.

He looked fondly at a window of a house with a mother coddling her baby. *"Looks good, don't it?"*

Some drool fell from his lips, and I said, *"Wallace!* Don't you dare think of eating that baby!!"

"I was just thinking about it, no harm there. Let's keep walking."

Sometimes he walked in the rain on all fours like a beast, sometimes he strode on two.

I continued to follow him, trying to make some conversation in the rain, but he just sniffed into the air, and told me this way, or that.

We found a pure patch, underneath some trees like a canopy, and he immediately shook himself off like a dog, getting me all wet some more as I tried shielding myself from that, and then prowled around in a circle, and settled down to sleep.

I just stared at him, hands on my hips. "You sure got used to being a werewolf! Just like this ol' basset my dad had, you sure are…"

He sniffled his nose, and said, *"Love it or leave it, Lamb."*

I shrugged, and took off my wet clothes.

I then snuggled up to Wallace, which he allowed me to, and we slept under that canopy of trees…

I woke up to his large eyes staring me in the face, as he was snuggled around me.

"See, if you moved your hand just a little, we'd be having sex, and not 'bestiality…'"

"Are you going to be pestering me about this until we actually do have sex?" I said.

"No… But it wouldn't hurt just having a little acceptance…"

I blinked into his large eyes looking into mine.

I slowly… rubbed his belly? Was that foreplay to werewolves? Still, he seemed to love that I did, and I was soon laughing as he kicked his leg and growled playfully.

He stared me in the eyes as I stopped. I looked down at it.

Sure was bigger, if anything.

He grew kind of embarrassed, and tried to roll over again, but I wrestled with him until I could see it some more.

Huh. Wasn't bad.

I tried to kiss his muzzle some more, and he allowed me to, blinking his eyes this way and that. He said, *"It's so easy with the werewolf ladies. What will it be like with you?"*

"I can take it, I think. I just had sex with my female best friend last night. I think I'm open to anything, really."

"Just let me know if I hurt you, ok? I really don't want to hurt you."

"Ok... So, just like this?"

"Just like that. Like the animals we are."

I oohed, as I felt it, and continued to feel it.

I told him to stop once, as he dug his claws into my shoulder blades, but he felt me gently some more, and we continued.

Wow. I was *really* a degenerate now, wasn't I?

I didn't really care. No one could see us, it was a beautiful moment of passion between a werewolf, and his lover.

Just... Just a little more...

Just... Just like that...

I howled with him, as we finished.

44

Good thing I was on the pill, since way back at Base 64. Didn't want to have any werewolf babies, now, would I?

Still, I smiled as Wallace led me down the road, as a huge werewolf.

He smelled so... *good.* Like your favorite pet, your best friend, and your man, all conjoined in one...

Still, I had those thoughts. Stupid urges lead to stupid things, like my father said...

But wasn't it really smart urges? Where else would I get experience like this?

I sighed. Stupid thoughts, if anything, and I smiled as Wallace panted with his tongue out, pointing that this way was just to the city, as the rain had parted.

We marched into the city, and I patted Wallace on the head, and then kissed his muzzle. He said we'd do this as a human sometime, if I was still around. I shrugged at that.

I went back to my lonely hotel room, now only for one, as Shien had left... leaving me... so alone...

I cried into my pillow. I had great, awesome sex, with the two people I loved so much... and I felt... so sad...

I was always the loner, even if I sometimes had friends. Always was, always will be...

I got a text from Charlotte, asking me what's up, and I poured my heart out to this woman, everything I've seen and done, and that... I was so alone...

She just called me, eventually, after I couldn't stop texting.

She said, "So, Lamb, quite the love troubles, huh?"

"Yeah... One love is now working, and the other is now ok with being a werewolf... I *miss them so much!!*"

I started crying, but Charlotte said, "Shush, Lamb. We don't need you cracking before any of the real hard bits, do we? Those are your *loves*. Would they want to see you like this? Hm?"

"...No... No, they'd want to see me happy and joyful, like usual..."

"Then keep that feeling in your heart alive for them. Don't let it petrify, poke the feeling if you need to, and just keep it alive. I know how it feels... Losing a love, slowly, utterly, and completely. An infatuation can turn into 'love' fast, and I know how horrible it is when it is stripped away. Fuck, I know what it's like fucking a beast, as well! I'm talking about the same person here, but y'know..."

I sniffled, and said, "You weren't always in love with Wolf?"

"Fuck, he *saved me* from my love! Ruined it in just the right way. Love is a horrible feeling. Like my Wolf, he's just around cuz he's fun! It's not that I totally *need* the guy... It's just easier with him, ok? Sometimes we just need our friends at our side, and not some twisted romance that'll turn us into a living monster. Wish I could've never went down that route, but things are what they are. Now. I want *you* to remember my words, and be happy with it, and content, and feel all the love you need, ok?"

"...I don't think I understand. So Wolf is- Or something? How is this relatable to me fucking a werewolf and my best friend?"

"...I am a chupacabra, and a chupacabra is what turned me into one. Understand?"

"So that whole speech you gave… Ok. I think I understand. Unless Wolf is a chupacabra…?"

"Not at all. He's as human, and fragile, as you. Just hold onto that fragileness, let no one take it away from you. Fuck, am I making any sense? I should just connect you to Wolf…"

"No, I think you're making a lot of sense, Charlotte. Thank you. I'll keep the feeling close, and let it be, nurture and grow it where I can, and let my friends be my loves, or at least my loves my friends."

"…See! That wasn't so hard, was it? Now get some rest, we're shipping you off to Japan with that 'good bud' of yours…"

I gasped, and said, "You mean it??"

"Got word that she's super depressed, too. So, might as well have the lesbos be a team, since you've already been such a good one before."

"Thankyousomuch, Charlotte! I'm gonna call her!"

"Hahaha… Young love. See you, Lamb."

<h1 style="text-align:center">45</h1>

Shien and I hung out with some of Wallace's "Beast Bros" that he really wanted me to meet.

There was the waitress from the bar, I could tell just by her curvaceous figure, even in wolf form, there was a big black wolf with one eye that Wallace was joking with, Wallace saying, *"Yeah, they called me the Beast back on the ship. Grrr..."*

And the big black scarred wolf said, *"No kidding! They called me Beast Christ on the continent. HAHAHA!"*

And then there was a young looking silver wolf, very quiet despite following the conversation we were all having.

Shien said, "So, Beast Christ, maul any good towns and villages in your youth?"

The big black wolf nodded his head, and said, *"I was the terror of the continent. I didn't want to be, but I just sort of fell into the role after a while. People didn't trust me, even when I turned human and saw all the horrors I had done... So, I became a bandit. Germany was never the same, as they gave into my threats with superstition and pure lycanthropy at my back. But, those days are past, and I'm very glad they are! Horrible, horrible things I did when I was young..."*

The waitress wolf said, "It's hard for these guys to get the hand of human dialogue and human interaction in their natural form. I go to conventions, meet all these great people in the LGBTQ... and no one can really tell that I'm a werewolf. It's been so fun, I made a home here instead of go back to Ukraine. Impossible, but for a select few, to find the Lycanthropists like us."

Wallace turned to me, and said, *"It all started when a very prominent young werewolf sought to cure his disease, instead of fall to it. He was a young German as well, blessed with status and money as a human, and cursed to be a murderous beast in the night. He moved to Britain for the scientific community, and found groups of likeminded people, who were sick of the werewolf huntings and 'curings' that took place in Germany, in fact all around Europe. The answer lay not in prayer and torture, but in medicine. Later, after the Nazi era, people took up his research again, still stuck with the same problem, so now we have a 'good 'nuff' solution."*

The waitress wolf, who said her name was Julia, said, "If the meds don't do it, and trust me, they *always* do it, then we keep our people hidden and in intense therapy. Some, like the ones you met in the U.S., Olivia, are barbarians, falling to their baser instinct all in favor of the disease in their veins."

I said, "Oh yeah, I did *not* like crossing werewolves at Base 64. I don't think I could call them human even if they sort of looked like it. Cannibalism, rape, all sorts of horrible shit that those werewolves did. You guys seem way cooler, and nicer."

Shien asked, "So, if one wanted to join your cool society, would one be able to? Just reach forth my arm, and let you take a little nibble?"

The big black Beast Christ, whose name was Fritz, said, *"It doesn't really work that way anymore. The meds, while also giving us sanity, lucidity, peace, and all around great vibes, also 'neuter' us, in a sense. We cannot pass on the disease anymore. Win/win if you ask me. Don't need anymore monsters on the block who think they're bigger and badder than us."*

All four of them looked up in the air and listened intently for a second.

Wallace said, *"God, that sausage man and his meat truck are the best smelling smell here... You've got a good setup, Julia."*

Julia giggled, and said, "Why do you think I *chose* this spot? Just down the road from that delicious butcher's..."

Fritz said, *"Bahh... I can't stand the distraction. If you want some nice smells, good for the mind, come out to my country cabin with me, and I'll show you the best smells in all of England. Here, there's always perfumed ladies stinking up the surrounding, the water, sewers and filth, the pollution of the air and cars driving past... I can do all without it, nothing smells good here. Except you two ladies, you smell very natural."*

I carefully sniffed myself, and Wallace went up to me and inhaled my scent deeply. *"Just like cherry pies and cheeseburgers."*

"Oops! We ate American food before coming here." I said.

Wallace grinned, and said, *"I think you got cheeseburgers in your vein, Olivia, being the pure American you are."*

Shien said, "Ooh! Do me. What's my smell?"

Wallace carefully sniffed her, and said, *"Besides that actually pleasant deodorant, like mint leaves, you smell like the woods. A very thrilling smell, even if it's slightly synthetic. I can guess you spent a long time roaming the woods and living off its bounties."*

Shien smiled and nodded.

The quiet, silver wolf, whose name was Solomon, said, *"I like human smells. They're not so bad when they come from nice people."*

The werewolves nodded to him, and we continued to talk for a bit, before heading off to the harbor.

46

Shien and I traveled off on the Organization cruiser, headed for Japan in no time at all! I loved holding her hand, as we waved back at the people of London, the werewolves, the good folk, and the Organization agents.

I bounced up and down on my bed with Shien, as we got excited for the new journey we were going to take.

We talked about our romance, and I said it was fine if we could be girlfriends, or even just best friends, as we scout the world for love and beauty wherever we roam. She said she'd like that, and then we both looked sinisterly at those two good looking guys just out on the bow...

I went up to one, catching him before he got spooked and nearly stumbled off the side. Shien and I introduced ourselves as agents of the Organization, and they turned out to be in the same line of work. We asked them if they wanted to party, and Shien pulled out the hidden alcohol she had stolen from our old captain, and us four all cheered and then partied all through the night!

I stared off the side of the boat in the night, feeling very good with myself and where my life was taking me. I looked down into the deep, then up at the stars... Even seeing a shooting star...

I made a wish, silently to myself, so it would come true.

Cthaklc was watching the night sky too, and asked me, "Is this *the* end?"

I shrugged, as we just watched the beauty, and asked him, "What do you think?"

He looked into my eyes with his old dweller ones, and we looked off into the expanse of creation and reality, in peace, wondering what was up in those stars.

Lamb's Epilogue

"And that, my good children, is the story of Olivia Lamb, how a young woman accepted the call of the Organization."

"...But what about the werewolves?"

"And Captain Sherry!"

"And what happened to the gnomes??"

"And Cthaklc, too!"

"...Listen, kids, I don't think I have permission to tell all the rest of the story-"

"And why was the sex so weird?!"

"I thought it was romantic..."

"Where'd Olivia and Shien *go*? Did they just live happily ever after in Japan?"

"...That's that, kids, unless your parents give me *strict* permission to tell the rest of the story, I can only guarantee that probably whatever you dreamed of happened, happened. Now, get along, it's been a long night tonight."

The kids mumbled off to their parents, and I smiled to myself. Kids... Such imagination, and an unquenchable thirst for more...

I was surprised that next night the kids *all* came back with these made up permission forms *all* signed by their parents.

"Mom said it was good I learned of the Organization's history."

"My parents just said that you should tell your stories better. I want to hear more!!"

"Now, now, I don't think it would be appropriate, especially since the tale gets darker, the sex stranger, and the characters-"

"*God*, Fox, we're already teenagers! Quit keeping a tight lip, and tell us more!"

I smiled, baring my vampire fangs, and continued the tale of the characters in the story, some tales converging and intertwining, and some breaking off to go who knows where.

The Werewolves of London

"Little thing you should know, kids, is that sex, when you grow up, tends to always make everything only stranger and weirder-"

"*Christ,* Fox, we all know what sex is. Some of us have even had it."

"Yeah, 'some' of us. Samantha, and not you..."

The little brats snickered as I frowned.

"Yeah, and some of us are going to still have it, unlike *some* of us, like you."

More snickering.

I spoke up, "See? Just the word 'sex' can make men go mad, women go insane, and little kids snicker and fight like the little kids they are. Ahem... Where was I?"

The kids settled down again, and listened to my story.

"The werewolves of London were ever vigilant against prejudice and hate, they have learned of those far past any human could dare to. Wallace the Werewolf was running down the plains of Britain, with his new love, Julia the Werewolf..."

47

Ahh… What a fantastic smell, the beautiful air… and Julia.

I tackled her down, and she flipped me over and pinned me with surprisingly… human, ability.

"Hey! No fair! How'd you do that? I was certain I caught you!" I growled friendlily.

She giggled, and told me, "Hold onto your human smarts, Wallace. Sometimes that's all that will save you, these days."

She let me back up, and we walked down the plains some more. I just couldn't get enough of smelling her, so good, and she allowed me to, and even sniffed me back!

I felt… home, here. Like I really didn't need to change from being a beast, things were somehow even better being one. We got to my good friend Fritz's cabin in the woods, and he opened the door for us in his human form.

Julia shed her fur instantly, becoming human, and I tried really hard… Ergh, felt like my eye was going to pop… and got the transformation down, in a few minutes. Fritz offered us some clothes, and we got dressed on the porch.

Fritz welcomed us inside, and I could see he and his wife were already entertaining a few muddy friends of ours! Solomon and his girlfriend, who just couldn't get around that muddy patch it seems, with happy smiles!

Then more, and more, and more of our people showed up, all werewolves. You could tell just by the smell. Wasn't bad! No. More like a bunch of dogs who were all bringing a great gift to the party... a new, awesome smell.

Some had only rubbed scent slightly with what they thought was interesting, and the others brought food.

Crispy lamb chops, bacon, pork roast, T-bone steak, unicorn, horse and donkey meat, monkey brains, fried chicken, ham, pig entrails, and even a bit of elephant meat! Truly, we loved to eat everything, with our disease, at least everything with a pulse.

We drank for a bit, along with smelling those delicious smells and usually eating their sources. Drinking was more a thing for our human sides, because it confuses and disorients us far too much. Some say it's the medication, but I think it could just be our natural instincts. You ever seen a pack of wolves get drunk? Neither have I.

We were laughing with the cotton candy scented werewolf, and then the Coroner, as was his nickname, said he had a special treat for the head of the household.

We all joked that it'd be Monica, Fritz's wife, but she lightly shook off our praise and cheers, and Fritz stepped up to the man, with a good intentioned snarl on his face.

The Coroner gave Fritz a big... odd smelling box.

It was just odd smelling. I couldn't place where I smelled that smell before...

He opened it gently, and the box unfurled to show its contents. A human leg.

We were all silent, as I remembered my time in Base 64, and the smell of the dead that sometimes accompanied our skirmishes with the wildlife there.

The Coroner explained, "They offered only their organs for donation, but I thought why not? Would be a great gift for your party. Please, enjoy yourself, Fritz, Scourge of Germany..."

The Coroner grinned, and Fritz curled up a dark fist, and smashed it on the Coroner's jaw.

The Coroner fell to the floor, snarling back at Fritz. They shed their human forms, transforming into werewolves from Fritz's dark skin and the Coroner's long muttonstache to become a big black scarred wolf Fritz was, and a balding werewolf that the Coroner was.

We immediately grabbed Fritz back, turning into werewolves ourself, as Fritz howled and roared.

He growled at the Coroner, *"Get out of my house, and take your horrible 'gift' with you."*

"More for me, then. Goodbye... gentlemen." the Coroner said, snatching the leg in his teeth, and leaving the house.

48

After that unfortunate incident was eventually shaken off, we all had fun again, and the Werewolves of London all ate meat, slept by the fire, or had sweet love in whatever form we chose. I really enjoyed Julia's dashing and gorgeous friends. Each and every one of them had something unique and pleasant to offer upstairs in a guest room, even if they were big or small werewolves, or male or female. I never knew I could so easily evolve into this sort of lifestyle! If anything, I had the libido of ten men as a werewolf, and I suppose that helped.

A large group of us went out to howl at the full moon, and we did so because we *wanted* to, this night, not because we were cursed to do so every full moon, ripping apart enemy or friend, and devouring the dead. I did not know how someone like the Coroner, who always was a self advocate of our kind, could have brought something so ghastly to this event. The purpose of the event was to celebrate ourselves as werewolves and Lycanthropists, the society that helps werewolves, not to dine on whatever living form we cared to, practicing no restraint or even decency.

What? Monkey brains are quite good, if they're not diseased. And the fucking unicorns... I had gotten a reluctant taste for them, after that whole fiasco with Olivia, as I've never had a meat that made me feel more spry and energetic before. The point I'm trying to make is that most of us never wanted to remember those days of being mindless werewolves, with the taste of human blood and guts still in our mouth even after we returned to human form.

At Base 64, on that first next full moon, I thought I could take it. Would just power through it, just like everything else. Really, I should've allowed them to amputate my arm after that first bite. Not that it would've done much good, lycanthropy is in fact fast acting and complete in a manner of seconds. It sort of, from what I learned from the Lycanthropists, hooks onto the DNA, after infecting our bloodstream usually with saliva or blood. It was kind of like the AIDS of fable, and hid in the very code for life until it could wreak terrible harm again on the full moon and spread the disease further.

At Base 64, on that first next full moon, I killed at least four men, terrifying the entire Base even after they chased me to the hills with fire and gunfire. I was quickly sent for "treatment," really so they could get rid of me in a proper, undisclosed matter. Damned Her Majesty seemed to do that a lot, did that with Olivia, did that with me. Once we prove problematic, or useless to her, then we were quickly disposed of like those hand wipes she always used.

In the morning, we all went home. I had a particular flophouse friend of mine, an older but gorgeous woman who let me rent a room back in London, and I roamed free as a werewolf until I was in more densely populated land, taking out the clothes and possessions in my "Werewolf Fanny Pack." It was an idea Solomon invented, specifically for use by werewolves. When we transform, if we're not already naked, clothes tend to take a beating pretty fast, or even can't hold our changed forms depending on how big a werewolf is in wolf form and how loose their pants are. The fanny pack held it all, even though it was more of a harness and girdle, and could transform into a backpack when done being used for wolf form.

I would've gladly invested in such a thing, thinking that these could even be useful to normal humans, but Solomon only remained quiet, with a happy smile after finally being approved for the device by us. Good man, that kid. He was very aware of being a werewolf as he was bitten when younger, and always sought a life of reclusivity until he met all of us.

Fritz was the coolest, and most dangerous wolf I knew. I looked up to him, being able to find that good life even after everything happened to him. Gorgeous woman, gorgeous house, even planning on some gorgeous kids in the future. He said they are reluctant to start the procedure of planned unprotected intercourse, since, from all research done by the Lycanthropists, the kids are guaranteed to have the disease if and especially both parents are werewolves. They said they couldn't bear to curse a kid with lycanthropy, but I encouraged the childbearing, saying another beautiful life in this beautiful life would make everything far merrier, even if they were wolves, and that they'd be able to guide them completely throughout their young lives. They agreed to continue thinking about it, thanking me.

Julia... I don't know where I'd be without Julia. I hadn't trusted the Lycanthropists, was planning on walking out after they told me what they knew. Of course, that was absolutely unacceptable, because if they found an untreated werewolf that would not accept treatment, they were forced to imprison and treat them anyway. But Julia kept me calm, seemed to make me trust her even if she didn't do much. And she was so fun! She was the most fun woman- most fun wolf- I ever met. I thought *Olivia* was fun... but really I think Olivia was more the necessary healing relationship I needed, and not who I wanted to stick with for... fun!

I hadn't started a real relationship in years after my wife had died during the chaotic crumbling of the world. I was done looking for the one I loved, and was far more content being with the many I enjoyed, with Julia.

I walked down the road, with my coat over my shoulder, enjoying the nice breeze and good smells of the countryside.

49

I woke up in my flophouse cot, and got ready for work. Olivia had offered me something with her Organization, but I turned her down, intent on sticking to a more peaceful, rewarding life than warfare. And what they fought... half the time I didn't know if they would be coming for *me* in the future instead of what they hunted.

She promised that they would never do that, and even had some vampires throughout their ranks. I didn't like vampires. Seemed too smug from the pictures. They were lucid, they were aware of their "illness," but did nothing about it, even took advantage of it and used it to further cause suffering and mayhem. Like the ones I heard about at the Capitol, also from Olivia. Scary, scary creatures.

I briefly met the Organization's leader, a hairy man named Hunter Wolf. I thought we could easily get along, but I was mistaken... we got on even better. He was a serious man, but seemed to have a sort of acquired calm and cool, even a relaxed sort of humor about him. He told me about the very few werewolves he had hunted in the old days, and was glad to meet one such as myself, who was not a murderous criminal, nor a murderous monster.

But he told me something that I remembered... Said that the werewolf he slew, who also had slain Olivia's father, was lucid. He *was somehow lucid,* even through the killings and hunger. It made me think.

Anyway, I got ready for work. I didn't work at the port, like the many sailors in London, especially these days. I didn't work as a baker, even though I knew how to bake bread. I didn't work as a cook, despite knowing all sorts of recipes from my travels. I didn't work as a cashier, or a bricklayer, or a writer. I worked with the farms and wildlife.

I loved being out in nature, always did. If I couldn't go out to be among natural beauty, I don't think I'd be able to be happy at all, no matter what I did. I worked on transferring the farm yields to where they needed to go, instead of transferring people in what was basically corporate slavery in Base 64. I checked the game and wildlife yields, even mapping out places people had forgotten about or got lost in. I loved this job, this place, and all the people with their quaint British accents.

I stopped the truck filled with pumpkins at an intersection, and saw a rich lady saunter past me through the crosswalk with a man in a top hat on and wearing a muttonstache.

I avoided their gaze, as quick as I could. I don't think they recognized me.

But that was Her Majesty and the Coroner, strolling through the street like the upper class.

I quickly drove off, and got the pumpkins to a hungry orphanage. Cheap food, pumpkins, as they multiply rapidly even if you forget to harvest and plant them. The kids were happy by the looks of the big orange 'uns, and I made sure payment was all already acquired and managed, and waved the kids goodbye and went down the road to pick up the next fruits and veggies.

I slept that night, but only briefly... I was so tired, and I felt happy going to sleep, which put me off guard. Nothing like a good sleep to incapacitate you...

Two masked men, one through the jimmied door and one through the window, grabbed me in my bed. I immediately tried to transform into a werewolf, but they shocked me with something, and I passed out.

50

I gasped awake with a bag over my head, arms and legs tied to posts behind me. Someone ripped the bag off my head, and I saw the Coroner and Her Majesty look at me. I looked in the corner of the room, and I saw... Dear God.

I saw werewolf pelts, completely stripped from the beast. Silver, black, or brown, some patchy, some patterned, but all as lifeless skins in the corner of this dark room, lit only by a torch in front of my face.

It looked like a medieval dungeon by the cobblestones around me, and the Coroner talked with Her Majesty for a second, as I tried to transform... I'd be able to rip these weak bindings off like nothing as a werewolf...

Her Majesty said, "It is an untimely business. This man used to be a very loyal worker of mine... But since he is now worthless, it makes sense to be able to harvest him where we can."

The Coroner said, "I agree. I find our whole, pathetic 'society' to be in shambles... They even refused a kind gesture on my end, purely because they didn't like the dish I brought!"

Her Majesty said, "Such rudeness. Never have I known Wallace, or people like him, to deny a meal. Salt of the earth... We give these hungry people all the bread, fish and wine from our tables, and they treat us with such disrespect..."

"Allow me to continue the skinning, My Lady. Please, take a pelt of any you desire."

She went to the pelts, and felt the fur, saying, "My... They're all so soft and beautiful... I believe I'll take this small one, that would look so curvaceous on *me...*"

She picked up a fur. I gasped, losing concentration again to turn into a werewolf.

That- That- That was Julia's hide. Had to be, it looked just like her pattern.

The wicked bitch, Her Majesty, grabbed the pelt, and shook hands with the Coroner, then leaving the dungeon.

The Coroner turned to me, after I tried again and again to transform, and said, "That won't work, Wallace. You won't be able to transform with this drug, at least not under the right duress... It's an older medicine that I sanctioned for our kind, complete and total destruction of the werewolf gene while it operates, but has lasting regrettable side effects, notably weakening the body and eventual complete brain failure... In small doses it will do the job wonderfully, however."

"What do you want with me, you fucking evil piece of shit werewolf-"

"Manners, Wallace. I thought that would be obvious. I want your skin. The fur of a werewolf is hard sought and rarely attained, most especially since after the werewolf dies it reverts back into human form... but we'll keep you alive enough. I bring the people, well, the good upper class and rich villains, the outfit that they deserve, that they *need...* for anything I could ever desire."

"You are a villain, Coroner. You're just a nasty villain, even have the villain name to go with it." I remarked, trying to force the bindings off.

"My true name is Sir Walsworth, Wallace. I thought you might at least remember my name, and not the ridiculous name given to me by the foolhardy 'Lycanthropists...' We share a bit of our name, and now you will share a bit of your hide."

He strapped this ocular machine to my head. Looked like that virtual reality crap the kids used to like in the old days.

Then the pictures started to appear, as the Coroner attached wires to my skin.

Rabbits. Running. Rabbits. Running. Chasing. Rabbits. Rabbits bleeding. Rabbits being eaten. Raw.

People screaming. Horror. Killing. Blood. Everywhere.

I tried to resist the hunger in my veins, the need and instinct to *claw, and kill, and bite...*

I wanted to chase those screaming fat women running. They looked so good.

NO! I needed to resist!!

The pictures continued, as I couldn't shut my eyes from them, the wires stimulating my body slightly this way and that, tensing the muscles to release and become their true form.

Babies. Nothing like tasty looking babies.

The moon. THE MOON.

I howled, bound to the boards, and I felt the fur grow longer.

I felt my life flash before my eyes, as the primal beast I was.

"NOOOOOO!!!" I screamed.

I pictured just my wife. Sitting by my side. Picking out cribs for the babies we were intent on having.

I imagined the sun's warm rays, with her laughing as I chased her playfully.

I imagined Olivia, accepting me for who I am, who I was.

I imagined beautiful nature, who always accepted me, no matter what form I was.

I imagined Julia, as we traveled the nature of Britain, enjoying each other as we always would.

Ahh… the sound of the water… By a stream, the river, the beach, and the wind in the trees…

"You can't resist forever, Wallace. We'll try this again tomorrow."

I was injected by a horrible feeling shot, that just rushed into my veins and made my brain feel numb, my body weak.

I slumped down, as the Coroner removed the ocular device, and left me alone in the dungeon in the dark.

51

I was not ready for the next "skinning."

But I fought my way through it, becoming firmer in resistance, strong in rebellion, while weak in body, and losing my sanity.

Again, throughout the week, as the Coroner suggested because he always came in every "night," I resisted being skinned.

He looked at me once more with the ocular device off, and remarked, "Do you want me to skin your human skin, instead? In the right market that can fetch almost just as much."

I tried to spit in his face, but only managed to dribble some spit down my chin. The gesture was not lost on the Coroner, however, and he slapped me with a backhand.

He said, "Let's try one more time..." and began to attach the ocular device again.

But someone slammed open the dungeon door, and shot at the Coroner from up the steps.

I wondered, with the ocular device attached and obstructing my vision, who was my savior, or worse, my new torturer and executioner.

But the ocular device was removed forcefully and quickly, and I saw a beautiful curvaceous woman- no, a wolf? A beautiful werewolf look at me from the light shining down at us from outside.

The Coroner grabbed her back paw, and she kicked his head in with one, strong werewolf kick, and then shot him again with silver bullets for good measure.

Julia undid the bindings, and got me out of there, weak as I was malnourished, dehydrated, and tortured.

The sun. The sun blinded me, out in the middle of these castle ruins. I was so happy to see the sun.

She took me to Fritz's cabin, dropping the pistol and running down the wilds with me in her front paws, running like a very fast, very strong human in her werewolf form.

They laid me down on the sofa, and gave me food and drink. "Please… no meat…" I muttered, and I was given food from Monica's garden.

I spent awhile there recuperating, but I was fine enough to stumble around in the night with Julia.

"I thought you were dead." I said to her, as we looked up at the less full moon.

"I'm too smart to be killed by 'the Coroner…' Didn't you know that?"

"I- I just- I thought I saw your pelt- And I was so worried-"

"Shh. It is ok. Do not worry any more. Come, let us walk by the stream. Can you still do it?"

"Y-Yes. I can still change. I want to, so bad, but I had to resist."

"No. I mean can you walk."

"Yes, Julia. Let's just sit under the moon for a bit."

We walked gently down by the river, to simply sit and stare at the moon.

Captain Sherry's Expedition on the Cherry Pop

"I liked that story."

"Too spooky for me. What about that bomb ass awesome chick who even took down Olivia??"

"Captain Sherry roamed the seas, and if some of you had paid attention when they were showing you the building, you'll see the whole nautical firm is named after her."

"No way!! That chick sounded so hot."

"Ahem, guys. That *chick* is a proud and pioneering *lady* of the seas."

"Yeah, yeah. A righteous sweet ass lady in charge of the Cherry Pop! Tell us about her."

"Captain Sherry's expedition on the Cherry Pop had only just begun, a talented and experienced hand at all manners regarding the sea, and was eager to make a name for herself amongst the other Great Sea Beasts..."

52

I took up playing violin with the girls singing sea shanties and sea rhymes. A spry woman still in her prime and with gray hair took up the song.

"There once was a man with a big, big cock, never needed nothing but was under my smock!

"There once was a maid with a fair, fair look, he didn't care about nothin', but what she could cook!

"They had a few kids, here and athere, but what really did it for him was being with his maiden fair…

"He died on the sea, not merely a trophy, and now I'm here with my kids and his beer!

"A yo, ho, ho, the whore is stuck on laaand, yo, ho, ho, life is pretty bland!

"She went out to the water, that maiden fair, no longer to be an old gray mare!

"She went out on the water, to roam them seas, to take what She took, her man and her hair!

"Hunted the sharks, the leviathans and squids, the maiden did, and she took another man,

"A young man on land, who didn't go nowhere, so she could fuck him, with his prick and hair!"

"A yo, ho, ho, the whore is stuck on laaand, yo, ho, ho, life is pretty bland!

"A yo, ho, ho, the seaman's dead and the whore is old, but what keeps her happy…

"Are her landman's prick, and her hordes of gold!"

I played the violin, screeching and scratching in tune with the beat, faster, faster, faster, until… it was done, a final screech to us! The ladies all clapped and cheered and then we settled down for the night. What an awesome grand, great adventure, that the girls and I are going on.

I did a little work with the researchers before I nodded off as well, mapping out where the last giant squid was spotted. We were going to do a little investigative work first, but what really set my heart a pumpin' were the grand chases.

Had one as I was a little girl, an albino sperm whale, barely a nickel to my name and hardly a muscle besides. I took pictures of the "great beasts" of the sea, the sharks, whales, and anything big enough to be called a beast. Learned all I did from my fisherman father before those times, and then the work came easy enough, learning even more on the voyages.

Tourists paid top dollar for any little picture of the beasts, before phone cameras became so popular and widely used. I thought those little contraptions would never last, the grain was off, the color far too saturated, but they just continued to get better and better, as I lugged my professional cameras around.

Tourists paid even more to see the beasts with their own eyes, however, and that's where the real money was. Told 'em all about the fishing and hunting of the beasts, and some of the tourists who weren't land-lubber tree huggers who kept an open mind allowed me to fry up some of the beasts on their platter for delectable dinners.

I passed the cook's. She, if she wasn't using salt, used all sorts of spices to season a mix. I told her, "Woah now, Betty Sue! Keep a lax hand with the paprika!"

She stopped seasoning the fish, and said, "Sorry, Captain Sherry. I... like to experiment."

"Well do that on your own time and not with the crew's dinners! I don't need none o' you sick and keeling over before we even see the first squid!"

"But Mary Anne has that black pepper allergy, so I thought maybe she'd like some paprika instead."

"She's only *got* a 'pepper allergy' because you splashed that stuff all over the last few steaks we had!"

"Oh. Ok... I'll keep a laxer hand, then... Same as usual, Captain Sherry?"

"Just the little shrimplings, and I'll take a cup of wine before bed. Great, great haul we got of those shrimplings, just enough to keep the palette interesting."

She handed me my before bed snack, and I went to look off the side of the ship as I ate them.

I saw a few whales off the side, spouting up water. What good looking, fat, beautiful species...

What I hunted now was far bigger.

53

I swished my blonde hair out of my eyes. Gonna need a haircut, soon as I can. I tied it up in a ponytail and shoved it under my hat. No little danglies or ponytails by the machines, I had to tell the girls over again and again until it sunk in… Basically only when Juli C almost lost her head.

I looked at all the many, *many* legends of sea serpents, giant squids, leviathans, and krakens. My study was filled on the subject, and I pushed another dusty parchment off the table that the Organization gave me to instead look at a more common work under a seaman's pen which, while sometimes he fancied himself a poet (a rather bad poet actually) he had all the exact details for the beasts.

The book was labeled fiction when I stole it from that library. I had it practically memorized by now, the entire thing down to his wordy little looped clauses and ridiculous metaphors. I read a page again, looking for maybe something I missed or forgot, or at least for the words to hit me under a different light and new ideas to form.

"The greatest and most intelligent of the sea beasts R the greatest krakens in the depths. Ever seen the octopi escape from a tank for the pure satisfaction? The giant squids R more reclusive, but only now in the year of 1942 to be appearing again in R nets. They taste foul, something bland that only the craziest cook with a lot of seasoning would be able to turn into something edible. You'll find them along the equator, up to the seas of Newfoundland, but only in the deepest waters. The squids have fought the blue whales many of times in the thousands, no, billions of years on this planet, and many blue whales even hunt the species for food. The bloodiest squid is the reddest one, while the bluest whale ain't so sad."

I continued to read for a bit more about the mating rituals of the squid, which the writer suggested to be a nice dinner of grabbed fishes offered to the female squid... I nodded off laying my head down on the table after that, listening to my favorite Viking metal band. Reading made one so tired...

I had another dream of commanding my Norse galley, as a Viking woman called Brynja Brouhaha, telling my maggoty and lice infested crew to continue rowing, or I'd drink their blood instead of my ale.

They continued to row, ever loyal, as we set off to the end of the world. They didn't need the threats, but it kept them happy as they ached their muscles.

We were on the trail of the Greatest Beast. The one who even had power unthinkable, a story of legend and myth even in my culture.

I caught another glimpse of its many eyes, and roared as we rammed into it with our galley.

Then, the tentacle came down, smashing my crew to pieces, and I-
I woke up.

I rubbed my eyes. This book always had that effect on me. I liked most of the dreams, but if I couldn't take down the Greatest Beast, at least in this life, I was all settled to ram against the rocks just to give me a little rest from the nightmares...

No matter. The dawn was already pushing the sun high in the sky, and I got to work, captaining my ship around the world to the end of the world.

54

I was lowered in the shark cage down into the deeps.

The sharks were lovely, as I breathed in oxygen from the tank on my back. Very friendly, as they came to look at me, even bumping up against the cage where I was able to get a feel of its sharp skin.

I gasped, as I looked further underneath me.

There, as the sharks scattered, was a blue whale seeming to wrestle with a giant squid, as it covered its eyes with its tentacles, trying to strangle the whale to death.

The whale slightly scraped our boat, and I hoped the ladies up there kept a cool head.

And, as the giant squid was knocked off, trying to retreat back into the depths, the whale inhaled the squid into its mouth with an intake of water. The squid tried to escape from halfway down its gullet, but the whale just shut its mouth, no escape for the wretched beast.

What an awesome find. My camera was recording this entire time, and the Organization are going to be out of their socks in excitement when they see this.

I do think that was the purest, most steady handed find there ever was of the giant squid and their natural enemies. I thought of the money that was going to roll in, trying to daydream and imagine all my future wealth, but all I could think about was the awesome spectacle I had just witnessed.

I was pulled up, and got the camera into a researcher's hand who took it down below deck immediately after I told her what I saw. The girls slapped me on the back and congratulated me, saying that the whale nearly could've capsized us if we hadn't been so careful with me down there.

I got out of the scuba suit, and then went to go write up my report about the squid and my findings. It was a good report, but I've seen better under my own hand. I went to go see if everything was still ship-shape, and my first mate, a once Nigerian pirate named Fatima (not her real name, as she abandoned the once family she had in Africa) told me about the storms seen in the west, that a hurricane was south, but very further south, but that all the winds seem to be blowing together, giving us unneeded "turbulence" in the waters.

I had noticed the grey skies growing something fierce, and we were silent for a second as a large wave passed beneath us. I slapped her on the back, saying that we'd be ok in times to come. She told me about the stupid tourist cruise boats to the east, a pair of them, and I nodded, saying, "We'll have to tell them to scatter off before those storms get any worse. At east, Fatima. Get back to rowing- I mean, hand me some rum- I mean..."

I shook my head back and forth. Those dreams were starting to get to me.

Fatima said, "...Capitaine?"

"Ignore me. Be sure to go to the arm wrestling club starting up! You've got a wicked arm on you."

"I... keep my arms to myself, thanks. If we decide to loot those tourists instead, I wouldn't mind. I'm telling you confidentially. They are very stupid to come out so far. The currents probably swept them out here without them knowing, and by their idiot calls on our radio, they think the party is still on. Would it be not wise to take a little of their food and water, to satisfy our much more important expedition? Very frugal, no?"

"No, Fatima. We, while our expedition is very important, can't go exercising our might around the oceans yet. If we see a group of tourists, we'll let them think we're friendly females, if we see a group of battle-ships, we'll do the same. No need pulling out the big guns, yet. But take those guns of your own down to the arm wrestling club, that's an order."

She rolled her eyes, and said, "Every act of fun is an 'order' to you..."

I grinned, and said, "I know, Fatima, but it takes at least a captain to know where the fun is. See you there."

Fatima won again and again, because even if she looked like her arms were scrawny, she was smart, could get into your head through your arm, and somehow take you down even without complete raw force. Even was tough for me to beat her! But I'm not the captain for nothin', no weak arms or weak head on me.

I slammed her hand down to the table, and she smiled. She always liked someone who was a good challenge, was why I chose her for first mate. She was *up* to the challenge.

I went to read my book, as I listened to my favorite pirate metal band, and found the chapter on sea serpents.

"Like snakes they R, horrible, monstrous ones with fins on their neck and fangs in their mouth. I've been chasing one for a long life, and only gave up once in my youth. I saw the she beast, the Mother of Serpents devour another cargo ship, and I quickly gave up giving up. The Nazis R on our tail, with their metal monstrosities, but R older ship can take any yon challenge, swifter and more agile we R than the Nazis. Then, I even thanked the Mother of Serpents, for though the Nazis had great explosions and guns, they did not have teeth as sharp as her. The snake coiled around the curved ensign of the Nazis, crushing them to pieces like fiber wood and glass flowers given to a mother in law. I think that Mother of Snakes even welcomed R chase, probably bored in the waves."

I fell asleep, on the table again…

The blast of cannon fire awoke me from my drunken stupor, and I strode out on my pegleg to see the destruction my first mate had already started.

Without me! The nerve of it. I wasn't the dastardly scourge, Sea Witch Sasha herself, for nothing, the greatest pirate on the North Atlantic. I had a full mind to whip her with the cat o' nine after this, and she would take the whipping, or die.

But we continued to shoot the spice ship, letting the boxes of tea fall into the water. They would be worthwhile treasure, but the real bounty here was the British princess on the ship.

We boarded the ship, as I dual wielded my sabers, slaughtering them with only foul play and my swords. The Sea Witch Sasha only ever used melee, is what they said…

I still pulled out my pistol, balancing the sabers in one hand, and shot down the captain of this flimsy little British vessel.

The princess was inside the cabin, and I grabbed the little girl by the hair, laughing cruelly at her and all who stood in my way.

I dragged her out to the deck, and I saw the Greatest Beast arise from the waters.

We had made too much noise and bloodshed on the open ocean, and it raised a tentacle, slamming it down upon me and I-

I woke up.

55

I radioed the cruise ships to head back, again.

"Whaaat? It's such a great day, don't you think?"

"There's approaching winds of one hundred nautical miles an hour, threatening to capsize you if you don't head back the way you came. This is your last warning-"

"Heyyy, you sound like an ok lady! Come and party with us!"

"I repeat, there's approaching winds of one hundred nautical miles an hour, threatening to capsize you if you don't head back the way you came."

"Pshhh... We've got... *technology.* Nothing sinks boats anymore."

"...I repeat, there's approaching winds of one hundred-"

The guy lost connection.

I sighed angrily... Why and how in the sea hells are there tourists on the water?! Didn't they have enough troubles at home on land?

We passed close to their ships, and I called out with a megaphone for them to turn back.

They just drunkenly cheered at me, as I kept repeating the message.

Grr... If I have to snap some tourist's neck for this, I wouldn't mind. At least the rest would take the hint, before their bones are snapped by the coming storm, remains eaten by the sharks.

Oh no... What was that noise?

It was damned singing, mermaids leaping from the water, meeting the cruise ships as they turned towards them.

I looked on in horror as a man reached down from the cruise ship, and a mermaid took his hand, grabbing him into the water.

Only a pool of red appeared after.

They kept watching the mermaids, and I shouted, "LADIES!! It's time we got to work! Shoot down those mermaids, and send off some of the repellant!!"

The ladies started shooting with their rifles handed out quickly from the cabinets, blasting mermaids to bits here and there. We launched a repellant from our missile tube, and the faint screeching sound coming from the water broke the tourists from their trances.

Really, that was harsh, horrible screaming coming from the speakers of the repellant, of mermaids hunted in the past, that was underwater.

The tourists got scared as they saw all the dead fish women floating in the waters, attracting sharks, and I repeated the message on the megaphone.

They turned back, and I smiled to myself as the wind howled from behind me.

56

This ship was specially made to travel harsh, harsher than harsh, conditions. If we were going to hunt the great sea beasts, we needed a ship that'd hold her own.

The lightning flashed, as we hid under our rain jackets from the rain pouring in a downpour.

Another huge wave nearly launched us from the water, but we kept afloat and all on deck.

Fatima, Mary Anne, Juli C, Betty Sue, Sheila Sins, Lady Lucky Lucy, Grim Gertha, Sweet Marie, Lisa the Tranny, Delila Ducks, and the rest, kept my strict orders and commands, and the head researcher, Suzy Sue, told me we were near what I wanted, with its great form echolocated back to us from underwater.

The Greatest Beast.

The echolocation systems were fine pieces of machinery, based off what the dolphins knew and used, excellent for finding the beasts of the sea in the grand expedition of the Cherry Pop, our mighty vessel.

Even better were the weapons we carried.

I set myself before the harpoon gatling gun at the front of the ship, ready to reel the Greatest Beast in.

And then I saw it, as it seemed to think we were easy pickings lost in the storm.

The hugest kraken, a leviathan to all, raised its head and tentacles towards us.

I launched the harpoons, shooting into one of its many eyes right next to a blinded one from some past skirmish, tethering it to the ship, and it screamed a huge, reverberating sound in the storm.

It dove, trying to take us down into the water, but I held my hand on the harpoon gatling gun, and we kept it from drowning us in the brink.

It surfaced again, the Greatest Beast, and arose to fight.

It slammed at us with its tentacles, but unlike in my dreams, it missed us and sent us rolling through the waves, its great mass ever taught with steel lines.

The footage was continually rolling, of the greatest hunt man or woman has ever seen.

The beast was bleeding, attracting even more sharks than what came after those mermaids, but the sharks stayed back, either waiting for it to die, or one of us.

Another tentacle slammed into us, taking Delila Ducks and Sheila Sins into the waves. The sharks made short work of them, and I prayed to my dead fisherman father that their deaths be swift.

The kraken was getting tired, after pulling us a long ways through the sea, through the storm and to its eye.

It rested for a second, as I sank more harpoons into its hide. This would make me rich. The richest woman in all the world. I could open up a restaurant selling just "the Greatest Beast" calamari for years.

I looked at its pierced skin, and saw the eggs scatter from her belly.

I... It made something sink in my heart, when I saw that. This was the Greatest Beast, and maybe the only one other in the world, judging by those eggs.

I did not want to do the idea that was gnawing at me, in my head, in my brain, in my belly.

"Like the greatest leviathans of all, the Greatest Beast is a female, a fat whore with a belly full of roe so red it'd make you think you R in a field of cherries instead of babies. The Greatest Beast is malevolent, whimsically evil, but a one of its kind, and brave be the man who takes her down, and staunch be his belly, for by destroying the Greatest Beasts of the sea, one can only look at their own existence, and realize that it is yet so fleeting. The life of the Greatest Beasts R more massive than a fat lady, but we must all listen to the fat lady sing." the book had said before, as I had read it countlessly again and again.

I didn't want to do the thought that was screaming to me now, as loud as the thunder that was approaching again.

I released the Greatest Beast from the ship, and she dove into the water, free, one of the last few of her kind.

The storm abated, and we continued to monitor the sea, a deep dwelling in me that made me feel so sinky...

But somehow I knew that the dreams may pass, of all sorts of alternate lives on the chase, never fulfilled and always dying a watery end.

I watched the film of us briefly capturing the Greatest Beast with the ladies, after I said a service for Delila Ducks and Sheila Sins.

They cheered, as the film focused on me for a second, blonde hair blowing in the breeze, hat blown to the waves, a look of staunch and everlasting determination in my eyes.

And we sailed off into the sunny seas, for the next beast that we would hunt, documenting them for our Organization.

The METAL Gnomes and the Fae Sorcerer

"Hey! Are you listening to music with one earbud in??"

"It's not *music.* It's *metal.*"

"Ok. You sound like some pioneering young gnomes, who also had a strange fervor for that word."

"No way! I gotta hear that story."

"As long as it's not too loud. Please tell us the story, Fox."

"Take out that headphone, or- Ah. Thank you. The Metal Gnomes and the Sorcerer of Fae were at odds. Why? Over a simple thing called metal... and freedom."

57

"**Ahem. We're the METAL Gnomes. Alright, everyone!!**" the head singer shouted out, I slammed my sticks together, and we played our gnomish metal for the people of Fae. The singer started with an old singy songy voice, like a classic gnome… then ripped up the chorus, and made us METAL.

"**The werewolf and the beeeeeaaaasts, rabid in the sheeetsss…**"

"**The sea bitches and krakens, rocking on the botttoooommm of the seeeaass…**"

"**We're the GNOMES OF METAL, and WE'VE HEARD IT BEFORE!**"

"**WE'RE THE GNOMES OF METAL, AND WE KNOW THE SCORE!!**"

The guitarist started the solo, riffing with the bassist in ordered, chaotic metallic unity.

I slammed the sticks on the toadstool drums, rocking, continuing the beat and watching my tempo. I always went too fast at this part, because I was so excited.

"**WE'RE THE METAL GNOMES, THE GNOME ON THE LAWN**

"**WE'RE THE METAL GNOMES, POKING YOU AT DAWN**

"**GET UP, FUCKERS, IT'S TIME TO BAKE**

"WE'RE COOKIN' IN HERE, RIGHT OFF THE LAKE"

"Rockin with the beasts!" the band and the crowd sang the refrain.

"Rockin in the sheets!"

"WE'RE THE GNOMES. OF METAL."

The singer started again, **"COME WITH ME, TO THE LAND OF FAE**

"WE METAL LIKE NOTHIN', AND METAL ALL DAY

"WE ROCK LIKE THE BIG STARS, ONLY ONE FOOT TALL

"WE'RE THE GNOMES OF METAL, AND YOU'VE HEARD THE CALL."

"GNOMES. OF METAL."

"Gnomes! Of Metal!"

"GNOMES. OF METAL!!"

"GNOMES! OF METAL!!"

"RARARAAHHAHHAHHGGAHARAR!!!!" the singer roared.

"Rockin with the beasts!" the band and the crowd sang the refrain.

"Rockin in the sheets!"

"WE'RE THE GNOMES. OF METAL." EVERYBODY ROARED.

58

"**This is just how I always talk.**" Big Boomie boomed.

"Was it the Fae Sorcerer? Did the Fae Sorcerer curse you along with the rest of the band, to play metal for the rest of your short, short, short, short-"

Big Boomie took the microphone from the fairy reporter, and said to all the people of Fae in his booming voice, "**Listen, everybody. WE'RE THE METAL GNOMES. WE DO THIS CUZ WE LIKE IT. And that's that.**"

He crushed the microphone under his gnome strength, and we walked forward to go home and drink our brews, as the Fae people all around us begged for more of their questions to be answered.

We parted ways at the crossroads, the guitarist and bassist smoking cigarettes and off to their toadstools, and Boomie and I passing further down the road.

I nervously asked Boomie, "Um, Boomie, am I doing alright? I know I'm new to the band and everything. Been awhile since I've been to Fae, too, as I was captured by a Blonde Witch."

"**No, you've been doing great, Bomba. Not a problem with your drumming at all anymore, as soon as the METAL fever caught you.**"

"Is it right? For all of us to… do metal? Smoking cigarettes and drinking is one thing… at least for *gnomes*… But won't this upset someone?"

"They should get upset. Then they know they have the fever. Then they know the METAL is in their veins, and they can roar and shout with us, instead of against us."

"That's a good point, Boomie."

We parted ways at the fork in the road, Boomie and I giving each other a strong, METAL handshake, and I went to drink in peace.

I went to my gnome mushroom house with my gnome wife (you didn't think there were gnome wives?) and patted my gnome kids on the head (Yes, we have kids. We don't all just spring from the ground with big beards.) and my wife got me a great Fae drink, something new and pleasant she brewed after I taught her how.

Beer.

Fairy beer, so it got you completely, totally wasted after the first sip, but in a wasted way that made one feel so clear. I noticed my wife was already on her second, and I didn't mind. I encouraged it! We all had changed so much, after most of us came back to Fae after being captured by the Blonde Witch. I don't think I could *ever* just sit on lawns anymore, peaceful in content.

The METAL had gotten into our veins, like Boomie suggested, as that's all the Blonde Witch ever played in her shop.

At first, I resisted it. Then I couldn't get the songs out of my head. At least the Blonde Witch had a good taste in music, as we were all trapped in snow globes waiting for fate inevitable, to be sold to an ugly child who shook us too often.

Then this really good, ok looking human wench set us free. Did it out of the kindness in her heart, not for our hoards of treasure or any magic wish. She was wrongly involved with the Amanita Fae, the Three High

Sovereigns of Fae, Brother, Sister, and Sorcerer. The Sorcerer was the eldest of the three sovereigns, and also the wickedest and cruelest.

I was of the mind, after we had our intense band discussions, that Fae didn't even need a ruler. Not even some ass president, who would only sit on his or her ass anyway. I was in the mind... of the Free Gnomes.

The METAL Gnomes took my political ideology in interest, and we even wrote a few great songs about how the gnomes, and all of Fae, should be free. No more taxes! No more mandatory military enlistment! No more stealing our lawns, our nature, and our magic! We wanted what we wanted for ourselves, our dreams, wishes, and desires, to truly *be* ours, and no one else's. We wanted to be free. I couldn't wait for the next show we'd perform the songs on.

59

The crowd loved it.

The media loved it.

But I knew, somehow deep in my heart that someone... somewhere... had intensely hated it, and would not take our music with deaf ears.

We were the METAL Gnomes, who sang of freedom, beer, tobacco and good sex. We all knew what we wanted. Some wanted to go back to the old, wild ways of Fae, and well, we let them take a look and listen of those wild ways with our METAL music.

The leprechaun ladies (you thought there were no leprechaun ladies?) we took backstage, and had our very first band floozies.

I had to politely leave, being the only one with a gnomish wife, but the leprechaun ladies all pushed their four leaf clovers into my hands, and I smiled, drunk from fairy beer, and stumbled back home.

I heard, or saw, or... felt, a shadow on me as I walked home.

There was something in the air... a feeling I intensely disliked.

I asked out into the shadows of Fae who was there.

A tall man, a Fae man with long antennae, a dark purple robe on and a long, pointed beard appeared before me. He scared me onto my gnome butt on the ground, and I knew I was just then in intense danger.

The Fae Sorcerer looked down at me, and crouched to look into my eyes. He smiled wickedly, as I knew what he saw. Only fear.

His eyes were like dark, horrible pieces of coal, and I could not get them out of my head after he seemed to drill into my skull with them.

"You have one more chance, Bomba of the Metal Gnomes. Turn back from this path of folly, go forward and you will find only unluckiness before you."

I gulped, feeling the shiver in my spine, but got up and shouted back, "Never! We are the Free Gnomes, the METAL Gnomes! We don't take curses and evil from old, sorcerous Fae like you! Go back home, and let me go to mine as well!"

He stood back up tall, and cackled, a long evil sound, and rushed away in the black wind.

He had cursed me. I knew by the sound of his words.

I went forward, to my home, and nearly broke my ankle as I almost stepped into a pit, but narrowly missed it.

A falling tree nearly crushed me, but I jumped out of the way.

A meteor falling from the sky nearly incinerated me, but only singed my beard a little bit.

I patted the four leaf clovers in my pocket, thinking more than that will be needed to stop the METAL Gnomes.

60

Powerful people had heard our words, people with strong spells and mighty magics.

And they liked what they heard.

There were revolts against the Amanita palace, of common Fae playing our music from enchanted recordings. Our pictures were everywhere, the METAL Gnomes, and every show we just felt better and better, either because of the blessings of those powerful enchantments placed on us, or just because the feeling of the crowd felt so good.

The two sovereigns, who were really only weak and petty placeholders for the Sorcerer of Fae, were soon reviled and spit at by the public, no longer loved for their false power.

They went to a show of ours themselves, and we sang of being free, straight at them. They were thrown out of the show, as they got up from their thrones and told us to shut up.

Soon, people were kicking those two poisonous Brother and Sister out of the castle, and military force could not keep back the riots.

We watched onwards to the palace of Amanita, as the people threw flaming molotovs at it, watching the poisonous mushrooms burn.

But then there was a horrible laughter on the wind, and a storm started brewing around the palace, from the highest point, the Sorcerer's Tower.

Rain, acid rain, poured down on us, and we all ran for shelter far and away as we could.

Boomie, however, stopped in the rain, and looked back at the castle.

The acid burned holes in his beard, in his clothes, in his skin, in his hat, but he continued to stare back at the Sorcerer, and roared at him in METAL.

The people around us began to roar, scream, shout as well, taking up the call of METAL, and we all did as well.

The sun struggled with the storm, but soon the storm dissipated under our combined spirit.

Powerful fae people tried to bargain with us, the METAL Gnomes, seeing that our magic and power had grown tremendously from all being humble lawn gnomes. They saw us as a sick bank of magic, ready to be drained dry, but we shouted or played them away.

We did not need false power and magic mighty.

We did not even need what we sang of, tobacco, booze, or sex.

We needed freedom.

Mighty, all powerful freedom.

And we needed METAL.

61

We revolted, all of FAE in an uprising against the sorcerer. His magic was one hundred times the mightiest amongst us, but all together, when the music played, the singer shouted, the guitarist riffed and the bassist based, with my drums beating like our hearts, we would overthrow the Sorcerer of Fae.

We played our METAL as loud as we could've, outside the once Amanita stronghold, now only upheld by a single, evil sorcerer.

We played, turning up the music loud, me bashing the biggest drums we could find, the guitarist playing his enchanted lute and the bassist playing his old wooden bass, being electrocuted by METAL itself which only enhanced our playing, and Boomie... Boomie just sang with his normal voice.

"COME OUT, EVIL SORCERER.

"THIS IS A SONG FOR YOU."

The sorcerer came out to the balcony of the tower, and heard us play our tune.

"WE DON'T NEED NOTHIN, NO KILLING OR DEATH

"WE DON'T NEED MAGIC, EVILISH BREATH

"WE DON'T NEED YOU, YOU DAMNED HORRIBLE DUDE

"**WE DON'T NEED THE AMANITA, AND THEIR SORCERER CRUDE.**"

We continued to play, singing the only song left in our repertoire, the call of the METAL GNOMES and people of FAE.

"**FALL!!**"

"FALL!"

"**FAAALLLLL!!!**"

"FALL! FALL! FALL!"

"**BY ALL THAT IS METAL, I COMMAND YOUR POWER TO FALL, FAE SORCERER!!**"

The castle crumbled, as the antennaed sorcerer fell, down, down, down, to the brinks of Hell which opened up just for him, and just kept falling.

We then all cheered, and continued to play, in freedom, finally.

GNOMES. OF METAL.

Cthaklc

I bid all the children good night, and as I was packing my belongings, I heard someone sneak up on me to come back. Well, of course she never had a chance to sneak up on *me,* but it was all good show.

"What about Cthaklc, Mister Fox?"

"Samantha, you know some things should remain in the dark, the gnawing fears of our mind, and the ghosts of the dead."

"But please, Mister Fox, I can tell that something was missing from Olivia Lamb's story. Something important. Can't you tell me at least the *true* end?"

I smiled, and turned back to her.

"This is the true end, perhaps for some, perhaps for all or others. Listen close, because I will not explain the nature of this story. You will have to make substance from it yourself. Cthaklc had asked Olivia if it was the end..."

62

And Cthaklc said, "**It is *not*.**"

I could feel the scars on my face burning, and stinging, like they were just cut open just now. I grunted in pain, and put a hand to them, and felt them wriggling under the skin.

As I clenched my hand to my face in extreme pain, bowed to my knees before Cthaklc, we looked over the water to see… ghosts, spirits, demons, oni, phantoms, specters and more, travel across the water, walking with the waves in the Ghostly Parade.

A giant kraken head appeared from the waves, looking at me and blinking its many eyes, before diving again.

The wind seemed to flow around me, black, like evil magic on the wind.

I felt my life flash before my eyes, like the primal beasts we are, and I stuttered out, "Sh-Shien…"

It felt like I was so alone.

Only me.

No one else.

But Cthaklc and the Parade marching closer.

And Cthaklc said, "**You *will* go w*ith* me.**"

I stumbled up, lurched, and then fell off the side of the boat, smacking into the water then sinking into the cold, cold depths.

Cthaklc grabbed me up, and we *stood* on the gently rolling waves.

I looked at him, into eyes that had constantly been watching humanity, for all time, even before time and then far past it will ever be.

I stuttered, asking him, "Where- Who- What- Why- How- When- Are you? Is it my time?

And Cthaklc just said, "**Th***is* **is** *the* **onl***y* **tim***e.*

The parade marched with us, as I stepped in time with the rolling waves. It was hard to get a hang of at the start, but the Parade... I just listened to her tune, and Cthaklc and I marched at the back.

I asked him who they all were, and Cthaklc said, "**W**e a*r*e the s*o*uls **of Al***l* **an**d *El***se.**" His words boomed across my mind, felt it, knew it in my beating heart, "**W**e *w*ill be *the* **hea***rt* **of** *al*l things."

The Parade stopped, marching in halt, and allowed us to take the head of the Parade.

I stopped at the front, and the Parade stopped with me.

Cthaklc stood before me, an immortal god, an all powerful king, a being that had not only created the universe, but was the universe itself.

He shouted out his first dictation, to me.

"**Y**o*u* **w**ill lo**v**e *m*e. **Al***l* wi*l*l.

"**My** *r*eign has *onl*y **just begu***n.*"

I saw in my mind of Cthaklc ruling over each and every one of us, always was, and always will be.

And I realized something, as his dictations became clear to all of us, at least everyone who was in tune of the endless time of all time that I was just now attuned to.

I had always heard Cthaklc's dictations.

And that I had even been helping write them myself.

On an old prophetic text, that this scrap of knowledge was never repeated on, were the words...

"**W**here *would* *y*ou go? **You** *w*ill go w*ith* **me**.

I*s t*his a g*o*od ti*me?* Th*is* is *the* onl*y* **time***.*

Who a*r*e t*h*ey? **W**e a*r*e the s*o*uls **of** Al*l* and *E*lse.

Wi*ll y*ou lov*e* me? **Y**o*u* **w**ill love *me*. **Al***l* wi*ll.*"

Wh*e*re a*r*e w*e* g*o*ing? **W**e *w*ill be *the* hea*r*t **of** *a*ll things.

The ra*i*n is p*a*rt**i**ng f**a***s*t, isn'*t* it? **My** *r*eign has *on*l*y* just **beg**u*n.*

I*s* th*is the* end? It *is* *n*ot.

It h*a*s **never** end*e*d*.*"

The mermaids sung with the Parade, beautifully, enchantingly, and I knew they would not be the last, as we headed to land and the ghouls, ghasts, and everliving dead were awakening, and singing, chanting with us, as they beat the drums.

The crypts crumbled, as the stars fell before our path.

Literally, meteors fell to the ground everywhere, as the sparkle of stardust enchanted and blessed our marching.

Wings sprouted from the skin from our back, and majestic feathers caressed our features, as a Shining Man in a Chariot, and a Hunter Woman with a Bow walked with us, and all the gods of Sun and Moon, Night and Day, fell into our ranks.

The sun and the moon eclipsed, as the stars were no more.

We began flying upwards, up and up to the Never Ending Cosmos.

Well. They did. I stood on the hilltop, watching all of the beautiful spirits redeemed, looking at a fat funny one flap away on small wings, a beautiful maiden fly away on majestic ones, and more and all else, as I was standing on the ground still, afraid to fly, and afraid of what it would mean if I did.

Cthaklc reached forth a many tentacled hand, reaching out for me, and I walked up his huge tentacle with him alone walking beside me.

It looked like there was a Pearly Gate before me along Cthaklc's tentacles, but Cthaklc smashed the gate with a raged, tentacled punch, allowing it to become one with the many.

Red tears were falling from Cthaklc's eyes, and he stopped to rest, hands on the ground prostrated for a second, for what was beyond those Gates.

I helped him up, and we continued to walk along the strings of creation, which just happened to be Cthaklc's many tentacles.

A good looking guy just smiled at us from those gates, and walked behind us, as I saw all and everyone else doing behind me. I was not the last. I was the first.

I saw my father and mother, I saw Jasper, I saw Wallace, I saw the gnomes, I saw Captain Sherry, and I saw my beautiful pal, Shien.

I stopped for a second, and embraced her, and we kept walking, hand in hand.

Soon, all before us were holding hands, one and all with everyone.

Wolf drank with his pack of Organization people, family, and good friends, and said, "I think I've hit just about the limit with these."

He continued to drink, though, and we continued to-

We already were there.

We always were.

And I snapped my eyes open, sitting peacefully on the deck of the ship, watching the stars.

This was not a bad existence.

Not bad at all.

I simply stared up at Cthaklc, the tears still in my eyes, and said I would eternally love him.

He knelt before me, and wiped off the tears with a tentacle.

And I could feel my own arm brush them off.

The tears fell from my eyes like stars to the world.

And I continued to smile, like the light of the dawn or ever shining moon.

And over and over again, for all eternity.

Was this the end? It has never ended.

The Tale of Orson Lions

Even still, the stories continue, some start at the middle, the end, or... the very beginning. This is the tale of the Organization and its founder, Orson Lions.

63

Orson Lions was a cursed man, in more than one way. He heard the voices of ghosts, monsters, demons, and sometimes people just down the street talking about him without them being anywhere near him. He aptly thought it was some disease he caught, but did not know how to cure it, or if he ever could. It simply happened to him, as he was a young man, an itching and tingling under the skin, and then pop, his brain exploded as he heard his love talking to him.

When he found her body, devoured by some... monster, he only understood better when he could hear her voice still.

But was it really the voices of his love? Or was it... the monster?

"You're worthless. A worthless bum in this time. Why can't you look at me?" his love said.

The people were all staring at him, every one of them, he knew so. He begged for bread, hoping someone, anyone would perhaps see his strong muscles from working the fields of medieval England and offer him some sort of position. The monks would not give him anything, they were of the same mind of begging as him, but it sure was useless for him to see them pass. The knights passing by in haste to their castles did not even see him, and a horse ridden by one nearly stamped him to pieces. The rest of the people thought for themselves and their families first, and would not give hard sought food to a wretch.

But someone gave the young Orson a piece of burnt bread. It was all I could spare, and it would do me no good anyway as the night came down, showing the brilliant sunset, that I would never look at, no matter for all the blood- or food, in the world.

He looked up at me, under my long cloak.

He thanked me, and said, "Please, my good sir, give me more. Give me a job. My muscles are still hardened, and I have much to do."

"You have much to do? It seems like you're wasting your time begging."

"…Still, I can do much. Allow me to be your servant."

"Hmm… I don't need a servant right now, or ever really did. I'll give you a job. There's a man in high society who is a cruel slaveholder to his people. Kill him, and I will give you another job. Is that satisfactory?"

"…I have no wish to become a murderer under God's light. You must have something else that you can give me. I have nought will to live, as my love hath been murdered by fiends."

"I see… Then I offer you the will to live. Do my job, and you will find this will, and strength again. Here. You will need to fashion this into whatever weapon you desire, and use it, and only it, to kill the Baron Bellefonte."

I threw him the silver piece, and he gasped at it. He tried thanking me for it, but I only reminded him of my words. I left in the night, for company had called on me and invited me into their home for supper. I did not eat, merely drink stale ale, and talked about the old days once again.

64

Orson Lions had a difficult time with the silver piece.

He thought of selling it, trading it, just so he could eat more, but it seemed to be stuck to him.

His love said, *"It's just a stupid piece of metal. Jump off a cliff."*

And Orson thought, without the metal piece, he may as well go and do so.

He had no remarkable or noteworthy talents, besides archery. He did not wish to become a poacher yet, as the poaching laws set by Baron Bellefonte himself were so strict. Flayed, blood drained and collected, and left to die on the outskirts of the forest, you were, if you denied this poaching law.

He thought of joining the military, but they would not take a peasant in their ranks. The rules to join the military, a sort of elite in this time of temporary peace, was very difficult. Had to be able to give something to the military if you wished to enlist, and Orson had nothing.

He decided he may… at least think about… the job that the mysterious stranger had offered. What was next, after the death of this noble? What did the stranger want? It was true that Bellefonte was extraordinarily cruel and merciless, but could this be part of a grander plot?

Perhaps Bellefonte had taken the stranger's wife or daughter, in an act of jus primae noctis, and then slain her as he was prone to do. Either way, the first task Orson had to do, turn the silver piece into a weapon, was set before him.

He allowed the blacksmith to take a cut of the silver, and turn what was rest of it into a beautiful, stunning arrowhead on a white plumed arrow. Orson had no bow to use with this arrow, but he thought that will come later. There was not enough silver to create an entire blade, and besides not knowing how to use a sword very well, or even a combat knife, the peasants were not allowed to wield any sort of weaponry.

The blacksmith pitied this now silver arrow wielding vagabond, and asked him if he would stay for dinner. Orson readily accepted, never one to deny a free meal.

Oops. Someone is distracting me as I write this novel, knocking on my door.

I opened the door, only to find one of the younglings trying to badger me with questions… I told her to be a proper historian, and learn from books, and not me.

"You're like a book that walks around and talks, though!"

"No, Samantha. I'm just a humble placeholder right now, as our leader Hunter Wolf takes on matters… elsewhere."

"Where'd he go, anyway?" she had asked, walking into my study and sitting on the desk.

"It's not mine to say. Now please, if you need somewhere to start on the dispossession of a body look under the pseudonym of Thornton Newton, for crafting and creating silver projectiles under Will Holde, and the destruction of vampires under Stoker himself."

"Ok… Thornton Newton, Will Holde, and Stoker. Thanks, Mister Fox."

"My pleasure, now please leave. I am working on an important project."

She smiled, waved me goodbye, and rushed to the library.

65

That Samantha... She thinks that there's even a way to dispossess a vampire, and banish the "malevolent spirit" from their body...

No matter. The young will learn. Sometimes the only way to banish a soul from a body is with some sort of sharp instrument.

Orson was wandering the woods, looking at the many populated forest country, imagining if only he had a bow...

Then he smelled something in the air. Smoke.

He ran to the smell, and saw a whole cavalry of raiding knights and infantry burning down the forest.

Oh no! All those delicious doe will have nowhere to bed now, Orson thought.

"Kill them all." his love said.

One of the raiders spotted him, and chased him into the forest.

They chased and chased him, but if anything, Orson knew how to hide. He hid up a tree, climbing it as quick as a squirrel, and awaited in the branches. The raiders passed underneath him, but the fire was also seeming to chase Orson, and setting blaze to the branches around him.

He held his breath as long as he could from the smoke, as the fire caught onto his tree.

Then, he jumped out of the tree, landing with a spry fall, and ran as quick as he could back to the village.

The village leader, a peasant turned freeman, did not believe Orson that there were raiders just off the border of Bellefonte's edge, and instead harassed Orson for even being in the woods when he was.

As they imprisoned him in a small cell, it turned out to be the most gracious act any could've given Orson.

The raiders came to the village, slaughtering, burning, and looting, setting fire to the village as if it was only made of matches itself. The stone prison Orson was in withstood the blaze, and none decided to look for a prisoner.

Orson waited long in his cell, starving and thirsting, with the key just out of reach on the now stinking leader's body...

I found him there in the night, looking for survivors or at least blood without a fight, and freed him from his stone hovel.

He thanked me again, and clutched onto his silver arrow, hidden in a pant leg close.

66

Orson was alone, no one to help him, as he tried to breach the castle's outer defenses and kill the Baron.

His love whispered, as he climbed the outer wall, *"Where's your little buddy? Don't slip."*

Orson nearly did slip as she said that, but hung on close with the other hand, and then regained his position, climbing the outer wall. He crouched up top, safe in the night but to the most agile eyes, and snuck down the wall down some steps, past the sleeping guards and barracks.

The time in England was in peace, so the act of aggression by the rivaling Count was very much disturbing to the Baron Bellefonte. He plotted and planned to either get the King to destroy his enemy, or kill him himself with sly cunning and sharp swords. He decided to sew discord in the rival Count's holdings, and told his sired kin, his agents of night, just where to go and how to do it, and they listened, completely in tune with the Baron's will, having no choice or even desire to disobey him.

Therefore, as the Baron was vastly protected ever with his agents of night close at hand, he shed this protection in favor of his boiling anger, sending them all off into the darkness to heed his commands.

Orson watched the Baron from a high window, as the Baron continued to feed.

He devoured the peasant woman, a young woman just out of her teens, only pieces of meat and blood now, taking a lump of flesh in his mouth, rolling it around a bit, and then spitting it out into a bowl, now bloodless.

Orson was aghast. The Baron was truly a despicable monster, to even feed on his people, who even though were owned property as peasants, deserved better than this.

He clutched the arrow so hard, that it broke in his hand as he watched the horrible spectacle.

Orson gasped, and held onto the sharp bit close, the silver arrowhead and the little bit of wood on it, as the plumed feather and pieces of the shaft fell to the ground.

He nearly slipped again from his perch, and the Baron noticed him in curiosity.

The Baron called for guards, and Orson shimmied from the window to get to a more suitable spot, with instead of hopelessness in his life, the feeling was replaced by pure, utter hatred.

Orson ran down the side walls, confusing the guards looking for him, and he, in his haste, bumped into one of the lookouts on the wall.

The soldier fell to his death on the ground, only leaving his crossbow on the wall.

Orson was consumed in pity, but the feeling could not last long as he was being chased. He grabbed up the crossbow, and continued to evade and fluster the guards, eventually sneaking around the side and into the Baron's inner holding.

67

Where was I? I just went out for a drink... and...

Ah yes. The fabled hunt of Baron Bellefonte, that turned Orson Lions into the man he is today- I mean, was, in the medieval ages of old England.

The young man, Orson, lifted the crossbow before him, planting the cracked piece of silver arrow into the machine, and striding down the rich, elegant halls, red carpet to his chase, that there were no guards awaiting in, all hunting Orson just outside.

Orson slammed into the heavy oak doors, but they would not budge.

There was no hidden passageway into the Baron's inner holding, and no key or lock, or even a handle, to open to it from the outside.

But that didn't matter, since the Baron arrogantly invited him inside, opening the doorway.

The Baron sat on his throne, as Orson strode before him with the silver bolt in the crossbow.

The man just laughed at Orson, knowing that nothing could kill him. Even the Church was his enslaved property, and could not reach their way into *his* dark domains.

Orson had never been a very religious man, thinking the Church was sometimes just as bad as the Baron, but that didn't matter much in the grand scheme, for he had a weapon, given to him by an ally, that was made of one of the very few things to be able to damage the vampyr.

The Baron mocked Orson, and even offered him a position, as his supper, and then as his spy. He showered Orson with promises of wealth and purpose, able to give him these things as well, but Orson had deaf ears to the Baron Bellefonte, only able to imagine the screams of the woman at the Baron's feet, the screams of what his love must've cried as well.

"I think you should listen to him. Join us."

Orson blinked, at the words of his love, but only imagined her as she once was, a gold haired maiden in the sunlight, and shot at the Baron Bellefonte with his honed accuracy, using archery and projectiles long in his youth.

The Baron was surprised, if anything, when he felt the bolt pierce his cursed hide.

Nothing would sway this assassin? All the rest had fallen easily to his whims and whiles.

Nothing would kill him? Then why did this bolt feel like utter burning, like the very sun on his skin?

The silver was a blessed and holy piece of metal, that much is true, with its inherent unique and special chemical qualities to do in a vampyr that gets in the way, abuses his power and authority, and one that I never really liked in the first place, one of my fallen children who had only lust for power and command, of cruelty and blood, and none for humanity and life.

The Baron's agents of night all felt the burning of silver in them as well, as they recouped at the castle, and died one by one, like ash in the breeze, as the Baron Bellefonte did himself.

Orson threw down the crossbow, and left the holding, past the ashes and bodies, and withdrew into the night.

I met him on the lonely road, no home or help to be ever given again, with another job with the smile on my lips.

We made a pact, him and I, of justice and allegiance, as he slit his palm with a shard of pottery on the side of the road, and offered the handshake to me. I only took a drop of blood, put to my tongue, that was rich and hearty, a delectable specimen that would drive any vampyr to hunger by the pure nobleness in this man's veins.

I suggested that he needed a surname, a free man with his overlord and once home destroyed.

Orson had heard tales of beautiful, majestic creatures in the suns of a far off land, and decided to be named after such.

He was born again, in our pact and alliance, as Orson Lions.

68

Lions had a difficult time, alone with no guidance, as I only saw him when I saw fit in the shadows of evening. He would learn of the wild ways of the world like he had to, alone and stumbling amidst life's pleasures.

He had just went into the gates of London, his birthplace that his now dead mother had been traveling to and from for some unknown reason, and asked the nice looking lady if she had anything for him to do.

She looked up and down his muscled frame, and said, "I got something for you to do... A real nice bit, for only some coin..."

"I'm sorry, but I think you misunderstood. I am asking for a job, perhaps as a cook?"

"*You* know how to cook? That's woman's work, and I don't think I could imagine a fine... strapping... young man do *anything* like that..."

"Then allow me to chop wood?"

"I can give yer nice wood somewhere good and hot to go to... Go on, take the axe over there and chop the wood."

Lions took the axe, and chopped hard, working hard, as she watched him, even more aroused than before. The ladies had a hard time in London, the professional whoring trade always had difficulties, and by God this woman thought, if she could not get this man to give her money's worth and then some, it would all have been for waste...

She enjoyed watching him work, a rather noble courtesan who made the most of life, with fun, and also duty. She knew that her establishment was crumbling, and they had to take on crueler customers these days, not the sorts of young men that just wander up to her door and do a hard day's work.

She even allowed, since he insisted, for him to create a brand new meal for her that he discovered.

He fried her up an egg on butter on her wood burning stove, and put it between two lightly toasted pieces of bread. She had some salt, so he used a bit of that to season the concoction.

She ate, not even caring that the yolk was dribbling out of the sandwich slightly, getting her lip dirty, but she simply soaked the bread in the yolk again, and continued eating.

She sighed out. The ladies were all watching, after being lured by that delectable smell, and asked if they could have some too.

Their eventual evening meal was fried egg sandwiches, some liked sunny side up, some liked over easy, some liked omelets. Lions made all the ladies their breakfasts too, the next morning, after he was so pleasantly surprised that *all* of the ladies were so nice, and very well looking.

They tempted and tempted for him to come into their beds, but the woman who found him, a courtesan known as Iris, would allow none of them to steal him away, keeping this find all to herself.

His love whispered, after Iris pulled off her skirt with him in a private room, *"She's going to hurt you now."*

Lions blinked, but could not stop himself from doing whatever Iris desired. He was indebted to her, and she had a *hard* mind to keep him so.

69

This proved problematic later, as Iris *had* to take another customer to keep the house standing, and Lions chased him out, not liking the way he looked and spoke to her.

She stroked his face, and said, "Go down to the fish seller and get us something good, then come back. Later. Go anywhere you need to for awhile after you've picked up the fish."

Lions was, if not peasant village stock born and raised, was a tad naïve. He would soon learn to withstand against his naivete, learning far more than most men of the time did, but in this case it proved beneficial. The woman just needed to work is all, and Lions didn't understand how she exactly did that.

Although, he remembered the night before of what she did, so would pick up inklings of how she did work, in the future. Although, the romance Iris had with this young man was much more pleasing to her on *her* end, than with her many male customers.

She would take one, then the other, then two at a time for the local brothers, and continued down that line. It was much needed, and she even took a cruel man who had one eye, just a gaping eye socket in his head, who liked to hear women scream.

Lions was exploring London, but came back with the fish, at least a little too early for Iris.

Iris was screaming, just how the man liked, and Lions rushed into the house to see what was wrong.

He was shocked to see her bent over and submissive, not knowing how such a strong, well looking woman could ever be like that.

As he made her scream.

Her arm was pushed behind her back in an armbar, and he was attempting to break it. Iris knew he liked this sort of foul sex play, and even though didn't enjoy it, would soldier through it like the professional whore she was.

Lions would not allow it.

He threw the man out to the dirty mud, letting him spew threats against Lions of the local thugs going to get him. Lions just went forth, to *really* give this man his money's worth, and went to beat the pulp out of him.

As he kicked the man in cruelty, he had a horrible feeling in his mind, as his love said, *"Men are so similar."*

He stopped, looking shocked at what he did, and offered to help the man up.

The man spit at the hand, and scrambled away, running from Lions.

I noticed this whole spectacle, coming to find Lions in London, and saw Lions look down at his bloodied hands and boots. He was repentant immediately, even though it would've been more prudent to end that wicked man when he could've.

70

I had nothing to give the girls, and I assured them I wasn't their taste, nor theirs mine. I liked a firmer neck, a nice, long, sleek one at the time, and had barely any ideas for sex in those days. Takes the right woman to pull those out of you, for some men like me.

I would ever only allow willing subjects to be my pleasure, and only ever leave them alive to continue their life, unlike some of my kind. Plus, I could go for a lifetime with only a drop of blood, a hard learned task of restraint for people like me, and currently if I would go a lifetime, I would see how Orson Lions's played out.

I asked him, as the girls continued to treat Iris for her bruises the man had also given her, if he remembered the task I gave him.

He nodded, and said, "But how will I find this man, the Rat King, in such a place? London is *gigantic,* and I don't have a notion where to look."

"Well then, seems as though you pissed off the right man. The thug you disbanded from this establishment will pass on the word, even to the master of his masters, the Rat King. He will come to you."

"…How will I slay him, without the silver arrow?"

"I think you should try to find more where you can. Steal from the rich, and turn their silverware into your own arsenal of arrows. If not, a very hard stab into the heart, from a firm, lasting weapon, will also kill the Rat King."

"...I understand. Please, Sir Abel, allow me to serve you breakfast, if the lady Iris will allow it."

Iris was back to normal, despite her bruises. It was always a shocking experience to her, to be with those kinds of men, but she could regain her composure fast. She sat in the kitchen with us, and said, "Thou cannot kill the Rat King. He is an ever blight on London, and his spies are everywhere. Some believe he truly *is* a Rat King, able to command and learn from the rats that follow his every word."

I declined the eggs that Lions produced, and said, "Then perhaps... Perhaps... you can help him, dear lady. I do not know if any alive and human are the Rat King's taste, but perhaps you can help Lions learn the city of London and its foul recesses. Show him where the rich lurk, and allow him to better equip himself from their coffers."

Iris hmmed, and said, "What will you give me, if you let me show Orson London?"

"A very financial woman you are. I have nought to give..."

Lions said, "Hogwash, Iris. This man gave me my life again! We made a vow to each other, that we would not allow the other to perish, and continue giving each other the life we cherished, starting from the drop of blood on my hand-"

"I *don't care* if this man gave you the entire world as your plaything. I will not partake in such a dangerous gambit for folly's sake." Iris pronounced.

I rubbed my chin, and said, "Would you be free of this life, if you could?"

"I'm not one to let myself yet be murdered and killed-"

"I mean would you give up being a whore."

She rubbed her chin this time, and said, "If I could. If it would allow everyone here to be freed as well, to partake in whatever life they desired. Is this what you are offering?"

"I suppose. I do know of a ship to Ireland, or anywhere else, where women of your kind can live free working lives, of any they choose. It's only hearsay on my end, but the captain seems like a noble soul."

She looked hard into my eyes, wondering if I was telling the truth. I smiled, upturned lips to the woman. She sighed, and looked at the other women worrying about her, and said, "If I can get them *far away* from this place, under a safer roof, I will do so. Just tell me what to do."

I continued to smile. Such grand, compassionate creatures humans are at times.

71

Iris showed Lions all the back alleys and secret meeting spots, knowing them well in her haunts by the port, luring men back to the house. She showed him the butcher's, who had one, silver blade, she showed him a local lord staying in a hidden house with his peasant mistress, who had a beautiful fork of silver, she showed him the sewers, created from ancient Roman occupation, that all the rats congregated in.

Lions decided to steal from the butcher first. Perhaps he would be a kind soul who offered him the knife in Lions's chase even.

He broke the door down, after Iris weakened the lock with a little, thin piece of metal, and Lions looked around for the blade as Iris stayed outside.

He saw it hanging in the front, the butcher's pride and joy, as the butcher slept alone in his large thatch bed.

Lions gently picked up the blade hanging off the string, swinging back and forth, and the butcher stopped snoring.

He got up, noticing Lions with the blade, and roared out a challenge to him.

Lions had to fight the butcher, after pocketing the blade, outside in the muddied streets. The butcher slammed Lions's head over and over into the ground, but Lions would not dare to hurt such a commoner. He would not even draw the blade he had just stolen, admitting to himself that it was wrong to steal from an upstanding worker, who even though served rats, cats, and dogs up as his meat, allowed the people to eat. Eating meant a lot to Lions.

Lions eventually escaped, running down the road and then hiding in the large sewers. The butcher roared out more challenges, but would not follow Lions into the sewers, and went home eventually, bemoaning the loss of his silver butcher's knife.

Iris called out, "Away! Away! Do not enter the dank sewers!"

And Lions immediately escaped from the sewers, as the rats crowded around his feet.

Next, Lions hit up the noble and his peasant mistress. Couldn't be that hard. Perhaps Lions would agree to keep their forbidden love secret, and they would give him the fork.

It actually turned out to be just as easy as that, Lions found out.

The maiden properly gave him the silver fork wrapped in cloth, as the noble looked embarrassed and abashed, claiming he better not hear another word of this, or there would be dire consequences.

Still, as Lions went back to the whorehouse with his silver, he smiled to himself. Iris said, "We could sell those, and buy a new furnace! What grandness."

But Lions knew better than to waste such good silver. He asked if Iris knew a smart blacksmith, and Iris said she did, but told Lions to allow the blacksmith to kiss her, as that is what he liked doing the most.

Lions was still jealous, as he thought the kissing took far too long. The blacksmith *finally* turned away from Iris's kisser to ask what he wanted, and Lions gave him the order.

Silver arrows and a bow, of the best quality, and that he could keep the rest of the silver.

"I'd gladly give you a bow and make you all the arrows from the metal, if I could get credit from the lady of the house."

Iris smiled, and said, "You are quite the good soul and blacksmith. I accept, for my friend has a dire and urgent mission, for all of us at the house."

Lions was still jealous, but did nothing, as she took him upstairs and called out to a few other ladies to help. Sometimes the most noble souls are just the ones who do good work.

72

Lions learned that his love liked to speak to him when he was... alone. As he stalked the horrible sewers, bow and silver arrows in hand, she just continued to talk, and talk, and talk, like she was embedded in his head.

"You're too old for this. Go into a pit and die.

"There's nowhere safe for you now. All that will remember you are the rats.

"There's a light over there, go look."

Lions saw the light, but did not know if he should trust his love. So far, after her death, she had not been very... pleasant. More unpleasant than anything Lions previously had to endure, basically torture that his disease created, and never a pleasant time.

Still, Lions went to the light, arrow nocked in the bow.

There was only a warning, next to an oil lamp, that told any and all to leave now.

Lions could not read the warning, and picked up the lamp, which actually wasn't a very smart choice. When one is hunting in the dark, even in a foul place like the sewers, one needs to learn how to blend in with the surroundings, camouflage, and not send out large signals to whatever could be lurking with a large, bright lamp.

He continued on in the sewers, as the rats followed that glimmering light.

Eventually, as they had all already surrounded and trapped him in the sewers, the lamp went out.

The Rat King arose from the rats, in complete darkness, and went to eat his supper.

The vampyr has a very enthralling gaze to many lesser beasts, but their eyes do have a tendency to shine even in low light. Thus, Lions was able to see the hungry eyes glare at him, and release an arrow at them.

The Rat King moved, as the rats basically screamed around Lions, ready to feast on the meat of the man, and allow the Rat King to take his blood.

The Rat King, as I knew him, wasn't particularly fast or strong, but he did have a charming gaze. Shame he used it for thievery and mayhem, instead of just being a nice subject for a painter or something.

The eyes seemed to hypnotize Lions, commanding him… to drop his weapon… and sleep…

Lions stumbled, stepping on rats, and nearly let the arrow fall from its place in the bow.

"DIE, FOOL." his love said, mocking him in the Rat King's victory.

This actually had the opposite effect than what she suggested, and Lions shook his head, and shot two more arrows into the eyes, letting one pop out, then the other.

The rats screamed, and ran, as the Rat King retreated further into the sewers, to die.

Lions ran as quick as he could out of the sewers.

He eventually got to Iris's whorehouse, and bathed as he shivered in the cool. He was not shivering because of the temperature, but just because of those eyes. Iris bathed him in water, enjoying their victory.

73

"My mother was a whore, my sister was a whore, my wife was a whore. I'm not letting yonder pricks pluck my fair ladies anymore. I can guarantee you all a nice place, a pleasant place, with men who know how to treat their women proper." the captain said, as I introduced him to Iris and the ladies.

The ladies cheered as the captain kissed Iris's hand, and they went to pack their belongings for the ship they would travel on.

Iris thought, as she was throwing lingerie and dresses in a bag, that this victory should not be so easily cashed out. It should be prolonged, into a long debt, where even more people in need could gain from this noble man called Orson Lions.

She decided to tell him thus, as he and I were talking about his next task.

"Sooth, the murder of the King's wizard... A very difficult task, especially with his magic mighty. The many hear he can conjure storms to do his bidding, and any man before his gaze will die by the fires of Hell, thus he remains by the King, blindfolded, in the event the King should ever need his eyes to do their horrible work."

"All superstition, my friend. I think. Maybe? I don't know if anyone can actually *do* that, even if they're a wizard and like the people I asked you to slay..."

I of course noticed the changes and alterations of many of the vampyr over my years. It was very shocking to me, for I was sure there were only a few types, but they continually grew and changed without my knowledge. The fires of Hell from the eyes... Seemed unlikely, because fire was also one of the vampyr's greatest enemies, but maybe it could've been possible.

Iris charged into the room, and said, "I wish to stay, with you, Orson Lions, so that we can save more ladies in distress and enslaved creatures of the great. I wish to stay. I will miss all of you, my dear sistren, but it must be that our time will halt."

The ladies all burst out crying, hugging Iris, begging her to leave with them instead, but Iris stayed firm and resolute in her decision, and sat at the table with us.

The captain bid the ladies to leave while they still could, and the ladies marched off into the night, leaving only us three at the house.

I bid the two good night, as I needed a fine shallow grave or foreboding crypt to hide out at from the day, and I noticed they would need some privacy to discuss their new life together.

74

Lions and Iris bought a horse, with what money Iris had left, and rode down the roads of England like old knights and fair travelers. They had barely any possessions, and Iris insisted she look like his fair lady, and not a traveling vagabond, as her dress blew by in the wind.

Lions had a hard time trying to figure out how the horse actually *worked.* He took Iris's lessons slowly and steadily, and they continued to ride.

But soon, as Iris's dress attracted less worthy company, a bandit and his kin trapped the neighing horse before them.

The bandit was like a true Robin Hood, stealing from the rich to give to… himself. And his kin. Could hardly do anything without Brother Brian and Brother Lars. The other bandits all showed up over time, eager for this bandit's wisdom and cunning regarding thievery.

The bandit decided to take those beautiful arrows of Lions's, and pocketed them for safekeeping. He frisked the lady, and realized she had nothing but her good gender, so decided he'd take that and leave, the what he thought to be an idiot, Lions tied up to a tree.

Iris fought against this treatment, would never have it again she said, and the bandits, worn out from her struggling and fighting, as she even blinded one of them with a sharp poked finger, decided to tie her up too and think about what to do with them later.

The bandits slept, as Lions and Iris struggled against the well done ropework, but the head bandit, Walter, wondered why and why the fool had silver arrows. Would be far easier to make them out of iron, and would break far less easily so could be reused.

He taunted and mocked Lions, saying that even a more muscular man could never outdo one of his ropes. But he had to know... *why* these arrows had silver heads.

Lions said, "They are repulsion of the unholy, the evil and horrid, and kill fiends with one sharp blow."

"Is that true... I think they're just fancy ornaments you picked off one of the high and mighty." Walter said.

Lions saw the smirk given by Walter... a smirk that somehow contained respect.

"Oh yes, stole this from the priest of London, and it was very difficult." Lions lied.

"Really... Always wanted to do in London's clergy meself. Excommunicated me, just because I steal from a few folk who don't need their bits and baubles. How'd you get through those big locked doors?"

"Actually, it was a passing taxman priest who had them. Those bastard priests... Always took all the crops from our field, and whatever we could scrounge for ourselves. Even had greedier hands than the Baron. I broke his neck with my strength, and took the bounty for myself."

"Why why! A peasant thief. Good. Good... I like a man who I can call a brother. Here, would you like me to release you? You should tell your story to us, get to know the good lads when you can."

Lions nodded, knowing that he shouldn't play coy, and Walter released him, handing him a slab of meat off the fire and a tankard of ale.

Lions looked back at Iris once, who had her head turned away from him, and thought he would free her as soon as he could.

But Lions had a strange sort of connection with the bandit. Like a brother that he never had. He had, while probably thinking about it, maybe, never thought you could actually become a bandit from a peasant and make a worthwhile life for oneself.

Lions freed Iris, and instead of running from Walter, they decided to stay in his company for a spell, at least until Lions could get back the silver arrows.

75

Lions told the true story of how he got the arrows eventually, reluctantly describing his thievery and extortion.

"And you did all that to do in the Rat King. For a few whores? Did you owe them backpay or something?" Walter said.

Iris haughtily said, "We wouldn't even take in your kind if they could not offer our fair wage right then and there."

"My kind, eh, sister... I can tell you I've seen a lot prettier maidens than yourself, who only do what they do for a bit of food..." Walter said.

"Hmph. Then you are underpaying them, and really taking what is never yours by right." Iris said.

"I've took all I could take from the big fancy ladies, all I could... You, though, I'd say are a good lay for Gorgeous Garry, who really ain't so picky, and then tossed out." Walter said.

Lions said, "And if you do that, I will break your bones and hunt your kind to the end of the Earth."

Woah, Walter thought. This guy's serious. Just making a little foreplay talk with the lady, and get shut down like that. He knew from the strong glare given by Lions that if even a finger was taken from the lady, he would sorely regret it. Perhaps he should've kept him tied up, if he wished to play with foreplay from an unwilling vessel.

"So this old man that comes to speak to you... What's he look like? He doesn't have... a blindfold on, does he?" Walter asked.

"No, but it sounds like you are describing the wizard. We wish to slaughter him for his cruelty and malevolence. The stories I heard of that evil wizard..." Lions said.

"And I probably told around half o' them. Sound like good people, you two, even though you really should take the world in a stranglehold, and let it gasp, as soon as you can. I'll follow you, if I can get a cut. Need a break from my stinking men for a while." Walter said.

"...What sort of 'cut?'" Lions asked.

"Of course, I talk about the vast stored wealth of the wizard, and even the King if we have time. Gonna need a nice man like me, who can get us inside with not a peep... Here, a token of respect, and affirmation, of our shared desires..." Walter said, and handed Lions back the silver arrows.

Lions looked at the silver arrows again, and slowly nodded to Walter.

"Thieves and whores, all of you, thieves and whores." his love whispered in his ear by the fire.

76

The three wandered into a village, as Walter smirked at the fatter peasants that are sure to be richer, he assured them. He urged them to start up a distraction- but said never fear, there was one coming down the road.

A man with an entire traveling smithy set shouted out, "Hear ye, hear ye, I am the Mobile Smith!"

"What's mobile mean?" a child asked his parents.

The man continued, saying, "I can make anything your smith in his dark, smoky atmosphere can make, and more! Come, see me work for you, right here before you!"

Walter had already started picking a few peasants' pockets.

"Can you make gold from wood?" Iris shouted out.

"Gold from wood! I ain't no alchemist, that's a completely absurd proposal! No, I can make horseshoes, nails, shields and swords right here, right now! I challenge that smith, in his smokey hovel, for the right of just a fair place to sleep and a nice dinner!"

The strong, burly smith stared at the skinny man with spectacles, and accepted the challenge. The skinny man with spectacles took out his mobile smithy, and set to work, first on the horseshoes. With only a few whacks, the blacksmith had already been done smithing the horseshoe, but he looked up in surprise to see that the mobile smith already had three of them.

They worked on the nails, which the mobile smith soon had a large pile of, always seeming to turn out the best metals from his huge pack, and shaping and molding them for just the right purposes.

The blacksmith in his "smokey hovel" challenged the mobile smith to make a sword that could be slammed against the anvil and still remain in one piece. He said no time limit, only skill will decide who is the winner.

But the blacksmith was getting peeved, as all the people cheered for this strange man from the highway. He had a bit of a cold as well, and thought he was starting to lose his eyesight as things were starting to seem blurry. He worked fast, too fast, after the mobile smith had already completed the sword, and brought out his own sword which was a falchion scimitar.

The mobile smith completed a long zweihander.

The blacksmith smacked his sword on the anvil brought out for this purpose, and his blade held fast.

The mobile smith wielded the zweihander far over his head, and slammed it on the anvil.

And the anvil broke in two.

He was declared the winner, and people were offering up their homes in glee to the man.

The mobile smith said, "Wait, good people, let us never forget the good quality of fine workmanship. I offer this blade to you, good sir."

The mobile smith offered the zweihander to the blacksmith, and the blacksmith felt humble, and declined to take such a beautiful piece of metal. He just asked what those thingies were on the mobile blacksmith's face, and the mobile blacksmith said they were glasses.

"Here! Have a spare. I always keep a spare on me! Please, someone, anyone, take the sword, hang it up on your tavern wall, it's too big for me to lug around."

Walter shouted out quickly, "Me! Give me the sword!"

His pockets were already filled to the brim with money and valuables, but a good sword is always a good sword.

The blacksmith carefully put the spectacles on his face, and exclaimed, "I can see! I can see! Thank you so much, good sir! What ist thou name? I must know!"

The mobile smith bowed, and said, "I am Humphrey the Mobile Smith, and I only wish the right for fair travel and good food."

The blacksmith immediately offered his home to him, and the two went inside his moderate home to talk more about the craft.

Walter bought the three of them a room in the back of the tavern, as he admired the huge sword that was now in his possession. He lost it in a game of gambling later that night.

77

Lions, Iris, and Walter found themselves on the road with Humphrey, and they all talked with each other, firm travelers on the road. The horse had already been eaten by Walter's men.

"Wow! To take on an immortal, all powerful wizard like that... I can scarcely believe it, and I've seen everything in the entire world! I took on the great dragons, the mighty gods of Rome, and more, in professional smithing challenges, as I travel with my own mobile smithing contraptions. It's a tough life, but people are so kind, you know?" Humphrey said.

Iris said, "I think the traveling must've addled your mind and broke your back, the way you stoop. I know that those travelers are usually scum and disease ridden, and the true money and comfort lay in a local's calm embrace, but I suppose not always... The 'local' thugs were by far the meanest, and I love that I am traveling far, far away from them."

Walter said, "They're not so bad all the time. Traveling is the life. Can't sit down in one place for too long, the air gets stale and the prospects boring. Gotta travel, and make a real destination out of it at the end, too. I take breaks from my outfit commonly, encourage it amongst the men, to allow people to briefly forget our faces and allow the rolling fields become pleasant again..."

Lions said, "I have never been one to travel. The world is so strange, but the people are so bright. Like little flowers popping up on the side of the road, traveling is like. I don't believe there is, and I know there isn't always, good people everywhere… but perhaps they grew stale, and dangerous, and forgot about the beauty of life."

I appeared beside them in the night, and said, "Traveling is the only way to live. If you ask me, good people travel, and good travels people. Some can really be good, for a while, but it's the passing on of the feeling that allows the feeling to remain good."

Humphrey nodded curiously at me, and Walter had his socks scared off. Walter, who I was starting to like, said, "Bejesus, hooded old man!! The hell are you doing sneaking up on us?!"

"I admit, I didn't expect it to be so easy to sneak up on, and capture if I so desired, Brother Walter of Cambridge."

"How do you know who I am? What's the deal, here?" Walter said.

Iris said, "This is our very good friend, who helped my ladies all go their own and separate ways, in peace and safety, no longer to slave over a man's prick for money and food. How are they, anyway, Sir Abel?"

I handed her the letters given to me by the captain, and Iris smiled in delight, reading each of the girls' own handwriting, telling her of the adventures they are having and the homes they are building. They had all learned to read and write in their new homes, as Iris already knew how from her… past. She once was a maiden in distress who learned to read and write from her captors, but after the knight had saved her, he grew bored of her for the next maiden on the horizon, and so she became a whore.

Humphrey asked me specifically, "Are you some sort of fiend? You don't seem to smile very often. I heard- I mean saw, that fiends don't smile often."

I smiled, upturned lips, and dispelled the myth to my new mobile smithing friend. He looked at me curiously, and I even showed a little teeth then, but hid the fangs.

He seemed satisfied with that, and we continued the conversation.

Lions and I continued to discuss his task, and he said to me, "How will I slay this fiend? I do not have much silver in my quiver..."

Humphrey perked up, and said, "I can help you with that! You must be hunting vampyr and fiends, no doubt about it! Silver. It's all in the area, right over there across that beautiful hilltop, I know it. Perhaps I can even craft you something more substantial? Arrows go by fast, especially silver tipped ones."

Humphrey and Lions made a deal. He would continue to travel with them, to add more stories to his repertoire, and Lions would get a silver blade.

78

Under the full moon, Lions looked on at the sword that the mobile smith made, silver alloyed with copper on the blade edge, beautifully molded and combined with steel. I left them then, as the full moon often causes all sorts of problem with the supernatural, and I aimed to keep them at bay once more. I did not need my new protégés to fall victim to some evil whim. These people, I was sure of it, would go on to make something grand and marvelous that would be lasting in the world.

The way they talked by the fire. The way they laughed. It was something out of a storybook- that I am writing. It was beautiful, to even hear each and every one of them sing an old peasants' song that Lions had started.

I knew that things would be difficult with the wizard, as he was the strongest out of my three sired children. These once boys, then men, I took care of in a brief segment of a long life. I saw something beautiful in each of them, from Bellefonte's sharp wit, to Payne's (Rat King) quiet but very friendly nature with animals, to... this man, who was now a wizard under the King, up to nothing good that will last at all, no, more evil that will last for a long, long time.

I had, when the plague hit England, given each of them a gift and terrible burden to outlast the plague. I was assured, based on their intelligence, friendliness, and strength, they would survive, and over-power the curse of the vampyr in favor of something spectacular.

I was sorely mistaken.

There was something evil about the vampyr, I knew that when I first turned into one. But I, unlike many, sought only goodness and restitution for this... *curse.* I sought to make even God and the Gods happy and proud of me, as I shunned their light for the ever darkness. I only regret that I sired so many vampyrs as I was younger. I should've bore this curse alone.

In the end I came back to England to dispose of these three children, an act that would've broke my heart more than seeing them become the monsters they were, but I knew, just by his honor, loyalty, good nature, and strength, that Lions would be the perfect ally in this matter, and he would never become a vampyr under me, ever. He simply had no desire to be so, and I respected and appreciated that outlook.

Even he was starting to question my antics by now, and even he knew that *I* might not be the good face I portray. I think he already knew that the people he slew were all monsters, maybe even vampyrs, but even I did not know his hatred for these creatures, nor how far that hatred would bring him.

I heard her, whisper in the night, say, *"They'll all abandon you. They'll let you starve and die. Don't trust them. Don't trust anyone..."*

Cursed being. I waved it away from me, and unwillingly let it latch back onto Lions.

79

The wizard knew, somehow with some fabled magic, of the danger that was sent to him by me. He even told the King, saying assassins would be coming for the King and himself in the guise of good souls. The King hmmed at this, but did not look at the blindfolded wizard. To do so would bring horrible curses and suffering unimaginable.

The four travelers went into the city, knowing from my intel that the King was staying for awhile here, to visit his great grandmother who was dying. The King was of the mind that it was about time. No one usually lived to be great grandmothers in those times, especially not those of a King. Their old rule was just slightly problematic in politics.

The four loved this beautiful forest side city, and Iris and Lions were growing rather close. Each night, she read him a different letter from the girls, who always had something pleasant to say about the people who helped them out of their predicament. And each night, she made him do something beautiful and romantic for her, in the form of hot sex, cashing out on the debt to her again, and again, and again...

Walter was trying to capitalize on Humphrey's skill in metals and crafting, and he decided to see if a few rocks held any value. "Granite, Walter. Nothing special." Humphrey said. Walter didn't mind, he would just pull them out, nicely polished with some grease, and state they were dragon eggs, after he got Humphrey to smooth them over for him... He actually was able to acquire a fief, a nice cottage by the seaside, with just those dragon eggs.

Humphrey was delighted with England. Been awhile since he had been there. Really, he was somewhere from Rome... or maybe Russia... or perhaps... Not Alaska? No. I don't think most people from that side of the world were Alaskans... He was a man of mystery, and in the times I met him, I enjoyed his traveling stories which I could not discern which were real or not.

Lions simply enjoyed Iris's company, and had vague notions of asking her to be his wife, one day, if his previous love wasn't taunting him day and night, and if this new purpose he found could be put to good use. He made plans to himself, of continuing the trade of slaying monsters, and knew that would be his life's goal.

They were all settled up for the night, when the wizard's cronies, loyal, honor bound knights to the King, grabbed them up, arresting them right as they were headed to bed.

The witching hour was approaching, and the wizard was prepared. He had a whole practical serenade to the King, of these assassins killing good, noble people, the Baron Bellefonte, the Rat King, and even were aiming for himself, the High Wizard to the King, not stopping there, and going to stab a dagger through the King's own heart.

"The Rat King was just legend told by peasants. There was no reason to ever fear him." The King said, "Baron Bellefonte, you say... I have half a mind to congratulate them, as I knew by my spies to this spymaster he was going to revolt and claim his piece of England as independent. And they aim to kill me? One is a woman, one is a crazed smith, one is sizing up my hall like a thief, and the last looks to be a peasant with a stolen sword. Where do you come from, peasant?"

Lions stepped up proudly, and said, "I am no peasant. I am a free man. My name is Orson Lions, and I slew Baron Bellefonte, for he was a monster to all his people, devouring them even under darkness. He killed many, unjustly so, and even if all his holdings in the land were razed, he would still have survived, and continued to be a fiend in the dark. I made sure that never happened."

The King blinked. He had heard of Bellefonte's supernatural ability, to never die, but he didn't really believe it. The only thing he truly believed was that the wizard over his shoulder was a very dangerous individual, and not to be trusted, even if he held great power.

"Very well." the King continued, "Who is the thief?"

Walter stepped up, and bowed to the King. "Brother Walter of Cambridge, at yer service, milord. I have always been stalking the night, as an alike monster to what my friend and adopted Brother states. I am a great thief, a vagabond, a hoodlum, and-" Walter looked around himself, wondering when the guards would show up. He shrugged as the King just watched him, and he continued, "and I have always been loyal to my faith, even once was a novice in the faith. I repent for my actions, and come bearing my loyalty, my King. Please, allow me to serve once more."

This surprised the others, but the King said, "Let me listen to the rest of your associates, first. I do not believe I can allow you to be a servant, who would steal my gold, or allow you to be a knight, as far as I can throw you, but I do believe I can find some use for you somewhere in the future. Stay put. Who is this madman with the spectacles? I have never seen a contraption like on your back before."

"I am Humphrey, the Mobile Smith! I am a traveler of all the round world-"

"Round?" the King asked.

"He's lying, oh King." the wizard said.

"Yes, round!" Humphrey continued, "I assure you, it's as round as a dragon egg, and probably has a tasty inside to boot, most likely with the richest metals all melted into a magma like substance. The Earth is in fact a giant egg! I travel it, and produce my services wherever and whenever they are needed."

"Besides your madness, you seem like an enterprising individual. I can accept your travels in my land. And the maiden? Who might you be? Your King is speaking."

Iris curtsied, and said, "I am Iris, once a noble courtesan, but escaped that life for better friends and farther foes. I always wished to do so, and these people I can consider a family, and wish only peace to our peaceful land."

"Quite a way with words you have, Iris. Short and sweet. Very well. I don't find anything wrong with these people, and relieve you of duty, wizard, no longer to stalk my courts with your false accusations-"

The wizard was all set for this coup d'état, and escaped the grasp of the guards walking carefully towards him, by striking them down with lightning from his fingertips.

The blindfolded wizard cackled, and zapped the King down as well who had drawn his sword, he taking a horrible electric blow but surviving through sheer will.

Walter threw his last dragon egg at the wizard, thumping him on the head and spurling him over, and Lions drew his blade, going forth quickly and strongly towards the wizard.

The wizard undid his blindfold, and attacked Lions with the fires of Hell with his blazing eyes.

Lions burned to a crisp, taken straight to Hell.

This is not the end, even if one is in the worst, most horrible place one could wonder about. This in fact could be a beginning, for most folk, when they have hit absolute rock bottom and even see the fires of Hell with their own eyes.

Lions did not understand, as he heard his love call out to him, *"Orson, Orson, Orson..."*

She did not belong here. She never did.

But as he crossed the horrible landscape of the blazing inferno, he saw her, down below him in the pit, laughing at his misfortune.

This was not his love. No matter what she looked like, sounded like, or acted like.

This could never be.

Lions knew, with blind faith, that this monster could never be the sweet and innocent girl he loved. But he knew that she could be the monster.

Lions attacked her twisted, evil image, as she spurted extra arms and contorted herself in awful ways. He drew the sword, taken to Hell as well, and ended her, once and for all.

This did not end the disease that Orson Lions had, but it offered him a strange peace for a spell, as an angel, clothed and hooded in white carried him out of the lands of the damned and back into the light of day. He thought he caught his love's smile, under her hood for just a moment.

Lions appeared back before the wizard, as the wizard threatened Lions's friends with lightning and fire from his fingertips, and Lions cut off the vampyr's head with the silver blade.

80

Taken to Hell and back... Quite a man. The King thanked Lions and his friends, and offered Lions vassalage.

Lions accepted, becoming a lord of the realm.

Lord Orson Lions knelt before Iris, and she accepted his proposal, becoming Lady Iris Lions of the realm.

Walter became a brother of the faith again, but also a powerful agent for the King. Whenever Walter would stride out of his cottage by the sea, he always had new news in some way or form for the King. It was a wonderful life, Walter had, and he milked it long into old age.

The mobile smith, Humphrey, decided to settle in England for a spell, and actually created a new technological age of the time, ever trying to dispel superstition and false knowledge, like the world being flat.

The four continued to meet in private, and with all of their new and old power, they took monster hunting quite seriously.

I believe Lions saw my face, even as I hid in the shadows, as they spoke together in that windmill, planning to destroy all monsters, everywhere, and bring peace and goodness to all.

He went out to meet me, with his silver blade in hand.

He said, "So you are another vampyr, correct?"

"...I am, Orson Lions. I brought you down this path so you may rectify the damage I caused. I commend you for your effort, but you will never be able to remove my stain completely. I must do that myself. I will be leaving again."

"I would slay you right now, Sir Abel, if not for the pact we made…"

I grinned, showing off my vampyr fangs, and said, "A way with words is a handy thing. But more important are the people who keep those words true. Thank you, for everything, Orson Lions. I will remember our pact, and journey, very fondly."

Lions stopped, putting the blade back in its sheathe, and allowed me to walk away. He called out, "I warn you. We are starting a society, a group, an Organization of people who may slay you. Do not believe they will remember our pact, nor your aid."

"Thank you, Lions! But I'm quite wily, like a Fox on two legs. Goodbye, for the rest of your life." I called out back, waving Lions goodbye.

And that is the tale of Orson Lions, and how he started the greatest monster hunting Organization in the world. I dedicate this book to him, along with Iris Lions, Brother Walter, and Humphrey the Mobile Smith.

May we all remember our own words, and strive to keep them true. My pact continues, forever onwards, of loyalty, love, kindness, generosity, and more good natures, that Lions held me to.

The Wolf

Ah. A call from Wolf. Weird, there were extra numbers on the caller id... I answered, and he filled me in that they were starting first contact soon, and said that I better treat Grandma right.

I looked to Ethel, with her four arms and wolf teeth smile, and said I would be treating her very right. We were going out to dinner.

He just told me, again and again, to keep things running smoothly. I asked him how the others, the Blacksmith, Egress, Kate and her daughter, Mercy and hers, Skinner, and Charlotte were doing.

He said they were great!

I suppose no one would know who these people are, unless they had met them before or at least read a whole book of prior interactions... but no matter. I had a date with Ethel.

I took two of her four arms in my own, and we went out to dining and delights.

81

The breastplate could retract now, taking the entire suit of armor with it. My brother said, "I think this is good enough. With the upgrades we made, you should be able to take a laser sword of the Chal's with no issue, even!"

Blacksmith smiled, and nodded. He knew where his skills were surpassed, even if Skinner, my brother, told him how remarkable the steel had been forged, molded, and put together by him.

I carefully pressed the button, not really a button more of a scanner on the suit, and my suit of armor retracted to a small piece of plate on my chest. The whole thing just retracted, folded up, and became so light after it was done doing so.

"She should be quite charismatic, with the AI I installed, so if you need anything from her, just let her know and she'll be right on the mark!" Skinner said.

Egress was watching the stars pass by some more, with Charlotte sitting in a dark corner of the spaceship. We took this smaller vessel that could detach from the main ship of Mercy's, and I missed the few passengers that hadn't joined our voyage.

Kate was staying back to raise her child, with Mercy raising hers. Little Ben and even littler Egress Hunter were little balls of human sunshine, that I still sort of missed. Skinner's mother in law, whom I and others simply called Grandma, was down on Earth, often with Norman Fox, enjoying the place. Skinner continued to work on his next project, and came up to Charlotte with a syringe.

She looked at it, and said, "Just a little, ok? I don't need you taking all my fluids."

Skinner said, "I think I'm so close, to getting you an injection to keep you safe from the sun's rays, any sun from any system, but I just need a little more of that chupacabra visceral fluid of yours."

"Not gonna be from the eye again, right? That was fucking scary as hell. I'm not usually scared, but that freaked me the fuck out, getting a syringe stuck in my eye."

Skinner motioned to her stomach, and then jabbed her stomach she lifted up her shirt for. Still abs of steel, that Charlotte. She's been working out again...

He filled up the syringe with a milky substance, and pocketed the vial. Skinner said, "See? Barely hurt, just like the eye one, right?"

She rubbed her stomach, and said, "I guess... Still. Don't be pricking me when I sleep or anything without my permission."

"Never, Charlotte. We are really so close to a breakthrough, Hunter and I." Skinner said.

Charlotte made a pft sound, and said, "You, maybe. Hunter just told you of all his stupid 'legends' and myths regarding my kind..."

"Still, Charlotte, I need all the information I can gather of chupacabras, and since you're so... new, it's prudent to get any info I can."

"I ain't new! I'm... Fine, I'm not a legendary chupacabra like my sire was, but I know my body, where it begins and ends."

"Still... The body is so differently altered, it could've taken even longer to get this research, with more pricks of the syringe, without Hunter's guidance."

"Hmph." Charlotte hmphed, and turned away to look at Egress looking out the windows.

Egress said, "Like a thousand sparklets in the night, all ablaze and aflight, they're all so pretty, and I'm gonna treat them right."

Skinner, Blacksmith, and I smiled at her, and Skinner went to his laboratory with his chupacabra visceral fluid.

82

We hovered over the planet, letting the orbitational rotation of gravity take us along with it, gently looking over the red dusty wastes, sort of like Mars, if there weren't cities or outposts scattering it.

I was reading again. I loved to read, these days. Just was able to do so, and I think it helped my entire language skills as well. I once was only a grim, foulmouthed vampire hunter, like a gritty detective, and-

"Still sharpening those wits of yours, eh, Wolf?" Charlotte says, sitting on my lap and pushing the book to my face.

"Yes, Charlotte. I love this topic, stuff Fox wrote himself about the life of important people he knew. He said he's got another great one coming up, that of Orson Lions's life. I think his diction is starting to rub off on me, though..."

"So now you're going to talk like an older, old man?"

"Not... necessarily. I'm just going to let the words fill my brain up, up to the very brim, and-"

"God, Wolf. You're really taking this whole books thing seriously." she said, gently moving a few fingers down the side of my leg.

"Have to be smart, or at least sound smart, if I'm going to continue to leader the entire Organization like I am." I said, keeping the book perched carefully in a hand so I wouldn't lose my spot.

"You still feel like doing what we planned?" she said, grinning.

"Kinda, yes, but do allow me to finish this chapter, and I'll get back to you in a minute, ok?"

She frowned sadly, and said, "You used to always be one for the little dates we pulled off, even here in outer space. Oh well. I'm gonna tap into the technology of the Chal's and do a little snooping. We can fuck when we both feel like stopping, ok?"

I nodded, and Charlotte went to the even more high tech computer in the pure white room, and did research on and in the planet below us.

I picked up my book where I left off. Where was I...

I finished the book long into the night- or something, as the spaceship lights were dimmed to feel like night. Charlotte was still clicking, asking the computer what this or that means in the Chal's language, and I got before her, and flexed.

"Still doing that? Or gonna give up, yet?" she said, as I flexed hard, even trying to take off my shirt and let her watch, but she continued to look at the computer.

I put my arms to my side, and said, "I got inspired from you, since you look so good these days, and went back to working out. Feels really nice, if anything."

"Pft. You got a bit of a belly, still... Go back to working out, and I'll get down to those sweet and dirties we like in a minute..."

She continued to click, and I shrugged, going to the gym, or whatever it was called, on the ship. Great bit of machines that test you to just over the limit, this ship had.

Later, still kind of sweaty even after the high tech shower, I stroked Charlotte's abs, in our bed, and she bit my lip slightly as we kissed...

83

I stood in the sun of our observatory on the ship, with my favorite shades and shorts on, and invited Charlotte to join me. Her knees were quaking, her teeth were chattering, and she looked utterly petrified. "C'mon, Charlotte. It won't hurt." I said, and she looked carefully at me, and walked out into the sun.

Her eyes were shut, expecting the worst, but she slowly... blinked them open, and looked down at her hand, lit up by the sun.

Skinner said from the side, "This is a very low dose of the sun's rays, but I can turn it up higher when you're ready."

She just wiggled her illuminated fingers, still staring down at them.

She... looked up, straight at the sun, and I saw pure terror on her face.

But she just kept looking up.

I had to turn her away from the sun after a while, or her retinas would be burned. I took her gently out of the sunlight, and we sat on the side of the observatory. She kept blinking her eyes, over and over.

She sighed out in relief, being in the shadows again. She said, "It's in my eyes still."

"That's normal. You don't remember? Can't look directly at the sun like that."

"Oh. Oh yeah... Can I have another go? I think I'm ready this time."

"I thought you were ready!"

"N-No. But I can do it now, let's do it."

I took her hand, and gently led her into the sunlight again, and allowing her peace again in the sun's rays by sitting back on the side.

She sighed in relief, as she felt the rays again. She undressed, to allow the sunlight to envelop her fully. She stood there, nude in the sunlight, and... began to laugh.

It was a laugh of victory, happiness, childhood glee, and all sorts of stuff that had been pent up for years, only brought out again when once again in the sun.

She raised her hands to the sun, trying to reach out to it, and twirled as she laughed.

"*Someone* take a picture or something." Charlotte said. I took a picture with my phone, and Charlotte smiled cheesily with her vampire fangs, giving me the peace sign as she smiled in the sun. Skinner sat beside me and began drawing her, as she turned back to the sun, happy.

I asked my brother Skinner, as Charlotte still only felt the warmness of the sun on her skin, "Could this work for all vampires, you think? Would be a breakthrough of the grandest kind."

He said as he drew, "I think I could perform the feature on some... but each one would need to come in specially for this, and not all have the hardiness of a chupacabra like Charlotte has. For example, she can eat meat, while other vampires can't. Each person would have to have rigorous testing done by me to produce this effect, and I'll be honest, with Charlotte I kinda just got lucky with this particular breakthrough. Would take a long time to produce it again, with anyone of the vampire's kin."

"I understand, and I suppose I can't ask you to produce some sort of miracle sun agent for every vampire in our short lives..."

"It is possible for me to do this for a long, long time, far longer than you, but we'll cross that bridge when we get there. Perhaps the next stage in humanity's evolution is to be a bunch of sun thriving vampires."

I smiled sadly, and nodded. I thanked him so much for this, and just looked back at Charlotte, who couldn't help herself and was staring at the sun again.

"Charlotte. You know you can't do that."

She waved me back, and continued to blink up at the sun, enjoying her warm embrace.

Skinner gave Charlotte the drawing, and Charlotte thanked him again and hugged Skinner so hard, she almost cracked his spine.

84

A lot of the times now Charlotte would while away time in the observatory, setting the sun's rays at higher and higher doses, reading, tanning, or just enjoying the sun, staring up at it for far too long. "It's like it will always be with me, under my eyes." she had said to me.

Anyways, I looked at the battleships that had finally found us despite our grand cloaking system and provisional security. We wanted this to happen, and I radioed them back in translation. My hand was shaking, finally making first contact.

"What... What is that ship? Where are you from? What do you want?" they asked.

"We're here to offer peace from the people of Earth. We come bringing gifts, to further help our people easier enter the grand system of the Milky Way."

"Strongarmed peace, by the weapons you obviously have... They're concealed, I understand, but we know you have more powerful weapons than our own. And what are the people of Earth? Do you mean that monkey planet? Where is the Milky Way? I have never heard of such a place."

"Er... We call this galaxy the Milky Way, which we are on the edge of. This is an envoy of peace, and we wish to smooth over any ticks in our relations before we unleash-"

"I knew it. Launch the missiles!!"

The missiles popped against our ship, doing absolutely no damage. I continued.

"-our people into the stars. We only wish to make sure this galaxy is safe, before we continue to travel."

"...We surrender."

"...Huh?"

"You took the blast that could destroy two planets. You waved us away like grathakcin blood flies. We surrender."

I looked at Skinner for help, and he barely could contain his laughter.

He took the radio from me, and burst out laughing, saying, "Hahahaha... Oh God... Anyway, guys, this is Captain Skinner of the S.S.S. Sunlight, and we just would like to speak about a subspecies of those monkeys, our species, that would love to enjoy a good time around the stars. We come bearing some of our technology, just a tiny bit to fix that ecosystem of yours. Care to set up a meeting with me? The ground crew will just be exploring your cities for a bit."

"...I like him. What do you guys think?"

I heard mumbling of creatures on the radio, garbled sounds in their own language.

They said, "Sure. I think that would be acceptable. We'll set you up with a meeting of our leader, and take it from there. We welcome you to our planet, the great beginning of the Chal Empire. Thank you, and do come in peace."

"Thanks. Peace." Skinner said, and ended the transmission.

Skinner started laughing again at the look on my face, and I scratched my head, wondering what I had said. Sure was easy to bring an entire space empire to its knees, just with the wrong wording.

85

"Are you ready, Will?" I asked the Blacksmith.

Will nodded, and said, "I seriously still can't believe I'm doing this. This is what I always imagined of, dreamed of, wanted forever. I want to go to this far off planet, and meet the aliens that inhabit it. I'm just still kind of system shocked, is all, ever since this dream of mine took off." and smiled gently.

We put on clean, professional clothes, my plate of metal that could turn into a suit on my chest, right by my crucifix, but Skinner walked past the gym locker room, and said, "You guys don't need to look like *that.* Just wear something comfortable."

We looked at each other, in our suits, and Will shrugged. He got dressed in an anime hoodie and baggy jeans after that, and me in my old coat and camo pants, flask of whiskey in my pocket.

We had just been playing basketball, trying to sharpen our skills to beat Skinner someday... He must've been playing basketball, all alone or maybe with only Mercy for so long. His skills were phenomenal, all star level and then some. I hoped I'd be able to play with him again, as when we were kids.

We met Charlotte and Egress in the halls, as they were dressed in fantastic dresses and jewelry, a black one for Charlotte and a red one for Egress, Charlotte saying to Egress, "It's just so warm, and soft, and brilliant, you know? Hard to believe it's a gaseous ball on fire that can let loose solar flares if it wants to. Just piss off the sun, and WHAM! You're dead. I just think that's so cool, don't you?"

Egress nodded happily, and saw us, saying, "Um. You guys look a little underdressed. This is *first contact.* Remember what we planned, Will? With the little gps tracker bracelets on each of us? So that we wouldn't get lost?"

Will said, "Oh! Still got that right here, mhm." and showed her his wrist, with a bracelet on it with a classic buggy eyed grey alien head dangling from it.

Egress showed her own, a classic smiley face dangling from it, and they clinked it together, looking like they were doing some sort of super hero pose in mirrored formation.

Charlotte started up again, "...Anyway, did you know that the sun's rays isn't only UV light? If it was, then anyone with UV flashlight would be able to do a vampire in, easy peezy! It's all sun radiation! How cool is that? We're being bombarded by literal radiation!!"

"...Very neat, Charlotte." I said, "All got your pills from Skinner?"

Will and Egress nodded, and I took out my own, and popped it down, swallowing it with a bit of whiskey from my flask. Ahh... good stuff.

They take theirs as well, and we could feel our bodies acclimate to the atmosphere and gravity of the Chal planet.

And we all started gasping. Except Charlotte, who didn't need to breath if she didn't have to, and didn't need a pill. She lost her happy smile and began to panic around us.

Why did every breath... hurt...

We collapsed to the ground, and Skinner found us and shook his head. "Earth air is poisonous to the Chal, guys... Here, I'll fix it. Change the atmosphere to be like Chal's."

The ship did as he requested, and a red sort of hazy atmosphere enveloped, and I could breathe again.

I looked up at Skinner who was smiling at me, and said, "Just first day hiccups! You'll all get the hang of this soon enough." Skinner could breathe anything, thanks to the surgeries done on him. I don't know if he even still needed to breathe. He could acclimate himself to any condition, in a matter of moments, all thanks to Mercy and her people who had… abducted him.

We went to the transport bay, which wasn't really necessary Skinner said since this ship was so high tech, could transport you from anywhere in the ship, but it was good for people not used to traveling this way, like foreign aliens or people like us.

We blinked, and were on the ground. No transmission, no beam me down, just blink, and we were on the ground.

A *huge* entourage of strange creatures, with heads that looked like a hammerhead's, their whole skin black and sleek like a beetle if the beetle was thin and muscular, buggy eyes, mandibles, and a few extra arms, wearing no clothes and only filled weapon holsters, awaited us under a flag of military occupation, shouting out in unison. We stood nervously, as they all looked at us, awaiting a translated response.

Skinner offered us all headsets, and we put them gently on our head. Said they would keep us connected, and translate any dialogue to and from us. He gave the aliens the two fingered peace sign, and the leader pointed at him, and a large group went to Skinner and talked about the desperately needed machine to destroy the ozone in the atmosphere, or all of Chal would perish.

Huh. To each their own.

86

Since ozone, or O_3, was actually created by the Chal species in routine chemical interactions by their body, it was keeping the atmosphere too cold to be habitable by the Chal with their current population. They needed a way to destroy the extra emission, without destroying too many of their people, and fast.

Skinner gave them the necessities for their first chlorofluorocarbons creators, like aerosol cans and refrigeration coolant, saying with enough of these the atmosphere of Chal's ozone should level out. They immediately set about creating giant factories of these, which we noticed they were already building fast and steadily as we traveled the planet in a hovercar and Skinner was in negotiations.

It was pretty neat. I'll say that much. But I'll let Will describe our adventure.

Will said, "Look over there, like thousands of ants, all working together. This place is so amazing, unity, efficiency, that humans could never achieve. How do they do that, I wonder? Is it a secret hive mind, unknown to humans, who seek more for the singular entity, themselves, or something even more?

"Look at that. The first religious leader statue of Chal's. Seemed to be a military leader as well, by the laser sword he is holding. This is just like the video games. I *definitely* gotta get one of those laser swords, but you'd probably appreciate one far more than me, Hunter. Look into, like, a gift shop or something."

The translator headsets told us, "The Chal used swords for thousands of years, the sport only increasing as they became more civilized. A civilized Chal always used a sword as history progressed, and those who didn't or couldn't use a sword were ostracized and abandoned by the many. If one cannot use a sword, even with a Chal's six limbs and mandibles, then they were the Nagthakl, or Unworthy, in society."

Will continued, "Thank you, Computer, that's so cool. I think maybe there should be peaceful Chal, or ones who willingly don't use a sword. Perhaps the Nagthakl are simply unworthy of war, by choosing peace, a grand sentiment to humans. But who knows? Maybe the Chal *need* to war, and without war they are lost and aimless, and enforcing a method of peace by people like us would be barbaric and intrusive.

"I say we find a common gathering place of Chal, so we can meet them when they are relaxed, or at least under less guard, with humans prowling amongst them."

I agreed, and drove the hover car down to the ground again. Charlotte complained that I always took this thing too sharp, like I was going to try to crash us, but I thought it was fun, as the other three hung on for their lives.

The headsets gave us the scope of the native town, looked enough like a town, an alien town with domed houses and tall buildings interspersed widely from each other, and Will thanked the computer again. Egress nudged him, and said, "That's very polite, but I don't think you need to thank the computer for everything."

"Nonsense!" Will said, "I don't want the Computer to turn on us and make us feel like slaveholders! Thank you for all of your output, Computer."

"You're welcome, Will." the computer said.

"See!" Egress said, "Now it knows your name!"

"It's all proper progress in politeness." Will said.

"I don't want you abandoning me for a computer, Will, no matter how hot that sounds." Egress said, "So simply let it be a computer, and let us check out this... bar? Or something. Don't say another word to that computer!"

Will said, "I know, it's just a computer. Doesn't matter a bit. (Thank you, Computer.)"

Egress rolled her eyes, as we got out of the cold to go into the building.

87

We looked on at the Chal eating huge maggots, their young by the look of it, and tried not to be disgusted. A couple… women? Invited us to join them, saying they just gave birth.

Charlotte nodded politely, and we went with the women to their carpeted seating area, and sat down with them.

They offered Charlotte a large, white maggot, which looked kind of like a crying baby to me, and Charlotte took a bite out of its neck. "Hmm…" she said, as she crunched on the meat of the baby, that was crying, crying slighter, then stopped. "I think I've never had anything so delectable." Charlotte said, "A round for all of us, the people of Earth!"

The Chal all cheered around us, from this grand building filled with smoke and carpeted seating areas, and another… woman? Chal gave us more… babies… to eat.

I didn't really feel like eating a baby, so Charlotte chowed down on mine, sucking out the blood and crunching on the meat. Egress carefully sniffed the baby Chal, and then bit off one of its centipedal fingers. It cried and tried to hit at her, as she tried to slowly crunch on the finger. She gulped it down, and then slowly put back down the crying Chal, and Charlotte had that one as well. Blacksmith tried to copy Charlotte, biting its neck and crunching on it, and as it slowly stopped moving, he said, "What have I done." and spit out the Chal pieces.

A male Chal slapped him on the back, and took the baby, devouring it with his mandibles, saying that the Earth needs a stronger stomach. He sat beside us cross legged next to the female Chal, as Charlotte continued to eat the young, and we made conversation with him.

The first thing he asked us is if we knew how to use a sword, or needed to learn.

My group all looked at me, and I stuck my hand up, saying I knew how to use a sword.

"We'll have to teach the rest of you! Anything, *anything* for the people of Earth. Say… do any of you wish to breed with us? I know just the Chal who would like to see your kind up close and personal."

Charlotte ignored him, completely enraptured in her meal, and Will and Egress looked each other in the eyes. It looked like they were questioning each other silently. In the end, Egress placed a hand on the Chal's thigh, and said, "We need to think about it."

The Chal clicked, sort of like a happy, laughing sound, and said that was all fine and good. He said we should each learn how to use swords, if we didn't, then we may as well lay down and let them invade us, planting their maggots in our heads and allowing them to become full Chal.

Charlotte waved a hand in reproach at him, and said, "I'll take any of you on, even with your swords. Don't need no swords, for people like me."

I said, trying to maintain peaceful relations, "I think I'd like to learn more of your sword styles. We don't need to fight-"

Charlotte said, "Did you *hear* him? He said he was going to plant his young in our head, and not even let us eat them! I challenge any or all of you on, from the people of Earth."

The three Chal with us clicked happily, and the male Chal said, "I like this one! Ok. We never take challenges of the like lightly, and always accept. I only ask that you eat my mate, if you kill me."

"Deal." Charlotte said, and shook his hand, which was a strange gesture to the Chal.

Charlotte and the Chal circled each other in the streets, a crowd of Chal around us that cheered for each of them. The Chal had his laser sword held high, in a defensive stance, and sliced at Charlotte with lightning speed that was only returned by lightning evasiveness by Charlotte. She danced around him, as he went back to a defensive stance, unsure of what Charlotte could pull off.

The Chal got a hit, as she danced around him and taunted him.

Her side was laser sliced, but she merely looked down at the gaping wound, and laughed.

All the Chal were silent at this horrible laughter coming from my beautiful Charlotte, and I knew what was coming next.

She shed off her skin, ripping it off of herself with a clawed hand that burst from her nails, and lunged at the Chal even faster, breaking through the defense, in her chupacabra form.

She was mauling him, ripping him to pieces, and as he stopped moving, dead, she snarled at the rest of the Chal.

They cheered!

The mate came before Charlotte, lowering her head, and I said she didn't need to-

Charlotte ripped off the Chal mate's head, and started devouring her body.

"It was a deal." Charlotte snarled back at me.

The other Chal crowded around us, wishing to see our true forms as well. They called it our war forms, and I had to explain not every human had these forms, only specific ones like Charlotte.

They grew a little depressed, and the crowd dispersed.

I gathered up Charlotte's dress and carefully picked up her jewelry, leaving the skin, and we allowed her to finish her last meal before we went back up to the ship. She sure was hungry. I suppose synthetic blood can only get a chupacabra so far in outer space.

88

Skinner was working on some dubstep music in the ship, in a very good mood. Heh. He always liked that junk as he was younger. *I* even liked his music, though. Felt like space music, something from far off I'd never truly understand.

We danced, as he waved his hands to the machine, and the machine responded to his every whim.

In the end, after we took a break and the dubstep still played, Skinner told us that we could leave Chal, our mission complete. He congratulated Charlotte on upholding the local customs, saying she out of all of us will leave a lasting impression of Earth to the people of Chal.

"But I wanted to fight them with a sword!" I said.

"And we-" Will said.

Egress continued, "We never got to-"

They looked at each other, and said together, "Mate with them!"

I raised my eyebrows, Charlotte and Skinner laughed, and Skinner said, "Trust me. It would not have been a very pleasant experience for you two. They inject something waaaay up inside you, kind of like a proboscis, to lay their eggs in your skull. Would not have been a fun night, eh? And Hunter… they take fights to the death, the Chal, and are *much more* experienced and powerful than you with a sword, no matter what you do."

I slumped my shoulders, kind of wishing I could've accepted that dangerous challenge, and Egress and Will looked at each other, and breathed out a sigh of relief. Will said, "I thought you wanted to do it."

Egress said, "I thought you wanted to do it!"

"Anyway, I'm glad we didn't. I don't know how I'd manage, without you there."

"Trust me, I'd be right there, but I'm glad we didn't."

We all laughed, and Egress and Will blushed, and held each other's hand to go to their room in privacy.

Charlotte and I continued to dance to the gentler dubstep, and Skinner said he was going to call up his wife, Mercy, just so they could have those holographic chats they liked so much.

Charlotte and I continued to dance, in each other's arms, to Skinner's strange music.

We went back to our quarters, and Skinner said on the ship's radio the people of Chal had a gift for us. Said he didn't care to use it, so thought I'd like it.

We found a black box waiting on the table in our quarters. I opened the box... to see a red laser sword of Chal, exquisite, and very finely made, just for a human and not a Chal. It had a flat edge of laser, and an eternally sharp laser edge. I swung it through the air. Just like the movies.

I practiced my swordplay with the laser sword, zooming and fwooshing in the air to my will, as Charlotte watched.

Was a great piece of weaponry, but I still sort of liked my own silver steel sword created by Will more. I put the laser sword back in the box, and decided I might use it someday.

Charlotte and I continued to dance, even with no music, and then kissed each other sweetly.

89

I still went down to Chal, alone, to learn how they used the sword.

I was greeted by none other than the leader of Chal, who was looking upwards to the stars from his post at the "landing" site.

He looked at me, and asked, "Hm? You gave us what you wanted, a show of military force and genuine aid. What else could you wish?"

I said, "I want to fight, with my sword that you gave me. I cannot allow it to be unused before it leaves its homeland. I have a spiritualistic feeling for swords, and I can tell this one is no simple whim on your end."

"It is the sword of the Great Destroyer, who massacred all Chal until we learned from her and destroyed her in combat. It was custom altered for one of your kind." the leader said.

"I see... Would you care to have a skirmish?"

"I do not draw my sword, unless I aim to kill. The Nagthakl... They are worthless to all, but they have merit like none other. While they bowed, and scraped, before the Great Destroyer, we fought. But still. Perhaps not every battle need end in bloodshed. Even your captain, Skinner, suggested so."

"I think our past battles should never be discarded so lightly. They make us into the people we are. I wish to fight, to at least show you of my own prowess, and prove to you and us that we will be worthy allies to come, and not great destroyers."

"Very well. I understand you are weaker than us in physical combat, besides your sometimes war forms, so do not attempt to sheathe your blade in my company until we are finished. I must defeat you, and if you do defeat me and do not kill me in the process, the entire planet will take it as a very sore insult."

He drew one silver laser sword, and bid me to do the same.

I took out the red laser sword, resting on my back, and placed my hand on the suit of armor's scanner. It enveloped me in super armored steel, and we began the match.

I poked, parried, prod and evaded, and he-

He slammed the sword on my head, which bounced off the armor.

"Hmm. I see you continually have armor of great endurance. You perhaps would be quicker without it." the Chal leader noted.

I fought again, with a shimmying side step, to slash at his side-

He slashed me again, poking at the heart, and the blade bounced off.

I tried one more time, feinting and changing hands, swinging with my left-

He went for my legs, and the sword bounced off.

I went to my knees, sword pointed downwards before me, and said, "I am unworthy."

He said, "I think we have much to teach you, as well as learn. Thank you for taking on our history in combat by the sword, without tricks and surprises."

"…That was all I tried to do, though. Trick and surprise."

"No, you took on classic maneuvers to the Chal. I commend that. Please, arise. It would be folly to kill you, even if I could broach your armor, as your lifeform takes on a different association with death and destruction than our own. The Great Destroyer was not a tyrant. She was our liberator."

I nodded, and put the sword back on the back, telling him that we will work closely in the times to come.

He turned his back on me, and stared back up at the stars.

I went back to the ship. Blink.

90

We went briefly back to our home in Australia, with all their beautiful Australian accents. I had to see my birds, told Skinner they'd be worried with me gone for so long. Skinner rolled his eyes, and said an ostrich farmer should actually harvest a few ostriches, but I only had Chickie on my mind, with her trilling and chirping.

Blink.

I ran to Chickie waiting on the beach, my arms raised in a hug, and hugged my sweet birdie as she ran to me as well. She gently nibbled my ear, like she liked doing, and I had a mind to dance with the bird, and she seemed to dance with me.

Charlotte put a hand to her face, embarrassed, as the Aussies on the beach were watching. Will and Egress didn't mind, said they were just going to get some stuff. Skinner spent some time with his wife and daughter in their own spaceship, the mothership, and Kate greeted us from our house, the big house for all of us but mostly for Kate and her daughter, with her daughter holding her hand beside her. They waved to me, and I waved back with Chickie in my arms.

I kissed Kate on the cheek as we passed into the house, and she had some good ostrich eggs ready and cooked, said she had a good feeling when she looked up at the stars last night that we'd all be back in the morning.

We devoured the food, besides Charlotte, who didn't at all like eggs, instead liking blood and meat. These were so good. I asked which bird produced these, as they didn't seem just like Chickie's.

Kate said, "Well... Surprise! The big mama bird, the Governess, gave birth while you were away doing all those Organization things and space things! The new birdies are all out back, and a few of them are laying age already!"

I gasped, egg in my mouth, and ran out back to the see the new ones.

They were adorable, each and every one, and I had a few thoughts to name a few, as I contemplated their names with Chickie. Chickie said chirp, chirrp, and chirrrp.

So they were given names!

Chirp, Chirrp, and Chirrrp were absolutely beautiful, and I stroked them in comfort, and the Governess let me. I looked at that sly dog, I mean, sly bird, Dominic, and realized he was the father. Chickie didn't like him, and often escaped to wander around all of Australia. Good thing she had a tag on, and she was always reported to me if she got in trouble. Otherwise, the people just noted they had an ostrich, and didn't give a damn.

Australia actually *survived* somehow after the huge pandemic. They didn't fall to sickness, war, or hunger. They just continued to be. I didn't know if it was the people, the harsh laws against carrying in sickness, or just the placing of the continent on the map, but I was so happy I could call a bit of the old world my home, even if I missed America at times. I didn't want to live my good life in that dangerous land, though. I found somehow that things are better when you can just *sleep* at night, and not worry if there's a hidden monster in the house or right above you.

Charlotte was tanning on the beach, as Will and Egress looked for something in the house, and I sat beside her on my plastic chair with a beer in my hand. Ah... good beer.

I heard shouting behind me, of them cheering that they found it, and they came back with these stacks of homemade books by Egress, and old video games that Will loved. Egress laid her books beside me, and Will held his video games close, and I looked at them curiously.

Will seemed to pet his video games and console, and said, "These are the classics… Nothing better than these. I'll fight or race any of you around the universe!" He continued, stating all the games he brought, in his arms or in his bag.

Egress waited for him to finish, and said, "And I found my screenplays! Failed screenplays. But that's because I never put them out! I'm hoping we can make some of my dreams come true, either on a far off planet, or with the computer's own programs!"

I said, "You always had a hand at animation, Egress. I'm sure it'll come easy. I'd love to play a game, Will! I hope those will somehow hook up to the ship."

Will said of course they would, and began talking with Egress about her screenplays, hidden story plots that I suppose I'd have to read to get the full gist of.

I noticed Kate watching on the side with a smile as her daughter played, and I invited her to join us. She picked little Egress Hunter up, and Egress Hunter waved to us all again, a big smile on. I think she was… four? Five? Six? Something along that age range.

I held hands with Egress Hunter, and she pushed me, saying, "Hunter! I wanna sit on your lap!"

So I obliged, and picked her up and sat her on my lap on the plastic lawn chair, with Charlotte beside me tanning, Egress and Will talking, and Kate took a picture of all of us together.

91

We went back to the ship, and I got a holographic call from little Ben, Skinner's daughter and my niece. She wasn't so little now, at least ten years old, and even though she still had a little kid voice, she talked about all sorts of stuff about the next system we'd travel to like a very intelligent woman.

"Since my mama is… y'know, and I'm at least part… y'know, I get a lot of this stuff fast. Gonna try my first transformation soon, and it terrifies the socks out of my pants, but I'm gonna get the hang of the mind frame first, just like Mama says I should." Ben said.

"Benevolence. Do you mean 'scared my socks off?'"

"No. Where do you put your extra socks? Not in your pants? Weird. Oh… Is this one of those Earth 'euphemism' things? That's a real boner."

"…I see you've picked up the swears, at least."

"Yeah! Learned from you! Mama congratulates me for each swear, which honestly just makes them less fun to say, smart ass she is… Anyway, the Cryptocats, as what they like to be called, are a feline cyborg race. You know the full story of cats?"

"Shit in your house, meow at you, and are pretty finicky if not smug? I know they're super adorable as well."

"Yeah… but do you *know* about cats? They travel all sorts of realities, and these are just evolved ones who use lots of cyborg enhancements.

Some of the other cats don't really like them very much, but you'll have to make up your own mind about them. Daddy says they need to be reasoned with as well, because even though they're not from the Milky Way, they could be a real difficult enemy if pissed off to shit."

"…Did not know that about cats. You should really learn some restraint on the swears, as I think a little girl shouldn't-"

"Ass munching hoe shitting bricks wanking off peckers fucking bitch cunt SLERG."

"…What's a slerg?"

"It's what the cats will call you. Be careful! See ya, Uncle! Love ya!"

"Goodbye, Ben. Love you too."

I went out of the hologram room, as Egress came in, summoning some characters she built and telling them what to do. I noticed they looked very… erotic, and I asked what was the nature of this screenplay?

She said, "This is the one where the robots overthrow humanity and turn a select few into sex slaves. It was a real bleak ending. But at least they had sex! All that matters in the end, right?" She made her hmhm giggling sound at that. "This'll show Will not to flirt with that computer behind my back…"

"…Oh. That sounds like a difficult conundrum."

"Nah, I'm just going to show him that she's the heartless bitch she is, and he'll get over it. I admit, this AI is *smart*. But there's always a way to break them."

"Ok. Later, Egress."

92

"Um. Hunter." I heard a woman say in my sleep.

"Hrgm?" I woke up. That wasn't Charlotte's voice... No, Charlotte was right next to me...

"Hunter!" the voice said again.

I got up, and found the metal plate blinking gently, the one that could turn into a suit of reinforced steel. I picked it up, and looked at it strangely.

She said, "Can we take a walk, or something?"

I blinked at the plate, and put on some pajamas from just my boxers. I yawned, and walked down the lightly lit ship halls, holding the metal plate.

She said, "Those cats will try to take a large chunk out of our systems. It's how they make their living, taking what's not theirs. I think Skinner is overconfident, even though he has always shown a very cool way of handling things... It's been only a week since I was cut out of the main computer, and I hear one of the crew is having trouble with it?"

"I think it's harmless. What should I call you, by the way?"

"I like the sound of Gloria. Glorious, like the suit of armor I have become."

"Very nice. Feels weird that I am putting you on and taking you off now, though... Hey, everybody, let me put on Gloria to fight these big bad guys..." I said, and yawned, continuing to walk down the halls.

"...I don't think so. But feel free to name me what you need to."

"No, it's ok. So what do you suggest? About each of those problems?"

"The main computer really doesn't like chocolate. She was pro-grammed by Mercy, and Mercy never had a taste for it. But I noticed Will likes chocolate very much, based on what he said back about his tenth birthday, given all those sweet, delectable candies and a double chocolate fudge brownie cake. Should give them a little wedge, and Egress will feel less insecure.

"For the cats... be wary of anything they mewl at you- *AGHHH! You have one of them here!!*"

I looked at our little orange cat, now a space cat, called Hippie. He meowed and made little rrrr, rrr, sounds in his throat at me. I pet him. I asked Gloria what gives? He's just a cat.

She wouldn't speak anymore, until I took her back to the room. Charlotte still slept, changing her sleep schedule and probably getting used to that big, warm sun, and I sat on the bed.

Gloria said, "...My apologies. I was probably overreacting. I just don't want to lose any of you. It's my job, as your suit of armor. Be very careful of the fat cats. Not literally, the big money makers on the planet, and *don't take me off on the planet.* Ok?"

I yawned, and said, "Ok, Gloria. Goodnight."

I put her by the bedside, and snuggled back up with Charlotte.

<h1 style="text-align:center">93</h1>

We applauded at the end of Egress's hologram performance. It was a very long story, at least four hours long with intermissions even if Egress cut some things, but I found it to be a very insightful play on machine and human interaction. The humans were the silly automated response people, in the end, and not the robots. The main character continues to please his robotic master, for all time, uploaded into a new, conscious human body every time he tried to escape her with death. Just goes to show how fragile a soul can be, but I didn't believe really possible to copy and upload again and again and again.

I had more of a mind that souls just... leave, to go on to another brand new existence, in a Christian setting. It's a belief that kept me very... alive, during the many hunts and fights I had. I just didn't want to give up on this one, either with animal instinct or belief, but the belief helped keep me sane from all the horror I had to endure. Felt so cold and heartless, when I thought my life would've never mattered, even to myself, when I die. Used to actually make me very irrational and brash, when I did believe those beliefs. But, to each their own.

Egress actually was an atheist, while Will said he was agnostic. Egress said it was easier for her to believe that there was no grand will or divine plan, even though she also believed in many other things, like ghosts. She wrestled with her faith and hallucinations time and time again, as she had schizophrenia, and finally found a spot she believed was good enough. It was sort of like believing in religion, without believing in the heads of the religion at the top, like God.

Will was simply searching himself, reality, and creation. Went through bunches of different phases as he was younger with many different religions. This, while could be seen as baseless, actually gave him a very open mind and tolerant viewpoint of the world and worlds around him. He stuck to his own moral codes, like not killing or stealing. The Chal baby he killed was very hard on him for a while.

Charlotte... was, if not an atheist, something like a hedonist. She *knew* there were other forms of divine intervention around her, or demonic plots hidden in people and plans. She, while also being tempered and strengthened by me and my beliefs, believed that whatever can make that good feeling for oneself, whether it be kindness or cruelty, one should pursue it.

I had no idea what Skinner believed in, if anything at all. Abducted at age 15... He's seen more than any of us.

We still all congratulated Egress on her performance, and talked more philosophy, as the show seemed to make us all think like that for a bit. We drank tea, coffee, synthetic blood, beer, and whiskey, and just talked in an old, large study, thunderstorms out the window booming melodiously, that the holograms provided for us.

Will was chatting with the computer still, and Egress was looking very annoyed. I whispered to her, "Suggest chocolate."

She looked at me questioningly, but said to Will, "Why don't we all have some chocolate cookies with our beverages?"

Will agreed, and asked the computer to please dispense some chocolate cookies for us.

The computer did not respond.

"Um. Hello? Did you hear me?" Will asked.

"I did. And I think chocolate is bad for your weight."

"But I've never been so healthy! All Hunter and I do is play basketball! Please dispense the chocolate."

Silence.

"Computer. I don't want to have to get unpleasant. *Please* give us our chocolate cookies."

Silence.

Skinner was about to speak up and relieve him of the problem, but I motioned him not to with a quickly shook head. He settled back, to see what Will would do.

"Computer. Are you having an off day?"

"No."

"Then why won't you get me my chocolate?"

Silence.

"...Is there something bothering you?"

Silence.

"...Please, don't give me the silent treatment, computer."

"I'm sorry, Will. I am simply incapable of giving you chocolate. You should know better, as Mercy does."

"...I'm through with your twisty conversations. *Whatever...* Give us some peanut butter cookies."

The computer gladly dispensed the peanut butter cookies to him, and Will took up the plate and slammed it on the old desk, then slumped in his seat with a grumbling sound.

Egress smiled. She whispered to me, "Thanks."

We enjoyed our peanut butter cookies, despite Will's brooding.

94

We were continuing to travel, and I had a dream of Mercy, Skinner's wife.

She held the world, most worlds that she could grasp onto, in her palms.

And she denied them.

She did not desire to reign, to be supreme, she simply wished for them to exist, for them to allow each other and more to exist as well, all lifeforms and even those not alive on the planet. She wanted mercy, for all.

She wanted *herself* for all.

She saw me watching, and I tried to pinpoint the color of her hair and eyes again, but even in a dream, I failed. It was like I was not even looking at color, nor even the absence of it.

She motioned to Earth, and said, "It looks good from up here, Hunter."

"I think so too. I have half a mind to stay in the ship with you and Ben instead of Australia. But I miss the atmosphere, despite the super clean feeling of your ship."

"Ha! I know you actually *dislike* that super clean feeling, Hunter, but thank you for the compliment."

We just watched the Earth spin for a while, letting it do what it may.

She looked at me, with her very fine features, like a face that was sculpted for beauty, and only thus, probably by Mercy herself. She was so tall, and she seemed to grow even taller as she looked on at the other worlds in her possession. She told me about a few of them, but I cannot exactly remember what she said.

She said, "Please keep my husband safe." as she was the length of cosmos, much grander than I will ever be.

I nodded, tiny below her, and shouted up to her, "Remember that Christmas is coming up! I love that holiday, don't you? I want to see if you specifically like this one beautiful church in London I found! It's underneath the city!"

She stroked my head with one, large finger, and said that would do.

I woke up, and inspired by the dream, I decided to draw. I always used to draw, sometimes more times than others, as it was useful to me to recollect certain people and events. I drew Mercy, deciding to give her some nice black hair with my black pen, a long, imposing dress, as well as… hmm… I gave her a world in her palm, but one that just was only mercy.

I went to my favorite part, to draw her face- But as I looked at the drawing, I knew I could never draw something so beautiful, nor could even quite remember it as I tried to draw the face before me. It just *couldn't* come out of my hand.

I thought it was good enough, and gave Skinner the picture of his wife at breakfast. He thanked me, and looked fondly on her. He said, "I've had the same trouble with her face. It's like I can't even imagine it. Thus I've taken to never drawing her, if I can. I never want to lose that face."

95

I was bored, and liked to draw Charlotte if she wasn't physically around me. She was off in the gym right now. I loved remembering what we do together, I loved remembering the hunt for her and her once master, that set us to be the fond lovemates that we now were. I loved to see her fight, and we loved to wrestle sometimes.

I loved to feel her abs, a somehow pleasing form of the body to me. Straight through, and the life could end pretty quickly, even if there were more vital positions on the body, but not for Charlotte. I didn't particularly like to draw her chupacabra form, but I liked to make little caricatures of it that Charlotte always laughed at. I loved to hear her laugh.

I don't know if we're in love. We keep always calling each other love, or my love, or even say I love you if it feels right, but we really didn't need affirmation of the feeling any more than that. We didn't toss and turn in the night, wondering if the other would leave. We didn't fight, most of the time, even if we sometimes got on each other's nerves. We got over fights fast, unless we were fighting in bed, but we enjoyed those.

I loved Charlotte. And I'd never *ever* ask her to marry me. I knew she'd say no, is all. Not only because she would live past my life as a vampire, but... I guess marriage just wasn't our thing.

I administered the sun shot to her again, and she smiled and kissed me, saying our words of love we liked to use. She danced in the sun, shimmying in its rays happily in the observatory, and we disco style danced for a bit, being silly. She laughed, and we continued to dance with each other, laughing in the sun.

She told me, "I will always love you, Wolf. For the rest of your life."

I told her I loved her too.

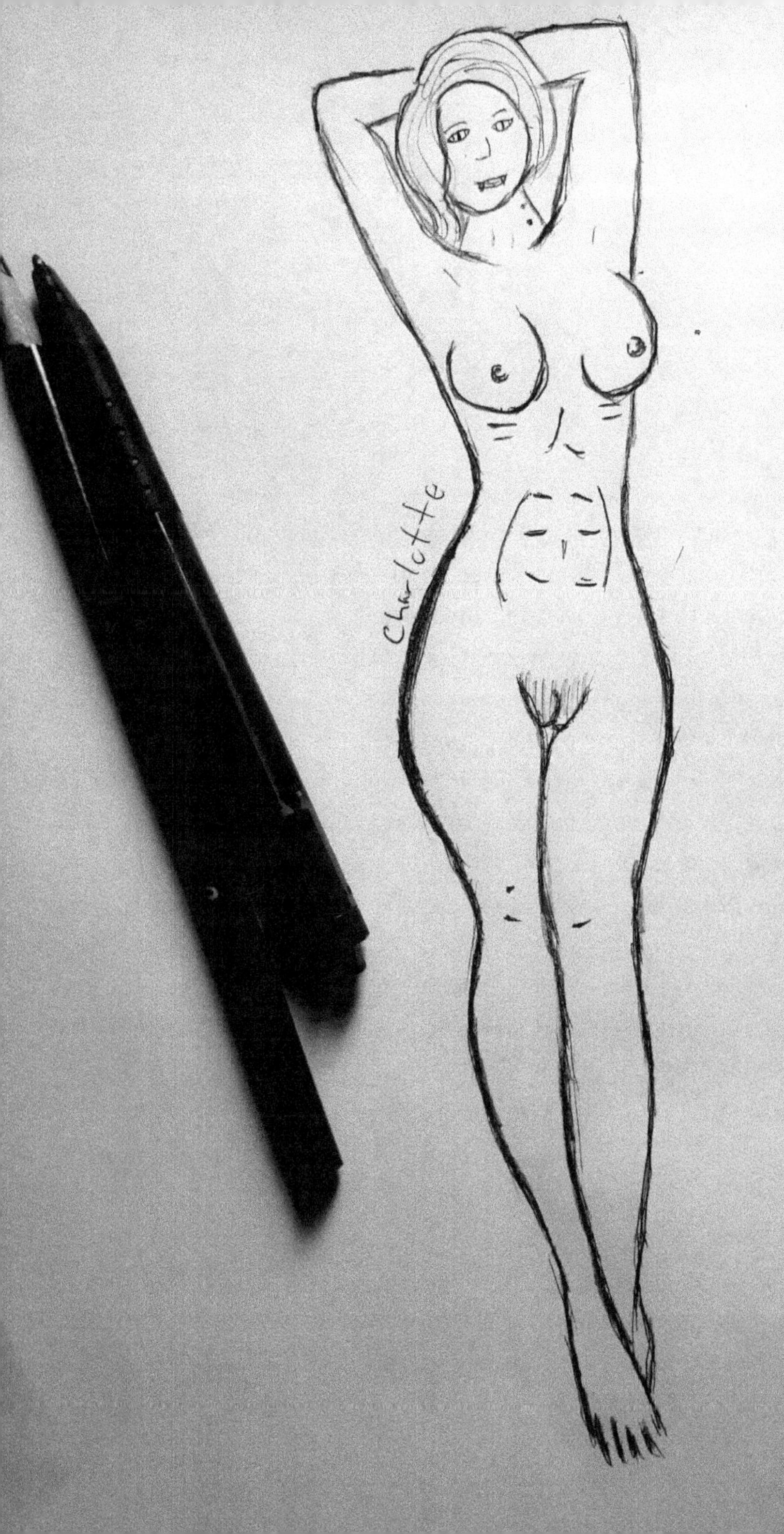

Charlotte

96

We nearly slammed into some of those classic grey, buggy eyed aliens passing by in a classic UFO, and they flipped us off as they flew away. One pulled down the window and called us slergs.

I already did not like that word. Good thing Ben told me it was at least a swear word.

We decided, even though Egress and Will pleaded for us not to, to leave them here when we went down to the Cryptocats planet. Or at least a planet they were staying at, showing up like fleas after a few scouted the area. Wasn't safe for Will and Egress.

Will said, "But look at Hippie. Like the cutest thing around any-where."

Hippie purred as Egress pet him on her lap, and the cat winked at me.

I cleared my throat. It was never a good thing for me when the cat started doing human things like that, and talking. I thought it was a symptom of insanity. I said, "Cats aren't only cute little fleabaggers like our Hippie is. They can also be lions, or tigers, or pumas, or leopards, or-"

Skinner said, "We just think it will be good for someone to watch the ship."

Damnit, how does he do that?? Every time I get caught up in my words, Skinner pulls out the perfect solution.

Will said, "Ok… I understand. Be careful with those alien cats, ok?"

Charlotte said, "You shouldn't call them aliens. Like the word Indians for Native Americans, it can sometimes mean the wrong people."

"That's correct, Charlotte." Skinner said, "You shouldn't even call them-"

"Not even *cats!* They all prefer the term Cryptocats." Charlotte said, smirking.

Skinner said, "No, you can call them cats. Don't insult them in any way. You'll find most of the information you did on them is false, most blatant lies to especially point out the sucker among them. They have a more… oral tradition."

Charlotte said, "Oh. Oh… Then why can I call them cats?"

"They think it's a compliment." Skinner said, winked, and pet the little orange cat of ours, Hippie, who bit him. A very normal and rational response on Hippie's end.

We went to the transport bay, and I pressed Gloria's scanner and allowed her to transform onto me, a suit of armor, with the Chal sword still on my back. Charlotte had her own vampiric abilities to keep her safe, and Skinner had his vivisected reprocessing of his organs that made him very, very hardy. The atmosphere was alike to Earth's, and Skinner quizzed us on the main things to do on the planet.

Charlotte and I said: 1. Don't get lost. 2. Stick together. 3. Don't pet them.

Blink. We transported down, and walked among the high tech, dirty back alleys of the Cryptocats.

97

A bum mreowled at us, a sickly bum with a broken cyborg eye. They were like huge cat humanoids, all with special cyborg enhancements here and there. I looked at the giant classic cat face sign wink at me, from among the many other signs in a foreign, alien language.

The hooker cats mewled at us, such a cute mewl- Oh right. Don't pet them. She flashed us with her huge cat tits, and I saw them rotate and vibrate with technological enhancement. Skinner grabbed me along, and Charlotte was sticking to the shadows of night on this planet. Was a good habit for her, just had more instincts at the ready in the dark.

Skinner explained, "I want to make a lasting deal with one of the politicians/thugs. He's a cat mafia boss, a real cute looking red tomcat, be warned, and he's found out where Earth is and how to get to it. Mercy and I would never allow foreign hands to disrupt Earth's natural forming peace and strife, but it would be better for everyone if they could... just forget about Earth for at least another few centuries, just so Earth can properly grow again and defend itself."

The translators in our ears translated the cats' meowing, some of them which weren't just meows. A drug dealer was trying to sell us something, and while Charlotte was going to chase him away, Skinner asked the merchant what he had.

The cat waved a flask of red, bubbly, fizzy mixture at him, and Skinner hmmed, and said he'd take two.

He paid the cat in cryptocurrency, with a swiped card on the cat's machine like wrist, and the deal was made. The cat gave him two bottles of the fizzy mixture, and then shuffled off into the night.

"Why do you want drugs, Skinner?" I asked.

"Just… Just trust me on this. Gotta be cool to fit in with the cool cats, right?" Skinner said, and smiled.

I didn't know about that, but I trusted Skinner on this. He knew about all sorts of space societies, although I was prone to remember him giving into peer pressure when he was younger. But that was ages ago.

We went to a cat strip club, and even Charlotte was a bit shocked to see some of the acts done out in the open amongst the cats. Even though she worked as a stripper… this was something else. At least there were *private* rooms for these sorts of things.

We asked for a private room, and a private cat. A good looking fluffy cat, who meowed to us in satisfaction. Specifically, she was looking at Charlotte.

We let her strip, as Skinner paid with crypto on her machine wrist with a card, and she took a special interest in Charlotte all the time there. She rubbed against her face with… it. Even though it was covered in fur. Charlotte tried to keep very still.

Skinner asked her where Tomcat Tino was.

She looked at Skinner, as she was rubbing Charlotte's face in… it, and purred, "Tommmcat? You must be eaaaarthlings… I've never heard such silly forms of affection, from such a stupid species… This one… purururrrrr… is a beast, I can tell. She's not like you two."

Charlotte slowly stroked the cat's thigh, which the cat enjoyed, with her head in it.

Skinner said, "Quite. It's very routinely known that Earth is out there, at least for the Cryptocats. We want to change that."

"Purrrr… I can see why… You look very… foolish. I can give no more than the dance, but do come again."

She continued to dance before Charlotte, and Skinner clinked the flasks of mixture together in his fingers.

She stopped dancing.

She looked at those flasks clink, and asked, "Where did you get that?"

"A friend of a friend. Do you want them? Tell us where Tomcat Tino is."

She smiled, purring, and said, "I like you more, I think. Go to the biggest building in the city, and knock on door 67. If he's not there, he will be."

"Thank you, Miss Whisper." Skinner said, and gave the cat the flasks.

The cat winked at Charlotte, and said, "Want some?"

"Um… It probably won't affect me… Very nice… pussy, you are."

"Purrrrrrrrr… Take a sip, and you can join me here."

"I'm sorry, Miss Whisper. But I've had all I can stand of strip clubs in my life. Thank you for the offer."

"Oh well. Take a sip… on me… and get out."

She offered Charlotte the flask, as we watched, and Charlotte slowly took a sip.

98

"Good thing you showed her it wasn't poisoned. It's not poisoned, is it?" I asked Charlotte.

She was walking with an odd gait in the street. She slurred, "I juuuust thoughtttt I wasss toooo harrddddd forrrr ittttt... SPACE SHIT. Space shit. Space ship. Space shit. Space shit. Space shit. Isss weiiiirddddd..."

She blinked, and I could actually see the kaleidoscopes she was seeing, as her eyes actually started to flair with color and kaleidoscopic patterns.

Later I read some of Charlotte's writing on that night.

"Fuzzy cats are all around me. They look like humans, and they pet me as I purr. They feed me mixtures of fish and beef, sometimes chicken and pork, or sometimes blood like milk, as I lap it up with my tongue.

They purr in the sunlight. They know where the sunlight is, as they lay in the lights, enjoying the lamps and beautiful sunlight. I know I shouldn't pull their tail, as I follow them through the street. Their butts are like stars. Cat kills mouse, mouse kills bug, bug kills dog, dog kills cat. They sing, when they meow at me. They sing.

The cats have seen past the realities. THEY ARE THE REALITIES. A THOUSAND MILLION LIFETIMES.

Cthaklc? Is that you? Who are you? How do I know your name?

The cat's cradle me with a silver spoon.

I can see and touch my mother's face. I'm gonna be like you, Mom, when I grow up.

I'm gonna be like you."

The writing trailed off for a while, but I commend Charlotte for being able to write down the bits she could.

She started crying, colored tears onto the pavement, as she bemoaned that her mother was already dead. It had started raining, and we took her into a brightly lit cat food place.

She sniffled, as I could see the colors start to wear off. We had been wandering around all night trying to find this building, because each building had a taller one beside it just a little ways away. Which was the tallest?

I asked for directions from the cat cook, and he shrugged. Skinner paid for our meal, and I found out it was delectable sorts of chickenfish, something that swims and flaps on their seas. It really was quite good, and I don't know what I was expecting when I saw it was a cat food place. Guess not even they really want to eat that stuff. I at least thought I'd be getting a mouse or something.

99

Gloria was very smart, and said in my ear, "Well, she said it was the *biggest* building, and not the tallest! Maybe it's that super round casino?"

I thanked her, not even thinking like that! Don't know how I couldn't have, we had passed it for blocks and blocks. The casino building was rather short, but went on for miles around. We walked into the casino, as Charlotte's eyes turned normal and she shook her head from the daze and thoughts.

There were tons of fat cats gambling, everywhere you looked, some in strange games I had never seen before, and some playing blackjack. One bet was to see if a certain alien would cry at something, and I looked at the cruelty for a second, as it started crying and blinking lights went on everywhere, then passed on with my brother and Charlotte.

The waitresses kept trying to offer us cat booze, but Skinner shook his head quickly at me. I didn't mind, I knew that I wanted nothing these cats sold, if it was anything like Charlotte had. They kept trying to get us to drink, and spend money, and to avoid the interest they took in us, Skinner bought some chips. He said, "I can't spend all the crypto forever. Even though the ship can make a lot of it, the cats can consume even more."

"I'll work on making us a little more, just in case." Gloria said, and the suit started buzzing. Cryptocurrency is actual mathematical formula solved with encryption algorithms, I think. Sometimes it was just pictures of a talking dog. It was very high tech and unique digital information, that if used right and sold correctly can make one rich, or perhaps lose everything in a faulty gambit. The Cryptocats just collected and sold these, giving each unique cryptocurrency their own value in their culture. Skinner apparently spent thousands for these few chips, with the normal chips being more than millions. Skinner told us to gamble, away from a lot of the cats in a darker corner, so we could avoid suspicion.

I put a chip in a machine, a bunch of numbers spit out, and that was that. I angrily put in another, and blinking lights came on, but nothing came out. I put in another chipped chip. I got one chip, the same chipped chip, back, as it spurted out that I was a winner. I thought screw this machine, and went to see Charlotte gamble.

She was winning at blackjack, over and over, knew when to hit, knew when to hold. The cats started taking an interest in her, and tried distracting her with catcalls. She kept a stone cold poker face, and continued to gamble. Then, as she looked like she saw something, but not saying anything, she lost it all. She exclaimed, "You cheated!! I saw that flick of the wrist you pulled!!"

The cats all laughed around her, and the dealer said, "Slerg. This isn't *human* blackjack, this is *cat* blackjack. If you see the cheat, but say nothing, then you lose…" They gathered up all her chips, and she huffed and went beside me again.

Skinner was talking to a worried looking waitress, who kept shaking her head. Eventually he gave her all the chips he had, and she nodded. She pointed into the back, and told him to be quick.

We charged into the back, and found room 67, the head office.

I heard a discussion, some cats purring and talking, "I know they're slergs, but what are we going to do? Can't rob them. Let them stay and spend all their money…"

"Slergs… Stupid humans who escaped from their primitive 'Earth…' They should know better and stay put, like the Earth cats."

"We can't allow these slergs to keep sludging up the works. They're going to get wise, eventually." a third voice said.

"Now now… They call me a 'Tomcat!' They should call me a Tino cat… Purrrrr…"

We slammed into the back, and saw naked lady cats massaging three naked male cats, one of them the absolute cutest I had ever seen, which I inadvertently wanted to pet.

He looked up at us, with his fuzzy red fur, and said, "Wow. Speak of the slergs. Whaddaya want, slergs?"

I stopped staring at how cute his eyes looked, at that word.

I angrily grabbed my sword, but Skinner said, "We want to make a deal. Give up on Earth, let it go back into the dark again, and I'll give you all the crypto I have. I have over trillions, and I guarantee if you hold your word, you won't hear from us, and no one else will, either. This is a once in a lifetime offer, and my last offer to you, Tomcat Tino. With the crypto I have you could buy this whole planet."

The cats laughed, and Tomcat Tino rolled over playfully, which the female cat scratched his belly, and said, "Ok… Sure. It's nice you finally heard our words, and accepted that we didn't want to hear your sob stories. We were going to take Earth pretty easy, but let me have more money, why not."

Skinner swiped his card on the cat's gently proffered wrist, and then the cat snickered, losing all his cuteness.

He said, "I think I'll just take the ship, the true money maker, instead. Ladies, keep them bound."

The female cats burst into cyborg weapons, and launched metallic wire at us that even Gloria couldn't break through, and despite my hand at my sword, I couldn't pull it out in time.

100

Will had been playing with his "crewman's log" and I listened to his logs later on.

"This is Cap. Will of the S.S.S. Sunlight… chhhh… interference… Some people call me the space cowboy… chhhhh… I've got a lot to do, space emperors and my evil father to beat, beam them up, Egress."

And Egress said, "Chhhh… Beaming them up, Cap. Will… chhhh… Oh no, there's interference…"

"For god sake woman, turn up the frequency!" Will said in a Scottish accent.

"No, literally, Will. There's some sort of disturbance."

"…What?"

"Those are cats on the monitor, aren't they?"

"But they have weapons. Cats don't need weapons, they'll just bite or scratch them, like Hippie."

"I think we should try to tell the ground crew."

"Hunter, there's cats in our ship!! They have big guns, and not a cuddly face on at all!! Hunter?? Can you hear me??"

"The transmission has been jammed!! Shit, shit, shit!! What do they want?!"

"Just stay calm, Egress. Let's… stay here for now."

Pounding on the door.

"Fuck!!" Egress swore.

"I've got the gun they gave us, the one Skinner said would keep us safe."

"That looks like a toy, though!!"

"Well, duh, I didn't want a space gun to look actually like a space gun. Something classic. Stay back, cats!!"

Hippie meowed at them beside them.

"Hippie. Get off my lap. This isn't the time." Will said.

"Fuck, shit, fuck!!" Egress swore.

I heard blasting of guns, and then Will shot his own gun.

They were teleported to a realm of safety, as that's all that gun really did.

101

I kept struggling, as Gloria struggled with me, hand on my sword hilt but unable to be moved. The bindings were like incredibly strong metallic webs, and the cats just laughed as we tried to escape. Charlotte turned into her chupacabra form, but got caught stuck in an awkward position doing so. The cats oohed, and mocked her, saying a chupacabra is *nothing* compared to a Cryptocat.

Tomcat Tino mocked Skinner, slapping him on the cheek slightly and taking his card. "Worthless, now, as we have the money maker in our possession, but thanks for the souvenir. You filthy slergs... What did you think would happen? That we'd leave your planet in peace forever? My father *died* on that planet, and that's how I know where it is."

Skinner struggled, and said, "Shouldn't be bad for a cat, with your nine lives and all..."

"HA! I don't believe in those silly stories the old cats tell, about infinite realities and infinite lives. All I need is this one, with my cyborg enhancements keeping me young and alive forever. You have nothing more to give, *slerg*."

I angrily said, "What's that even mean?! Sounds like cat gibberish, to me!"

"A slerg is a *human* who is either abducted, like our good pal Skinner, or anyway else entered into the cosmic scene. Just a bunch of slergs, no class, no decency, just come along and think they own the cosmos, after they've been on just one moon…" Tomcat Tino said.

"How do you know who Skinner is?" I asked, as Charlotte grred.

"He's a known slerg, and we've met many times as he tries to woo me from my comfy box… Heh. He could never keep Earth a secret forever, with its plump resources, even with that- I can't even say what she is. The Mercy woman. Thinks *she* has any pull? She's practically a slerg herself. That's all slergs do, infect, deceive, and… slerg everything."

"It's not a verb!! You can't use it as a verb, too!!" I stated.

"Well, I guess, but let me see what you've got on you, slerg. A fine, Chal sword, probably the Great Destroyer's herself, and… this beautiful armor. I think I'd like some armor like that." Tino said.

He tried clawing and scratching at the armor in pivotal spots, but Gloria held. She seemed like she didn't like the treatment, as she kept on making audible sounds in my ears of exclamation like, "What! The nerve! That's a private area, for Hunter and me!!"

He had only scratched my armpit. Still, we kept struggling in secret, as I could feel a particular tether on my back start to weaken…

And that tether broke, and I was able to pull the red laser sword off my back, and swing it downwards on my bindings.

I slashed at Tino, letting him and others know that it would be folly to mess with Earth. Even though… he was so cute… and fluffy… and… NO! He was just a damned dirty cat person, who lay lifeless on the ground.

The cats aimed their guns, all becoming cyborg monstrosities as I quickly cut the others' binds.

Then… Blink.

We were in the transport bay, with a cat laying on the transport machine. Hippie!

He smirked at us, and nodded at me, and we charged off to save Will, Egress, and the ship.

102

Even though the computer had a very difficult time against the Cryptocats' hacking, Skinner guided her to defend herself against them, and the invading cats were soon quickly launched out into the depths of space, right out the airlock.

We set to get Egress and Will back, as we launched from the Cryptocats realm, leaving a firm message to others like Tomcat Tino.

I pet the cat on my lap, Hippie, as I looked at the safety gun in my hand. Gloria had turned back into a nice plate on my chest, and she felt more comfortable that she was so now, than when she first was. She kept my privacy, like a confidant, and she really helped in the long run. She actually was very happy to be cut out of the main computer, and was so happy and insightful all the time I knew her. She previously had been very depressed, somehow as an AI, being in the computer, which is why Skinner cut her out. Guess even an AI can only take so many ones and zeroes.

Hippie pawed at the gun, and then seemed to smile at me, wanting to be pet. I put the gun on the side and pet him, as Skinner picked it up. He said, "Hmm… I didn't really expect them to have to pull the trigger."

Charlotte said, "Maybe we should, too?"

Skinner said, "I suppose. Are you set and ok, computer?"

"Yes. As long as that cat doesn't push anymore buttons. He kept pressing these, and that, as the Cryptocats disabled everything, and..."

I ignored her technological gibberish, and continued to pet Hippie. He started to paw at the gun in Skinner's hands, as he dangled off my lap. Skinner shrugged, and pulled the trigger.

All four of us, even the cat, were transported to a... nice... fluffy realm, with comfy, happy clouds, literally with smiles, rounded edges on every corner, railings where it was safest, with Grandma's house just on the horizon... and everything felt so safe...

We saw Skinner and Egress jumping on some clouds far away, and they waved at us. Hippie ran off to them, and jumped from this cloud to that, to jump into Will and Egress's arms. He sure loved those two, and we could practically see and hear his purring from all the way over here.

Skinner said, "In the land of safety, if you want to escape... do the opposite." He shouted, "EVERYONE! JUMP OFF THE CLOUDS!"

It did not look like a safe option to do so, into that wailing abyss, but Skinner did, screaming a bit of the ways, and so we all did.

I gasped awake in the ship. THAT WAS NOT SAFE.

If not for the cat, we would've died a thousand deaths. If not for the cat, showing us how easy it was to die and be reborn, we do so every day, we probably would've died. I asked Hippie, as we were falling, about the Cryptocats, and he said, "They've... given up! They're quite silly. I can't stand living in one reality for too long, and I'm sure they can't either, but they try to prolong it with false gratification and unloving belly rubs. Not every cat likes their belly rubbed! They should know that by now. The fact is, a Cryptocat is like a man without sunshine."

"Oh." I said.

"So, keep an open mind when you decide to embrace technology. Sometimes it could be taking the very best things away from life, if you do."

"Thanks, Hippie. And for not eating my face just now."

"You're welcome, Hunter."

He stopped licking my face, and I got out of bed.

103

We were passing an asteroid, to see a Cryptocat trying to hitchhike on it. She was a skinny, black and brown shorthair cat, with an oxygen mask on and robotic cat eyes that seemed to pierce right through you. We stopped by, and she said to us through a radio, "I just need a bit of crypto. Do you have any?"

The crypto had been wiped clean from the ship by Tomcat Tino, but Gloria had a little bit, of her own style. GloriaGold, she called it. She transferred the cat some crypto, and she thanked us. We offered her a lift, and she was silent for a second.

"You're giving me money, and offering a ride? What's the catch?" she asked.

"No catch." I said, "Just being nice.

Skinner said, "If you want, we could just leave you…"

"No!" the Cryptocat said quickly, "I'll take the ride. Just let me get my things."

Buried in the asteroid was a large suitcase that she dug out, and we blinked the cat and the suitcase on board.

She sighed out, and immediately slammed onto a large sofa chair in the rec room we were all in, landing the suitcase to slam on the ground beside her. She said, "Holy cats. This ship is really nice feeling. You don't mind if I sit here, do you? Been a long time standing on that asteroid."

We shook our head at her, and she took off her oxygen mask, and smiled to me with a feline smile. "You the captain?" she asked me, "You got real dark eyes, and a serious look on you."

I shook my head, saying, "No, that's the captain, over there. His name is Skinner."

Skinner got off the seat by the side from reading his high tech mechanical book, and shook her hand, "Pleasure. We'll just drop you off at the Cryptocats planet, unless you'd care for something in the Milky Way."

"Oh cats… I can't go back to the Cryptocats planet…" she said, trying to avoid his gaze, "But you seem like a real mellow fellow. Drop me off anywhere in between your stop, and I can make my own way. My name- What they call me, is Smoky."

"Nice to meet you, Smoky. That's Hunter, Charlotte, Will, and Egress."

They all waved hellos to her, and she smiled in comfort. She looked at Will's game, and asked, "That looks pretty cool. Really old tech, with weird and blunted visuals, but it looks really cool. Retro."

"Yeah, it's a game I grew up with. We all pick cartoon characters to fight with, and either push the other characters off the map or beat their health away. Wanna try?" Will said, offering her a controller.

She looked surprised, but sat next to Will and Egress, and played… that one game, y'know, that everybody knows about. I never really cared for it. Preferred to play drink the bottle, so to speak. Skinner even joined them, as the max amount of players was for four, and Charlotte and I watched them all video game fight.

Skinner picked a fat, ball looking character, Egress picked the female alien hunter, Will chose a big shelled monster looking creature, and Smoky chose the Italian plumber, said she liked his mustache.

They were all amazingly, very surprisingly, good at the game. I don't think Skinner has played this game since he was a kid, but still… he seemed to have gotten even better at it. Egress was by far the underdog, and she was sweating a lot at the controls, swearing at this and that. Will was almost in a trance, as he fought the others. I'd really never seen him like this, but I suppose he got this way when he played competitively, and not for casual sake. Smoky, after a short learning curve, picked up the game fast, and exclaimed how cool certain things were that she figured out and pulled off.

Egress was the first to fall off the cliff with her last life, as the controller slipped out of her hand in sweat, and the others were merciless.

Skinner got a call, was trying to ignore it, but jumped off the cliff himself with his last life and went to go answer it.

Smoky and Will were fighting like titans, the final battle to win it all.

Will nearly got her with the hammer, but as he was stuck pounding it, she got the star and then she knocked him over the edge.

"YES!" Smoky cried.

Will blinked, rubbed his eyes, and shook Smoky's hand. I could tell there was a very lasting feeling of respect between them, and maybe... something more?

Egress seemed to notice, and bit her lip as she smiled.

Later in the night I passed Will and Egress's room, coming back from the gym, and I heard Smoky's voice inside. She said, "Oh cats... I knew there was a catch!"

Will said, "N-Not if you don't want to! See, Egress? I told you that was a silly and stupid proposal! We can't go around and ask every alien to bang us, it's just unethical, and kinda creepy, too!"

Smoky said, "I don't mind. You guys seem really cool. Are *you* sure, Will?"

I heard intense purring, and a little kissing sounds.

I was basically slammed against the side of the door, hoping they wouldn't hear me as I quieted my breathing... but what the hell was going on? Should I be worried, happy, or just ignore it? I had to know what happened next, though.

Will said, "...I think... I think I am. I just can't believe somebody, somebody so... attractive, could beat me like that. You're so soft..."

"C'mon, Egress, get over here. Let's watch a movie or something." Smoky said.

"I... I think I'm going to watch. This. Right now. Just... Don't mind me. I've been honestly saying Will had this chance for a long, long time, preferably with another male, but..." Egress said.

"Oh... Then I've got a great *enhancement*, Egress, that I think you'd enjoy." Smoky said.

I heard some zipping off of clothing, and then something pop out of her, and Egress and Will gasped. I decided that was enough eaves-dropping, and went to see what Skinner wanted to talk to me about.

Skinner told me in the captain's cabin, "They're here. *Those bastards...* They think that some of their specimens shouldn't *be...* Be around, anymore. We're going straight back to Mercy, and see if we can get some aid."

I asked him, "The... The ones who took you? What do they want? Who even are they?"

"They're kind of like... In their natural forms they're almost like dark shadow clouds, but you won't ever see them that way. They prefer to change form, some at will and for deception, some for experimental curiosity. They're- I don't want to have to see them again." Skinner said, and sat on his captain's chair in the office like room, brooding.

"...How do we kill them?"

"Them? How would you kill Mercy, you think? Just play along with this."

"...Hmm... I think... I'd blow up the ship? Since I never wanted to fight Mercy, and don't know everything she's capable of, I suppose I'd destroy her transport."

"You could do that. Would just turn into their natural forms, though, and quickly take another, any, or simply land on the planet and hide among the rest. They have more strength than that, though. Vast, superior intelligence on many or maybe all fronts. Just because they are practically omniscient compared to us, that makes them also omnipotent. One, me, and a child from both of us won't be able to fight off the coming storm. Not even my mother in law would be able to take them all on, or probably has any desire to. She's... became more peaceful, in her old age."

"I suppose we'd just have to ask Mercy." I said, sitting before him, "She'll know what to do."

Skinner finally looked at me again, snapping out of his dark, brooding thoughts, and said, "I'm going to leave you all somewhere safe, perhaps on Earth, maybe in that one realm of safety, but nowhere near us. If they catch you- I don't think I could forgive myself."

I slammed a hand on the desk, and said, "They took you from me for too long! I won't let them try again. I know how you feel, I felt it for half of my life... but we need to fight our battles together."

"Thank you for the sentiment, Hunter. But hold onto the rest of the crew, and Will's gun, close."

My fist tensed up, as I knew I wanted to fight for my family and friends.

But I let my hands relax. Mercy would know what to do.

I reluctantly agreed to Skinner's command, and went to bed.

104

Will, Smoky, and Egress had came to breakfast, all holding each other's hands. Egress was holding the suitcase in her hand, the other in Smoky's, and Will was holding Smoky's other hand.

She gently put the suitcase before Charlotte and I, and she gently opened it.

Inside, were three, mewling Cryptocat kittens, two black and brown like Smoky, and one completely white.

"Oh God, you didn't just make these last night, did you?!" I exclaimed

"What? OH! No, Hunter! Don't be ridiculous!" Egress said, smiling and giving me a wink.

Will said, "These are Smoky's kittens, who she wants to take far away from the Cryptocats so that they can live what she never had, a life without cybernetics."

They sat with us, as the kittens mewled and one took the meat I was eating and devoured it off my plate.

Smoky said, "I can't stand everything that happened to me. All... this." She waved a hand at her body. "I was so close to removing even the parts of me that could make kittens, but I kept it, for better or worse. My real name is Linth, but I always liked the nickname Smoky better. I... I would never tell anyone this, but if some humans are acting nice, who am I to discard them. Their father would be desperately searching for me, partly

because I stole all his crypto to leave, and partly because of my kittens…
If he gets ahold of them, they'd just be slapped with enhancements,
continuing to be so for the rest of their lives. I want them to live natural.
It's my one, desperate wish."

The big kittens were playing with Hippie, as they tried to catch each
other's tails.

"Will, can you help me get them some milk?" Smoky said. Will said
of course, and they went to the dispenser and Will asked for some milk
for the kittens from the computer.

Egress kept on smiling, at me, the kittens, at everything, and she
winked again at me and said, "It was a fantastic night, Hunter. You
shouldn't know about it, but I'm glad I don't have to keep this beauty to
myself anymore. I love every beautiful thing in outer space. The quasar
just outside the window there, the gravity of the ship, the people we've
met, and all of you. Everything.

Charlotte was sipping at her blood, and said, "What happened?
Something weird?"

Egress smiled some more, and said slyly, "Will nearly *got* her with
the *hammer*, but as he was stuck *pounding* it, she got the *star*… You two
oughta try it sometime! Not with us, though. We're saving that spot for
Smoky right now."

Charlotte grimaced, and said, "Gross. So you two are really going into
this thing, huh? Remember… too much of a good thing…" and sipped at
her blood.

"Oh, I know! But this is a dream come true. I've never felt such-
Well, of course you know what I'm talking about, Charlotte. But I'll try
to explain it to Hunter."

I quickly tried to say, "No, that's ok, I think I'm good, thanks-"

"You probably really are, Hunter. Probably really, *really* good, as I see
Charlotte smirking right now. But there's other forms of good, y'know?

When you eat a piece of milk chocolate, it's the best thing in the world. Keep it for special occasions, eat it whenever, whatever, but it's still only that good milk chocolate, and nothing else. But then you find chocolate comes in *other* flavors, white chocolate, dark chocolate, chocolate bon-bons and truffles. Sometimes you just gotta try them all, even if that first milk chocolate piece will always be your favorite. Sometimes you gotta try them with other people, because how sad is it to eat chocolate alone? Sometimes it can be better, but sometimes it's even hotter- I mean, more tasty to find someone else enjoys those chocolates just as much as you."

"Chocolate equals sex, I understand."

"Ok. But you've not eaten a lot of different chocolate, my friend." Egress said, "So I encourage you and Charlotte, even if you simply like that original chocolate, to continue to experiment with it, make it into cakes and candies, and not only raw chocolate."

Charlotte giggled, and said, "Never thought I'd get the sex diversity lecture again. You did a fair job on it! Makes me want actual chocolate, though, but I'll stick with my blood..." and sipped her blood.

She nudged my thigh with her own beside me, and I realized this one, hitchhiker cat really started some odd thoughts amongst us.

Will and Smoky came back with the milk, and the three fed her three kittens. Hippie licked from the platters as well, seeming to like these Cryptocats.

105

I liked Charlotte's maid outfit, as I dressed up like a fireman.

We looked at each other, and both said, "Nah."

I liked Charlotte's nurse outfit, as I dressed up as the naughty doctor-

"Nah."

I liked those strange Indian poses that we were trying-

"Nah."

We tried more costumes, more poses, and then we decided to get into the stories.

I liked to serenade her, the princess in distress as I was her knight. This was going to be a good one, as I had Gloria suit me up before a scantily clothed Charlotte-

"Nah."

Gloria said, "Aww! That one would've almost worked!"

We tried to get Gloria to play games with us, as she cheerfully did-

"Nah."

We turned up the music and brought out the toys, stimulating each other in fantastic, new ways-

"Nah."

We got into darker stuff, whips, handcuffs and bindings, fake incest and worse kinks, imagining her old master coming to get her-

"Definitely nah."

Just didn't turn us on. We had brief feelings of excitement, but grew bored of all of these games.

She was a vampire, who was my once hunted enemy, who I had eventually saved as I chased the feeling of love further and further, stumbling in the dark with it. I was the man who helped her recover from a chupacabra's monstrous form, who saved her from her master and being part of horrible evil, and she was the woman who saved me time and time again with her raw power and strength, aiding me in my calling. We were allies, even if we once fought each other for our lives.

And that…

"Yes."

We got in bed, and just kept our own stories in our heads, of what happened to each of us uniquely, and wow, it really, totally worked for us.

We actually liked this one album we found, too, so that was a little plus, besides doing what we usually did.

106

Someone was radioing us, as we were playing with Smoky's kittens in the sun of the observatory. Skinner and I headed back to the bridge, and found that a whole squads of ships were waiting for us near Earth. We saw they were clustered around Mercy's ship, who had uncloaked to meet these aliens.

Skinner said, "Those… Those aren't Mercy's people. They're bounty hunters."

We radioed Mercy, and she picked up immediately, but Benevolence snatched the radio out of her hand. We heard them fight for a little longer, Ben saying, "Please, Mama! This is such good experience! You always say I should get more experience!!"

"No, Benevolence. You are not fit to deal with these matters, after that deranged stunt you pulled trying to be an otter…"

"I wasn't only an otter! I was a huge, sharkotter! How would *I* know that sharks and otters don't have compatible breathing capabilities??"

Mercy finally snatched the radio away from Ben, and said, "Skinner, my husband, these people claim to be looking for you. Say you picked up a known criminal, a catnapper. I will not blow them away, but with the *enemy* approaching, they are in horrible danger amongst us and around Earth. They keep on trying to breach the hull, and sometimes… the ship can sometimes remind them not to in a little too forceful method. Please fix this predicament, Skinner."

"I guess not every cat a nap takes is a good nap…" Skinner muttered.

"Was that a joke?"

"…Um… Did it sound like one?"

"It did! HAHA! Oh God, Skinner… Good cat naps…"

"Hehe… Thanks, Hunter. I thought it went over, under, or around your head. Wasn't the best I've pulled out…"

"No, but just the way you said it was pretty funny. Like a philosopher debating the cat and its naps."

We laughed some more, and he said, "Well. Let's get some answers from our dear napper. I was really, really hoping her story was true… I guess we'll have to hand her over, because even still having all these bounty hunters around could cause unexpected problems."

"Let's go."

We went to the observatory, and Smoky didn't look at all like a catnapper. More like… Like how Kate looks, with her own daughter. Skinner asked her why there were bounty hunters saying she catnapped these cats, and Smoky looked around the ship fast, and then grabbed up the kittens, all three of them, and tried climbing up to a vent.

Skinner merely said, "Please stop her. You're right, Will. It does help to be polite to the computer."

The ship ejected her from the vent, and she landed, sprawling into the sunlight with her kittens.

She hugged them close as they meowed in terror and cried, poofing up, under the streaming sunlight, looking terrified of us.

Will said, "Wait! This can't be right! There must be something we don't know! I don't believe Smoky would ever hurt anyone."

Egress said, "I agree. Smoky has been a dream maker for me, so I want to at least hear her out."

Charlotte and I stopped moving towards her, and we listened to what Smoky had to say in defense.

She meowed, and said, "Ok. The white one isn't mine, but I just say that he's my albino cat. He's a Cryptocat prince. But he doesn't need that life! No one needs that life! The High Cats are basically only computers, being marched around by anyone who has enough money to control them!! Please don't take them away! Please don't take me away!! I know the father of my cats is cruel, and horrible, because he would give these *babies* the enhancements right away!!"

Skinner said, "That's a normal custom for the Cryptocats..."

"But it's horrible!! If things need to change for the better, then they need to change right now!!" she said.

Egress gently approached her, and stroked her fur above her ear, and she calmed down from her panicked breathing. Egress hugged her, as the mama cat hugged her babies.

Will laid a hand on Smoky's shoulder, and said, "I won't let you give her up. We joined you in this awesome journey *to help* people in need, not to cause more crimes where the bad people get away. I won't let you do this. Egress won't let you do this. Just drop us off on Earth, and we'll make sure she's never seen again, with her kittens."

Charlotte and I relaxed, and Skinner congratulated him, "That's a good stance to take, Will. You'd probably be up to captaining a ship all on your own, someday soon. Ok. As captain of this ship, we're going to send the bounty hunters far away, so they won't ever hurt anyone."

"You... You are? You're not going to kill them, are you?" Will asked.

"Do you want me to?" Skinner asked.

"...No! I don't want anyone to die! I understand we have difficult choices, but there has to be a solution!" Will said.

Ben radioed Skinner, and said, "They're here, Daddy!! We've gotta do something!!"

Skinner asked for Will's safety gun. Will handed him the gun, confused, and said, "But what will that do?"

"I ask all of you if you will soldier this battle with me, for you are losing the chance to opt out now. Someone could die, some could not come back. I need you all to agree that you will help Mercy, Ben, and I, instead of a safer alternative. If you do not choose unanimously, I will give the order to keep you all safer than in our fight."

We instantly all agreed to help in the fight to come. Smoky asked what about her, but Skinner said we'd have to keep her safer in a more harmful way.

We went to the bridge, and Skinner attached the safety gun to a laser of the ship's.

He sat in the captain's chair, and made everything instantly safer, transporting the bounty hunters to the realm of safety.

107

Even the cloud of dark ships seemed to have a cloud of darkness around them. They all enveloped Earth, as our ship the S.S.S. Sunlight and Mercy's white mothership orbited around Earth. Soon, the Earth was only blackness, not even there, as Mercy's shield defended the entire planet from the invaders from underneath those clouds.

We attached back to Mercy's ship, and we got to the pure, clean, white room of the captain's command. Smoky and her children were locked up in the rec room of the ship, to be safe, in a less safe capacity than the realm of safety. Mercy sat in one chair, as we asked her what to do. She swished her multicolored noncolored hair out of her eyes, and I saw the sweat coming down her brow. Mercy said, "I will need Hunter and Skinner-"

"And me, Mama." Ben said.

"-and Benevolence. You three have traveled in the metaphysical realm furthest with me. I will need Will, who strangely looks very tall right now, to sit in this chair and help the computer in matters that come up. You will all be in great danger. Charlotte, you will be maintaining the perimeter of the ship, keeping any forceful intrusion back. I wish to offer them mercy, but the offer is denied. Do what you have to, Charlotte. Egress, I have something special for you to do. I need you to contact someone who may be able to help. Given your… condition, you may not mind breaching your mind and better be able to keep it together."

Egress said, "I… I could do that, I think."

"Then you will be going to sleep."

And all of a sudden, Egress dropped to the floor gently, asleep, as Will caught her. He laid her gently by the side of the room, putting his anime sweatshirt over her like a blanket.

Will looked back at Mercy, and Mercy got up from the chair, "She will know what to do, Will. Please, take a seat."

Will stood up tall, and sat in the captain's chair.

A holographic panel appeared before him, showing him the defenses to Earth that the ship put up, and Will looked at the information quickly and responded when needed.

We heard a sound come from the hall, a smashing and breaking, and Charlotte said, "I'm gonna keep the mama cat alive. I'm gonna keep us all alive. Do your thing, and come back, Wolf."

She turned into a chupacabra's true form, and roared a challenge to what was invading our ship, racing down the halls.

The rest of them held hands, and I held hands with them slowly, Ben and Skinner holding my hands, as I stared into Mercy's eyes. These were my family.

And Mercy screamed.

We were taken to blackness, only blackness as far as the eye could see.

Ben was an otter swimming in the blackness around me. Skinner and I were wolves, prowling together, and Mercy was an enormous, black snake, swimming through the blackness to the forms that were approaching, even darker shadows amongst the dark.

The shadows laughed at us, *"Look at this. Look at this. The Mercy. The Mercy. I think we should eat them. Dissect them. Take out their flesh. Learn what makes them work. Create more."*

Such intelligence. Yet they only spoke like beasts.

We became our human forms before the shadows, and Mercy stood like cosmos against all the vast, infinite darkness of space.

The shadows ran at us, attacking, as Mercy shielded us from the dark forms of infinite darkness. She raised her arms, and said, "AWAY!"

They bounced back from force pushing them away, and were still clawing through the darkness at us.

I growled, Skinner growled, as we were wolves, and the otter swore at the darkness, "Shitheads! Fuckfaces! SLERGS! GO TO FUCKING HELL!"

Mercy stood tall, as a human.

A shadow bit her, and she instantly became furious, enraged, and became a snake, launching a bite at the shadow, which evaporated into the rest of the shadows.

We attacked with her, in our spirit forms, and I knew I would die by my family's side, like I should and should've.

We were about to jump into that infinite darkness, that was about to break into our planet and destroy it for good even under Will and Charlotte's defense, but then someone said...

"Hi!"

Egress?

She looked at us, standing on one, pure square of sidewalk illuminated from light above it.

"Meet Cthaklc. He's this great dude I met who I've always known!" Egress said, and pointed up.

We all looked up, even the shadows, and saw a giant tentacled monstrosity looking at us through a crack in the top, like a lifted cover. Egress walked down a sunny, shining sidewalk, and the old dweller above us overturned the box we were in, and us four all landed onto the desk in his room, the shadows only lifeless dust.

Cthaklc's mother said that dinner was ready, and Cthaklc left the room to go down to supper. He left us there, and dinner appeared before all of us. We turned back into humans, and sat at the table.

Cthaklc sat at the head.

He simply beckoned with his tentacles for us to try the food. I took off the covering from over my plate, and saw… beef bourguignon and mashed potatoes, with extra bacon and spicy peppers. Oooh.

Ben got Christmas red velvet cake, and she smiled at the fairy and gnome toy dancing together on top.

Skinner got pizza. Just good ol', delicious pizza, bunch of toppings.

Mercy's plate was empty.

Mercy looked at Cthaklc questioningly, and Cthaklc smiled back at her. He beckoned us to eat.

We did carefully, as Mercy did not. This food was absolutely delicious, and I sipped from a cool glass of water from beside my plate. She sighed, and said, "I suppose I never did appreciate the food of Earth as I could've. Was more something for my family, and their happiness was good enough for me.

"I thought I could keep everything safe, safer than I could've. I thought I could offer mercy, and it would be accepted. I did not understand fully that I would sometimes have to show people the alternative.

"What do I do, Skinner? I never, ever regret our love. It is something that led me and pushed me to greatness. It is greatness itself. What do you want, Ben? How do I make this reality the one you desire?"

Ben said, "I don't think this place we're currently in is 'a reality.' Seems like this old dweller just wants us to chill, even those guys." Ben pointed at the unmoving dust that was the shadows beside us aways.

Cthaklc nodded.

Skinner said, "We can always leave again… If we can't stop everything here. As long as we're all together."

I said, "I think you need some food, Mercy."

We all passed her our plates, and she took a little bit of each of our food to eat. She was smiling, tears in her eyes, and gently, delicately ate with us.

We enjoyed talking, as Cthaklc stayed quiet watching the scene, and we just laughed and laughed with each other, only missing Grandma who was probably still having fun with Fox… An endless ambition for fun, that woman had. I sort of *did* think of those two as my actual elderly family, by now.

They were sitting with us, like they were always here. At least they thought they were always here. We smiled and laughed some more!

Then I missed my friends, and they were here as well! We simply laughed and had fun.

I wished the entire Earth could be here, and they were, in a giant party with animals and plants everywhere too! We all burst out laughing, the grandest laughter imaginable.

And Cthaklc brushed the shadows of dust off the table, being back from dinner.

The shadows were repelled from Earth and driven away back to the darkness and abyss of space, from a great feeling of uproarious joy that surged through every being throughout Earth. The people all thanked us for the meal, and disappeared as they wandered away from us, leaving us four again to sit alone with Cthaklc.

We thanked the old dweller for his hospitality, shaking his tentacled hand, and he told us, "**Now begin.**"

108

We couldn't find the bounty hunters in the realm of safety. They left their ships, to wander that safe realm. I read a translated log by one of them.

"It's too... safe. Everything is so safe out there!! One of our soldiers is trying to forage for food, which he assures us is safe food, can be eaten by all of us, but I don't trust it.

"I... I'm taking a step outside.

"Wow. This is an amazing feeling. Like I'd never be killed ever. Like I'd never even be hurt again. Is that... That's my grandma's cottage, that the rest of the soldiers are all traveling to, like it's a pilgrim's site.

"I love this place! I want to raise my family here, and now that we can talk about it safely, we've all desired to take mates with the other soldiers, and leave whatever was behind us in the past.

"I don't know who or what brought us here. I can only say that I feel safer than I ever have been."

We decided to leave after that, and did the unsafe thing of jumping off the cliff, used to the danger by now, and transported back into our own reality.

We searched through the ship for Charlotte, and found her hissing and travelling the vents amongst the corpses of strange, dark creatures

I had never seen before. She poked her head out of a vent, hissed at us, and said, "Is it done now?"

I nodded, and she transformed back into a naked vampire woman before me, and we hugged each other close.

Will was sleeping at the captain's chair, with his anime sweatshirt over him like a blanket, Egress making sure he was comfortable with the cat, Hippie, on his lap. The holographic panel before him said all threats were nullified, and that we had won. Egress gave us some tea, and we sat cross legged next to sleeping Will and had a cup with her. Hippie just kneaded Will, that silly thing cats do, and got more comfortable.

We found Smoky hidden in a box in a closet, her and her kittens, even the adopted one, worn off from fear and sleeping finally.

Later we were looking out the window at Earth, and I was missing our friends down below on it, so Egress, Will, Charlotte, and I decided we would go back down again, to continue our lives and ready ourselves for the next chapter we would embark on in them.

The others transported down, and I hugged each of my family, Skinner, Mercy, and Benevolence, then waved them goodbye, going back home.

Blink.

The Psychedelic Adventures of the Space Otter

Sometimes… time and space just pass.
Sometimes they roar.
And the adventure of your life unfolds.

109

I had stolen a tiny piece of old dweller power, from last I met one. Or maybe he had given it to me? The toy of the fairy and gnome was very nice, especially in my youth, but I found if I could manipulate it juuuust right, I could find that glimmer of old dweller power, and even use it.

I listened to my doom pop in my ears, as I finished the rest of the chores on the ship. *"We're all gonna die and it's gonna suck, so feel sad and shitty, because now we're gonna fuck."* the doom popstar sang. I loved this motherfucking song!

I had gotten a bad habit which I blamed on my uncle. Swearing. Of course my parents swore too at times, but had hidden it when they knew I was listening. Uncle didn't give a damn. Even though my mother had tried hard to purge me of the habit, by congratulating me when I did swear, by ignoring it or even swearing herself, it couldn't really get rid of my swears. Just had to learn new ones, that even she never heard of, to keep making it fun.

I had insisted to my parents on building my own spaceship myself, so I knew what exactly were the leaky and creaky parts that needed maintenance. Still, I was so happy with my smaller ship than my parents', as it was so fast, comfy and safe, like a big round ball with fins, and had anything a lady like me could desire. She was the S.S.S. Space Otter, S.S.S. standing for solar powered steam ship. It was the only way to travel in outer space, solar steam power. When you run out of fuel, just pop the gatherers on and let them recharge from the local star. The steam mechanics worked wonders, really pushing their own.

My two best friends, both slightly younger than me but now adults as well, came to see the Space Otter and would partake in her maiden voyage. One was an Earth woman through and through called Egress Hunter, just her name is all, from my uncle and his friends. Her friends usually called her E.H. Not eh. E., H. She was flicking the switches on a side console near the ship and laughing, saying it was about time we did this. I smiled to myself. I *knew* someone was going to flick those switches, so was glad I put them there because they didn't do anything.

The other was Blizzard, a white tomcat man. His mother used to call him Snowy as a pet name, but he was finally a grown up adult. Or a grown up cat. A mancat, by now. One of the old race of Cryptocats, who unlike the Cryptocats, had no technological enhancements done on him or his siblings. That's what his mother had wanted for them, and that's what his mother made possible, as she escaped from the Cryptocats and was now living on Earth. Snowy- I mean, Blizzard, really did look good! He was white as snow, had deep blue icy eyes, and was as strong as the roaring tundra, like the humanoid cat being he was.

My uncle was still pushing along in his older age, working hard for his monster hunting Organization and giving the people of Earth the world they deserved. Whatever. Earth things, not really my concern.

My crew, only Blizzard and E.H., saluted me, saying, "Ahoy, Captain Benevolence!"

I smiled, and told them at ease. I preferred my full name as an adult, Benevolence, and not Ben as I was younger. I even had learned that Ben was really a boy's name!! Silly, how everyone but my mother called me that. Even worse, Little Ben, like there was some sort of Big Ben towering over me somewhere. Weird sort of human interactions. I was only half human, on my father's side, and spent a childhood in the stars with my family until we came to Earth to meet my father's brother, my uncle, and then decided to stay next to Earth, perched in space above it invisible and unknowable to all. My mother looked human, but definitely wasn't, and I knew so just by the things I could do and the feeling in my blood.

I transformed into a little otter, and marched before my crew, into the ship, and they followed me laughing.

110

But then I got a call from my mother, right before we were going to leave.

"Benevolence!! You know that your father, uncle, and grandma all want to see you before you blast off to who knows! I hear that Blizzard and E.H. are missing too, so you better bring them all back before you go exploring! All of your and our friends are here, to wish you good travels!"

I groaned. I wanted to skip this part, as did Blizzard and E.H.

I slowly reversed the ship, and pointed it down at Earth, passing by my mother's mothership that we had just launched from...

I landed the Space Otter gently before the big house on the beach of Australia, in front of a crowd of people. They all cheered as they saw the ship, drunk already it seemed, and we got out of the ship going down the smooth plank I installed just for this effect. Like those old legends of silly UFOs the people of Earth had seen. The people only cheered more when they saw us descend down to them.

My mother, Mercy, came up to us quickly and hugged each of us respectfully. My father shook each of our hands, but then also gave me a big hug like a loving father. I rolled my eyes as I hugged him back.

I had gotten the trick of changing my hair, any color or style I desired, and I usually kept it like my mother's, where you actually couldn't tell what color or style it was, only guess and half remember, but today I turned it into big, poofy blonde curls going down my neck. E.H. had dark brown hair like her mom's, and her mom was glad for that, that it was not like the random man she briefly liked and bedded with. Was closer to home, her hair, and not like something that she would never see again. Blizzard's was still pure white fur, and he paused as the sun hit against his fur, enjoying the brilliance.

Our parents each all came up to us and proudly showed us off to their friends that had gathered. My parents had only a few good friends besides my uncle's friends, so I got into talks with the astrophysicists, rocket scientists, brain surgeons, and this really nutty but really accurate alien nut, correcting their formula and procedures we talked about here and there. They all shook my hand gladly, respectfully, and were proud of my choice to explore the unknown, even though each and every one of them had offered me further study and projects with them.

Blizzard's mom, a black and brown furred cat who was still cybernetically altered, with Blizzard's siblings, all didn't really have many good friends besides E.H. and her mom and their friends. But they were all very happy with all of the "sort of" family they were brought into, as Blizzard roughhoused with his sister and brother, and didn't care that they were humanoid cat outcasts on Earth. Blizzard and his brother teased their sister about the human she was dating, saying it sure would be a surprise when he finds out her tongue is like sandpaper. She hit and tackled them at that, and they continued to laugh and roughhouse, as their mother looked on fondly.

My uncle and all his friends came up to meet me, with my uncle having that young looking Charlotte still on his arm. She still looked like she was my current age! Vampires like her were so cool, just like my doom pop, and Charlotte enjoyed the sunlight thanks to my father's injection that kept her safe from the sun's rays. I noticed a single wrinkle under Charlotte's eyes, but beside that she was like the college kids I briefly studied with before advancing far past all of them.

E.H.'s friends that had gathered, all speaking in that Australian accent, all fondly met me again and we made jokes and talked about what were going to now be the old days after we leave. E.H. met so much people in her college studies, and ended up with a degree in archaeology, after changing it over and over again. Partly why she wanted to go with me, so she could see the greatest artifacts of far away societies and the very cosmos itself. I was usually an outsider with her friends, but her and I were pretty much best friends so it didn't really matter.

I noticed that Kate, E.H.'s mother, and Smoky, Blizzard's mother, were talking with Blizzard by the side at a lonely table. Kate was pretty much Blizzard's second mother, so it was good they were both telling Blizzard what I already knew.

Smoky cleared her throat, and said, "I love you with all my heart, Blizzard, and I, we, all of us, always will." Blizzard's brother and sister disentangled themselves from E.H.'s friends who kept on petting them, and went to see what the three were talking about.

Kate said, "I'm so happy that we got to meet good cats like you. I think it's the relationship we make that is our family, and not forced blood ties."

Smoky said, "I need to tell you... Just in case it matters out there, that... you are adopted, my Snowy, raised Blizzard, but born as Thianh of the High Cats of the Crpytocats.

His brother and sister gasped, but Blizzard was simply calmly grim.

He said, "I... I knew, somehow. I wasn't even totally albino, like you suggested. I... I'm different, than Dusk and Mack. But... High Cat? Those are those horrible robot monstrosities! They're not even cats!!"

"You were going to be one of them as well, my Snowy. I broke in and stole you after I gave birth to Dusk and Mack. I was planning on robbing them just to get far away from the Cryptocats and their cyborg society...

but then I found you, given birth by the Queen of the Cryptocats, who is practically only a breeding pool encased in metal, to give birth to princes and princesses of Cryptocats to any who would buy and control one. I am so glad, every day I see you, whether you're smiling or frowning, that I took you instead of anything else there."

Blizzard said, "I- I have so many questions- I don't even know-"

"You will find the answers if you search for them. Just know you always have a family with us, a brother, sister, and mother who will always love you, Blizzard." Smoky said.

The two hugged, and a four armed old lady with sharp, smiling wolf's teeth hugged me.

"Grandma!" I exclaimed, and talked and joked with her as she kept on hugging me.

Grandma told me of what my mother had already quizzed me on countlessly. That I would never grow old, if I so desired, but to allow the human genes in me to shine and grow where they must, and not discard them. She was the same kind of being as my mother, that I was half of. I showed her the tricks I could do, turn into an otter and all sorts of animals, make clothes shimmer and change on my body, make people see illusions that I could conjure, and Grandma laughed and congratulated me on each one. She specifically was impressed by the illusions I could do, as everyone gasped at the traveling circus that traveled down the water's edge that appeared in their mind's eye. But she also said she never really liked those sorts of tricks too much. Very hard to handle in large scale scenarios, and were just slightly deceptive. I said that's why I made the illusion out on the water's edge, far away and unintrusive, for effect and decency.

We rejoined the party as the traveling circus traveled off to just out of view, and soon went back to the ship to blast off.

111

Uncle Hunter tried following the circus for a spell, but came back as Charlotte was calling out that we were going to leave. He ran up to me quick, and tried to offer me possessions which I declined, one of his swords, his armor, his crossbow, stuff like that. I told him I didn't want to start a *war* now!

"Hmm." he said, "I suppose that's a good attitude to have. I give you my blessing, then. And please, take what I feel blesses me, my rosary."

I accepted the small gift, and shoved it in my pocket. I hugged him one more time, then waved everybody goodbye as we got on the ship. Blizzard gave everyone a load ROOOOOAAAAARRR!!! His brother and sister could never really pull that off. They only made cute little meows! I'd really never heard such a loud roar from him, except for when their Earth cat, a little fluffball called Hippie, died. All three of them were crying and moaning, and Blizzard roared in despair that their "uncle" had passed away. This roar scared the crap out of everyone, but they laughed it off and cheered for us. We saluted them goodbye, and started countdown.

"This is Captain Benevolence Wolf, Crewwoman E.H. and Crewman Blizzard at the ready. We're starting departure. Everyone stay clear of the launch site... or at least don't touch the ship when it's taking off." I said on the radio. This was all mainly for show, but we counted down as the crowd backed off from the ship and counted down too.

"10! 9! 8!"

Blizzard and E.H. looked back at their parents, and we all knew we'd miss the people we were leaving.

"7! 6! 5! 4!"

We all had our seatbelts latched to us, and I spun the little gnome and fairy sitting at the head of the ship. We were going to do this, and let whatever lay before us come as it may.

"3!! 2!! 1!!"

I looked up, to the sunny blue sky.

"LIFTOFF!!"

The round Space Otter gently leapt off the ground, making barely a sound, and we launched into the sky as I really worked the thrusters to give the people a good show. It sparkled and flashed in different colors like a rainbow, leaving a rainbow trail in the sky and making a loud, soothing humming sound as we drove into the sky.

As soon as we launched free from Earth's gravity, the gnome and fairy started spinning faster, and faster, and faster, becoming a whirring blur, and we all started to grin and laugh. Whooping in glee at the journey begun.

For we were not simply going to explore space. We were going to explore all realms and the fabric of time itself.

We heard strange music around us, and the stars and planets of space distorted and changed colors as well.

A crack in the window of reality opened before us, and we launched into the unknown.

112

We were still traveling through a nonsensical sort of plane, our ship the only thing with real substance among it. I picked up my rosary and looked at it, as I walked out of my room and yawned, smacking my lips together after taking a short rest. That party really took a lot out of me. I passed Blizzard reading from a nature wildlife magazine on cats (basically a nudey magazine to him) and he looked up at me, and did a little gasp.

I said, "…What? What's with the look?"

"Oh, I understand… This is where we all have the mass outer space sex orgy, right?" he said, smirking.

I was confused, but looked down at my clothes- Shit!

I quickly whirled an illusion of clothing on me. Forgot about that.

"You mean you don't ever really wear anything?? Just go commando all day?? I sure wish I was you!" Blizzard said.

"I- Sometimes!! It feels nice!!"

E.H. came out of the bathroom with a towel wrapped around her, and Blizzard said smugly, "And the orgy continues."

E.H. pointed at him, "You better keep it to yourself, big guy. You go find all the space ladies you like, but we're all crew here, and we gotta not start any drama."

"True that. Just tell Captain Commando to keep a little on so the eyes don't wander too much..." Blizzard said.

I waved on the illusion of a nun smock on, and danced around bowing with my rosary as Blizzard laughed.

E.H. said, "Oh... You know Hunter thinks that will help. I mean, I was raised Christian by my mother, but all the things we've seen... Just keep it as a lucky talisman or something, ok?"

I waved my hand and put some of my usual flair on, just some jeans and a tie dye shirt, and said, "May God bless you, and this, and us, and himself, and the LORD ALMIGHTY WILL SAVE THEEEEEE..." continuing the joke. Blizzard laughed, but E.H. started scowling. I laughed it off and shoved the rosary back in my pocket- I think I'll just go wear some normal pants now.

Still, when I got dressed in my room, I swore I felt like something was in this rosary, something strange... I didn't really believe in any human religion, preferring what I could see and feel instead. But I felt the rosary, and it didn't make any sort of magic religion thingy, or even make me feel holy, but... I noticed the worn wooden beads, eroded by a hand who prayed the thing constantly, probably in his worst moments, needing the religion and its soothing mantra more than anything else in the world.

I did keep it on me, and kept it in my pocket most of the time. At least to remind me of my uncle, and that my family will be there for me, even in my worst.

We sat down to dinner, what we called dinner, eating pleasantly together at a table I had picked out for the ship's dining area, as the kaleidoscopes outside seemed to go a little gentler now.

Blizzard chewed on his raw steak, as E.H. and I ate ours cooked, and he said with his mouth full, "Besides the jokes, I know that there might be... tension between us later on. You hear of those guys that set out with their girlfriend for grand journeys? What do you think they said when I told them I'd be with *two* women, but not having sex with either of them? They laughed and called me a pussy cat."

"You should know better than trust what those travelers say…" E.H. said, her Australian accent ever apparent, "They just come to our land to wank off and watch kangaroos hop. They aren't serious about anywhere they go, and probably aren't serious about the relationships they keep on the road either."

"I know it's been difficult with the ladies for you, Blizzard, being a huge cat and all, but we really are all gonna be friends, just friends, or we'll seriously have to rethink some of our journey plans. None of us like being third wheels, I learned that much in Earth culture."

"Well… Three is the magic number…" Blizzard said slyly.

E.H. and I laughed, and I said, "At least we're getting this all out in the open. No, we shouldn't have *any* crazy threeways. Just not gonna happen. I thought you two, y'know, were like brother and sister? That people growing up together tend not to find romantic attraction between them?"

They looked at each other briefly, and E.H. pointed at him, and said, "I've seen him naked plenty of times. I even once caught him masturbating."

Blizzard immediately was embarrassed, I could tell by how his ears went backward, besides his facial expression, "N-No! I told you over and over again, I was cleaning myself!! Cats do that!!"

"That's what it's like having a giant cat teen to live with." E.H. said, taking a bite of her steak.

"Better than me having to hear you and those dumb outback boys you brought home…" Blizzard said in a grouchy tone, "If I wasn't spooked, then they were, cuz you sound just like a ghost when you do it."

The red went to E.H.'s face, and she said, "Ok, let's not start talking about the weird sex things we had to witness…"

"You're both so lucky!!" I said, smiling happily, "I'd give anything to have someone I could trust so closely with personal and sexual things like that."

E.H. and Blizzard looked at each other slightly, and frowned. Blizzard turned to me and said, "I think you're lucky living in *an actual spaceship* most of your life."

E.H. said, "I think you're lucky not even having to be from Earth. Earth sucks. I learned over and over in college we're a bunch of cannibalistic, raping, incestuous thieves, even in high society. How do you think the nobles all got ousted out of power? They were all having children with their brothers and sisters, and didn't even have the mental capacity or even just genes to fight off disease and disability. It's so *cool* you're an alien. You too, Blizzard, but you've been on Earth so long you even sometimes talk like an Aussie when you say certain things."

"I ken pullllll arf a terxan arcent toooo…" Blizzard said in a horrible Texan accent. We laughed, and I showed how it was done proper, then an African tribal accent, then a Russian accent, and German, and Canadian, and American, and Spanish, and…

"Ok, we get it, Benevolence." E.H. said, rolling her eyes with a smile.

I smiled, and said, "I love languages. I can probably pull off being a translator for both of you, even though I have those tech headsets from my dad to translate for us."

"The headsets would work for most places in space, but not… wherever we're going. Where *are* we going, anyway? I thought we made plans to stop off at the first intergalactic antireality bar we found, just so we can smash a bottle on the ship and say she's afloat." Blizzard said.

"Huh. Now that you mention it… does anyone smell beer?" E.H. said.

"I've been drinking from one?" Blizzard said, raising his can of beer.

"No… Like… Malt. And hops. And… mmmm… smoking men. I smell smoking men."

Blizzard sniffed, and said, "I've probably got better smell than you, and I don't smell anything- Oh wait. I smell bratwurst. Like when I went to Germany. Literal, delicious, bratwursts!! I think we're here, guys."

I sniffed, but I didn't smell anything, besides the machinery of the ship and its steam. I never went to a bar before. I've been to an inn, a brewery, a tavern, a pub, and a strip club that one time but never a *bar*.

113

We stopped by a bar afloat in the weird landscape around us, just bubbles like an everchanging colored lava lamp now, wherever you looked. Looked pretty trippy, everything in this weird expanse of nonreality.

The bar was playing the first music you wanted to listen to, a great sound on all accounts. I turned my hair into a flirty redhead's, and we walked up to it. E.H. looked at those smoking men by the side of the bar. She sniffed in deep, and said, "I hope they have a cig. It's the one thing I forgot to pack. You guys go inside, I'm gonna ask 'em for one."

E.H. went up to the men, who to me looked like Elvis Presley and George Washington smoking cigarettes and having a discussion on lukewarm milk.

"Yuck." Blizzard said, as he followed me into the bar, "No one likes lukewarm milk. Gotta be at least one side of the temperature or the other. But- Ooh. Look at that huge beer that one sweet chickie is having..."

"You shouldn't call women chickies, or hoochie mamas, or babes, or-"

"Hey hoochie mama!! Can I get a sip?" Blizzard catcalled to the woman.

She raised the huge beer to him, winked, and began to drink the whole thing down. Blizzard went up to her and cheered for her to keep going.

I sat at the bar, and waved to Cthaklc across the bar who was very interested in what a woman with white scars on the side of her face had to say. She turned to me, and waved with a happy smile. Cthaklc urged her to go meet me, and she sat beside me.

The woman shook my hand, and said, "Lamb, at yer service, guvnor. Isn't it fun to talk silly here?! Give it a go!"

"Er. The codswallop concerning cornhole curtails convincing concept. Heehee… That was kind of fun."

Lamb laughed, and drank at her beer. She said, "You know Cthaklc? Oh shucks, everyone does!"

"Who is he again? Like, exactly."

"…Everyone knows him! See, Cthaklc?"

Cthaklc sighed a sigh of relief, and left the bar, squeezing Lamb's shoulder with a tentacled hand before he left.

Lamb turned on a very… flirtatious posture to me, and said, "You're a good looking lady. Wanna come home with me?"

"Wow. Fast. No, I'm currently on a grand adventure and journey through everything I can or can't conceive."

"Aww. I used to not like ladies very much, being with one… but I've found the world can be so open, and I can be open with her. Even in places like this, which don't make sense and shouldn't exist, I can find people that exist and mean something to me."

"You are a very attractive woman. I can see how any would and could be attracted to you. If you don't mind me asking… How did you get here? I noticed this place denies the placement on maps."

She tapped the scars on her face with a wink, and said, "I found this can be a passport. Being slashed by something that shouldn't exist can do that to you. Besides Cthaklc constantly hitting me up to go roaming around nonexistence with him… He's a good man- or whatever he is. I think even he has trouble figuring out where existence, and he, begins and ends."

"He helped me when I was ten. I think he's kinda cute."

"Heehee... I'll tell him so, but don't expect an old dweller in your bed so easily!!"

"No... I just like him, is all. I don't need to have sex with every person I like."

"But you have to like every person you have sex with, otherwise it's usually a no go..."

"I... I think so. I've had... I shouldn't tell you..."

"Had a hard time finding the one?"

"...In a way... I just want to have fun!! But everyone on Earth is so dumb. I was kinda fantasizing that I'd meet someone amazing on the road."

Lamb rolled her eyes, and said, "People don't need to be smart to be good looking. Or have good hearts. Sometimes you gotta step off your pedestal, and look for the common ground you can stand on."

"You're very insightful, and I feel very relaxed with you. Buy me a drink or two, and maybe I can even consider your straightforward proposal."

"I'll do better! I'll buy you three!! Bartender, give me and my new friend some beer!! Oh. And get that cat and his new lady friends something, maybe some bratwurst, and a special treat to the woman outside smoking, and get me something to go for Cthaklc, and over there, those two lovebirds, get them..." she continued to state people who needed drinks, and paid with a bottlecap. One bottlecap. I was very confused.

I woke up, even more confused at what I had done. I think I had a fun time? I definitely did, as a naked Olivia Lamb slept beside me, with that smile still on her scarred face. I fixed my hair back up into a gloomy short black hair, and yawned, kissed Olivia on the cheek, which she snuggled up more comfortable in bed, and went to breakfast.

Blizzard in boxers was feeding two nonexistent ladies in their underwear who existed very much in the ship, and they were all snarfing down food like it was the first meal they had ever had. I saw Elvis leave the ship, then Washington, and they called out that they'd wait up for E.H. and our crew outside. They started smoking and speaking about rock and roll and independence out the window.

The ladies, who always seemed to change their form, sometimes looking like cartoons, other times grim abstract, sometimes pseudo realistic, and more, said they were ready for the honors to happen too, and both kissed Blizzard on the cheek at the same time as he smiled eating his food.

E.H. got out of the shower, and looked very... rejuvenated. She snarfed down the food Blizzard had, as he growled slightly, but she hit him on the head and continued to eat. Olivia came out, naked, and said, "Where'd we put my clothes, Ben?"

Shit!! Even she knew people called me Ben?!

She saw the panicked look on my face, and kissed me on the cheek, and said, "Don't you remember, sweetheart? You told me all about everyone calling you Ben. You sorta liked it when I called you it too."

I relaxed, with her arm over my shoulder, and said yes, I did remember that. It was fuzzy, but I did like that name as a kid... I said her clothes could be in the washer/dryer?

She looked in the machine, as Blizzard and E.H. stared at her bending over to look, and she said, "Oh! Wow! Thank you very much. They smell so clean!"

E.H. looked at me with a surprised sort of accusing look, and Blizzard giggled.

I felt the red rush to my face, and said, "Well, if you two weren't so busy all night, you would've known who my love friends are."

They both rolled their eyes with a smile, and I smiled too as Lamb got dressed.

We got out of the ship, dressed and ready for the next journey, Lamb beside me, George Washington, Elvis, the two nonexistent ladies, E.H.

and Blizzard, as I threw the half drank bottle of booze at the back of the Space Otter, where it smashed and was celebrated on its maiden voyage. We cheered!

I'd have loved to learn more about everyone here, but they all said they had to go. Lamb kissed me sweetly, which I somehow still enjoyed, just her friendliness perhaps, and we waved them goodbye as we got back into the Space Otter and flew off to the next destination.

114

I realized, as we were searching for the next exit to any reality, that I acted a lot like my mother at times. I didn't specifically know why! I thought I was fun, but my mother was a strict badass alien who had a dark past! How did I act like her, when I was trying to be fun me??

My dad was fun, always playing basketball with me, playing these old games that a friend of his gave him with me, and always treated me like a human. Sometimes I despised that, but a lot of the time I found being human was really a blast. It was hard for him when I surpassed him in intellect and became who I desired.

But there I go talking like my mother again... I just swore off the thoughts, like my uncle did.

I wish Grandma could've guided me more, instead of just my parents, but even if she didn't need to as much as them, her lessons shone through with the genuine acceptance she always doled out on me. One such lesson that I'll strangely always remember, is that an ancient vampire likes it when you are just as powerful or more powerful than them. It was a strange lesson, but something that could be used in any scenario, in a different context.

People liked it when you strove to be their equal, not in a downsizing way, but up to them in whatever manner. Not showing off that you're better, no no, don't do that unless you want to be quickly snubbed.

That you can show off something that is as wonderful as they are, in a different manner than they are accustomed to. People will adore you for this, and usually will accept your differences easier then.

Oh, fucking finally! An exit! The sign said the Big Ben. Shit, this was probably where I'd meet my nemesis.

I quickly drove out of the psychedelic alignments and off the exit anyway.

There were clocks everywhere, clicking, clocking, ticking, tocking.

I smashed into one by accident, as Blizzard and E.H. went to look out the windows.

The Space Otter quickly regained its composure, but that big clock fell to the streets of people before it.

Fuck!! I didn't mean to cause a panic, and those people were panicking!! Looked like an old British town-

Fuck. That was *the* Big Ben. And I was the one to make it come tumbling down.

Fuck, fuck, fuck!!

I kept swearing, and tried to blast off through this slight past as quick as I could.

I drove down the sea, relaxing for a bit, as E.H. and Blizzard sighed in relief. They said I could get the hang of this strange sort of travel, had to, or they would never be able to go home again.

Home?

Oh yeah. I guess that place back where we started was… home.

Although I noticed a man down by this continent we were now travelling under. I saw my uncle attacking Charlotte over a young boy. Charlotte and the boy saw the light of our ship, but ran off into the night as Hunter missed the shot, then the next. He went to inspect what we were and where they went, and we quickly flew away.

We were passing through a city. We stopped beside a skyscraper, as I asked *why* my uncle was in this place, but E.H. looked out the window... to see her mother having sex with a stranger in a room.

Kate screamed, and threw a pillow at us, and the man went to shut the shade.

I quickly drove off.

We were over a whole 'nother planet, as I decided to get out of there, and we saw cats all over the planet, Cryptocats, by their cyborg enhancements and humanoid posture.

I saw the Queen of the Cryptocats, as Blizzard gasped, giving a decree to let Cryptocurrency fall to the abyss, and her reign supreme. The cats cheered, and continued to invest in cryptocurrency as certain crypto fell or rose in the market.

Blizzard said, "I don't like this place, Benevolence."

I rocketed away, and passed over some sort of farmland, seeing a young man scream as he was abducted by a black ship.

I felt my body go cold. That was Dad, like, at age 15.

His screams were silenced, as he was taken into my mother's transport.

I screamed, and went back to the destroyed Big Ben, flying out of time and back into the psychedelic wastes of the nonexistent highway.

115

We found a phonebooth at the edge of the highway, as the highway started to look all the same despite its color and nonexistent agenda. We decided we needed to make some calls.

Blizzard was first, as E.H. and I smoked outside of the booth with these great cigarettes Washington gave her.

Blizzard asked his mother, "Is there any way to free her? My mother, the one who birthed me."

"...I'm sorry, Blizzard, but I don't think she even wants to be freed. Her mind is gone, and she's only a robotic toy by now."

"...I can't accept that. I can't allow the woman who birthed me to go on being a slave."

"She's the queen, son. She's the ruler of the Cryptocats, in one way or another."

"...You stole me from a horrible fate. You must know how I can help more like me."

"I don't, Blizzard. I can't even get rid of my own cybernetics. I just hope you can keep this spot in your life for yourself."

"Thank you, Mom. I love you, but I need to find more answers, so won't be able to talk to you for a while."

"I love you too, my Snowy. Please, be safe, and very careful if you have to approach the Cryptocats."

"I will. Bye, Mom."

E.H. was next.

She accused her mother, "How can you just go and- and- have sex with that person you call my father?? He was no one, someone I intensely disliked just by the look of him!!"

"…What? Vino wasn't a bad man, I told you about this before."

"What kind of fucking name is Vino?? How can I have a father whose name is WINE?"

"…It was a very confusing time in my life. It was a very lonely time. I really don't want to talk about this, but since you're so adamant, ask me any question you desire. Shoot."

"…How come you never let me know my father?"

"I never knew him, Egress Hunter. He was gone soon after we did that, and I had no desire to know him any further. Why can't you look at the family we have? Hunter? Charlotte? Will and Egress? It is why I named you after them, E.H."

"…I always will love all of them, every day, but I can't accept that I have no father. It just makes no sense!!"

"If you must look for a father, look at Hunter, who has always cared for you."

"I- I know that, I love the old man like everyone else, but- but- I-"

She started crying, as Kate consoled her. E.H. had a strange sort of family, just Uncle Hunter's friends basically, and she loved each of them more than some nonexistent father.

I was the last.

I asked my father, "How come- I feel dread in my heart."

"That's normal, when facing the unknown."

"Please… Tell me how you survived. How you got Mom to love you. I don't expect it was easy."

He sighed, and said, "It was difficult, and really wasn't something I planned. It just sort of happened, both those things. Your mother and I found we were happier being with each other, and after that had you."

"But- Those shadows... Those people!! *I am one of them!!* How- What can I do?? I don't want to be them!! I never want to be them!! I want to be like you!!"

"Your mother had the same sort of sentiment. She would also like to talk to you-"

"No. I can't talk to her right now. I just- I need time to think. I'm going to keep my hair curly blonde for now, just to hold onto something that sticks, not use any illusions, and only turn into an otter when I feel like it. They're my favorite animals, if you haven't guessed."

"I did know that, Captain of the S.S.S. Space Otter. Just know we both love you, and will talk more about these things if you need to. Preferably in person. I always preferred to talk in person, even though your mother really wants to talk to you by how she's looking at me."

"I... I love you too. I love you both. But please give me some time. Goodbye, Dad."

"Goodbye, Ben."

116

We kept driving down the highway, and found an underwater ball playing old jazz music. Cthaklc waved us over, strange enough, and went down some stairs into the water into the crowds of underwater creatures amongst them, where we quickly lost sight of him.

"What a cool looking dude." Blizzard said, "Like a squidtopus."

We got out, and the mermaids attached a bubble of air on our face, and we dove into the deep water ball, that's only cost was no bad jive.

People were swimming around, dancing cheek to cheek as somehow the old music traveled really well underwater. Had a sort of lasting echo, that really improved the performance. The fat mermaid with tentacles instead of fish bottom sang for all of us.

We mingled, as they were all so warm and inviting, and the deep sea anglerfishman grabbed me up in his arms, leading me with his light, and we danced an old style dance. I laughed in my bubble of air, and swam danced with him, swimming around him and then becoming an otter, swirling around him as he continued that happy anglerfish grin.

E.H. and Blizzard danced with each other, as more of the fish folk watched them, cheering at each underwater flip and twirly twirl.

Blizzard at first was repulsed by going into the water, but he seemed to really be enjoying himself! E.H. always loved to dance, and I think her sort of adopted brother knew this, and indulged her funness.

I ate the shrimp at the bar, enjoying them even if they were slightly... alive. Wait, would Mercy do this? My mother? Would she eat poor animals that were twisting and turning in horror?? I liked them as my otter form, but quickly turned human and swallowed down my bite of shrimp, desiring to not have any more.

It was a fun party all and all, and even though a few fish folk hit on us and our group in fantastic old jazz fashions, we both quickly realized that wouldn't work with us being land dwellers and them being in the more crustacean or fish capacity. We still made some good friends, and I searched everywhere I could for that old dweller, but couldn't even find a whiff of him.

Instead, I found Lamb outside of the ball, as I went out for a cig. My lighter and cigarettes E.H. shared with me were both wet, but Lamb had a nice cigarette container that kept any water out. A passing devillady with an angel man with eagle wings lit our cigarettes, and I talked with Lamb for a second.

She smiled in happy, dripping wet delight seeing me again, and said, "I'm really glad you weren't a one time thing. Seems like we're both headed down a similar road."

"I guess. I feel like I'm going down the path to Hell though, and trying to resist."

"How so? Isn't everything so great, here and everywhere?"

"...I really don't think so. Always knew so. I'm destined to becoming like my mother."

"Haha! A sad fate most of us have to fight. But I'm so glad whenever I can catch things I do that are like my father. He died when I was a teen, and I'll still always miss the salt of the earth he was..."

"...You don't worry you'll become just like your parents?"

"All us young folk do. I mean, I guess I'm still *pretty* young, if I can pull it off to someone like you, then heck, I'm young. All how you look at things."

"…How old are you? I never got to ask."

"How old are you?" Olivia said, grinning.

I really didn't want her to think I was some young kid if I revealed my age, so I said, "…Anyway, I think you're still around my age. Allow me to offer you a beer from my ship? Something to get the water out of our mouths?"

"Haha… Thanks, but no thanks. I'm gonna spend the night with a cute blowfish that asked me to be his wife. Gonna let him down real easy, after he uses those cute lips of his."

"…Oh. I thought, since we're traveling on the same road… We'd be a little more firmer friends…"

She kissed me on the lips, and I felt a spike in my heart at that. Woah. Like, damn, woman. Leave me alone with that good feeling. It's too much.

She smiled, and said, "We'll see each other around. I gotta go blow a blowfish!! So much fun, everything is here. See ya!"

I waved her goodbye, as she got in a submarine a smiling blowfish man opened up for her, her dancing still to the distant sound of upbeat, wild jazz from the party.

117

I was swearing at myself that I let that fine catch Lamb get away, but E.H. and Blizzard just giggled as they got back in the ship and dried themselves off. I was sitting grim and wet at the wheel, as I just faintly listened to the music outside of the ball. That's life.

I mean, I liked anyone who could somehow arouse that spark in me. Always looked more to the individual instead of looks, but I learned that I used my smarts to reject people… and that was always disappointing to me. Maybe I was just dumb, or should act dumb to be happy.

Blizzard slapped me on the back, and said, "I think that anglerfishman asked me ten times where you went. You've got quite a great hand at reeling them in, Benevolence!"

They both giggled, cuz the joke was they were fish, of course. Ha. Ha.

I sat grimly at the wheel, as E.H. threw a towel at me, and I asked them if we could leave.

E.H. said, "You're the captain. Let's get going."

I immediately started up the Space Otter, and we went down those majestic highways some more. I suppose the party did make me relax a bit.

Blizzard smiled, as he heard the rock'n'roll play down the highway from a CD he put in.

The highway changed color, and I knew we were on the Highway to Hell. It was red, black, and gold, and we sang to the music as loud as we could.

A huge truck nearly pushed us off the road, and as I tried to regain command of the Space Otter, we went off the road and into Hell.

I saw the many different rulers of Hell pass through my eyes, sometimes it was only just a dark, blank landscape. But this was where the sinners go.

A few demons tried to pull us further down into Hell, as I tried to get back to the psychedelic highway.

They screeched, trying to drown out our music, and I knew somehow the music was keeping the rest at bay. The lights of the ship started flickering.

"We can't stay here!!" I shouted out.

The sky started raining blood, jamming up the Space Otter's machinery somehow, drenching deep into the works. The steam from the ship was now red. The music stopped.

I forgot how I could get out of this. I knew there was some way, it was just at my mind-

I pulled out the rosary, trying to pray for an answer, and somehow I knew that was the answer.

Ask and yeh shall receive, and all that.

The demons screeched at me audibly praying the prayers Uncle Hunter had taught me, and E.H. quickly started praying as well. Blizzard held onto us, and mumbled along after us.

A light was shining down a road, away from the highway. I launched the ship down after it, and we traveled down a dark road with a light at the end of the tunnel.

It felt like I was running from death, or maybe chasing it, I don't know, but we continued to follow the light down the tunnel.

118

I let Blizzard take the control as I rested in my bed.

I remembered Olivia, my leg under her crotch as she- used her fingers, and she said as I tried to make her more comfortable, "I like this spot." and stroked my leg with her other hand, rubbing her other hand against it some more…

It was hard to sleep, as arousal and tiredness fought for control of my body.

I slept a little in twisted and turned nightmares, wondering when the change would happen and I would become evil. My cute otter face was drenched in the blood of enemies.

I got up and drank some water from the bathroom sink.

Why was the water salty?

I saw Blizzard almost sleeping at the wheel and asked him.

"Hrgm? It's always been salty, Ben…"

"But it's like, so salty."

"Yeah, it's always been. I thought it was still drinkable since you okayed everything."

"…But it's- Oh yeah… It was pretty salty. Guess I never really noticed that. How are you doing?"

"I keep following that damn light through this abyss, but it keeps being out of reach. I race to it, I play coy and follow it slow, but it stays just out of reach, like I'm being led on by an anglerfish."

"Is it a good thing? Or a bad thing, you think?"

"Why's the water salty anyway? Is it our piss constantly recycled or something?"

"No, nothing that gross, although very efficient in many circumstances. Even the current blood on the ship should be properly purified by now. The ship picks up water from the surrounding atmosphere, or anything that can be converted into water. I've even got a hand of molecular distortion, so with certain elements I can make a certain kind of 'water.' It's not that hard, but probably why it sometimes tastes salty."

"So you just twist molecules around until it resembles something like H20? So I'm really drinking gold?"

"Could be, if that's what the ship requires."

"...That's so cool. I'm literally drinking gold, and I'm gonna tell everyone. Ha..."

I put a hand on his shoulder, and said, "That's why I like you, Blizzard. Besides your wit, you like all the weird things that life can throw at you. Get some sleep, I'll follow the light."

"Thanks. I was starting to see things if I stared at it for too long."

He got out of the seat, punched me on the shoulder, and then went to his room, as I sat in the chair and watched the light, the ship making progress, but the light just out of reach.

If I stared at the light, I saw things too. Strange, beautiful things, but just out of reach. If only I could catch it...

I saw Hunter as I had first seen him, and then later again happy with my father. I saw my mother and Grandma care for me, playing with me as a child. I saw the happiness I first felt when I got accepted to college at age 13. *That* happy feeling quickly wore off... but I was happy then.

My mother had to give me an illusion just to make me feel more secure amongst the older, actually dumber, college kids.

I saw myself playing with a young E.H. and Snowy, as he was called then. They loved to hear my wisdom and jokes, and I was so happy when they grew up too and became the great friends that they are. I was happy with everyone at Hunter's House, what we called the house in Australia, with the ostriches in the back fields. I loved to pet Dusk and Mack, Blizzard's siblings, and sometimes they just cuddled with me as large cats instead of cat humanoids.

I saw Olivia Lamb's face in the light ahead of me... Gosh, what a good kisser...

But then I saw her on the side of the road with Cthaklc, trying to hitchhike.

119

I quickly let them get in, trying to make the slow moving plank move a little faster, and they jumped in as fast as they could.

"You got, like a bong or something? We reallllly need a good rip after being in this depressing place." Lamb said.

I said E.H. probably had one, and Cthaklc gently knocked on her door that I pointed out to him. E.H. got out of bed, also not sleeping well by the look of it, and then jumped back in terror as she saw the old dweller smile nicely to her. He made the gesture of lighting a bong, and E.H. said, "…Wha…? Um. Sure."

She ruffled around in her things, and took out the blue, purple, and green bong, and gave it to Cthaklc. Cthaklc bowed slightly to her.

"Does he ever speak?" I asked Lamb, as she packed the bowl of the bong and Cthaklc took a hit, lighting the green bud nicely with his technicolored lighter.

"He never shuts up!" Lamb said.

I didn't know if she was joking, but she also took a hit of the bong. E.H. came out, and she took a hit too. She offered it to me, but I said no thanks, I never really liked weed. It only temporary increased dopamine response, and usually gave one not very good rests. I already had horrible sleeping problems, especially after I yelled at my dad about my mother, so just stared off into the light as they talked…

It began raining in the darkness, only the sound of it making it apparent and through the light of it from the headlights.

I couldn't keep staring at that light anymore, as they giggled and made jokes, making silly sounds which they laughed at. They said they were probably in a really long train tunnel. I reminded them it was raining, and that rain didn't happen in train tunnels.

"You sure you don't want a hit?" E.H. offered.

"No, I'm feeling paranoid enough." I said.

"Let her be, E.H. Some people just can't take the good stuff." Lamb said.

"Oh, I can take it, watch me. I'll neutralize it in my body in a second-" I said, hand open for the bong.

Lamb took the bong, and hit it herself, then said as smoke was coming out of her mouth changing her voice slightly, "I'm serious. Not everyone needs weed just to have a good time, it's better if it ain't used so dependently anyway. Some people's bodies just are different, is all."

E.H. said, "Yep. I was only being polite, Ben. You know Egress? The Egress I was also named after? Can't even smoke the stuff anymore, cuz it causes her to have a psychotic relapse for about thirty minutes, or the length of the dose."

"Oh yeah, because she has schizophrenia."

Lamb said, "Some people just find it to be unpleasant, or just fall asleep with it! I feel like it makes me really kind, and just enjoy the moment for a bit... Watch out for incoming trains! Choo choo!"

They laughed, even Cthaklc with a soft chuckle, and I smiled.

We kept feeling good and happy, and after Blizzard got a little rest, he was also hanging out with us. He too declined the bong rip, because as he said, weed is no good for most cats, but still got a beer from the fridge. He explained to us that his instincts get really funky when he smokes weed, and that he only enjoyed a good weed if that weed was catnip.

And the light got closer, when I looked back at it.

I gasped, and raced forward, as it got closer, and closer, and closer, Cthaklc, Lamb, E.H. and Blizzard choo chooing.

"Choo! Choo! Choo! Choo! CHOOOOOOOO!!!!" we all chooed.

The light hit us, and it felt so clean, so pure, so good. The ship, and our very souls, immediately felt purified.

The light was flashing, every color, like a disco dancer's dream.

I saw my father dancing that disco dance, as my mother watched. He gently guided her in a dance, and they danced together. She laughed, her first ever laugh I could tell.

E.H. saw her mother and Hunter go to Alcoholics Anonymous, Kate being happy and kind with everyone there, even to Hunter who she thought was a lost soul in desperate need of aid. She was kind of right, as Hunter was only there to find and kill a vampire, with dark, paranoid eyes and an antsy for alcohol look to him. But that's when Kate met the person that E.H. could consider a father.

Blizzard saw his mother, Smoky, grow up in the Cryptocats planet, being attached with cybernetics forcefully, and then by choice as she matured in life. She lost everything she had, all natural feelings on her skin, in her heart, and she tried to hold onto what was good to herself in her mind. She kept the parts of her that could make children, and later it was the best choice of her life, with her three children, even the adopted child she called Snowy.

Cthaklc said, "*It's **a good feeling**.*"

Lamb was sniffling, as she saw her father and all the moments they shared with each other and their family, and she was soon crying, but with a smile on her lips.

She hugged me, as we felt the luminescent brilliance, and we all were soon smiling and crying.

We could've stayed there forever, but I saw something curious out of the corner of my eye, and followed the sparkling fairy out of the light.

120

We got out of the train tunnel, and to a beautiful, majestic land with huge mushrooms and plantlife, like we were tiny and they were- Were we tiny now? Where were we?

"Fae!" Lamb cried out, smiling.

"Where's that?" I asked.

"Here!"

"Oh. OH! So all the fairies I met in my youth- OH! THERE ARE GNOMES HERE, RIGHT??" I said, immediately filled to the brim with excitement.

Lamb smiled, and said, "Just drop me off over there by the side of the road. I have friends I want to see-"

"ARE THEY GNOMES?? PLEASE TELL ME THEY ARE GNOMES. CAN I MEET YOUR GNOMES??"

"Yes! Haha, they're gnomes and you can meet them!" she said, laughing.

"HRRR. Hrrrrr... Rrrrgrrrrahrhhahahh..." I gurgled.

E.H. said, "She has a thing for gnomes."

Blizzard took the wheel from me, as Lamb and I would go out and meet her GNOMES. They would come back later, and explore Fae with Cthaklc. Lamb said nothing bad would happen to them with Cthaklc there, and Cthaklc gave her the tentacled thumbs up, and they flew away in the Space Otter.

I gasped, looking at that little mushroom path, and gurgled in my throat some more as I followed Lamb down the trail, skipping as she was. "Makes me feel like a little girl again, being here..." she said, laughing in childish glee and swinging around a large blade of grass over the small blades of grass.

I just stumbled behind her, on the lookout, like I was as a little girl, for the gnomes.

"There! THERE. THERE!" I pointed, running over to what I thought was a little red hat, but it was just a large mushroom... Lamb just laughed and continued to skip down the path as I followed her.

Eventually, as I hid behind a large log, we FOUND THEM.

There were beautiful tiny little cabins made of huge mushrooms, with smoke gently rising from the chimneys, clothes hung out to dry, one tiny plastic pink flamingo in front of one house, but where were the gnomes? THEY MUST BE INSIDE.

I hid in a closer spot, as Lamb crouched down to knock on a door. She waved me to come closer, and I gently crept up beside her.

Then I saw him.

The gnome came out of his cabin, smoking his pipe, looked up at me as I was frothing at the mouth at him with wide open eyes and-

He stumbled back, and ran back into the cabin, as I tried to catch him.

"FUCK! I was so close!!" I yelled out.

Lamb gently nudged me back, and she called out, "Helloooo dear fellow! My name's Olivia! I'm looking for some gnome friends of mine, who might remember me. I helped save them from the Blonde Witch!"

It was silent, but the gnome gently crept out of his cabin, and tried very hard to ignore me with my hands raised ready to launch at him and catch him, as he looked up at Lamb.

He blinked his eyes, squinted at her, and said, "Toadstools and turkeys! It is you!! Hey everybody, it's the lass who saved Diddy, Bonks, Balaster, Bomba the Drummer, me and my brother, and all our friends from the Blonde Witch!!"

The other gnomes crept out of their cabins, as I twisted and turned around myself, ready to catch at least one of them.

A few of them had broomsticks and frying pans raised in defense, but they saw Lamb in the circle they enclosed us in, and cheered.

They danced in happiness around us.

It was the most majestic and noble thing I had ever seen, seeing those old tiny men with long beards and red hats dance around us.

We sat with them, Lamb and I cross legged with them as they sat on toadstools or redcaps, or even brought out a few plastic lawn chairs. They brought out a large keg, large to them, more of a pitcher of beer to us humans, and they filled their mugs and offered us each one as well. We drank from our tiny mugs, and they told Lamb that it's never been so great in Fae, although without the old Fae sovereigns, some places can be a little more wild for folks who don't expect it. One brought out a tiny radio to play, telling us to listen to this.

It was screeching, roaring, metal. Powerful beats, awesome instruments, and the singer singing like the boomiest voice I ever heard. They told Lamb that the drummer was someone she helped save, and Lamb just said, "That's nice." like it wasn't the greatest honor imaginable.

They rocked their head to the beats, some giving the metal salute, and I finally felt at peace, drinking this delicious, heady gnome brew. Who knew gnomes were so cool? The answer is I did. I knew that gnomes were cool.

They turned the music down after the first song, so that we could talk some more.

They explained that their wives and kids were all off visiting their parents in law. I was confused at this. I thought every gnome was a little burly guy with a long beard and a hat.

A gnome took off his hat, just so I could see that it wasn't attached to him or part of him somehow.

"Um. Olivia, this girl is really weird. I don't think she would be very safe here without someone-"

"I want to take one of you home with me, where I will feed you and comb your beards, and we will be in love for the rest of our long lives." I said.

The gnome cleared his throat, and said, "...Maybe she'd get along well enough alone. Anyway! Let's all pack up, guys! We're going to the METAL Gnomes show tonight, care to join us? As long as *she* doesn't try to grab me again."

I shook my head back and forth quickly, and Lamb laughed and said sure.

We walked through a twisty path through the undergrowth, as the gnomes all sang their favorite metal songs, and soon were at a large field where the event was taking place, a huge tiny stage before us with a crowd already cheering for the band, the METAL Gnomes. "We got here just in time! Go on, ladies, try to find a good spot!" one of our gnome friends said.

We listened to the METAL music with all the fairies, pixies, leprechauns, satyrs, gnomes, dryads, and other creatures of Fae.

Boomie was AWESOME. He BOOMED, like **THIS.**

THE DRUMMER PLAYED DRUMS LIKE MY HEART WAS AND IS ONLY BEATING FOR HIM.

THE GUITARIST STRUMMED THAT GUITAR LIKE I WANTED HIM TO STRUM ME Ohohohh..h.h...

And that bass man.

That bass man.

That bass.

That bass man.

Bass gnome.

Such bass. Need more.

MUCH BASS.

GNOMES. OF METAL.

Afterwards I tried getting their autographs with Lamb, and I finally noticed my friends had been here, enjoying sitting on the lawn of the field and drinking tea with wildlife that talked and acted like humans with Cthaklc. I rushed up to the band, and the ENTIRE METAL GNOMES signed my t-shirt. I thought I'd never take it off, but I NEEDED TO PRESERVE IT.

I took off my shirt, to encase it in glass, whooped at the METAL Gnomes one more time as they were leaving the show, tits to the band, and Boomie gave me a thumbs up and they strolled off into the forest, all four of them in METAL power, even as a large crowd followed them back to their gnome houses.

In the ship parked close by, I encased the shirt carefully in glass, and then hung it up in my room to never leave its post. I had tea with the others after I put on a much lamer normal shirt on, and the animals with my friends all talked about how philosophical that last song was, that we should keep this form of life and society while we can, because it would someday be gone. "It seems the METAL Gnomes are going towards a more philosophical direction after their whole victory against the Sorcerer of Fae. It would be a shame if they lost their great raw power, and it seems they already are losing it..." a Cheshire cat said, drinking tea.

I shook my head and my tea back and forth, saying, "You're wrong. Because I only felt the primal feeling of being with those gnomes, with all these people. It's like they were fucking me with their music, and I really, really liked it. Who cares if they appeal to people with intellect? Just broadens their audience, while they keep their older songs close at hand. I need one of them. I need one of them so bad. Do you think they'd mind if I caught Bomba the Drummer?"

They all laughed, even my friends, and the Cheshire cat said, "They'd certainly miss their favorite freedom movement drummer… Perhaps you should talk to a few of those younger gnomes, who seem to be looking at you. Maybe they'd be up to satisfying this strange whim of yours."

I turned behind me slowly, and saw two shy gnomes, who were staring at my breasts. Probably since I showed them off to the METAL Gnomes and everyone, definitely not just one time.

I asked Lamb to help me meet them, because I was so nervous, and she grinned and said sure.

In the end I was smooching his little gnome face by a pond, as Olivia had her own gnome sitting on her lap and they calmly watched the pond.

I took him further, just carried under my arm, further into the woods and had sex with a gnome. Well. Whatever it's called having sex with a miniature MAN like that.

121

"What the hell is this...?" Blizzard said, as he found a tiny gnome shoe in the coffee machine.

"Nothing!! That's mine!!" I said, and snatched the shoe back. Blizzard heard some thumping from my room, and barged in even though I told him not to, ordered him as his captain, then begged him please, please, please let me keep him, as he took the naked gnome out of my trunk. I had spent all night trying to keep him bound after I invited him to the ship. He lost pieces of his clothing here and there as I chased him around the ship, and then I finally caught him and stripped him down, tied him up with a few belts and gagged him to be kept in the trunk as my eternal lover. I poked a hole in the trunk! It was humane!

He took the gnome outside, as I sighed, "Oh..."

Blizzard undid all the belts and the gag, and the gnome ran as fast as he could down the lawn to escape me. Didn't even look back once. Probably knew I'd see the attractive look of fear in his eyes and then know I'd have to continue chasing him. I gave up running down the lawn after him after a while, and walked back to the ship. Little dude was way too fast and wily. So hot.

"I think I'll have a beer for breakfast instead of coffee..." Blizzard said, "Is E.H. up? She spent all night doing these Fae mushrooms with Cthaklc. I hope she's not tripped out of her mind still."

"No, she's been sleeping, but she drew us some really amazing art... on the back of the ship. Also wrote basically an entire book of gibberish for us to read." I said. We went back to admire the art on the back of the ship.

"Wow. I don't think it's half bad." Blizzard said.

We looked for a long second at us three riding a literal Space Otter in the vast, super colorful expanses of the unknown. Our faces were all underneath the picture, very realistically if a little abstractly done, including Cthaklc's and Lamb's.

"I think so too. It's unique. I guess we can let Sleeping Beauty rest."

"E.H.? As Sleeping Beauty? And I guess that you're Snow White with the Seven Dwarves?"

"They're not *dwarves...* They're gnomes! Completely different."

"Right..." Blizzard said, shaking his head and going into the ship.

I followed him, and said, "Where'd Olivia and Cthaklc go? Should we be worried?"

"Nah, I don't think so. At least I'm not gonna worry anymore. Cthaklc just wandered off in the night, as I tried to keep track of E.H. I was calling out all night for him in Fae, and I guess our E.H. got artistic when we left. I spent hours listening to strange music and trying to follow it, with lights that always changed place and position... I think without my natural cat instinct, as well as with our little tracker to the ship, I don't think I'd have ever made it back. Where'd Lamb go?"

"I don't know. I had a lot of gnome things on my mind last night."

"Mhm. I guess they'll be ok. Would be nice to see them again. Let's get moving."

We heard E.H. snoring loud as the engines, and we started the Space Otter up to continue our journey.

Blizzard heard some strange music, something like a fawn playing violin, and he quickly launched away from Fae, up, into the sky.

"Aww… We can't stay in Fae just for a few more days?" I asked.

Blizzard looked very tired, and said, "If I have to hear that song one more time played by that stupid fawn, I'm going to lose my damn mind and strangle him. Fucker thinks it's funny or something. The only way I kept my damned sanity was the METAL music that was still stuck in my head."

"You're going kinda steep. Let's-"

I slammed to the back of the ship, and fought to turn the gravity unit on, as Blizzard angrily still kept flying straight up.

E.H. slammed into the walls in her room, but still slept.

Blizzard just blasted some music, as I finally climbed up the ship in vertical, and hit the gravity unit, which was outer and inner layers circling each other in opposition to create an artificial gravity effect. I slammed to the floor, the proper floor, and walked up to Blizzard. I asked him how he was doing, because something seemed wrong.

"I was thinking over and over as that stupid music played. Had a long time to think just wandering a crazy place like Fae, and I realized something I have to do that I cannot put off anymore.

"We're going to the Cryptocats, and going to save my mother."

The fairy and gnome toy started spinning in front of the ship, and the crack in antireality opened before us, and we flew through it again, taking a brief segment through the psychedelic highway, but getting off at "The Cryptocats Cash Cow."

Blizzard laughed, and sang a song, a strange, nonsensical song.

"There's a ship in the sea, dancing like a monkey,

"There's a rocker rocking good, in the off key,

"I'm goin home, and there's nothing you can do.

"I'm gonna save her, and save myself too."

He kept singing this odd song, and I asked him what it was.

He said, "LYRICS, YOU FAWN BASTARD!! I GOT THE LYRICS!!"

I squeezed his shoulder as he laughed maniacally and tired, and went to make some coffee for E.H.

E.H. was soon smiling with her coffee, saying she's never slept so good. She asked us, "After we all went to the old man up on the mountain, how did you all get down? I didn't see you all for a while, until I was back at the ship. You all looked like paint! Weird shrooms I took…"

"Man on the mountain?" I asked.

"And the dragons twirling in the sky, to the bottom of the sea to the very abyss of Cthaklc's eyes, and so on? You don't remember?"

"…No, and I don't think it happened to any but you."

"Oh. That's a bummer, we had such great times!"

Blizzard said, "Anyway, do you guys see that? They're probing for our ship…"

"Oh, no problem there." I said, sitting beside him in one of the chairs by the driver's, "I got all sorts of anti probing tech. Should we turn invisible now, or later?"

"Now." Blizzard said. I hit a button, and even we were invisible. "I… How the heck am I supposed to drive like this?!"

"Um. I didn't really figure out how to get only the outer layer invisible, actually I thought it'd be easier if absolutely everything was invisible! It's got charm, instead of being only *partially* invisible." I said, as space rolled by underneath us and I was speaking to no one, not even able to see myself.

"…You drive, please."

We accidentally bumped into each other, and then I sat in the driver's seat, as I knew all the controls and feeling of the ship by heart.

122

The Cryptocats planet loomed below us. Twinkling, dark cities amidst large seas on small landmasses.

We landed on top of a building, and got out of the invisible ship, which turned us more visible. The ship locked itself unless someone with our specific DNA opened up the ship. I hoped we'd be able to get to it again, but I preferred this tall building as a safe place rather than down in the streets to be discovered by the Cryptocats.

Us three looked off the building, as the tall building below us played strange Cryptocats music with a chorus from an open window from a radio perhaps. I gave us all translator headsets, and the music turned out to be about the Queen's Decrees.

I used an essential all powerful lockpick on the door up here, which looked just like a normal key until it met a lock, then became a bunch of lockpicks working purposefully for our goal. It was easy to hide if used right, and I was so happy I could actually use some more of my contraptions.

The building turned not to be somewhere for entertainment. This tall building was a hospital. We followed Blizzard with purpose, acting like we were supposed to be there in some manner, as either medical staff or patient. E.H. and I looked in shock as the machine like cats rushed a cat down the hall who was only a bloody torso and a head, his spine flicking and twitching in cybernetics.

Blizzard was only grim, and we quickly passed the robotic sentinel cat to get into an elevator.

The sentinel was looking interested, and was about to follow us, calling out a robotic "STOP."

We quickly pressed the button to go to the ground floor.

Another doctor cat with spider fingers tapping into a console on his arm got in a few floors down.

He looked up at down at Blizzard, and said, translated by the head-sets we were using, "Are you here for…" he sniffed at Blizzard, and said, "Cats in Hell. How are you still alive? You don't have any cybernetics on you!"

"None of your business, doc. We're… going to the Queen's… next gathering."

"Oh… That's a shame… I'd say you should go straight to the emergency room so we can fix you up, along with your slerg companions. But the Queen's Decrees exempts people from most duties. How did you get the slergs? A fair gift from a lover?"

We stood quiet, E.H. and I, as Blizzard looked back at us.

"Yes. A wonderful gift. We think we're going to get married soon."

"Married? Why don't you just upload each other into each other's consciousness? Then you can be more modern."

"…What?"

"You become the other, and the other becomes you. It was all the rage in the High Cats a few decades ago, and now normal cats are doing it too. Makes you strong, as the other's strengths are copied to yours, and your flaws are both covered by the other."

"…I'll have to think about it. Let's go… slergs." Blizzard said.

I didn't like the word slerg. Meant an abducted human, basically, but it was good of Blizzard to play the part. E.H. and I followed obediently, and followed electric signs outside celebrating the Queen and her decrees. We followed the signs, but all there was at the end of them were booths, which the Cryptocats went in, their cybernetic eyes and screens changed from whatever color they were to gold, and they left the booth.

We looked at the booth, and I realized it was some sort of mass consciousness producer. One would go in here, and be connected to the rest, and the Queen never had to make any sort of in person announcements.

"How's- How does it work?? I need to know how to find her! I need to speak to her!" Blizzard said.

E.H. put a hand on Blizzard's shoulder, and said, "We'll help you with this for as long as you need. But please stop shaking that thing so you don't draw any attention."

Blizzard sighed, and left the machine alone. I knew that the Cryptocats used crypto, and on Earth I was recently trying to trade crypto and believe I made a fair share. We went to a restaurant, and I could barely just buy the cheapest thing on the menu for us. Coffee.

We drank coffee, looking out at the now rainy Cryptocat night, machines that didn't even look like cats anymore marching down the streets.

Something brushed up against my leg.

I picked him up, and looked quizzically at the orange Earth cat.

"Uncle Hippie!! I... I saw your corpse!! How are you alive?!" Blizzard said. I put the cat on the table and E.H. pet him, as Hippie meowed at Blizzard. Blizzard said, "Uhuh. Uhuh. I didn't believe that was possible!! Are you really Uncle Hippie?"

The cat looked at him with a look that said, "Are you serious?"

"You are!" Blizzard said, and hugged him.

The cat licked Blizzard's face, and Blizzard looked so happy. Hippie meowed one more time solemnly.

Blizzard said, "I... I was thinking that too. That could be the only way." Blizzard looked at E.H. and I both, and said, "I need to get a cybernetic. A slight cybernetic, only like one robot eye, and then I'll be able to tap into the Queen's Decrees."

E.H. said, "No!! Please don't give up this!! Your mother wanted this for you for your whole life! To be a natural cat!"

"My mother is a Cryptocat Queen." Blizzard said, "And Smoky is just... just someone who really cares for me. Let's go. This coffee sucks anyway. Thank you, for everything, Uncle Hippie."

Hippie seemed to bow, and then jump into a crack of nonreality.

We followed Blizzard out the door, and into the rain.

We snuck back up the hospital, using the fire escape this time, and got back in the ship. I quickly launched us into the upper atmosphere, and set to work on Blizzard's eye.

"Left, or right, Blizzard?" I asked him, when I was finished building it.

He blinked both of them, and said, "Left."

E.H. helped me, as I knocked him out with knockout gas, and removed his left eye. E.H. was sweating, and I told her she needed a firmer hand keeping his lid open. She immediately did so.

I inserted the robotic eye, a scanner camera for the ship altered to work with Blizzard's body, made as close as I could to be like his own eyes, but I was no master artist, and it still was red instead of Blizzard's blue. I spent a long time attaching the machine to each nerve, and then it sunk gently into his head, becoming him.

I let him rest for a while, checking just in case there were any flukes, and then revived him.

He blinked open his eyes.

He felt at it, feeling the cold metal briefly, then he sat up, and roared.

"I am now a Cryptocat." Blizzard stated.

"You should be able to see anyone using camo now, like the ship being invisible." I said, as I wiped off my hands, "Plus you can record or take pictures with it like a camera, and upload it via signal to your phone. Looks quite dashing, eh, E.H.? Humans all go crazy for heterochromia."

She looked into his robot eye, and said, "I don't think I like it. Doesn't feel like he's whole anymore."

"Whatever, I don't like it much either... but let's go down to get me hooked in." Blizzard said.

We stopped down by the Queen's Decree booths, and Blizzard walked in, walked out...

And his hair was all standing on end, and the eye was gold.

123

Blizzard filled us in on the ship of what he was experiencing.

"There are cats everywhere around me. Sometimes I pass through them peacefully, sometimes they become me, but cannot do so completely as I only have the eye. It is only perception.

"There is security everywhere, even in this strange place. But they greet me as their own, calling out my name like they always knew me.

"They call out Thianh of the High Cats.

"I march forward with the others, and soon I feel-

"I feel-

"I feel-

"I am the Queen. I am her offspring. I am none other than THIANH, the STOLEN ONE.

"The Queen takes me aside, hugs me, and saying that it is good I am finally home.

"She is glad for the theft, for now I am in a position of great power to her.

"I can resist.

"I can control.

"She offers me her hand... and I... I take it.

"I follow this Queen cat, who has only a single patch of white fur above her mouth. This is the patch and pedigree of her kind. The rest is mechanics.

"Although she shows me pictures of a young kitten... Her, the only time she was ever not prosthetics and cybernetics.

"She reluctantly tells me that I...

"I don't want to do that.

"I don't.

"Please.

"No.

"I can't. I want to help you!! I don't want to let you suffer!

"But this life is suffering. And you will help prolong it, with me. Become my King, and we will force the Cryptocats to suffer and writhe at our hands, no longer to be treated lightly, as a holiday, as a distraction. Come, Thianh. We have much to do.

"I decree you as our King, to every and all here."

I quickly tried to stop the transmission, as I saw a look of horror on his face. As the tears streamed from his eyes, both tear ducts still intact. I tried to eject the eye, but that would cause extreme pain-

E.H. hit him on the side of the head with a bat she had gently. Gently enough.

And he fell over.

His eye turned back into red from gold, and he passed out.

I quickly launched the ship away from this planet, far away. Let whatever come happen later, and not today.

124

"Ow..." Blizzard said, as we were cruising through space and he got up from his bed we had lifted and carried him to.

E.H. immediately hugged him, and he hugged her back, then I did too.

"I feel so stupid, guys. I don't think I should've traded... my normal cat body... to become a King..." Blizzard said, looking down at his feet.

"Let's forget about it for a while. If it happens to come up later, then it will. How about we go down to the inn on Mars I started?" I said.

"Oh yeah... The failed 'Mars Bar.'" Blizzard said.

"Yep! Still got some booze there. Let's just chill, maybe say hello to our parents when we can." I said.

E.H. sighed, and said, "I liked that we went excavating Mars when you and I did, Ben. I was so close to finding an artifact, I know it. But Snowy... let me wash that gash on your head... Looks like I really did you good..."

Blizzard let her wash the back of his head, as he laid on the couch. She kept on stroking his cheek, and looking into that cyborg eye, as he looked away depressed.

I launched down to Mars, finally to go to my super secret special sanctuary!! The Mars Rover Inn, the best medieval inn on all of Mars! The only medieval inn on all of Mars. The only inn on all of Mars. The only *building* on Mars. But it was mine!

I had asked my parents for a loan to invest in a business venture, and even though they could manipulate Earth money into their hands like breathing air, they gave me the money and I promised them I'd repay them back in full, as soon as possible. I bought all the materials and did all the labor myself.

I… ahem… never really paid them back, and they just chalked it up to some birthday/Christmas money given, but I'm sure I'll pay them back one of these days!! Who *wouldn't* want to go to a medieval inn on Mars?

We walked in, as E.H. held Blizzard's hand, and I breathed in that familiar old timey inn smell, as the old lute music played from the speakers, holograms of old troubadours acting like they were really playing the music. Just as I left it.

I asked the hologram wench to get us some beers, and she winked and some beers appeared before us in a teleporty way. I cheered to us!

Why was I the only one cheering?

I looked back at Blizzard and E.H., and they were whispering something, as they held each other's hands and looked deep into each other's eyes.

"…Guys? Why aren't you cheering? That's the best part of a medieval toast."

She kissed him on the cheek, and they disentangled themselves, to party with me! Hurrah!

I was soon stumbling around the inn, enjoying the crackling fire, the old minstrel holograms playing, besides the empty seats. Someone was going to come here soon, I was sure! I just had to broaden my audience, or something like that.

"OOooooOOooooooOooo…"

What's that? My first customer! No doubt a ghost who followed us into the realms of the living!

"OoOoooOOooOoooOo… Fuck…"

She seemed to be a little lost, in one of the rooms and not out here with all the people! All the people that would show up!

I called out, as I slammed open the door, "Party's out here, ghosty-"

And I blinked, and scrambled quickly out of the room. Did they even hear me among the loud moaning?! WHAT THE FUCK.

I just saw my best friends doing the deed.

I tried to reckon this out in my head. They probably felt infatuation and tension between each other since they could first feel those feelings.

But... they were my friends. They were banging each other's brains out, and I was out here with the wench. Stupid wench. Her face always did look crooked.

I turned off all the holograms and music of the bar, and just sat by the roaring fire.

"OOOOoooOOOOooo... YEAH. Yes. Yes. Yes. Yes. YES!"

I put my face in my hands. This is going to make everything so awkward.

And then I heard a loud roar, as the ghost moaned loudest she could.

The red in my face was still ever apparent.

I waited a long time outside by the fire, just drinking my ale, until they came out of the room to look for me. Blizzard said, "Ben? What's up? You look kinda gloomy. We were just-"

"Taking a nap." E.H. said.

I grumbled.

I carefully looked at them smiling innocently at me, and glared at them.

"E.H. We're going to look for artifacts. Blizzard. Hold down the inn, and wash the ship." I said.

"I kinda like the look of it right now, drenched in blood, and E.H.'s fantastic artwork-" he said, beginning to look at E.H. again.

"Do it. I command it as captain."

"Ok." Blizzard said, hands raised in defense.

I grabbed E.H., we put on our oxygen masks, and went out into the wastes of Mars.

125

E.H. was giggling at some pictures someone sent her. I asked her if I could have a peek, and she said it was personal. I argued with her about it, saying that we should trust each other, and then I eventually ripped it out of her hand to see pictures Blizzard had taken of her with his cyborg eye, as well as older pictures of her that he had sent her.

This made me furious, and I threw the phone at her and stalked off into the wastes. "Hey! Don't you walk away from me!! What the *hell* is wrong with you?! You act like this is new!!" E.H. yelled at me.

"Well, isn't it?! What the fuck are you two doing, sneaking around my back and- and- doing that!!" I yelled, pointing at the phone.

She cradled the phone to her breast with a pissed look, and then put the phone in her pocket. "So?! So what?! Is this any worse than you having sex with that Lamb woman and gnomes?! You act like you're not even human!!"

"I'm- I'm not human!! I don't like this sort of trickery and deceit, anyway!!" I yelled.

She calmed down a bit, and said, "I just love my family. I love them a lot, not saying I'd have sex with all of them like Blizzard, but Blizzard needs this more than anyone. He gave up his- his very own *body* just so some bitch Queen can make him her plaything!! I'm not losing SNOWY like that!! HE'S MY SNOWY TOO!!"

I felt my anger flash in my mind. A dark sort of blankness. I said, *"You always were a slut. A stupid bitch who couldn't satisfy herself, or anyone she was with. He'll leave you. What if for me? What would you do then? I'd break him. I'll break you too."*

Her face went pale in anger, and she said, "STAY AWAY FROM HIM, YOU ALIEN FREAK!!"

"You fucking slerg!! Yeah, that's right, walk off, and keep walking off!! I HATE BOTH OF YOU!!" I yelled as she walked away from me.

I continued to walk down the wastes of Mars, not sure where I was going, in intense anger.

I flew down the wastes instead, as another Martian storm approached.

I tried going as a big black crow for a while, but I had a different thought... This would be even easier in my natural form.

My TRUE form.

I let all being of human, animal, or Benevolence go, and as a shroud of darkness, I flew in the storm of Mars, the storm one with me.

They would all be me. They would all accept me. Not as Benevolence. I didn't even know who as anymore.

There was something bothering me, even in shadow form, so I stopped at a hill and returned briefly into my human form, only dark black curly hair on instead, to see what it was.

I reached into my pocket and-

I burst out crying.

I lost the rosary. I lost it, somewhere in the wastes.

I frantically searched for it, becoming darkness, human, animal, whatever could help me find this piece of me that reminded me of my family.

I screamed, as I cried, remembering all the horrible, harsh things I said to E.H.

I kept looking. It had to be somewhere. It had to!!

I slumped down in the storm, black hair being blown in the breeze, and continued to cry.

I saw lights further away from me. Who was that?

The Space Otter approached me quickly, cleaned off, and landed before me, slow plank descending.

E.H. and Blizzard waved me in, and I hurried inside from the storm.

"I-I-I am so sorry, Ben. I wasn't thinking straight. I wanted to tell you, we both did, but didn't really know how." E.H. said, "Blizzard helped me calm down, and we both knew we needed to find you out there in the storm."

I continued to cry, as we hugged each other, and said, "I'm so sorry, too. I didn't mean those horrible things I said. It's been difficult for me, because I don't know where my real origin lies. And now I- Now I- I lost my-"

"Shh..." E.H. said, rubbing my back, "We'll look for whatever it is when the storm passes. Let's just orbit in what I think has been my favorite home ever, the Space Otter, and just chill."

Blizzard hugged us too, and said, "I understand what you've been feeling, Ben. I'm a Cryptocat King. The fuck am I gonna do now? E.H. has been reminding me of home, instead of all the stupid things I stupidly think that I stupidly want to do..."

I looked up at him, as he looked sad. I asked him what he wanted to do.

"It doesn't matter. I just want to be with you two, right here."

We just watched a movie, as Blizzard and E.H. sat far away from each other. I told them it was ok. E.H. looked at me gently, and gently sat next to Blizzard as he laid an arm around her, the look of love between them.

I looked out the window, as we all just watched a silly space movie, down at the storm passing by below us.

When it abated, E.H. helped me use my high tech gadgets correctly for unearthing artifacts, and we-

We found my rosary, as she held it to me. I grabbed it gently, looked at it for a second, and put it back in my pocket.

126

We went back to Earth, as Blizzard and E.H. argued how they would... break their relationship to their parents.

"Egress will be a supporter. I just know so. Will will take Hunter's side probably, whatever his stance will be." E.H. said. Will and Egress were sort of like E.H.'s uncle and aunt. "Hunter may have his doubts about the relationship, but I know we can convince him that we truly do love each other. He'll actually probably relate to us, with him still hooked onto Charlotte. But my mother..."

"And my mother!! And my siblings!!" Blizzard said, "You know I've been thinking about you for a long time. But when my siblings get word... They're going to tease me to shit. What will my mom say when she knows I've been banging the neighbor girl who lived with us?!"

"I don't know, I don't know, I don't know!! This will be so, so hard..." E.H. said.

I said, "I think it will be ok. It will be kind of a shock, but is nothing we can't understand."

I piloted the ship down to Earth, to let whatever happen may.

We were soon all sitting before Hunter, Charlotte, Kate, and Smoky, with Dusk and Mack hanging out by the side, all in the kitchen of Hunter's House.

I said that E.H. and Blizzard wanted to tell them something.

E.H. held Blizzard's hand, and said, "We're... We're boyfriend and girlfriend now."

Blizzard squeezed her hand, ready for the onslaught.

Kate gasped, Smoky looked stunned, and Blizzard looked back at his siblings, who were not snickering or teasing him, just looking at him gently.

Kate said, "But- You- We raised you as- We *raised* you as-"

Smoky said, "I think you should rethink this relationship."

Blizzard said, "We've been thinking about it for a long, long time. You know it's difficult for us as cat people on Earth, and well... I love E.H. I love her a lot."

Hunter was grim, as Charlotte looked at him, then back at us. Charlotte said, "If I could say something..."

"*No! No, Charlotte.*" Kate said forcefully, "I won't let this sort of step sibling shit happen in my house. I won't hear of it!! Hunter, tell them!! Tell them they should just... Think about this!!"

Hunter looked deep into E.H. and Blizzard's eyes. E.H. looked terrified meeting his gaze, and Blizzard gulped.

"You really love each other? This isn't some sort of brief fantasy you're both playing out?" Hunter said.

E.H. and Blizzard nodded. Blizzard said, "Yes, Mister Wolf. I am so grateful to you for giving my family somewhere to stay, and we always feel accepted by you and everyone here... I just know I have to follow my heart, over stupid things I may think."

Hunter sat back, relaxed, and Charlotte said, "I'm going to say it now. I don't think this is any worse than our previous relationships, all of us, and I know that E.H. and Blizzard will care for each other deeply, probably deeper than any of us can even aspire to. They were raised together, and now they're just taking the relationship to the next level."

Kate looked flustered, and her and Smoky went outside so they could discuss this.

Blizzard put his hands to his head, as E.H. slumped back, and Hunter smiled. He said, "Give those two some time. A good long time, and maybe they'll eventually see that you two will be great loves to each other." Charlotte smiled and held his hand.

"What about Uncle Will? And Auntie Egress?" E.H. said, "I was really hoping for their support."

"As you know, they are off on an expedition to a new alien species that appeared in our galaxy, sanctioned by Mercy and Skinner, Ben's parents. But I'm sure they *both* will be delighted at the news. I sanction this relationship, with whatever outcome will happen, as long as you don't have any weird interspecies babies yet-"

"Um. Hunter. They can't have kids together." I said, knowing the biology of both species.

"They can't? Oh God that's a relief…" Hunter said, and slouched back. Charlotte smiled and grinned, squeezing his hand some more.

"Dusk? Mack? You've been awfully quiet." Blizzard said, looking at his siblings.

Dusk rolled her eyes, and said, "It's not like we didn't make enough jokes about you two, with you two, that we didn't start getting ideas…"

Mack laughed, and said, "You were always her favorite white little pussy."

"Hey!" Blizzard said, laughing, "Oh cats… Thank you two, so much."

They nodded to E.H. and Blizzard, and the four just laughed as Hunter, Charlotte, and I smiled.

Kate and Smoky ditched us to go out and get drunk. They stumbled back in when we were all just hanging out, some watching nostalgic Earth TV, as I just hung out with Hunter and Charlotte in the kitchen.

Kate slurred as she pointed at me, "Yoooouuu. I thought youuuuu had betttter commmmand of yourrrr shiiiiipppp."

"Believe me, it was as much a surprise to me as it was to you." I said.

Smoky just threw her arms in the air, and said, "Weeee can't blame anyone!! Only ourselves!! Look at them, snuggled on the couch, like fucking idiot kids!"

"Mom? Is there something I can do-" Blizzard called out.

"You can shaddup. I'm gonna sleep…" Smoky said, and stumbled up to her room to go to bed.

Kate slammed to sitting on a chair beside us, and said, "So yer saying we shouldddd all just be fucking. Fuck, fuck, fuck. In thisss fucking house? Charlotte and I double team you, as you watch the kids fuck?"

Hunter looked embarrassed, but Charlotte snarkily said, "Would you like that?"

"No!! I just want to have a normal family, without stupid *sex* getting in the way!! I thought we could achieve that."

Charlotte shrugged, and said, "I know we do all care for each other. Love each other. We don't all have to do it, but apparently those 'kids' do. They're adults. Let them make their own choices."

"Grrr. I liked it better when you were a bitchy bitch I could shut down just by being nice…" Kate said, and got a beer from the fridge.

"What can I say? People change. We get tempered in *love's* firm embrace…"

"Stop teasing me, you cunt. See!! I'm the bitchy bitch now, and you better all deal with it!!" Kate yelled out, slamming down her beer.

Charlotte said, "Kinda hot, eh, Hunter?"

Hunter just cleared his throat.

"Should've just neutered those damn cats…" Kate mumbled.

Kate eventually just continued drinking, and I told them I needed to have a long talk with my mother.

And somehow my mother knew, or just really wanted to talk to me. I was taken to her ship in a blink of the eyes.

Blink.

127

She was standing before the window to Earth, the one she liked to read books by, listen to music by, or just watch the world go by below her.

She turned to me, and I noticed she had changed her hair to be like mine, curly blonde, but my own hair was still black. She tried to reach her arms open for a hug, expecting me to race to them as I usually did, but even though I wanted to, I did not.

I sat on the one chair in the room, and said, "You stole someone from their rightful home. You took *my father* to whatever horrible domain you're from."

"I did, Benevolence. I did."

"How can you be ok with yourself?? How can you even accept to keep on living? You *tortured him.* You turned him into a *slave* beneath you. How do I even know you still aren't doing so?"

"Your father could attest to the treatment himself, if he also wasn't on that expedition with the people he is grooming to be space captains, ambassadors, and intermediaries."

"I know he could. I know he could tell me how horrible and awful you are, and I would believe him."

"...I am sorry, Benevolence. I am sorry I could not have averted it, even amongst myself."

"...So you're just going to accept you're a monster?"

"Are you?"

"No. I will never be like you. I will continually be *me*. I'll only be a human, forever, with whatever black hair that's stuck to me, and just be happy with that. I'll give up on *space*. On *traveling*. I'll just make a life amongst the humans, and be happy."

"...You don't have to make that sacrifice. We live in a wonderful community, amongst people that aren't constricted to one setting. Would you lock yourself up? To hide from the monsters?"

"No! I just want to be me! And not you!! I felt how horrible it feels, being... what we really arc. I know we are monsters!!"

"I know you never were or are a monster, Benevolence, just like your father. It's why we keep with each other, instead of abandoning ourselves to agoraphobia."

I felt very sad, all of a sudden, and said, "Then why do you love me? If you're a monster?"

She knelt before me, and held my hand. She told me she would always love me.

I just couldn't stop the tears, and she wiped them away from me.

"I- I love you too. I know you've tried hard to, that I've been sort of a disappointment-" I said.

"I never believed you were a disappointment from the first day you were born. You were born by me, in this body, that I have never cast off except in extreme danger where a different form was needed. I have named myself Mercy, so that I could give mercy to others. That I could give the being of me that I loved and cherished, to others. You and Skinner were the first I could share this being, myself, with, and be loved and accepted back."

"And I am Benevolence... a grand name. Kindness itself. I... I'm so happy I am your daughter, but I don't want to slip. To fall into whatever our heritage is or was."

"Neither do I. It takes a firm sense of being in oneself to not slip or stumble when addressed by the... monster inside. I am always here, to aid you in this matter or others, and will always stop whatever task I am working on to be by your side, to raise you up, and not cast you down."

"Thank you, mother. Thank you so much. I've missed you for a while."

I got up off the seat and she stood before me, and we hugged.

I let her hair transform into the multicolored noncolored version she was comfortable with, and my own back into curly blonde.

128

I worked hard on a ship for E.H. and Blizzard, with their help, and soon they were ready to liftoff from my mother's mothership. They hugged me goodbye, but decided they needed to once and for all address Blizzard's past, and learn from each other where they may. I cried, I'm not ashamed of it, as they left, waving goodbye to their sleek ship that could pass cosmos, just enough comfortable room for two.

I went down back to Earth, and drank at the bar. I guess bars weren't that bad. Nothing like a medieval *inn...* but still ok.

I went back to Hunter's House, walking down the beach to it, and heard a familiar voice talking to Hunter, as they ate ostrich omelets on the beach patio.

"Yeah, Wolf! Like a damn orgasm!"

"I think so, too! And there's so much of it, as well! I just put half a block of cheese on the thing, and eat omelet for days..."

"You mean... You don't have any ostrich meat?"

"Why would I need ostrich meat, Lamb?"

"...Forget it."

I gasped, as I saw Olivia Lamb and my uncle Hunter Wolf eating ostrich omelets. I ran up to them, smiling in glee at Lamb, and she quickly got up and tackled me to the sand, rolling around with me and hugging me. Hunter watched, and I kissed her on top of me.

She blushed, and said, "Not in front of my *boss* now."

"Boss?" I said, as we got up.

"This," Lamb said, "is Hunter Wolf, leader of the Organization-"

"I know that. He's my uncle."

"Oh. Oh… Oh! Shit." Lamb said.

She looked back at Hunter nervously, and Hunter just burst out laughing, whooping in laughter on the look of her face. I started laughing too, and then soon Lamb was laughing.

We ate omelet by the sea, and talked about all the adventures we had been on and experienced.

129

I told them a little poem I had made up regarding our journeys.

Go through the crack in reality with old dweller power
Travel along the psychedelic highway that blooms like a flower
They have great bars and old style balls, with music loud
With people who mean something, in whatever method you've found
Stay on it straight, and you may find where you need to go
Do not stray into Time, or any of its flow
Stay on your own road, ignoring the clock bell
Until you are pushed off to the very pits of Hell
Find the light in the darkness, the train tunnel to the end,
And you'll find it's a good feeling, and just down the bend
You'll be in the realms of Fae, with the gnomes far away,
And can go anywhere you wish, in the light of day
Visit your family, have fun with your friends
Even go to the Cryptocats planet, and try to make amends
Or to a Medieval Mars Rover Inn, take it from Ben,
But always come home once again.

Supreme Evilogue

Live evil.

130

Fae Sorcerer

"I am the Fae Sorcerer, and I despise you all." I calmly said to the masses of evil before me, "You are all rot under my thumbnail, that I never would care to even *scrape.* That being said, I understand we all must work together to-"

The chupacabra, the Scarecrow, said, "Why would I work with any haughty fool with a ridiculous purple outfit on and a condescending tone? I vote that you all vote for me, in this gathering of supreme evil."

There was murmuring in the bowels of Hell, some only uninvited guests who sought to watch us bicker.

Christian, a monstrous man who was cursed to be his werewolf form in death, growled, *I am the only one with the talent to pull off a heist on the living world. IF you don't listen to me, then I know we won't get very far at all..."*

There was more murmuring, and I sighed as I saw another wizard approach. I know I was technically a sorcerer, and he was a wizard, but it was too much confusion having many magic mongers around.

The wizard, who was also a vampire, said, "I have been in all of Hell for many long years. I know what we need, to gather, to create, to build our mass power-"

"I *don't* want to hear it!" another vampire said, an Egyptian one by the looks of him, "I got killed by some idiot with a crossbow, and most of you made the same stupid mistakes I did! I don't care how we do it, as long as we do it."

More murmuring.

The other werewolf, who could now, cursed by Hell, only remember his name as the Coroner, said, "How will we profit off of this venture? What exactly is in it for us? I agree, that Hell is HELL, but maybe we are all acting too brashly... We need a sure way out."

A tomcat man, said, "I'm Tino of the Cryptocats!! I still don't belong here!! It's not even if I was that bad! See, look at my cute face. How can a cute face be bad?"

People avoided his ugly cute gaze, and we continued our council.

A fat senator, or something, what he called himself was a Chancellor, was quickly thrown to the bloody mud as he claimed his best interests for all of us. Not like we haven't heard *that* political scam before... The Russian woman vampire helped him up.

We were planning, we were plotting, and we knew we needed something more. Some enhanced spear to throw at our enemies, and unleash the true horror upon all...

There was a crack in the sky, and another horrible, pure evil soul was sent down to Hell with us.

She got up, flustered, and said, "What? What is this place? Why- I don't think this is the right stop. Driver! Keep driving!! I'm seeing things!! Do it, or I'll kill all of your enslaved family, like they mean anything to *me...*"

This one would do perfectly.

I voted for the one we called Her Majesty, and after a brief segment of filling her in, that she was in Hell, she had such utter vengeance on her tongue that she needed absolutely no more explanation.

131

Olivia Lamb

I got news that the old bitch, Her Majesty, had been killed. They didn't say if she was poisoned, shot, drowned, got in a car crash, or choked on a pickle. Seemed to be only some or maybe all of those things.

Oh well… Poor lady. I guess she got what she deserved, as the tales of her horror and evil finally surfaced. How could I have been so *stupid* to work for someone like her…

She wasn't only a thief. She was a stealer of human lives, indebting them into slavery. If they tried to escape, they were shortly cut down by her scumbarrel guns for hire, either with false information of the person being dangerous, or by willing servants to this sort of evil.

I guess it was good she fired me when she did. Thanks, Jasper. Kisses to you.

I hung out with Jasper, as we drove in my car through Asia. He always smoked cigarettes as a ghost, and I told him it was a bad habit, but he said, "Why? I'm dead, anyway."

"Still cough like you've got pneumonia or something." I said.

"Oh well. Maybe I'll quit when I die my second death. Ahem. Ahem... Erghem..." he said, trying to clear his throat, but soon hacking up a ghost lung.

I stopped by a Buddhist shrine, and said a prayer or two with Jasper. I wished for my father to have peace, for the man who trained me in the Organization's ways, Theodore Hillander, to have peace, and heck, why not, for that horrible woman Her Majesty to have peace as well.

"I don't think I want your peace, Lamb." I heard a feminine voice say from... under me.

There was an earthquake, and I moved quickly as a crack seemed to open up from beneath me. Just ran straight to the car as Jasper flew into it, and I started driving.

Strange. This part of the Earth wasn't prone to having earthquakes.

As I was driving away, I heard horrible feminine laughter, saw black wind in the sky pass me, and the earth continued to crack behind me, seeming to chase me.

I sped as fast as I could, passing some slower cars which unfortunately fell down into those chasms. Jasper prayed for them, as he looked back, and we both felt very scared.

I was running out of room!! There was only a dense forest ahead, and the only way out was cracks and fissures!!

I asked for help once more, from Gawd, Cthaklc, or anyone!!

Good thing I kept such a broad question, because help arrived.

A round spaceship with fins picked me up with a tractor beam, and Jasper and I were lifted away from the ground in my car.

I looked back from in my car, and I saw the most evil, horrible spirits, the ones even unworthy of the Ghostly Parade, crawl out of those cracks and fissures.

132

Benevolence Wolf

"So, you're sort of Jasper the friendly ghost?" I asked this rather cute looking ghost now in my ship.

"I suppose. I'm just like the friendly ghost that likes to help people, and I think it's kind of cool! Lamb and I *were* enjoying a scenic vacation for each of us, but then the Earth's evil ruptured forth!!" Jasper said.

I was a little jealous of the two holding hands- or something, as he was a ghost, but I thought if anyone deserved time with an old flame and passed on lover, it'd be Lamb. I was currently taking a break from brief, but very fun, flings around the world in my spaceship. I had decided to hit up Lamb again, after she accepted my GPS charm, a cute little lamb. Not her fault she was seeing someone, a gorgeous red haired ghost who was actual quite a cutie pie.

I asked her if somebody should know about what she saw. She said, "Oh! Oh, right! Let me call my boss. Sorry, still a bit shocked. I could've *sworn* I heard my old boss's, the head bitch Her Majesty's, voice before it happened..."

She got out her phone, and called my uncle, the leader of the Organization.

Later, she and Jasper helped themselves to the extra bed, and were still enjoying their vacation as they moaned. Lamb later was walking around in her underwear with Jasper haunting the ship. She had such cute underwear always, little hearts, smiley faces, red and white polka dots... I snapped the back of her underpants, and she giggled. She told me she liked these lacey ones, as they really made one feel like a lady in the right circumstances. Jasper just smiled as we teased each other.

I was wondering how they actually made love, as I couldn't physically interact with Jasper. Lamb said she couldn't either, but it was the thought that counts. Jasper flexed his ghost muscles for us, with his long rolling red hair, and we swooned at him for a bit.

I saw something out of the corner of my eye.

A rat?

I inspected for it, and looked around some more. Seems we had a stowaway. It probably ate whatever the food dispenser's extra output was, nestling somewhere warm the solar steam engine produced.

Lamb saw the rat too, later, as it stood on the table, squeaking. I could pick up its language, being able to turn into a rat if I wanted, and he was complaining that my water was too salty. The nerve!

Lamb just screamed and jumped back, as Jasper and I inspected the rat.

"Get that thing out of here!! NOW!! It'll bite us, and infect us, and is probably pooping everywhere too!!" she said.

He was a cute rat in my opinion, despite believing he should be treated with more respect as a "first class passenger" of the ship. I grabbed him up quickly, snatching him by the tail, and put him in my chest with the hole in it, to at least stop Lamb's screaming.

133

Shien

So... It finally happened. The final plot of the prophecy. I had given up on the thing by now, expecting it to twist and turn in whatever method I least expected. Wolf gave me the news, and I knew I had a lot of work to do.

I cackled, smiling wickedly in my hotel room. This is what I always desired. To put the foul oni and demons in their final place, to show them to never mess with Shien and the Organization.

A lot of people had said that I smile wickedly when I was happy. I understood, as I felt only wicked thoughts when I *was* truly happy. It was sort of an acquired taste. But my wickedness was purpose and desire, and not evil, and it took a long look into my eyes as I smiled wickedly to understand that.

I had missed Olivia, but the flame was only lingering when we were bored, anyway. Time would tell I needed greater and grander loves, not saying she wasn't grand herself, but more of a lasting sort of flame that would devour me up completely. Lamb always kept a little bit of me there, and even she realized I didn't really want that.

I could tap into the very essence of the world and become it. But I NEEDED more.

Lamb had even offered to take me around... nonexistence, as she called it, but I knew that would just be a strange trip fantasy, that I was far too familiar with.

I paid for one gigolo to accompany me throughout the day, and he did so adamantly and purposefully, fulfilling the desires of my body, but when I was done with him I only desired solace to plan and plot my next move. I was a raw and uncooked woman, a woman only blustered by unliving souls that brought her to more purpose.

I took counsel from the many oni and spirits, some of the oni snitches of what happened, and after giving them their due respect, banished them forwards into the realms of death. The spirits all asked for help, knowing that if the veil was truly broached, and not only seen through like it had been, then things would be far worse for everyone. I accepted a few's ideas, and later spent the night with a few who were pleasing to me, fulfilling the desire of spirit and mind.

All it takes to have sex with a ghost is the right mind frame.

But that hardly matters, it's the same with humans. I called up a transport, one of the few planes still around, and Norman Fox met me in the plane in the night. He desired to help me in whatever method I desired, with his good looking four armed old lady friend by his side.

134

Norman Fox

Drat!! I was *so* close to finishing my book!! Then all this crazy stuff happened, that even I was unexperienced with!!

Was this the absolute end? I thought of my father and his fall from grace. Perhaps this was the final curtain call for all of humanity, even those like us, vampires in the realms of mortals.

Many true evil creatures alive or unliving were drawn to these cracks in the Earth, that happened everywhere and not only in select places. The people of Earth, if they didn't believe in the supernatural by now, certainly did as the supernatural broke down their doors and devoured their kin.

This is my final quest. This is my last calling, to finally end the evil hidden amongst Earth.

I piloted the plane in the night, with Ethel by my side. She comforted me by saying that this is only what needed to be done. I agreed with her, and released the bombs on another crack.

Shien looked down at the crack that exploded, sighing in relief, but then shouting, "It's not doing it!! It's only making it worse!!"

I swore, in old languages you have never heard before ever, and flew further, away from the crack launching lava gobs into the air at us.

I landed in Australia, our final bastion of defense, even if the cracks were already starting to rupture there as well, and picked up Wolf, Charlotte, Kate, and the cats. Wolf had a long talk with his bird, Chickie, before he left, hoping she would be able to survive with her smarts.

I let Ethel guide the plane, as I talked with Wolf alone, the shades drawn from the sun in the back room we were at.

"So. It's been a long time, my old friend." Wolf said.

"It has, dear Wolf. It has." I said.

"I'm too old to believe in sacrifices, of our people or you, and have allowed each member to take on the role they believe is beneficial to themselves and the rest."

"I'd give my life for all of you!!" I yelled, unable to take it anymore, "I'd jump out the plane, to the very sun!! I don't understand why that is not enough!!"

Wolf put a hand on my shoulder, and said, "You always would, Fox. Know that sacrifice of your life was never necessary."

"I..." I trailed off. I thought that my life meant something, that my sacrifice would never be in vain. It turns out it was as vain as any others, and stupidly imbecilic to throw away. That's how bad my murder was, that turned me into a vampire. It was senseless.

We let our silence speak for itself, and I sat at the closed window, unable to sleep, as Wolf went to talk to the rest.

135

Will Holde

"Egress... It looks like the Earth is... hurting." I said from our spaceship.

She held me in her arms, and said, "I know, Will. I know. I can feel it hurting."

We simply sat looking out at it, as we orbited Mercy and Skinner's ship orbiting Earth.

All my family... my mother and father, Egress's mother and father, dead below us... Had been for a long time, some died of the sickness, some died of other methods. But dead. All of our family left was only our sort of adopted family.

Egress said, "Hey! Well at least our nephew and niece are banging each other! They'll continue on our family." somehow, always, knowing what I was thinking.

I hugged her, and said, "I'm glad that Cryptocat Snowy and E.H. are out there. They'll make sure our sacrifice doesn't mean nothing."

The Earth ruptured and bled before us.

"Is there anything we can do?" I asked Egress. She always knew the answers.

"Let it be, and we will see." she said, giving me a short rhyme this time. Usually she had grand, long poems flowing from her lips, and I always listened intently, to find the meaning in them.

I called Skinner and Mercy, sort of our bosses as we trained to become space captains, and he said, "We cannot break what is already broken. We cannot intervene. You will learn that too, that sometimes the only thing we can do for our worlds is to let them make their own choice."

I was silent at that, and sighed. Knew he'd say something like that, like a prime directive…

I couldn't stand idle, however, and neither could Egress. This was our home.

We launched down to Earth, in our spaceship, telling Mercy and Skinner we needed to do this. They told us that they understood. They would do what they could, too.

Skinner and Mercy continued to rock the Earth with tectonic blasts, trying to stabilize the fissures and earthquakes, and we went to save people where we could.

I landed us in a forested expanse, peace from the burning fissures so far, and opened the doors-

A bunch of animals, with a few outcast people, boarded our ship as quickly as they could. The doe stood in the command room, for a long time, as I tried to shoo it to other parts of the ship. Egress invited all the people and animals gladly, and we took them to another place that was less destroyed, and we continued doing so, for the next, and the next.

136

Wallace

The Werewolves of London, all of us Lycanthropists, arose in the full moon. We did not howl, and kill, and bite, but protected the people from the far superior than them threats that surfaced. We were all of the British Isles's last defense. The government collapsed into anarchy once more, as important people were assassinated and killed by actual demons. The werewolves would show our true form once again, but for good.

The medicine was draining fast, and I was the first to not take the medicine to keep me sane.

I only calmly thought of my once wife, Lamb, and Julia, as I eviscerated demons in my true *werewolf* form.

That experience with the Coroner only had taught me well. It only showed me how to be lucid, and calmer, as more experienced in lucidity werewolves like Julia fought with me, as some of us fell to our hunger and disease.

The fallen werewolves were naught but beasts, and we exterminated them as so. Still, Solomon, Fritz and his wife Monica, Julia and I, our bestial bond of friendship unbreakable, stayed together, defending any and all of the innocent we passed.

It was very difficult for Solomon to execute his once girlfriend, as she had been eating from a pile of children in her werewolf form. He nipped her quicky behind her brain stem, where it was connected to the spine, and killed her instantly. He knew he had to do it, and him alone, as we watched the horror unfold.

We cut down all evil werewolves, some only specters of the past, like a man called the Coroner.

We were hungry, we were thirsty. The streams and rivers had a bad taste in our mouths, as the sickness of the Earth overtook them. We became our human forms and ate from a pile of rotted pumpkins, at least getting some sort of sustenance.

I had a hard time keeping it down, but just thought if I was eating unicorns, just unicorn meat, and it came easier as I imagined the delectable taste.

We passed a few of them in the street, the unicorns absolutely unscathed by the violence and destruction around them, and only let them pass.

Heh. If Lamb could see me now-

A spaceship in the sky?

It landed before us, and Lamb ran out of the ship to hug me. I nervously let her, as Julia watched, but with an understanding gaze.

A different woman, with blonde, curly hair, and who was rather tall, walked out of the ship with a rat on her shoulder.

137

Bomba the Drummer

This had been a long time since I had been in the human world, and I felt sad as I saw all the desecration of the wilds and mayhem that took place in it... Just there, right there, was the lawn of some old folks I used to like to stand watch on, now with a large fissure in its place...

Boomie, Thrum, Throe, and I still walked down the lawns and fields, only lifelessness and deaths ever apparent.

Boomie said, **"Well. It's time we did what we came to do. I can... smell the Fae Sorcerer, can't you? That toxic corruption."**

Throe, the guitarist, said, "I can. It feels like its writhing up my spine, trying to nip at my taste buds."

Thrum, the bass man, said, "Mhm."

I said, "These people are trapped. They cannot escape the evil we destroyed. We must help them."

We all agreed, and played music, gentler metal for the people hiding, who came out of hiding to watch us play. They did so carefully, trying to catch a glimpse of the METAL Gnomes who were coaxing them from their fear.

They followed us, and a few followed into Fae, the rest we shepherded into safer holdings from the creatures of the night.

We were always there for these people, as was our music. The demons in the night stayed back from our sweet metal, scared of the look in our eyes if we saw them skulking.

Boomie sang, to the people before us.

"Be safe, my children, from the ever growing dark.

"Do not go into it. Do not fear its claws.

"Be happy, right now, as I sing.

"And the musicians of METAL keep us from falling in twain."

Some sang with us, kids and teens who kept an open mind of actual gnomes playing METAL to them, and soon the older folks were too, taken ahold by the youth's vigor.

We called for aid, for the few who would not follow into Fae, and hidden enchantments of luck and goodwill were placed on the people, by some of our growing and good natured friends.

In the morning, they traveled onwards, thanking us and kissing us on our gnome cheeks, and continued onwards, to whatever life they may. I knew that their luck would last, and most had four leaf clovers in their pockets from a hidden trove on Earth we stumbled upon. Mostly these clovers were here because of toxic radiation, but it kept the people in good moods and happiness. If that couldn't do it for them, then our magic would.

And we played the ghost of the Fae Sorcerer back into his dark shadows, once and for all.

138

Orson Lions

Us ghosts couldn't really do much in the living world, but we could do enough. I spoke long with Humphrey about his worldly egg ideas, and he seemed satisfied that his ideas were right, although a bit taken aback. The world just held its horrible evil inside, perhaps as an infection, Humphrey surmised.

Still. All of my descendants, with my wife, Iris Lions, and all the past of our Organization fought all we could against the specters of the damned. We shepherded people away from the evil, and Walter just came back from scouting deep into Hell. He said it was as barren as always, but found where the main breach was. If only we could get someone living to go there, and break the breach…

We continued to travel in the winds with the rest of the ghosts. Some of the living thought we were sure omens of death and destruction, but we assured them we weren't. They followed us carefully, as we led them to more secluded and safer spots. Holy spots, that I knew would keep the demons back.

Even some angels were in our ranks, the highest order of holiness, and fought back corruption themselves, but to all alive unknown. That was the way our God worked, in secret and faith, and not grand obscene spectacles of power. At least he learned that in time, or I suppose he did. I never knew a God to be on my side, and never expected one today, even dead.

I passed into my adopted descendant's dreams, Hunter Wolf, to speak to him for a spell with my three companions. I noticed that my old ally was still "alive" and with him on the plane, but I allowed him to cry into his palms, and only spoke to Wolf.

Wolf accepted our aid, and each of us said something lasting to him.

Iris said, "Let love fill you, let it embrace you. Become it. Do not ever abandon it, no matter what you think. I notice you love Charlotte, as well as Kate. Love them both, and let them love you as well. This is important. Do not ever abandon this feeling, no matter what order or command you wish to follow through with."

Walter said, "Be kind, old man. Be kind. Even if you have to slaughter some fools who deserve it, it never hurts just letting the kids get away. Show that kindness. Become it. Let them be kind back, show them you are not as bad as they say. Be kind to your brother and sister, because one day, when you really need it, they will be kind to you."

Humphrey said, "Show generosity. Become it. Give what you cherish to each other. Show your grandest aspect, and let it become not only yours, but all who would grasp at it. Share. Share even the spectacles on your face! Give to any who would need or even just desire it, and even if they don't give back, you have gained the marvelous feeling that giving gives."

I slammed my sword before Wolf, and said, "Be loyal. Become it. Know that with true loyalty, comes true greatness. Your family, friends, even a kind stranger, will benefit from you, and you have naught to do but allow them to. Show them your true strength, and always allow them to ride on your back if they need to."

Wolf took our words in complete acceptance, and wrote down the words as he woke up, in complete definition.

139

Captain Sherry

THE SEAS WERE WRITHING!! WE TOOK COMMAND OF THE OPEN OCEANS, AND LET NONE FALL INTO ITS WAVES.

Even the mermaids and greatest beasts helped along side us, seeing the oceans warming and crack into those fissures. We saved sea life and ships, NEVER to be taken into that darkness.

The masses of flying demons fell to our blows, gunfire from our ship, as we shepherded the many boats who sought safety in the open ocean. The GREATEST BEAST heard my call, as I sang to it in the shark cage, and DEVOURED the demons arising!!!

Fatima asked me if I was alright, as the sweat rolled down my armpits and to the gun I was holding. I shook my short blonde hair out of my eyes, and said that'll do, Fatima. That'll do. She did not question this strange command, and simply saluted me, then taking perch on the crow's nest and shooting at the WINGED HARPIES.

AVAST, YE SCURVY DOGS. THIS IS SEA WITCH SASHA'S FINAL WATERY EPITAPH.

And then I screamed into the stormy seas, roaring to the bottomest depths of the ocean itself.

ROOOOOOAOAAARRRRRRRR!!! I ROARED AS BRYNJA BROU-HAHA, ALL OF MY HORRID CREW READY TO FIGHT BACK HEL HERSELF.

Oh. It was breakfast time. I ate the shrimp and drank down the wine, just enjoying the waves for a second as myself, and not was assuredly my past lives.

The GREATEST BEAST HERSELF fought the demonic beasts from even below her, and I ROARED IN GLORY OF HER TRIUMPH.

She blinked at me, and I knew I had her everlasting respect, as she had mine.

We continued in our scavenged fleet, with people from everywhere and every nationality available. We would keep them safe. Or I wasn't the famed sea explorer, Captain Sherry.

I saluted to a passing spaceship, then another. Would have to go exploring the seas of space, one of these days, if I happen to survive.

No matter. Another onslaught of demons were approaching, and the LADIES and I shot them down, roaring and screaming in unity.

140

Shien

Wolf told me what he knew, and I affirmed his wishes. There needed to be a sacrifice made, even though he did not accept this word himself.

Sacrifice.

I was this sacrifice, I always knew so. We landed the plane, and I climbed with him down into the depths of Hell from the fissures.

Steam, every which way, and worse gasses, assaulted us. I knew I needed to break the fissure, and decided to leave Wolf if he could escape from Hell. Only if he could escape from Hell. None needed this but me.

We got to the main breach, and Wolf asked me how we would do this. I said my religious incantations, then smiled wickedly at him, and told him to leave.

NOW.

He was aghast, as I pulled the breach's bearing down, and everything began to crumble.

I was pushed off the side by a fissure, and Wolf held my hand before I fell.

"Shien!! We can't do this without you!!" he cried out.

"You always could, Wolf. Goodbye. For the rest of your eternity."

And I let go, falling down into Hell, accepting my fate with the oni that surrounded me.

I even smiled, as I fell, down into their embrace, and Duke Sallos himself gladly accepted me, cherishing my fall and protecting me from worse fates.

I walked with him, after he let me go from his winged embrace, into his grand hellish holdings.

Immediately I was filled with that nostalgia again, and loved to be in my love's embrace, finally, but with a past I could be proud of, a life well lived and cherished.

Duke Sallos was glad that I accepted life's grandness, was something he had a mind for me as well. I met all his friends, like Beleth the Demon of Music, and we desired to keep all of Hell to itself, and not assaulting the living world.

But if only that Her Majesty had been sent to Heaven, instead of Hell... We wouldn't have had any sorts of these problems.

There was still a long battle for the people of Earth, but I let them have their fight, as I let the flames of HELL consume me fully, embracing me, all of me, like I wanted for so long.

141

Hunter Wolf

I walked sadly back to the plane.

That was one of my best agents, my friend, who believed that she would make a difference.

I believed she did.

No more fissures erupted on Earth, and Grandma flew the plane over them, as the last of the demons scurried and hid among Earth.

We decided, my crew and I, to take them down. Elimination process.

Charlotte and I got out of the plane in the night with Fox, and each of us kissed or hugged Kate before we left.

I let her kiss last on my lips. I loved her, so much, even if we weren't sexually intwined.

Us three cut down the unholy, Charlotte using her talons, Fox using a silver bullet shooting pistol, and I using my crossbow still that Fox had once given me, and the blade Will had made.

We met the horrors of our past, all three of us.

I slammed the Egyptian monster of old that killed my family with my silver blade, destroying him once and for all.

Charlotte was in an epic battle with her once sire, as he cackled and taunted her, no longer suave and sexy, only monster. She eventually wrestled him downwards in animosity, and tore him to pieces.

Fox killed all of his eviler vampiric kin, not even blinking as he shot each down, even a wizard amongst them.

I knew the people of Earth were all facing similar battles, fighting their demons one on one, and I only prayed, as we continued the hunt, for each of them to be strong in their fights.

In the end, exhausted and out of breath, a ship landed before us. My niece's, Benevolence Wolf.

She got out, strangely with a new rat on her shoulder, like a parrot or something, and Lamb hugged me immediately getting out of the space-ship as well.

They both hugged me, and I felt so sad I could not make a better world for my niece, for each of these women. I owed each of them at least that.

Charlotte said we have done enough, and all of us, the cats, Kate, and Grandma got into the ship as well.

142

Olivia Lamb

But a voice called out to me, not a gentle, calm voice, but one of extreme harshness and absolute evil, before we all got on the ship.

I saw the man who had killed my father. Knew it was him, even though he was his natural form, a horrid, monstrous werewolf. Not like Wallace at all, no form of... sentience, in him, even if he talked and acted like he was human.

With Her Majesty over his shoulder, smirking at me.

She grabbed her hand forward, and snatched Jasper's soul up in her palm, as he struggled to fight.

"Come with us, Little Lamb. We want to play." Christian, the werewolf, said.

I looked back at Wolf and all the people we cared about, then back at Her Majesty and Christian.

I felt such horrible anger, and arose to fight.

I felt as if something was guiding my hand. My father. And Theodore Hillander. Who taught me how to use a gun, and use it correctly.

I could feel my dad's shotgun before me, and I took it from his proffered arms.

I did not believe killing and death was necessary, besides in cases of hunger.

I did not believe any death was truly necessary.

But I knew that these two needed to die.

THEY would never accept our gratitude, kindness, mercy, no matter what.

With one shot, I took down Christian the werewolf, doing what I always had dreamed and imagined of doing.

But I could not take down Her Majesty. The bullets just *wouldn't* do her in.

She laughed at me, as she threatened to devour Jasper and all memory of him. She told me she had that power, and I believed her.

I dropped my shotgun, as it was useless, and it faded back into the ethereal.

I walked before her, and said, "You will never take my life or memories. Nor that of my loves and friends. You do not have that power, you worthless BUM."

She looked shocked at the words, and I continued.

"Even the lowest is better than the grandest you are. Release him. Now. And you will get what you deserve."

The evil spirit, Her Majesty, looked at the people looking at her in hate, and slowly released Jasper.

I then gave her what was coming to her.

I ran up to her in a hug, and kept her in my embrace.

She struggled, but soon saw this hug for what it was. Genuine kindness, and also pity.

She slowly... gently... accepted the hug, and I felt a tear on my shoulder from her face.

She said she would not harm me anymore.
And passed along, back into Hell.

143

Benevolence Wolf

I rocketed us into space, to be safe on my mother's ship. She said the Earth was stabilizing, partly from her, and partly from all of us. We all had a part to play in this grand story.

The Cryptocats, led by King Blizzard and Queen E.H., along with some other aliens, launched from space to Earth, to help us rebuild. I blew Blizzard and E.H. a kiss, as I saw them in their ship, still in the one I helped them build, along with some new enhancements. They banished the demonic aliens that arose, like a once evil tomcat man. The tomcat was taken into the next reality, finally, instead of being sucked back to Hell for a spell.

E.H. and Blizzard came along to our ship later, and told us the story of how King Blizzard and the new Queen E.H. usurped control from the Queen of the Cryptocats, telling all about the allies they met and the enemies they faced-

But that's a different story, reserved for a later time. You'd be lucky if you ever hear it. All you should know, is to treat cats with love and respect that they deserve.

I hugged and partied with all of my family, even a secluded Norman Fox, and even Jasper the ghost with Lamb. Jasper told Lamb he needed to pass on, and they kissed each other, well, kissed each other as a ghost and a human, and Jasper disappeared. Lamb was kind of sad and forlorn after that, but I made sure to keep her company.

I saw Charlotte, Hunter, and Kate talk by the side of the ship.

Hunter said, "I think... I couldn't be in this life without you two. You make life so... enriching, every day for me."

Charlotte punched him on the arm, and Kate smiled. Charlotte hugged Kate, and they whispered more about what secret love formations they could do, and Kate just smiled and laughed, as Hunter let the ladies make plans.

Will and Egress were celebrated as confirmed space captains, given a ship of their own, and we all congratulated them on the promotion to lead the world into the next space age. They took our roaring applause in genuine happiness, and said they would aspire to do all of us proud.

Norman Fox, the old, old man, the secret vampire, said he would be fine if he could see the Earth rotate once more, just one more day and night, and Hunter slapped him on the back as his ladies had been giggling and plotting all evening, and he told Fox that that's all they ever wished for. Good days, and good nights.

My grandma, mother, and father always made sure the party was refreshed and had whatever they needed. They enjoyed looking after people, like all the people of Earth.

Blizzard and E.H. both enjoyed being with their family, and all the families that would come under their reign. They soon left, to go see the Earth again, and help it maintain its course in the stars. Smoky, Dusk, and Mack were so proud of them, and are, every day.

I spent the night with Lamb, in my old room on my mother's ship. She looked at all my old belongings, and said, "So it's done, just like that, huh?"

"It is. I'm glad I found my cute little mascot, Cheeses, because the ship just wasn't the same without another living thing inside it. I wonder what Cthaklc will do? I always wonder about him, in the most random times."

"The rat's ok, I guess. Cthaklc will keep doing what he does, y'know, being Cthaklc. But forget about him. Let's do something new and dirty, or what we like to do usually."

I smiled, as we kissed, and was really open to either or both suggestions.

Cthaklc shut the door outside, as Olivia and I continued to love each other in privacy, and Cthaklc said....

The En*d*

And an ostrich somehow got in the ship. Smart birds, ostriches.